CALL TO ARMS!

"Perhaps, if my brother, Henree Steevuhnz, speaks of his sorrows to his brother chiefs, wrongs to him may be put right."

At Milo's suggestion, Henree rose, and like a summer storm filling a dry stream bed, his words rushed out in a flood. He told of a peaceful party of clan hunters set upon in treachery by a caravan of eastern traders, his third eldest son murdered, two younger sons and a daughter captured and borne back eastward to what terrible fate no one knew.

"Therefore, my Kindred brothers," Henree concluded, "let us move quickly to cross that mightiest of rivers, that we may sooner free from the filthy men of dirt my little sons and my daughter. It is a duty owed by all of us to our Holy Race and to the honored memory of our Sacred Ancestors."

And with Henree's final words, the clan chiefs rose up, vowing to ride together on the bloody trail of revenge. . . .

HORSECLANS ODYSSEY

A Horseclans Novel

by
Robert Adams

A SIGNET BOOK

NEW AMERICAN LIBRARY

SIGNET, SIGNET CLASSIC, MENTOR, PLUME, MERIDIAN AND NAL
BOOKS *are published by New American Library,*
1633 Broadway, New York, New York 10019

FIRST PRINTING, APRIL, 1981

7   8   9   10   11   12   13   14   15

PUBLISHER'S NOTE

This, my seventh book of THE HORSECLANS, is dedicated to Gordy Dickson, superlative writer and good friend;
To Ken Kelley, whose fine covers have helped to make the series a top seller;
To my sister, Loula C. Adams, a calculating woman;
And to Sheila Gilbert, an editor in a million.

Author's Introduction

In the previous Horseclans volumes (*Swords of the Horseclans* through *The Patrimony*) I have moved consistently forward in time from the initial volume of the series (*The Coming of the Horseclans*); but this volume and the next few which will follow it are all set *before* the time of *The Coming*.

If some of my readers are confused by this, I am sorry, but I had deliberately left the initial volume open at both ends because I was planning just what I have now done.

The books to follow this one will deal with the origin of the prairiecats, the discovery of the breed of mind-speaking horses, certain of the adventures of Milo of Morai prior to his return to the Horseclans, and much, much more.

May Sacred Sun shine always upon you all.

Robert Adams
Richmond, Virginia
28 July 1980

HORSECLANS ODYSSEY

Chapter I

The Great River, which had shone bright-blue at a distance, rolled muddy-brown as it slid under the blunt prow of the broad row-barge. Senior Trader Shifty Stuart occasionally spat from the cud of tobacco in his cheek into the river, but he did not bother to look at the water, nor did he look back to the west, at Traderstown, which the vessel had just left. His eyes were for the east, for Tworivertown, where he would shortly make landfall with his cargo of furs, hides, fine hornbows, matchless felts and blankets of nomad weave, beautifully worked leather items and a vast assortment of oddments obtained by the far-ranging horse-nomads of the transriverine plains by trade or warfare from other folk farther west, south or north.

This was not Stuart's first such return from a long summer of trading with the nomads. For sixteen summers he had roved the plains country in a caravan of trader wagons—endless days of baking heat, choking dust, swarms of biting flies and other noxious insects, the incessant lowing of the huge oxen that drew the oversized, high-sided wagons on their five- or six-foot wheels from one clan meeting place to another or, every fifth summer, up to the semipermanent Tribe Camp for the quintennial meeting of the chiefs of all or most of the sixty to seventy clans of horse-nomads that had ruled the plains for most of the five or six hundred years since the fabled Mercan civilization had gone down in death and destruction at the hands of some far-distant enemy who must have suffered equal or worse devastation and deci-

1

mation, since no invading armies had ever followed up the bombs and plagues.

Stuart had heard all the tales, and he even believed some of them, for he had seen with his own two eyes the cracked and splintered shards of the network of fine roads that had once crisscrossed the land, and the long-dead and overgrown, but still impressive by their far-flung hugeness, cities of the plains. On three occasions, he had overruled the superstitious maunderings of his wagoners and associates to camp in the ruins of one of the larger of these, that one that the nomads called Ohmahah, and on each visit he and his men had garnered several hundredweights of assorted metal scraps out of the ruins, for all that the nomads had doubtlessly combed and recombed them for generations.

Others of the old tales were believed only by fools and children, opined Stuart, such as the yarns concerning men traveling to and walking upon the moon, or living beneath the sea or crossing the sea in boats lacking either oars or sails. Silly, asinine nonsense, all of it!

The senior trader leaned his weight against the massive timber beside him—one of four, two each at prow and stern, which were built into the flat bottom of the barge and ran through every level to more than twenty feet above the top deck, where they supported the iron rings through which was let a hempen cable over two feet in thickness and extending from the ferry dock of Traderstown to the ferry dock of Tworivertown, enabling the ponderous, topheavy barges to bear men and women, wagons, livestock and goods across the wide water in any weather and in complete safety.

He cocked up one leg to rest a booted foot upon the low rail and began to calculate his probable profits. Then a hand was tugging gently at his sleeve. He turned his head to see Second Oxman Bailee.

"I'm sorry to bother you, Mistuh Stuart, suh, but it's thet there nomad gal, she wawnts to git out to squat. Ever sincet I beat her good fer messin' up the wagon, she's done been real good 'bout thet. D'you rackon . . ."

Stuart waved a hand impatiently. Bailee was a good oxman, when he wasn't drunk at least, but he took forever to say anything in his whining, nasal, Ohyoh-mountaineer drawl.

"Yes, yes, Bailee, let the little slut out. It's safe to now— we're almost halfway across."

As an afterthought, he yelled at the oxman's back, "And when she's emptied herself, bring her up here to me."

The trader settled back against the immobile timber baulk with a self-satisfied smile. In his recent calculations he had clean forgot to add the probable sale price of the girl and of the two other younkers, as well, not to mention the three fine, spirited plains ponies. And even if she and the boys were to bring Stuart not a penny, still the last few weeks of use of her slender, toothsome body of nights would be almost recompense enough.

The treks outward, in the springtime, were not so bad, for the trading trains most always carried along comely young female slaves for sale to the nomads. Unlike most of the eastern, civilized slave buyers, the horsemen of the plains cared not a scrap of moldly hide whether or not their human purchases were virgins. Indeed, they would pay more for a pregnant girl or one nursing a new brat than for the very prettiest virgin or barren slut. Therefore, all the traders and many a common wagoner or oxman usually had a softbreasted bedwarmer every westward leg of the year's trek, until she quickened or was sold into some clan or other.

But the returns usually were companionless. Providing food and water for any chit that had for whatever reason not been sold by the end of trading was unbusinesslike. Nomads would not take a sickly or lunatic slave girl even as an outright gift, and many a trader drove these unprofitable leftovers out into the vast sea of grasses to fend for themselves. But Stuart was a bit more kindly. He had a guard or oxman slit the creatures' throats and leave the carcasses for the wolves and buzzards.

The horse-nomads only bought, however; they never sold slaves of any description. For all that, the rarely captured nomad women brought high prices from eastern buyers, while a trader lucky enough to acquire even one little nomad boy could practically name his own price from the slave mongers who had journeyed inland from the coastal lands of the Ehleenee, no trader who valued his yearly custom and his hide would so much as mention his willingness to deal in nomads to any of those shaggy, smelly, fleabitten, but grim and ferocious warriors and chiefs with whom he dealt.

Nor could an enterprising man simply snatch a few of the immensely profitable nomad spawn and bear them back eastward with him, for his own guards—hired here and there, from this clan or that, for the season—would not only desert him, but would bring back the fierce warriors of the closest clan to wreak a horrible vengeance upon the kidnappers and free the captives.

"You're a dang lucky son of a bitch, Shifty Stuart!" the trader told himself for the umpteenth time in the last three weeks. "If them four savages had come a-riding into camp even two days earlier, wouldn't 've been a dang thing we could have done 'cept to give 'em a feed and a mebbe do a little trading for them raw hides and horns they had. With them dang Clan Muhkawlee guards still in camp. I'd 've just had to watch a small fortune ride back off from me."

Through the sleeve of his tough linen shirt, Stuart gingerly kneaded the healing but still painful stab wound in his upper arm, thinking, with a prickle of justifiable fear, "It were a near thing, though, fer all that. If thet young feller had got away. . . ." He shuddered, his thoughts going back to tales he had heard of what had been done by vengeful nomads to would-be kidnappers of their kin. He shook his head. "Whoever would 've thought a little squirt—he couldn't 've been more'n fifteen or sixteen, an' dang skinny, to boot!—so groggy he couldn't hardly stand up from the drug we'd snuck into his bowl of stew, could of kilt two growned men outright, hurt another so bad he died thet night, an' stabbed or slashed four or five others, got on his horse and been on his way, afore ol' Lyl sunk thet dart in his back?"

Fleetingly, the trader once more regretted the loss—unavoidable as it had been—of the third nomad boy, then shrugged, ruminating, "Ain't no good to fret over spilt milk, I reckon. Mean as thet little bastid was, likely he'da had to be beat plumb to death afore a body got any use outen him, anyhow."

Stuart grinned again. "Three hundred dollars apiece, mebbe more, them two younkers oughta bring me, oncet I gits 'em to Fanduhsburk, mebbe twicet thet if I decides to take 'em plumb to Looeezfilburk. Hell, mebbe I'll do 'er, been coon's years sincet I'z in Looeezfilburk, an' I'll have me the gal to play with till we gets there, too. 'Course, she's gotta be gentled down some. . . ."

He had been the first to take the girl, and the little minx had fought him like a scalded treecat—pummeling, punching, kicking and clawing until his arm wound had started to bleed again, not to mention tooth-tearing his bristly chin and very nearly biting his right ear off; which last injuries she had wrought on him *after* he had had her wrists and ankles securely tied to the wagon sides, nor was he the only man she had savagely marked. That he had successfully resisted the impulse to give her back as good or better with his big, bony fists and strictly forbidden any of the others with whom he shared the use of her to strike her face had been based upon a good, sound principle of business—broken noses and knocked-out teeth lowered the value of female slaves.

He had not, of course, expected her to be a virgin, nor had she been; no nomad girl ever was so for any length of time after attaining puberty.

"But," he mused and again grinned to himself, "they says them there slave doctors in Fanduhsburk could make a virgin outen a thirty-year-old whore. Mebbe I oughta git 'em to make this gal inta one? Hmm, I'll think on it. She'd sure bring more thet way, eastern buyers likin' virgins the way they does."

He returned to his mental calculations for another few moments, then Bailee was shoving the girl to a place beside him at the rail, and he lost his train of thought. A glance downward gave him a glimpse only of the top of her head of dull, matted, dirty, dark-blond hair, for like all her people she was small, barely as high as his armpit.

The girl's baggy trousers and full-sleeved shirt were both somewhat the worse for having been violently removed from her body on several occasions, as well as being filthy from having been lived in and slept in for the weeks since her capture. Her short boots of red felt and brown leather had survived in better condition, since she had been carefully locked out of sight in one of the big wagons for most of the journey.

She stood at the rail for some minutes, then shyly edged closer, closer, until her slender body was in contact with Stuart's. Her grubby, broken-nailed, but slim and graceful right hand hesitantly extended to touch, then gently massage his genitals through the stuff of his clothing.

Stuart grinned. "Cain't git enough of me, can you, baby doll?"

Without turning his head, he said, "Bailee, you can jest go

on back, 'bout your work. Me an' this here little gal's got us some palav'rin' to do up here."

The trader closed his eyes in ecstasy as the captive girl rubbed and kneaded and caressed his flesh, and he was completely unaware of her other hand's activities, not even feeling the easing of the silver-hilted knife from out its sheath in the top of his right boot.

When he did feel the girl's body begin to crouch lower, he began to turn to face her . . . and a white-hot agony lanced in behind his right knee! Even as he suddenly realized that the right leg no longer would support him, the girl—still firmly clutching his scrotum in her wiry grip—launched herself forward, over the rail. Stuart, screaming his agony and terror, was dragged over and down and into the muddy brown water of the Great River.

Chapter II

The shock of striking the water and its coldness stunned Stehfahnah for but a moment. She let go of the man and put the blade of the knife between her small white teeth in order to free both hands for swimming. Surfacing, she shook the water from her eyes and breathed deeply, treading water and moving her arms to keep her body erect in the water.

Gasping and coughing up water, her sometime captor was floundering about a few yards distant, just beyond the rhythmic file of splashing oars, which meant some eighteen feet from the side of the barge, the upper rail of which was now lined with men, all shouting and pointing.

Taking another deep gulp of air, Stehfahnah swam purposefully in the trader's direction. Once close behind him, she grabbed the back of his wide weapons belt, jerked loose his big dirk and its sheath, then shoved him deliberately into the path of the heavy oars.

Stuart did not even have time to scream before the hardwood blade of one of the sweeps, driven by the strength of four brawny slave rowers, smashed into him. He sank for a long moment, then bobbed up, to float, face-down, with the current.

By the time several of the bargemen and wagoners had swum out, attached a rope to their leader and managed to hoist his limp, battered, broken and bleeding hulk back onto the barge, the girl was nowhere in view.

Remembering the shrewdly cast dart that had pierced and

slain her elder half brother, Broh, on the dark day she and her younger brothers were drugged and made captive by the treacherous traders, Stehfahnah swam underwater until she was beneath the flat bottom of the second barge, fifty yards behind the first. As the lead barge had halted, the barges behind had had no choice but to follow suit, but the column could not remain immobile for long, else the insistent tugging of the river's current at their bulks would place undue pressure upon the transriverine cable.

Stehfahnah, too, was menaced by the current. She clawed at the rough, slimy boards, hearing just a few inches above her the clashings and janglings of the chains that held the oar slaves to their benches. At last she found a hold that would allow her to extend her head slightly and break surface at the waterline to take air while she did what she must do.

Her lungs once more filled afresh, she sent out a telepathic beam—a type of communication that her people called "mindspeak," fairly common in those of her blood, but rather rare among these alien folk. She did not really know if one or both of her younger brothers were aboard this barge, but she could hope. . . .

"*Djoh, Bahb!*"

"*Stehfahnah?*"

"Yes," she affirmed. "I have escaped. I jumped off the water wagon. I think I slew the swine, Stooahrt, so a small part of our clan's vengeance has been taken, perhaps. I am under your water wagon, but there is no way I can free you, as well; you must find a time and a place to accomplish that for yourselves."

Twelve-year-old Bahb's acceptance of the situation was beamed clearly, but the younger boy, Djoh, asked silently, "But sister, there are so many of them and they are all so big and strong. What if we cannot get away?"

"Then you must go to Wind, little brother," Stehfahnah replied. "You must get or make a weapon and force them to slay you . . . but, for the honor of our clan, you must try to take at least one of the pigs with you. Be not overhasty, though, in aught you do. Depend upon Bahb's judgment—he has the mind of a full-grown warrior, for all that he has seen but twelve summers."

The barge had commenced to move forward, the heavy oars rising and falling rhythmically to the resounding strokes of a mallet on a hollow board. Stehfahnah took one last, deep gulp of air, then let go her hold and began to swim with the current, angling toward the western bank of the river.

The bargemen, long familiar with cases of near-drowning, had pumped the water out of Trader Stuart's body. Then his own men had stripped him of his soaked clothing and carefully bedded him down in his personal wagon. It was not done out of love or even liking for the man, but rather out of respect—respect for him both as a man and as a fighter of some note, not to mention the fact that he paid a decent wage for hard work. Never had he been known to try to cheat an employee out of monies due him.

Senior Wagoner DonnHwyt dropped heavily to the upper deck from the tailgate of the wagon. The aging but stocky and still powerful man was the nearest thing to a true physician that the caravan had. He was paid an extra amount for doctoring horses and oxen, but he practiced on the men as well whenever there was need. Now his thin lips were drawn even thinner into a grim line.

Three men awaited him—the two junior traders who had chanced to be on the lead barge, Hwahruhn and Custuh, plus Stuart's bodyservant-cum-sometime-bodyguard, "Clubber" Fred Doakes.

Custuh, almost qualified to be a senior trader himself, was the first to speak. "Well, man," he lisped through the gap left when the nomad boy had smashed out his front teeth with the pommel of a saber, "will he live or not? If he will, ith he tho badly hurt he won't be able to command nekth yearth venture?"

Old Don shrugged, his broad shoulders rising and falling, his big, callused hands spread wide, palms facing outward. "Lordy, Mistuh Custuh, I ain't no real doctor. And it'd tek one to tell yawl awl thet. Mistuh Stuart's left shoulder is broke, bad broke—thet oar done as much damage as a iron mace, and even if some surgeon don't tek the arm off, he won't never use 'er much agin.

"And the outside tendon a-hint his right knee's done been sliced clean in two, but thet ain't awl. His bag was damn near tore loose from his pore body by the there damn lil bitch. It's a pow'ful good thang he done a'ready got him a son 'r two, 'cause I 'spect he ain't never gonna git him no more younguns of no kind awn no woman . . . if he does live, thet is."

"The real question is," commented Hwahruhn, scratching at the scalp beneath his silver-shot black hair, "dare we—any of us—go back on the plains next year, since the gal's gotten free? If you'll all recall, I was against the whole dirty business from the outset—the treachery, the killing, the kidnappings, not to mention the way that gal was abused during these last few weeks. If she gets back to her clan . . ."

Custuh snorted derisively. "Bert, you maunder like an old woman, you do! 'If the gal gits back to her clan,' indeed! Did you ever hear tell of anybody swimming this here river with all their clothes on? Huh? And too, while all the rest of you were set at getting ol' Stuart out'n the water, I had a pair of darts ready and was watching to see her haid come back up . . . and it never did, so she prob'ly drownded."

But Hwahruhn shook his head, unease in his voice and worry in his dark-brown eyes. "What you aver is just possible, true, but these nomads are tough, wiry, resourceful people. They're survivors, Liasee. If the child you all insisted upon wronging gets out of the river alive . . . God help us all!"

Stehfahnah had not intended to come out of the river in close proximity to the trader town, but she certainly would have preferred to get out of the cold, swirling water much sooner than was the case. When at last she was able to drag herself up an inclined and muddy bank on the western side of the broad waters, she could but lie for a long while on the brush-grown verge, her muscles jerking and twitching with the fatigue of her efforts.

At length, as hunger began to nibble at her belly, she sat up and commenced—as she had been taught—to think out her situation, to take stock of her possessions and gauge their potential usefulness for accomplishing her purpose.

She knew that she was far, far east of the last place her clan had been encamped. She and her brothers, one of dozens of farflung hunting parties, had been a good two days' ride from camp when they had been taken, and the wagon train had lumbered on for nearly three weeks after. Therefore, she estimated that a span of not less than three days' ride west would bring her near the tents and yurts of her people . . .

but she had no idea just how far south the river might have borne her this day. Also, she had no horse or any hope of easily acquiring one, unless she should chance across one of the increasingly rare wild herds and could mindspeak the king stallion into allowing one of his sons or daughters to accompany her on her quest. She knew better than to approach any of the scattering of dirtman settlements; such would only mean slavery or worse.

She sighed, then spoke aloud to herself. "So I must walk. Sun be praised that the wolves are well fed this time of year."

But if she must plan upon making a journey of such length solely on foot, it might well take a month or more. Winter storms had been known to come very early, and if she was to survive alone, dismounted and friendless upon the open plains, she must have many things she now lacked—more and heavier clothing, more effective weapons than one large and one small knife, some kind of food that could be packed without quickly spoiling, a container for water, a means of making fire.

The last necessity was fulfilled almost at once. When she got around to closely examining the weapon she had torn from the trader's belt, she found not only a knife, but a number of smaller enclosures within the leathern sheath. A hone stone occupied one pocket, another held a flint and a steel for fire-making, and two smaller ones contained a tiny steel eating skewer and food-knife plus a small silver spoon.

The belt knife itself was a heavy, handsome, formidable weapon—a full foot of thick, broad blade, honed to razor keenness along all of one edge and the first third of the other. Below the polished steel ball pommel, the wooden hilt had been well covered with black leather and wound with many yards of silver wire, and the number of deep nicks in the blade side of the shiny brass guard showed that the weapon was not simply a gaudy showpiece.

Knowingly, Stehfahnah weighed and balanced the knife, finding its weight properly distributed to render it an effective missile. A design had been etched onto both sides of the blade, and Stehfahnah grunted satisfaction when she closely studied these. She had had little experience at the arts of reading and writing—not many of her people had, for few books had survived six hundred years of chaos, and neither of these two talents were necessary for survival on the prairies, high plains and mountains wherein Horseclansfolk dwelt—but she could write her own name and that of her clan, so she easily recognized that the letter S was the central motif of the designs and at once felt that Wind had intended this fine, deadly, lovely weapon just for her, Stehfahnah's, hands.

The boot knife was typical of weapons of its type—a leaf-shaped, double-edged blade of some half-inch width and some four inches in length, guardless and with a plain hilt of deer antler. Stehfahnah found that it fitted securely into the sheath built into her own left boot top.

Her gnawing hunger partially assuaged by a few handfuls of berries and the raw legs of a large frog she was fortunate enough to catch, the Horseclans girl sought and found a willow tree, and her nimble fingers had soon produced a quantity of twine from the inner bark. After locating three game trails in the riverside brush, she constructed as many simple snares of whittled twigs and twine nooses, plus a log deadfall where the mark of cervine hooves was plain; if even one of the traps proved effective during the night to come, she would have fresh meat, a skin or hide of some description, bone and possibly sinew or horn with which to fashion other tools and weapons.

By the time she returned to her starting point, the late-afternoon wind had completely dried the shirt and trousers which she had carefully draped over bushes. Dressed, she began to cast about for a safe place to spend the night, finally settling for the spacious crotch of a huge mimosa tree. Cold she knew it would be, but safe from any prowling predators, poisonous snakes or the like. That decided, she cut armfuls of springy pine tips and coarse grass and filled the depressed crotch with them. She debated kindling a fire with which to warm herself before she climbed aloft to sleep, but decided to not do so, for if her former captors were searching along the river for her, smoke or flame might give away her position.

Twice during the long, dark night, she awoke with a start, gasping and trembling and imagining herself still confined within that hateful, wooden-walled wagon, defenseless prey to the lusts of the hateful traders. Throughout all the suffering, the horrors and deep humiliations she had been forced to undergo, Stehfahnah's fierce pride had sustained her, and she had refused to allow her tormentors the satisfaction of seeing a Horseclanswoman's tears; but now, alone and high in a riverside tree, she wept, violently, uncontrollably, and at long last she slept again, so deeply that the warming beams of Sacred Sun on her face finally wakened her to the first morning of her new-won freedom.

Two of the snares still gaped empty, but the third had caught her a fine, fat rabbit. With practiced ease, she broke the neck of the struggling animal and went on with the furry carcass slung from a loop of the twine.

"Wind be praised!" she breathed fervently at the site of her painfully constructed deadfall, for beneath the heavy log lay a buck, so recently dead that the carcass still was warm. True, he was much smaller than most varieties of plains bucks, but his dearth of meat and smallness of hide was fully compensated for in the girl's mind by the pair of slender, needle-tipped and almost straight horns standing a good two feet up from his head.

Good fortune remained with her. Two days later, now armed with a brace of horn-tipped spears and a hand-carved spear thrower, she slew a large white-tailed doe. With the sinews of her two largest kills and the knife-shaped trunk of a redbark bow-wood tree, the wood roughly cured over the heat of her carefully shielded cooking fire, she began to fashion a bow. Arrows were whittled down from lengths of birch, fletched with owl feathers and tipped with fire-hardened bone shards. Birch bark and strips of partially seasoned deerhide were fashioned into a combination bowcase and quiver.

She also began the involved process of converting the doe's second stomach into a water bag for her journey. She felt pressed for time, being fully aware from a lifetime on the plains that she still was highly vulnerable to the elements and that the first freezing storm of winter could swoop down upon her with amazing suddenness.

Stehfahnah's first warning that she was not still alone in the riverside woods was the smell of smoke. She had been ranging farther and farther afield since she had finished her makeshift bow. Armed with it and her balanced pair of spears, she was seeking feral cattle or the large, curved-horned bucks for the thicker, better-quality hides they grew, knowing that her thin, flimsy riding boots would need heavy reinforcement soon.

Then she found an otter in a steel trap. The sinuous shiny-brown creature's frantic struggles to free itself had only broken the flesh of its pinioned leg, the remorseless bite of the metal jaws cutting the flesh to the bone. The beady eyes were full of pain and terror, and the whiskered lips writhed back to bare the white teeth.

The fine, large, water-resistant pelt would have been a most welcome addition to Stehfahnah's growing hoard, but her recent ordeal bred within her a kindred feeling with the trapped and suffering animal. Recalling that some animals, predators in particular, could often be reached by mindspeak, she made the effort.

She had mindspoken horses and a few of the prairiecats—the huge, long-fanged felines which had for hundreds of years lived among and made common cause with the Horseclansfolk—but she found the water dweller's mind significantly different from the other two animal sentiences. Silently, she offered to free the trapped creature if, in return, it would agree not to bite her.

The otter mind was a roiling maelstrom of agony and terror and bloodlust. *"Hurt . . . kill . . . kill . . . kill!"*

Broadbeaming a message of soothing, Stehfahnah repeated her offer. "Furry brother, if you will not bite me, I will free you from the hurting thing." After a number of repetitions, when she had almost despaired of reaching the pain-mad beast and was upon the point of ending its suffering with a well-placed shaft from her bow, the otter abruptly ceased to struggle against the trap, although its muscles still jerked involuntarily with the pain.

"Stop hurt thing?" he queried. *"Not bite if stop hurt."*

Laying down her spears and throwing stick, unshouldering her bowcase-quiver, Stehfahnah approached the otter, wondering if he really understood her. With some trepidation, she knelt near the trap, which was chained to a deep-driven wooden stake. The otter was big—almost four feet long—and could seriously hurt her before she could draw a knife and kill him if he had misunderstood the tenuous mental messages.

Nonetheless, she gripped the blood-slimy jaws of the trap and tried to pull them open, but the leverage was not right and her fingers kept slipping from the smooth, wet metal. Her well-intentioned efforts were only hurting the otter more, and his snarls were not reassuring to her.

Reaching behind her, she drew one of the spears closer. Drawing out her big knife, she worked the blade in near one hinge of the biting steel jaws, then gingerly twisted the knife. Haltingly, the trap opened a fraction of an inch, then a smidgen more. When it was open to the extent of over two fingers' width, she mindspoke again.

"Now, furry one, pull out your leg, quickly!"

Scurrying as rapidly as three legs would carry him, the otter disappeared into the brush in the direction of the nearby river. Stehfahnah, unable to either pull up the stake or break the chain, finally squatted over the trap and urinated on the device, knowing that the strong odor of human urine would warn animals away from the hellish instrument.

Within the next several hours, she chanced across half a dozen identical traps. Each one of them was empty, and she used a spearbutt to spring them all, also disturbing the ground about them, spitting to be certain of leaving twolegs scent. Such was her preoccupation with the traps that her day's hunt proved fruitless and she trudged back to her campsite that afternoon empty-handed.

She had just lit her squaw-wood tinder and laid a virtually smokeless fire in the little hollow and had lowered a quarter of venison she had hung high on an oak branch preparatory to slicing off enough meat for her dinner when she suddenly realized that she no longer was alone within the brushy-banked hollow.

She let go of the deer meat and whirled, crouching, her big knife held low, ready to stab or slash or throw. But then her blue-green eyes widened in stunned disbelief.

On the river side of the fire pit were no less than three otters. The largest she recognized as the big male she had earlier freed from the steel trap; the other two were significantly smaller, although obviously adult animals. Before the trio, in the weeds, lay a big catfish, still flopping and feebly gasping.

Sheathing her knife, Stehfahnah mindspoke, "Welcome, furry ones. Will you share this meat with me?"

The larger mustelid had sunk into a crouch, taking his weight off the three legs now, perforce, doing the work of four. It was he who answered, although Stehfahnah could feel the attentiveness of the two smaller beasts.

"Why female twolegs stop hurt thing and let this one go

free, why not kill like kill other furry ones and take hides? Why hunt out and kill other hurt things of male twolegs?"

Stehfahnah herself was not really sure just why she had passed up the opportunity—Sun-sent—to add the otter's fine pelt to her racks of seasoning skins, or why she had then wasted all of one precious afternoon in disarming the line of traps rather than preparing for the grueling journey which lay ahead and which must soon commence if she was to live to see its end.

She replied, "This twolegs hunts for food as well as for hides. She tries to kill quickly and not hurt. Also, you furry ones remind her of others, furry cats, with whom she grew up. This twolegs would be your friend, would share her meat with you. If you will allow her to do so, she has certain herbs she can apply to your leg to stop the hurting for a while and help the flesh to heal quicker."

The larger, male otter, it developed, thought of himself as Mighty-and-Invincible-Killer-of-Much-Meat-in-Water, a sobriquet he had assumed after, sometime in the past, having attacked and torn the throat out of a swimming deer, then guided the carcass to the bank. After he and the two female otters had gorged on raw deer meat and Stehfahnah had avidly devoured the tender fillets of the fish, he sat motionless, snarling only sporadically while she cleaned his lacerated hind leg, plastered it thickly with a mixture of herbs and deer fat, then bound it with a strip of cloth torn from her only shirt, warning him to refrain from chewing off the cloth for at least three days.

The smaller of the two females was somewhat shy and "spoke" but little. The other, however, "chatted" on at some length throughout the meal and while the girl tended the hurt male.

Mother-of-Many-Many had once borne and successfully reared no less than six kits in the same litter, though her present litter numbered only three. Fast-Swimmer also had a litter of three kits, and the two females were sharing the single den, as well as hunting responsibilities for and protection of the six kits. The male, for all that he also used the same enlarged muskrat burrow, hunted only for himself, and, from the various "conversations," Stehfahnah was never sure if he had fathered both or either of the litters. Otters, apparently, had never developed the close familial ties of the prairiecats or of the nomads' breed of horses.

Shortly after nightfall, the three otters took their leave and waddled swiftly into the brush toward the river, the bellies of all three bulging with a surfeit of rich red venison. The two females bore, as well, strips of the deer flesh which Stehfahnah had sliced from the quarter specifically for the waiting kits in the riverbank den.

In the following days, Stehfahnah did her hunting to west and south, studiously avoiding the north. The otters' information about the trapper had been disturbing to her. He was occupying a "den-of-dead-wood" at some indeterminate distance northward and within sight of the river.

She reflected that since it was imperative that none of the local dirtmen—the nomads' epithet for farmers and all other folk who lived in one set place—suspect her presence, here, she had been very foolish to spring and upset so many traps without touching the baits. The single bloodstained trap might have left the impression in the trapper's mind that the animal had managed to pull free of the cruel jaws, and if she had taken away the baits from the sprung traps and smoothed away her footprints, he just might have attributed the deliberate spoilage of his line to a possible wolverine and maybe even moved into another territory.

Now that he, through her unconcerned carelessness, was certainly aware that someone was nearby, Stehfahnah took pains to be extremely cautious in hunting and in everyday living, going so far as to forsake her warm, wind- and weatherproof lean-to for that tree crotch wherein she had spent her first few nights in these woods; though now she slept warmer and in more comfort for the two deer hides over the mattress of pine tips, and the odor of the fragrant needles went far toward masking the reek of her blanket of half-cured rabbit skins.

Fearful of being surprised at night, while sleeping, the girl kept all her weapons aloft with her and within easy reach. But the dreaded confrontation came by light of day.

On that ill-fated day, Stefahnah had, early in the morning, come across a spoor she had long sought in vain—that of one of the cattle whose ancestors had gone feral after the death of the earlier civilization, had in many areas interbred with truly wild bovines and slowly evolved into the long-horned, shaggy-coated and ill-tempered beasts known as "shaggy-bulls" and still roamed the hills and backwoods in small herds or individually.

The girl had first tracked, then stalked the huge old bull for hours, at last getting sufficiently close to drive three arrows almost to the fletchings within a palm-sized space just behind and below the massive left shoulder. After a time of roaring and stamping about, the behemoth sank suddenly to his knees and began to vomit up vast quantities of frothy blood. Then, slowly, the head came to rest on the blood-soaked ground and the mighty beast's near-ton of hulk thumped onto his right side, chest rising and falling spasmodically, the thick legs driving the deadly cloven hooves in the final agony.

Recalling the words of the hunters of her clan, the slender girl patiently waited until the big animal had ceased any movement, until the urine and dung gushed through the death-relaxed sphincters. Not until then did she approach her stupendous kill and set herself to the long, arduous and singularly messy job ahead of her.

Alone, without an axe of any description, she had known ahead of time that she would be able to take only half the fine, thick hide, but that would be more than sufficient for her purposes . . . if she could get the heavy, unwieldy thing back to her camp.

When she had hung as much of the carcass as she could manage to hack loose high in several nearby trees, she gorged on rich, raw, bloody liver and used her thongs of deer rawhide to tie the half hide into a load she could fasten to her pack frame, with the rest of the liver, the succulent tongue and a kidney stuffed into one of the bovine's stomachs added to the load.

It was near sunset when she stumbled, bone-weary, out of the brush and down the incline to her camp. Weaving with utter exhaustion under the heavy packload, she was just too tired to take her usual precautions or even to notice that the camp was not as she had left it.

Just as she shrugged out of the straps of the pack frame, something crashed against her temple, and Sacred Sun Itself seemed to explode inside her head. Then there was blackness.

Chapter III

For a week after Stehfahnah's spectacular and sanguineous escape from the ferry barge, the men guarding the two kidnapped boys moved warily and in augmented force about their charges. Heeding their sister's wise counsel and their own native cunning, however, the Horseclans boys seemed model captives, successfully giving the impression of an increasing passivity. Therefore, as seasonally hired men dropped off along the way to seek their homes or some winter employment, the boys' guards grew fewer and far more slack.

A fortnight of travel eastward from the Great River had brought the vastly diminished caravan of wagons, pack beasts and horsemen to within two days' journey of Pahdookahport—a true metropolis of about five thousand souls, largest river port on the western reaches of that mighty waterway called the Ohyoh River and always bustling center of the east-west trade.

Within and without the towering granite walls which protected the riverside capital of the Republic of Pahdookahport a visitor might see men of almost every race, creed and color—each attended by his hired bravos. Merchants from near and far haggled over bundles of furs, bales of hides of deer and shaggy-bull, bison and elk. A hundred or more forge fires fouled the air around the quarter of the smiths, wherein rusty or corroded metals dug from the ruins of the long-dead Ancients were reconverted to the uses of living men. Factors of the far-eastern kings, princes and archdukes

19

sat in their guarded carriages clad in rich clothing and sipping at richer wines in arrogant disdain whilst their hordes of well-trained agents scurried hither and yon sniffing out the best of the wares of incoming caravans and barges. In other guarded carriages lolled an Ehleen or two—swarthy, bigboned men, their black hair shiny with pomade, their full lips like as not encarmined, their golden swordhilts bejeweled, the nails of their heavily beringed fingers lacquered—sneering at the "barbarians," any not of their own race.

Urbahnos Kostanis was such a one. A native of the Kingdom of Karaleenos and scion of a noble house of that realm, he had nonetheless—once irrevocably exiled to this assignment in punishment for having killed the son of a powerful man in a duel—applied his keen mental faculties so assiduously that in the bare ten years he had lived among the barbarians he had become a very wealthy merchant and was even now exchanging letters with those who would arrange to purchase his pardon from the Royal House of Karaleenos, King Zenos and his ministers being always ready to see justice done if the price was right.

Unlike the other two Ehleenee resident in Pahdookahport—Pehtros Ziplonos of Kehnooryos Mahkedohnya and Kenos Trindis of Kehnooryos Ehlas—Urbahnos' knowledge of the merchandise he was offered and sometimes bought was as thorough and as detailed as that of his agents. So it had been a long time since he had been deluded or cheated as his two racial peers often were.

He rendered the other two as much courtesy as their blood heritage entitled them (which was damned little, really, for both young Pehtros and the older, corpulent and flatulent Kenos were, though much darker than most of the barbarians, clearly not *kath-ahrohs* or Ehleenee of pure lineage, as was Urbahnos), but that was all, for he felt that any man so stupid and stiff-neckedly arrogant as to not learn every facet of the trade or profession which earned him a livelihood was fully deserving of all misfortunes which chanced to befall him.

Puffing at his bejeweled pipe, Urbahnos snorted silent derision. For all that Kenos had been in Pahdookahport nearly twice as long as had he, the old fool still could not even tell the difference between a fisher fur and a mink. While just last year that young ass Pehtros had paid good, silver *thrahkmehee* for several bales of shaggy-bull hides (from which extra-heavy leather the best boots, bucklers and other war gear were fashioned) which, when opened for repacking prior to shipment, proved to be mostly poor-quality horsehides, interspersed with thin sheets of hardwood to give weight and solidity to the bales.

The full lips of the stocky Karaleenosian twisted into a thin, crooked smile at the memory of how the effete, stripling-slender Pehtros had howled. Naturally, an assassin had been retained to put paid to the account of the larcenous agent who had arranged sale and purchase of the spurious bales, but while the barbarian's well-earned death salved wounded pride and served clear notice to others, his corpse and hovel yielded up precious few of the Mahkedohnyan silver pieces.

Urbahnos snorted yet again. And the ninny would, had he not been there to advise, have sent his own well-known bodyguards to take revenge upon the unwashed flesh of the scoundrelly agent, which action would likely have brought down the wrath of the duke upon not just Pehtros but himself and Kenos, as well.

Observing that the barge he had been eying was now securely moored and that slaves were manhandling into place a broad ramp from deck down to wharf, Urbahnos dismounted from his carriage, shifted his jewel-hilted slashing sword rearward to make for easier walking and, flanked and trailed by four of his scarred, well-armed bodyguards, set his booted feet to the slimy cobblestones of Dock Street.

As the usual dockside crowd of slave stevedores, boatmen, agents, pimps, thieves and idlers from the town, above, grew denser, the largest of Urbahnos' bodyguards—and Nahseer was large by any standards, towering almost two full meters from pink-soled foot to shaven, dark-brown pate, with a big-boned frame which carried little fat but at least one hundred and thirty kilos of rolling muscle covered with a scarred and callused skin the shade of an old saddle—took the lead, his bulk clearing the way for his employer as the metal-shod prow of an ocean-going warship cleaves the tossing waves.

In the lee of the docked barge, a few swings of Nahseer's long, brawny arms cleared the foot of the boarding ramp and the party ascended to the deck, whereon the captain, himself, waited to greet the well-known and thoroughly respected Lord Urbahnos.

In the small, cramped cabin, the Karaleenosian sipped once, for courtesy's sake, at the contents of the copper cup served to him—that vile-flavored distillate of various grains known as "hwiskee" and as much savored by the barbarians as if it had been a decent, civilized vintage wine—then got down to business, speaking the barge captain's drawling dialect of Mehrikan with the ease and fluency born of long practice.

"To judge by your deck cargo, Hynz, someone must be building a new wharf or refooting an old one. Is timber all you're carrying, this trip?"

The burly bargeman sighed gustily and shrugged. "Damn near, Lord Urbahnos, damn near. It's the dang duke. He wants to build him a new pier and all up river, for to take some of the pressure off'n the ol' port, here, and wouldn't nothin' do but bal' cypruses clear from down to the drownded lands."

Urbahnos raised his carefully trimmed eyebrows. "You went that far south, friend Hynz?"

The captain rumbled a chuckle and shook his balding head. "Aw, hell no, Lord Urbahnos, only far as Tworivertown. Some of your kinfolk—Southern Ehleenee—they brung the logs up far as Mehmfisz, and Ol' Djordj Gaibruhlz he brung 'em inta Tworivertown and then I laded 'em there. You knows how 'tis, Lord Urbahnos, them Southron Ehleenee, they sure lawd won't come no futher north than they jest has to."

The Karaleenosian did know how it was, although he really could not comprehend just why the so-called Ehleenee of the vast Southern Kingdom felt cause for being so standoffish, since there had been so shamefully much intermarriage and interbreeding with the indigenous barbarians in those lands south and west of Karaleenos that the folk of that kingdom were all but barbarians. Only in Karaleenos (and, to a lesser degree, in Kehnooryos Ehlas) were *kath-ahrohs*—Ehleenee of pure lineage—any more in numbers than a rapidly dwindling minority.

"Then this timber is your only cargo?"

The barge captain nodded. "Aye, Lord Urbahnos, only save fer a dozen barr'ls of hooch, barley hwiskee it be."

The Ehleen repressed a gag; corn hwiskee was bad enough, God knew, but the distillates of rye and barley were positively nauseous to a civilized man of refined tastes.

"But," the big bargeman added, with a grin that showed brownish, rotting teeth, "I got me some news I bet will interest you a mite, Lord Urbahnos." Then he leaned back and applied himself to his hwiskee, resuming his conversation only when his guest had stacked four broad, silver *thrahkmehee* on the dirt-shiny table between them.

"Ol' Shifty Stooahrt, the plains trader, he be laid up in Tworivertown, and he won't be a-doin' no more plains trading, neither, not never again. Seems as he and his train got them a chancet to catch them some Horseclans kids—a gal and two lil boys."

Urbahnos leaned forward. "The boys—blonds? Redheads? How old?"

Captain Hynz treated him to another rotten grin. "Now, I jest knowed *thet* would tickle your fancy, Lord Urbahnos. The gal, she's the one what crippled pore Stooahrt—took his own dang boot knife and cut the tendon ahind his knee, she did, then jumped right off the cable barge 'tween Traderstown and Tworiver, a-draggin' the pore feller after her by his pore balls! Then when they both was in the river, she shoved him to where a oarblade crushed up his shoulder so bad the doc had to take the whole dang arm off him.

"But the lil bitch got what was a-comin' to her—leastways, mosta who-all was there thinks she drownded in the river, for all nobody ever foun' her body.

"But the train's still got them two boys—one blond and one redheaded, one about twelve and the other about ten— and they only 'bout two three days out from Pahdookahport, too, comin' in by land, crost the Old High Road."

Calmly lifting his own cup of the abominable tipple, the Ehleen meshed his keen mind into high gear. Fair-skinned blond and red-haired slave boys brought high prices in all the Ehleen lands of the east, especially were the slaves prepubescent and high-spirited—and in that last regard, he need have no fear if the captives were truly of Horseclans stock. Of course, the men who now held the boys were well aware of these facts, too, and would consequently demand and likely receive a stiff price for their "merchandise," especially if they

went onto the quayside slave block for open bidding by Urbahnos and the other traders, factors and merchants.

However, the Ehleen mused, should an enterprising man
act upon privately obtained information and ride out to meet
the incoming train . . . hmmm. . . .

Unbeknownst to the two men closed in the tiny cabin, a
sailing barge from upriver had furled sails, put out long
sweeps and rowed in to berth on the opposite side of the pier.
For all that she bore a small amount of miscellaneous cargo,
this vessel was basically a passenger boat, but a single short
glance at the passengers who lined the rail of the newcomer
as the boatmen made bow and stern lines fast to ironbound
bollards was enough to send most of the docksider pimps and
petty criminals off to seek better-heeled or less dangerous
prey.

Within a cabin of the passenger boat, a long-limbed, fair-
haired man sat brooding, his big hands clasped about the
well-worn hilt of a fine broadsword, his blue-gray eyes seeing
not the greasy, soot-stained wooden wall before him but
rather the rolling, green leas of the land of his birth, a land
now forever lost to him, the County of Geerzburk.

At a tentative rapping on the closed door, Martuhn of
Geerzburk gave over his bitter reveries and turned his head
to face the closed portal.

"Come."

At the basso rumble, the battered door swung inward to reveal a stocky, short-legged man known to all the world simply as Wolf. Hideously scarred was Wolf's face, by both
blade and flame. Neither ear was intact, and a piece of
waxed leather covered the empty socket which once had held
the mate to his ebon right eye, while his hairless pate
resembled an eroded and deep-furrowed hilltop. The plain
steel helm which normally covered the bald head was
presently held in the crook of Wolf's right arm, the hand of
which had long ago been lopped off at the wrist. The arm
was tightly laced into a leather cuff, to the tip of which was
affixed a heavy knob of steel.

Wolf fingered his nonexistent forelock, executing a short,
jerky bow. "M'lud count, the boat done docked up and
they's a-shoving the planks out. Duke Gutly's likely a-wait-
ing."

Count Martuhn smiled thinly. "Wolf, old friend, you'd best watch your tongue, else our employer may have it and your ugly head, as well. Surely you know that there is no man so proud and hypersensitive as a new-made noble? I like the corpulent old pirate no better than do you, but he pays well . . . and punctually, if you will recall."

The nobleman arose, having to stoop in the low cabin. He was armed—a corselet of finest Pitzburk plate, worn and nicked but polished to a sheen, short kilt of scale mail, arm and elbow guards and the ornate greaves which were the mark of an infantry officer of the far-away Middle Kingdoms. Not until Count Martuhn had buckled on his broad, steel-mounted dagger belt did he settle the even broader leathern baldric onto his right shoulder and snap the links of the sheathed broadsword to it so that the weapon occupied its familiar place at his left hip. That done, he lifted from the table his fine but battered helm and turned to stoop lower and to the side so his height and bulk might pass through the cabin door.

By the time the nobleman-become-Freefighter came on deck, his young ensign, Flairtee, and his six big, burly sergeants had shouted and chivvied and beaten the five dozen recruits into a sort of formation. One brief glance at these fruits of his eastern recruiting trip was all that the exiled officer could bear—thieves, certainly, rapists, likely as not, murderers, more than one he was sure, broken men, outlaws, brigands; all men who, for one reason or another, had found it expedient to put a good thousand miles of territory betwixt them and their homelands.

But even as Martuhn winced at the tatterdemalion sight of the "formation," his keen mind was consoling him with the thought that some few of his recruits showed definite promise. Back at Tchehshcerportburk, out of which he and his staff had operated and gathered their recruits, that slender, brown-skinned, silent Zahrtohgahn had demonstrated enviable skill in casting accurately dart, light axe, knife or stone; he was also a shrewd and accomplished wrestler. The middle-aged Harzburker (he denied Harzburker antecedents, but, to Count Martuhn, his accent gave him away) was obviously of gentle birth and even possibly, like Martuhn, a broken nobleman, for he was a first-rate swordsman and the habit of command was natural and automatic to him; mentally, the former lord of Geerzburk was already priming the Harzburker for either sergeant or officer, likely the latter.

The third he considered a real treasure. This man, like the first, was also a Zahrtohgahn, but older, heavier of build and much darker of skin. His weapons skills were passable, but his true value lay not in the pursuits of war. Quite by accident, during the journey from the east, Martuhn had learned that the blue-black-skinned man who had signed on as Ahkmehd al Ahsrahf was a highly skilled and talented physician and surgeon—something so rare in a Freefighter company as to be almost unheard of.

When he had donned his helm, Count Martuhn returned Ensign Flairtee's intricate flourish of steel with a hand salute, then drew the junior officer aside and spoke in a low voice.

"Keep these swine aboard, Rahnee. The last thing we need is to be held responsible for turning the likes of them loose on one of the duke's precious ports, much as this one does need a thorough cleansing.

"I would suspect that, when I report to His Corpulence, we will be ordered to garrison the new fortress at Twocityport. At least those were the plans when we were sent east, to recruit these reinforcements for the company."

The freckled young officer nodded. "You think we'll be sent by water, eh, your grace?"

"If I were the duke, that's what I'd do," affirmed the commander. "He dislikes and distrusts even the best stripe of easterners, and you may be certain that his spy network has informed him that our little contingent is composed of the very dregs. No, he'll not want this lot marching through his towns and grain lands to Twocityport . . . though Wolf and I may ride over; I've had enough of this damned boat and its foul, cramped stink. Give me a good bit of horseflesh between my knees."

Old beyond reckoning and built upon still older ruins, the City Republic of Pahdookahport was ostensibly independent, free of homage to any lord save the hereditary Council of Merchant-Lords which had ruled from time immemorial. In grim reality, however, the port city had not exercised any latitude of self-determination for the twelve years since—besieged by a huge rabble of river pirates and in very tight straights—the then council had sought the aid of the Duke of Twocityport. At the head of his hundreds of disciplined, well-armed and battle-hardened mercenaries, Duke Tcharlz had not only broken the siege but had virtually annihilated the several bands of temporarily allied pirates.

Then had the council made its most serious mistake. All but bankrupt from the cost of the siege and the hefty sum exacted by the shrewd duke for his troops' services, their port facilities in need of extensive repairs before they stood any chance at all of refilling their coffers, the councilors had irrevocably doomed their long-standing free status by contracting a sizable loan in specie, materials and slave labor from their savior.

Since that date, Pahdookahport had been a client-state to Twocityport in all save name. The duke's interest rates on the loan went far beyond mere usury. After twelve long years, and despite large, twice-yearly payments, the principal of the loan still stood untouched and the interest still continued. Even the densest head in Pahdookahport now realized that Duke Tcharlz's stranglehold on the small republic would be loosened only by his death.

Not feeling really safe inside his captive city, for all that his own troops patrolled the streets and docks of the close-packed aggregation of homes, warehouses, taverns, brothels, countinghouses and shops, the duke had raised up a fine, strong and commodious residence atop a low hillock a half mile away from the city on the road which wound to Twocityport. He alternated his residence between this edifice and his palace near the capital.

Deliberately grinding the noses of the citizens of Pahdookahport into their hated serfdom to him, Duke Tcharlz had partially demolished several of their public buildings to face his new residence—christened Pirates' Folly—and had stripped public buildings and the very homes of merchantlords of fine furnishings, statuary, wall hangings and artwork, allowing only fractions of their true value to be applied against the city's indebtedness to him.

Chapter IV

After a tramp through the noisome streets of the city, Count Martuhn and Wolf grudgingly parted with a copper that a man at the fountain near the north gate would lave the filth from boots and greavès. Then the former nobleman overawed the junior officer commanding that gate and commandeered for Wolf and himself a brace of poorly gaited hacks for the remainder of their journey.

In the outer ward of Pirates' Folly, the hostler on duty looked with contempt at the sad specimens of horseflesh from which the two mercenaries dismounted . . . but not until he was leading them away, for the reputations of Captain Martuhn and his taciturn bodyguard were well known in all of Duke Tcharlz's lands, and few sane men would risk running afoul of such cold, merciless professional killers.

The duo stamped into the spacious anteroom—which constituted the only public entrance to the ducal audience chamber and the private apartment behind—and came to an impatient halt before the long, polished table which served as a desk for the noblemen who took turns screening visitors (and almost always exacting all that the market would bear in fees from said visitors before granting them audiences with Duke Tcharlz). And suddenly guardsmen in all stages of dress and undress crowded out of the wide doorways of the two adjoining guardrooms, some openly grinning in anticipation, all anxious to be actual spectators to one of the rare confrontations between their duke's most valued and trusted captain—a man either respected or feared by every soul in the duchy—and one of Duchess Ann's precious and un-failingly supercilious young noblemen.

The duke made a practice of conferring knighthood only for military achievements, but the duchess awarded such honors for less grim and sanguineous reasons—once, for a handsome performer who composed and sang to her a song praising her beauty, grace and wit; to another, for his skill at dancing; such things as handsomeness of face and dress, inventiveness in the matters of new games or dance steps or refinements of tortures to be used upon the prisoners chosen at random from the crowded dungeons at Twocityport—whereat Duchess Ann made her court and which her husband visited only grudgingly and solely for reasons of ducal duty.

Duke Tcharlz utterly detested his fat, ugly, arrogant and frigid wife, and he fully intended—indeed, spent long hours in pleasurable contemplation of—having her murdered, painfully, the moment that he felt his power such that he could hold all his lands in his own name against either external aggression or internal dissension. His deliberate delay in disposing of Duchess Ann was but another manifestation of the mature sagacity that had seen him succeed his ducal predecessor and onetime bitter enemy, Ann's late father.

Unable, for some mysterious reason, to sire any save useless daughters upon any one of his several wives and host of slave mistresses, the last hereditary Duke of Twocityport, Myk the Wise, had been most favorably impressed with the cunning and stark bravery and tenacity displayed by young Baron Tcharlz of Newtownport in the defense—with vastly fewer forces and inferior armaments and warships—of his minuscule principality against the old king of Mehmfizport, who was then attempting to enlarge by conquest his already sizable holdings.

Not much thought on the matter was required to show Duke Myk that when Newtownport fell—as it assuredly must for all the astute strategy and stunning tactics of its young lord—Twocityport would, soon or late, be next. Therefore, the old man had mobilized his existing forces and hired on every free bravo within reach, even granting amnesties for past wrongs to certain bands of pirates operating just beyond the fringes of his borders in return for their manpower and ships.

Through a stroke of purest luck, a fierce and wholly unexpected storm capsized, swamped, dismasted or drove ashore more than half of King Djahn's huge fleet even as it proceeded northward on the river to meet this new challenge, and the pitiful remnant were fallen upon and utterly extirpated by the duke's fleet, while Baron Tcharlz and his sketchily armed partisans hunted down and slew or enslaved almost every one of the now unsupported and unsupplied troops remaining ashore.

Hard upon the heels of this great mutual victory over what had been staggering odds, Duke Myk had suggested an alliance between his duchy and Tcharlz's barony. This alliance was to be permanently cemented by marriage between his eldest legitimate daughter, Ann, and Tcharlz.

Baron Tcharlz knew just why this magnanimous offer was tendered him. If, with no sons of any description, the aging duke should attempt to pass his titles and lands to one of his daughters, a protracted and bloody civil war was certain to ensue between his cousins, nephews and more distant relatives; if the internecine strife did not shatter the duchy into a number of tiny, all but defenseless statelets, the borders at least were sure to fall to aggressive neighbors. But with a strong, war-wise son-in-law, still of an age and temperament to raise or hire troops and take the field against internal or external foes . . .

Tcharlz and Ann conceived a mutual loathing upon their very first meeting, but the duke's eldest daughter, with no choice or options in the matter, had intelligence enough to accept the inevitable with as much grace as she could muster, while Tcharlz would gladly have wed himself to a fat sow from out the ducal swineherds, if that was what it would have taken to see him inherit upon the death of Duke Myk.

There still were rumors lurking about that the demise of the old duke—less than six months after he had formally declared his new son-in-law ducal heir—was speeded along by either said heir or his agents. But there had never been any real evidence to support the rumors, and the spreading of such gossip had proved risky, and sometimes fatal, business. Only the old nobility and retainers of Duke Myk might have been sufficiently moved by tales of his murder to retaliate against his heir, and there were but a bare handful of them left alive in the duchy in this twenty-second year since the ascendancy of Duke Tcharlz. The most fortunate of them had died of age's infirmities. Some had fallen upon the battlefields of Duke Tcharlz's early and widely supported wars of expansion. The wisest had left for other and safer desmesnes within hours of the death of the old duke, bearing with them all their fluid wealth. Those neither wise nor warlike nor aged had died in duels or at the hands of unknown robbers or had simply disappeared mysteriously.

But still the duke was leery of disposing of the wife he had loathed from the start and now hated with every fiber of his body. The reason that he allowed that hated Ann to live lay not east of the river but west, in the person of Alex, the Duke of Traderstownport. Not only had his great-grandmother been a legitimate sister of the late Duke Myk, but he was wedded to one of Ann's younger sisters and so felt that he had far better claim to Twocityport than did Tcharlz, whom he openly named "the Greedy."

Tcharlz, on the other hand, publicly had named Duke Alex "the Grunting Shoat," and the two duchies had, during the last decade, come within an ace of outright war on several occasions. All that bound them together now were the thick, dual cables that stretched from bank to bank of the broad, treacherous river, providing an easier and safer crossing for in- or outbound traders and serving as the lure which drew the tremendous amounts of trade that had rendered both duchies rich and powerful.

In the lifetime of old Duke Myk, when relations between the two river-separated duchies had been most cordial, the operations and maintenance of the precious cables, their docks, barges, related equipment and row-slaves had been the sole province of the Bi-Ducal River Cable Company—a privately owned stock company, headquartered in Twocityport, paying equal tax levies to each duchy and with about forty percent of the stock owned between the two rulers. It had been a highly profitable arrangement for all concerned for almost forty years . . . until the fude between the dukes erupted.

Duke Alex it had been who first began to use the cable company against the man he considered a murderous usurper of his—Alex's—rightful claims to the Duchy of Twocityport. As usual, fees were collected from freight and passenger traffic upon boarding the barges—so much per ton, hundredweight or gallon of cargo, so much per head of livestock or per passenger. Now, however, each day's receipts went directly into Duke Alex's coffers, rather than to the company countinghouse at Twocityport, and he himself undertook payment of the salaries of the employees stationed on the west side of the river.

Duke Tcharlz had, of course, volubly protested both by letter and by messenger, but each reply had been more ugly, and insulting and libelous than the last. Complaints from the cable company headquarters had been answered by an invitation to transfer said headquarters to the western side of the river and set about forming a new company, assured of the full support of Duke Alex's every resource, with the eventual intent of stretching a new and larger pair of cables from a point just north of his ducal seat to a point within the County of Kairoh, across the Ohyoh River from Twocityport.

This message was supposedly secret, but thanks to his extensive espionage web, Duke Tcharlz soon was fuming over the dastardly machinations of his peer. But the new-made duke was a man of action rather than of words. Within less than a month, he had invaded and conquered the smallish county to his north without bothering to declare a state of war and butchered all its ruling family, save the one, sickly and feebleminded scion he deliberately spared to serve as his puppet count. But he forbade plundering or any of the usual rapine and spoilage which has been the ages-old lot of the conquered, and he saw to it that his newest province was ruled even more generously and fairly than his older possessions, so that before many years had passed, the natives of Kairoh, prospering under his rule, would not have returned to a semblance of the old regime.

Since he had seen his plans so thwarted, Duke Alex had been reduced to insults, libel, scurrilous gossip, the dispatch of an occasional assassin or agitator eastward . . . and truly meaningless saber-rattling. For he knew as well as did Duke Tcharlz that a real war between their two realms would be at best folly and at worst suicidal, for powerful enemies—north, south, east and west—required but the slightest hint of weakness or inattentiveness to ally, descend and try to capture for their own the rich lands, richer cities and strategic locations on the principal east-west trade route.

If it did nothing else, however, Duke Alex's growls of war caused Duke Tcharlz to maintain a larger and better-equipped army of mercenaries than he otherwise would have done. Also, he kept hundreds of slaves and free artisans employed on various fortification and harbor projects. But he could well afford such expenditures, for all that his income had been halved by the knavish thievery of Alex.

His commission to his best and most favored captain to journey eastward and hire on recruits had been in anticipation of the early completion and garrisoning of his newest, largest and most important fortress—a huge and impregnable structure of stone, so situated that its cunningly designed engines of destruction could effectively cover almost all the waterfront of Twocityport and the mighty river itself to nearly midstream. Also, he had had the western terminals of the cables extended from the cable dock to new moorings within the fortress, so that in the event of an invasion by cable barge, his garrison might wait until the bulk of the enemy force were embarked, then sever the cables and send them all downriver on the strong, merciless current.

There had been loud, agonized screams and even a few muted threats when Duke Tcharlz first seized several square blocks of Lower Twocityport and commenced to set his slave gangs to leveling existing structures and even digging out the foundations; but all the merchants and other property owners had been reimbursed—a few, almost fairly. And now, even the most flagrantly robbed grudgingly admitted to the grim beauty of the new fortress, with its smooth and eye-pleasing lines—from the wide, deep, stone-lined and river-fed moat girdling the whole, through the high, thick walls of dressed granite and the cunningly situated and shielded engine emplacements, to the soaring watchtower, higher than anything else in Upper Town or Lower.

What Duke Tcharlz told none of the admirers of his fine new fortification was that although it could give easy lodging to a score of hundreds of warriors, a mere two hundred could hold it indefinitely. He knew this because one of the few men he had ever trusted had assured him of the fact, often relating to him how—long years ago and many miles eastward from Twocityport—he had himself held the archetype of this fortress for nearly two years with that few fighters and had, with his food almost gone, even managed to demand and receive favorable terms for himself and his folk from besiegers who could ill afford a further protracted campaign.

Duke Tcharlz well knew the military expertise of this man

and truly respected him as he did precious few others still living. The stark new fortress was but one of his more recent accomplishments in the duke's service, which, bloody and varied, stretched back more than fifteen years.

When Tcharlz's most efficient espionage service informed him of the imminent landfall of the sailing vessel bearing Captain Martuhn and the new mercenaries from the east, he deliberately invented an errand for Sir Andee, then stationed in his antechamber, and replaced him with the current "guardian," Sir Djaimz. It would do the strutting young blowhard good, thought Tcharlz gleefully, to have the very dung scared out of him this day. Perhaps then he would waddle back to Duchess Ann—who had knighted him for something or other having nothing to do with fighting or military affairs, and whose spy the duke had known him to be even before he had arrived here—and thus leave the affairs of menfolk to those possessed of balls and beards.

It would have been most impolitic for the duke to openly watch the encounter he had arranged—as much as he would have loved to do so—but he had ensconced himself in the room immediately adjoining, where he could make use of the cleverly concealed peepholes and earholes.

Far, far to the west of the river, out upon that limitless prairieland which men now called a sea—the Sea of Grass—there was unaccustomed movement in the face of the fast-encroaching winter. There, where mosses, grasses and black earth all but covered the broken fragments of the cities and towns, the hamlets and farms, deserted by man and dead for more than half a millennium, were now more men, women, children and their animals than had lodged upon the land in one body for long centuries.

The traders from the caravans had remarked among themselves over the past spring and summer on the remarkable number of "new" clans—clans that had come up from the southern and down from the higher, western plains. But few had thought deeply upon such movement, for it was the way of the nomad clans to wander wherever graze and inclination took them. The traders had simply thanked their luck or stars or gods and accepted the enhanced trading possibilities presented by these new customers.

But the newly arrived clans were not, as the traders surmised, simply following their herds; no, they had been summoned. In an expanse of prairie where in recent centuries a season might have seen three or possibly four clans gathered now were camped more than six-and-thirty of the principal clans of the Kindred. Nor had their chiefs chosen the sites of this coming winter's encampment, toward which they now were slowly moving. The sites had been chosen and clearly marked out by a man whom few had met but of whom almost all had heard—a war chief of all the Kindred clans, elected by the Grand Council of Chiefs empaneled at a special summer tribe camp three summers ago, a chief named Milo of Morai.

Chapter V

A true scion of the Tidewater or "Old" Ehleen nobility, Lord Urbahnos went to great lengths to avoid forking a horse, bred to his firm belief that carriage or war cart was the only acceptable transport for a refined gentleman. Only in direst necessity would he chafe and bruise his flesh, painfully strain muscles of thighs and buttocks and chance injury to his privates upon the back of some sweating, smelly beast, and never whilst wheeled transport was available.

But Duke Tcharlz's roads, especially the stretches between Twocityport and Pahdookahport, were deliberately a very bane of light-wheeled vehicles—although trader wagons and army vehicles, with their heavy construction, high road clearance and large, powerful teams regularly navigated the miles of ruts and mud and sinkholes. Since Lady Ann too detested riding horseback, this road was another barrier against her undesired presence in the duke's sumptuous new residence.

Therefore, the Ehleen had left Pahdookahport in the next best thing, to his mind: a spacious, well-padded, covered horse litter slung—at fore and aft—between a pair of rented Northorses. The monstrous iron-gray geldings were rare and hellishly expensive to buy, coming as they did from some land far north of the great inland sea; but the breed were all gentle, smooth-gaited, stronger than draft oxen and, standing an average of twenty-two hands at the withers, perfect for easily bearing a weighty horse litter above the virtual river of mire which autumnal rains and heavy traffic had made of the road to the east.

In the wallet attached to Urbahnos' swordbelt reposed three drafts upon his account at the Ducal Bank of Pahdookahport, all requiring only his signature and seal to render them negotiable, and he hoped to use one or more of these to buy the two valuable slave boys. However, knowing full well the preference of the plains traders for hard, ringing specie, he wore under his clothing a weighty leathern money belt, abrim with ducal gold and Ehleen silver coins. And this was why Nahseer and six other well-armed bodyguards trotted on surefooted riding mules before, behind and on either flank of his litter, hunched and miserable in the chill, drizzling rain despite their oilskins.

Protected from the wet by the canvas roof and sidecurtains, from the chill by paddings, pillows and a thick, winter bearskin, the onetime Lord of Kostanispolis sipped delicately from a commodious flask of strong honey wine and mused silently.

"Even if I have to part with every ounce of metal in my belt . . . and one of the drafts besides . . . my profit on just one of the little darlings will more than reimburse me . . . or should. Hmmm . . . let's see . . . perhaps . . . perhaps, if I sell the less pretty one . . . say, to a buyer in Kehnooryos Ehlas, and then present the prettier as an outright gift to Lord *Thoheeks* Nikos, King Zenos' principal adviser. Or should I gift the little bastard to the king himself? No, that's right"—he sighed gustily and shook his head of oiled ringlets—"like his father before him—God grant that that old scumsucker is burning in the deepest pit of Hell!—the young king is said to care only for women. Must be the barbarian blood, for he seems a cultured, civilized man in all other respects, from what I've heard. But not to take a pretty little boy now and again? Remarkably uncouth, to say the least!

"So! Then the boy must go to Nikos of Sahpahntispolis, who is at least gentleman enough to appreciate—to *properly* appreciate—the rarity and value of the gift. Why, this pair are the first Horseclans boys through these parts in years.

"As I recall him, *Thoheeks* Nikos is—for all his other failings—a true Ehleen gentleman of the old school, and if he gives value due to value received . . . and he *must*! I . . . I'm *dying* in this barbarian pesthole!"

Feeling tears starting to well up from his eyes, Urbahnos fumbled for a soft cloth and dabbed lightly at his eye corners, taking great care not to smudge the cosmetics on upper and lower lids or to disarrange his long, curling false eyelashes. Restowing the cloth, he took a long, burning pull at his flask before settling back again to his musings.

"So, then, the prettier . . . probably the younger will be prettier . . . the prettier will go to Nikos, and he *must* be untried, too, for the tastes of so refined a gentleman, so I had best send him east with Nahseer. Yes, that's perfect." He smiled. "That Zahrtohgahn bastard will butcher anyone who even touches the little sweetling, and, lacking himself any man parts, there'll be no chance of the guardian's being tempted."

Urbahnos had never had cause to regret his purchase of the hulking Nahseer, years before, when the Zahrtohgahn was placed upon the riverside slave block in Pahdookahport. It had been upon the first occasion that the huge man had saved his life and purse from a band of footpads—taking wounds in the process, since, prior to that time, his master had been loath to arm him—that the Ehleen had considered manumitting him . . . but he had yet to do so, for all that he frequently used the brown-skinned man to convey and guard especially valuable merchandise to the eastern coastal areas—furs, jewels, young and beautiful virgins and the like.

Now in his mid- to late-thirties, Nahseer claimed to have been of a high-caste family of the Kaliphate of Zahrtohgah, a mighty warrior of high rank in the armies of that land and possessed of wealth and power. His downfall, he went on to claim, was his intemperate lust for a girl who chanced to catch the eye of the *kahleefah* and be taken into his *hahreem*. Such had been Nahseer's bemusement that he had plotted to take the girl from *hahreem*, palace and city by a combination of stealth, force and bribery and bear her off to his own faraway city—aware that once her flower was taken, the *kahleefah* would have no interest in her and would, eventually, forgive him, since, in his almost constant state of war, he had far more need of competent captains than of just one among his hundreds of women.

However, as the Fates would have it, someone had betrayed the bold scheme and Nahseer had been set upon by a host of the *kahleefah's* guardsmen the moment he dropped from the top of the inner wall to the springy turf of the *hahreem* garden. Knowing full well his fate if taken alive, the mighty man had drawn both *yahtahgahn* and long dagger and fought with awesome effect. With strictest orders to take the intruder alive, the guardsmen had suffered terribly, taking crippling wounds and death thrusts and deliberately foregoing many opportunities to slay Nahseer in combat.

Finally overcome by force of numbers and sheer exhaustion, Nahseer had been dragged before his ruler. In a foaming rage at the numbers of warriors the prisoner had cost him, as well as at the attempted violation of his *hahreem*, *Kahleefah* Yusuf had had Nahseer severely flogged, gelded and sold for a slave to a party of traders from Ohyoh.

Despite the loss of his manhood, Nahseer had proved most intractable. Few of his early masters had owned him long, and all had been glad to see him go, often selling at a hefty loss to speed his departure. Finally, having become infamous and unsellable in all the Kingdom of Ohyoh, a river trader had bought the mass of brown-skinned muscle and bone for a pitiful sum on the speculation that he might bring a decent price in Pahdookahport or Twocityport, where strong male slaves were usually in demand for the oar barges.

Urbahnos surmised that the big man's loyalty to him was the result of his boundless thanks at being spared the long, hideous, drawn-out death sentence that was the lot of slaves and felons doomed to the oar barges. Had anyone told him that in the heart buried within that massive chest the Zahrtohgahn slave to whom he regularly entrusted both life and property hated and despised him, Lord Urbahnos of Kostanispolis would have openly scoffed and forever after have considered that person an idiot and utter fool.

"The lord *thoheeks* knows what I want, of course," Urbahnos mused on within the swaying litter. "He knows what an injustice was done me by old Zenos, that barbarian-loving, moon-blood-lapping dog turd. After all, I only pinked the ahrkeethoheeks' son. It wasn't *my* fault he died of black rot, was it? Of course not! And to accuse *me* of using a poisoned blade . . ."

Urbahnos almost always conveniently forgot how, on his way to that eleven-years-done duel, he had several times run the full length of his blade into the stinking, well-rotted carcass of a dead pig.

"So, the sooner I get the boy slave to Karaleenos, the sooner I may expect a pardon and a royal recall to my lands and city. Let's see . . . perhaps Pehtros will buy my house slaves; God knows he needs them. Why he's not long since died of some loathsome disease living in that pigsty is more than I can fathom. I suppose that I really should free Nahseer, but I'll surely need money to reestablish myself in the proper style, and if I can find a buyer willing to pay a really good price for him . . . but I won't sell him to the barge owners . . . no, not unless the other slaves and the house bring less than they should.

"As for Lylah, I might as well not go back home if I drag along a barbarian wife; no true Ehleen would even spit at me were I to do so monstrous a thing. Besides, we're not really married; barbarian rites aren't legal in any civilized, Ehleen principality that I know of. I'd sell her for a slave, her and the brats, too, if I thought I could get away with it. But she's freeborn *and* her parents were citizens of one of those little southern counties, and if the duke found out . . ."

He shuddered, seeing himself overtaken on the trip upriver by one of Duke Tcharlz's fleet of sail-and-oar warships, dragged off the passenger barge and brought in chains back to Pahdookahport, where—his diplomatic immunity be damned—the old pirate would likely rob him of every *thrah-kmeh* he owned in fines, then send him to his death on the benches of a row-barge. No, it would be far better to forgo possible profit and simply throw Lylah—his once-pretty wife of seven years—and their six children out of the house once it and the furnishings and slaves were all sold and he was ready to start his journey back east to the land of culture and light.

Often Urbahnos wondered just why he had wedded the chit, for what with her producing a child a year and her bouts of moon sickness between brats, his manly needs drove him to spend about as much time and money at the bordellos as he had before he wed. Nor were his forays into the higher-class brothels in any way cheap. The girls were expensive enough, but such few as would even deign to cater to men of cultured tastes and provide boys were astronomical, especially when one took into account the fact that the proffered boys were invariably passive, spiritless and a bit older than he preferred . . . not to mention often ugly and whip-wealed.

Urbahnos still gagged when he thought of that morning,

some years back, when he had awakened after an hours-long bout with an almost-new slave boy to find that the little bitch had used a knotted sheet to hang himself from an iron wall sconce. Recalling the contorted face, protruding eyes and bulging, blackened tongue had brought up everything Urbahnos ate or drank for days on end.

After having been for so very long denied a really prime, young, untried love boy, it was perhaps natural for Lord Urbahnos to drift into fantasies of breaking in the other Horseclans boy, the elder one, of course, not the younger, prettier one—that one must go, untouched, to Karaleenos. So, lost in this pleasurable fantasy, warmed by the honey wine and the bearskin, lulled alike by the swaying of the litter and the patter of the rain, he fell asleep.

For all that the road was in abominable condition and not quite straight in places, mounted men with decent horseflesh between their legs could traverse the full distance between the two cities in under a day, but as the ox-drawn trader wagons never moved fast enough over dry, level ground, it was closer to a two-day journey for them. In the days of the old duke, traders had camped overnight a bit off the road in a sheltered area that had an unfailing spring.

Duke Tcharlz, however, early in his reign, had recognized the possibilities, located a proved entrepreneur and entered into a silent partnership with him, advancing monies from the ducal purse to build, stock and man a sizable, well-built and reasonably comfortable serai in the area around that spring.

The duke had been astute in his choice of a partner. Portuh Frank had proved himself unprincipled and larcenous enough to reap handsome profits from the operation, yet sufficiently intelligent to realize that he was surely being closely watched by one or more of his employees and that to attempt to cheat the duke would be suicidal.

The main structure of the serai was the counterpart of countless others the length and breadth of the land—a large, rectangular building of stone and timber, rising two and a half stories over a full cellar and capped with a roof of hand-cut shingles; floored with planks of pine, the serai's main room was fifty feet long and thirty wide, with a huge fieldstone fireplace at either end for heating, all cooking being done in a nearby outbuilding, while the small private rooms on the second floor were heated by individual braziers.

In addition to the cookhouse, there were a score of other structures, all necessary for the proper hosting of guests, their animals and running stock—huge, commodious stables for horses and mules; a sizable corral for oxen, partially roofed over to protect the beasts from the weather; a big smoke-house for cured meats and a springhouse of equal size for keeping butter, fresh cheeses, milk and suchlike. The smithy adjoined the shop of a wagonwright, with the fabulous six-holer privy being situated hard by the spacious pigpens. For easier egg collection, the hens were kept confined to the environs of their roosting house by a tall fence of woven reeds. Nonetheless, the roosters and some of the more adventurous hens were always roaming the innyard to be chased and occasionally caught by the hounds whose presence was thought to discourage the inroads of fox, skunk, weasel and other vermin.

Another covered pen usually held a few blatting sheep, for mutton was a favored fare among the inn's clientele, while a small herd of milk goats were rapidly converting a growth of young trees a few hundred yards behind the inn into a stubbly field. Portuh Frank and his current woman dwelt in a small, snug cottage near the inn, and the remainder of the staff bunked in one of the three structures designed for the purpose.

The commodious cellars beneath the main structure held the bulk of the serai's provender—barrels of flour and meal, dried beans, peas and lentils, cured and aged cheeses, casks of lard and honey and oil, dried fruits and vegetables—apples, peaches, pears, plums, raisins, garlic, onions, pumpkin, herbs, mushrooms—kegs of beer, pipes of various wines, barrels of hwiskees and stone jugs of cordials and brandies. In the darker, cooler reaches, wooden bins held root vegetables and fresh cabbages with casks and barrels of pickled foodstuffs stacked between. The cellars also gave lodging to a trio of brown ferrets—a hob and two fitches—the very presence of which guaranteed an utter dearth of resident rats and mice. The only entrance to these magazines lay without the main building, and the only two keys to its massive iron lock were never out of the sight of Portuh and his master cook, one Dik Tchertch.

Being by their very nature parsimonious, few traders of any class would pay the slightly exorbitant prices Portuh demanded for lodgings within the private, lockable rooms on the second floor, usually either sleeping with their men—rolled in skins and blankets and quilts—on or under the tables and benches which furnished the first floor—or in the familiar discomfort of their huge wagons. Therefore, few of the upper-floor rooms were any longer furnished, those that were being but crudely so, since their most frequent use was to lock up for the night either slaves or especially valuable merchandise.

So, when the slightly drunk and overbearing Urbahnos and his party of bravos descended upon the serai in the deepening dusk of the wet, gloomy day, demanding a suite of well-heated rooms, a hot bath, food, wines, brandy and cordials, Portuh found both himself and his staff hard pressed to accommodate this unusual and scathing-tongued guest in less than the best part of an hour. Never before had he, either in this place or in his former locale—far to the northeast, whence he had fled by night only a skip and a jump ahead of the grim and hard-eyed retainers of a certain earl—had had as a guest one of these eastern Ehleenee, and if all were as impossible to please as this one, he thought that he could just as easily live out the remainder of his life without the custom of another of the insultingly supercilious bastards.

But Portuh was nothing if not capable and unstintingly patient wherever money was involved, and in time the suite of rooms was cleaned, furnished and brightly lit to the Ehleen's grudging approval. The drafts of cold, wet air which would certainly have entered through the small, high window holes had been forestalled by stuffing the openings with rags and covering these plugs with small, bright hangings. Then the fine charcoal in the braziers was started with red embers brought from the blazing hearths below.

Portuh himself sprinkled the aromatic herbs and gums atop the started charcoal and supervised the setting up of a long copper bathing trough and its filling with many steaming bucketsful of fresh-boiled spring water. The arrangements of what would be the Ehleen's sleeping and bathing chamber once completed, Portuh set himself and his staff to the larger, outer chamber.

With the final meal of the day still cooking, the only hot

foods available were mutton broth and hwiskee punch, but
Portuh had a large pot of each placed in the center of the
table, with a heaping platter of cold smoked ham, several full
loaves of crusty bread, crocks of relishes, pickles and fruits
preserved in honey, a cold joint of veal, a brace of cold
boiled hens and decanters of various wines, cider and brandy.
Then, with bows far lower than his girth would seem to per-
mit, he ushered the ill-tempered Urbahnos up the stairs to in-
spect.

The first few days after the flamboyant escape of their
older sister, Bahb and Djoh had been kicked and cuffed by
their angered, frustrated captors. But the boys had borne this
abuse as stoically as the long captivity, snarling curses at the
men who struck them, saving any tears for times when they
were alone and unobserved. And this behavior had won them
the grudging respect of most members of the trader caravan.

Although the traders assumed them brothers and although
they addressed each other frequently by that term, the two
boys were not that closely related. Bahb Steevuhnz *was* a full
brother of Stehfahnah—both having had the same mother
and father—but little Djoh's mother had been a concubine,
not of Horseclans stock but rather taken in a raid somewhere
up on the far northern plains. However, this alien woman
had died in his bearing and he had simply been added to the
other baby then being nursed by another of his sire's
women—this one a third wife of Horseclans blood—and at
his current age of ten winters he considered himself to be a
Horseclansman, for all that he almost totally lacked mindspeak and had darker skin tone and bigger bones than most
Horseclans folk, with brown eyes and hair that was coarse
and, when not bleached by sun, a light ruddy brown.

On the other hand, Bahb looked his heritage, was a true
scion of the Sacred Ancestors in all ways. His telepathic abilities were great and well honed; he could mindspeak horse
and prairiecat and the more intelligent of wild beasts as well
as he could carry on everyday silent communication with others of his clan and tribe. And from his crosslegged seat on
the thin pallet in a corner of the chilly room in which he and
Djoh were immured, he was using this talent to "chat" with
the horses on which he and Djoh and Stehfahnah and their
now dead older sibling had ridden into the trader camp. Al-

though too small for the majority of the big traders to ride, the wiry horses had proved fine for load-packing and so had been retained. But, according to the plans of the traders, they too would go on the block at Pahdookahport.

But Bahb Steevuhnz had other plans, and it was the implementation of these that he was discussing with the most intelligent of the four mares, Windswift.

"Sister, Djoh and I have been working at the two bars of iron that block the wall opening in the place where we are. The opening is far too small for a man's shoulders to go through anyway, so whoever set the bars did not set them deep and now only a hard tug is needed to clear them away. Little Djoh can slip through easily, and I can make it, too, and one of the trader wagons is against the wall but a spear length below. But do you understand what you must do? Everything depends on you, horse sister."

The middle-aged mare beamed assent, adding, "But such a ruse could work only with stupid twolegs such as these who have enslaved us—twolegs lacking mindspeak, who have no real understanding of my kind. My brother will bespeak me when to begin?"

"Yes, horse sister, and it will be well after Sacred Sun has gone to His rest. No moon or stars this night, and just as well, too—the darker the better, for our purposes."

"But, brother twolegs, if this plan fails," added the mare grimly, "my sisters and I, we will not be taken alive by these ignorant, brutal twolegs. At your behest and at your twolegs sister's we have been meek and spiritless as so many silly sheep. But no more—after this night we fight!"

Bahb agreed just as grimly. "Belike, this night, we all will fight, sister; we shall regain our freedom or go to Wind."

After the serving of the evening meal—plain food, but plentiful—there was a brief period when the traders and their employees simply lolled on the benches and stools about the fires, chatting desultorily, picking at teeth, belching and otherwise going about the early stages of digestion. A bit apart from hoi polloi, Hwahruhn—who had been chosen as his successor by the wounded and crippled Shifty Stuart, whom they had had to leave in the home of a physician back in Tworivertown—and Custuh held their own, low-voiced discourse.

"It's boun' t' be them boys," averred Custuh firmly. "I done had lotsa truck with them damn Ehleenee. City borned an' bred, all of the shaved an' oiled an' sweet-smellin' bastids, an' it takes suthin' more'n jest extry fine furs 'r the like fer to mek 'em leave ther dang houses an' towns, even in good weather. So, fer thet there fancy-dan Ehleen asshole up there to shuffle his stumps 'long a muddy road this far from Pahdookahport, he's jes natcherly got him a dang good reason, Hwahruhn, ol' buddy; an' it ain't but one lot we got would set a dang Ehleen to itching. Ever'body knows 'bout how they dotes on pretty lil boys."

Setting mug to lips, Custuh drained off the last mouthful of beer from it, then nodded and stated, "You jest watch what I says, buddy boy—afore long, thet there Ehleen'll be down here or, likelies', he'll've sent one of his bodyguards down to fetch us up there to his rooms. An' you bet it'll be them boys he's after, an' we play him right, we'll mek us as much off'n them as ever'thin' elst put t'gether."

Trader Hwahruhn said nothing at once, sipping at a beaker of fine wine and sinking his gaze into the darksome depths of the vintage. He still felt strongly, had indeed felt so from the very beginning out on the prairie, that only calamity would be the result of the cruelty and treachery with which Shifty Stuart had enslaved the three nomad children and slain their elder brother. He had seen the maiming and crippling of the senior trader as but the beginning of this doom.

He had been pondering upon the subject much of late. The poor abused girl was dead, as likely as not, and the boys could definitely not be released to return to their clan. If such were done, no trader would be safe out there until that clan's thirst for blood was slaked. But neither was it really needful to sell the lads into slavery—especially not for the hideous, unnatural bondage for which Ehleenee were infamous.

Hwahruhn had begun to wonder if the fearsome doom he could feel pressing upon them could be averted if he took the boys home with him and reared them as sons. He had meant to look in on the boys this night to explain realities, broach his plan and give them the ways and means to appear so weak and sickly that the auctioneer in Pahdookahport would most likely not even accept them in his holding pen, much less put them on the block. But now, with that damned, odious, effeminate easterner in the very serai, both time and opportunity had flown. And he felt ill, queasy in the face of a dire and certain danger—apparently sensed by none other, but nonetheless now hovering so near that he could feel prickling hairs or gooseflesh over every inch of his body.

Custuh had arisen and stepped over to a beer barrel to re-fill his flagon, and so rapt was Hwahruhn that he nearly jumped out of his skin and did slop out half his wine when a throat was loudly cleared just behind him. He turned to be-hold the dark-skinned chief bodyguard of the Ehleen.

Although he had shed both his armor and sword, Nahseer looked—and was, in truth—no less dangerous with the long, wide-bladed dirk depending from his belt. But his manner and his tone were formally polite and deferential.

"How is the master trader called . . . ?"

Hwahruhn shook his head. "I'm not a master trader, nor is Custuh, over there; the master of this train was badly hurt a few days back, and we two sub-traders are simply acting as agents in his interest until he recovers enough to catch up with us."

Nahseer probed, "But you do have authority to sell goods?"

Hwahruhn nodded again. "Of course. In what might you be interested? We have some very fine hornbows for sale, real Horseclan-made. Three or four of them are of much better quality than you normally see offered."

The Zahrtohgahn shook his own scarred, shaven head. "I am a slave, sir. I have no money to buy weapons or anything else. And my master is interested only in two boy slaves he has learned you hold. He would speak with you and your as-sociate . . . at once, please; I will escort you."

Upon being ushered into the suite that was to be his, as long as he could bear to remain, Urbahnos had not hesitated to voice his extreme displeasure loudly and insultingly. The rooms were, by his lights, small, smelly, dirty, drafty and musty. The bed was lumpy and sour-smelling and the blan-kets were thin and stained. The filled bath was too hot, scald-ing; but yet the addition of but a single full pail of spring water rendered it "too cold."

The Ehleen dumped the tureen of mutton broth in the middle of the fresh-scrubbed floor and topped the mess with the hot hwiskee punch, then heaved the punchbowl at—and

but narrowly missed—Portuh's head. Had one of his usual
guests done even a quarter as much, Portuh's well-honed
knife would have brought forth some blood to add to the
other liquids on that floor. But he now restrained his temper,
intimidated as much by Lord Urbahnos' known connections
in high places as by the seven big, well-armed, tough-looking
bravos.

But finally, with the arrogant Ehleen ensconced in a bath
of the right temperature, Portuh brought in men and girls to
rescrub the floor, scoop up the mess and replace the fouled
carpets.

Once bathed, oiled and freshly scented, clad in clean garments from one of his chests and relieved of the chafing
weight of the leathern money belt, Urbahnos had Nahseer
bear the ham, the veal, a loaf of bread, some of the wine and
a couple of the cordials to his bedchamber, and only after his
stomach was filled did he allow the hired guards to go down
to partake of the serai's evening meal. They were sent two at
a time, so that there were never less than four of them and
the hulking Nahseer to guard him and his gold. The
Zahrtohgahn was granted no access to the hot meal below, receiving only the leavings of his master.

When the last pair of hired men had returned and when
the belowstairs tumult had quieted somewhat, the Ehleen sent
Nahseer to summon the master trader to the suite. With luck,
only a single night would be spent in this filthy sty of a barbarian pesthole. No matter what he had to pay for the two
boys, if the bribe one of them would constitute accomplished
its purpose and allowed him to return and live out his remaining days in a clean, decent, civilized land, the expense
would be trifling.

As for the other, the less comely boy . . . well, he would
provide sport and release for Urbahnos himself this night and
many a night thereafter until the Ehleen tired of and sold
him.

An experienced trader, Urbahnos knew men and could
quickly and accurately type most of them upon first meeting.
The plains trader Custuh, he immediately realized, was, for
all his stinking, barbarian antecedents, a man much like himself—avaricious, cold, cruel, cunning and completely amoral.
Were enough gold and silver stacked on the table between
them, Urbahnos knew that he would speedily have this Cus-

tuh's mark on the bills of sale that he had had drawn up before he left Pahdookahport.

But the other man, Hwahruhn, the Ehleen just as quickly surmised, could easily present problems, make the transaction overly long and force him to spin fanciful lies as to the eventual fates of the little slaves. He silently prayed that Custuh was in charge.

Ahzee, the elder of the two wagoners who had been assigned to supervise the captive boys and care for their needs until they were sold, had moved immediately the food was brought into the main room of the serai. He had chosen foods which he had known from his years of service with Shifty Stooahrt on the prairie and plains would have the appeal of familiarity to his charges—boiled mutton in its broth, hard cheese and soft, chewy chunks of dried fruits, a two-quart beer pitcher of frothy, fresh milk. Before sending a servant to fetch the milk, Portuh had loudly questioned why these slaves could not be content with his good beer or cider. But wise Ahzee knew that even the best grade of beers and wines had a decidedly unsettling effect upon the innards of Horseclansfolk, and he also knew that Mistuh Custuh would be a man to be avoided for some time if the two boys were suffering a bad case of the shits when put up for sale.

Before Ahzee and the other wagoner, Klahrk, could reach the foot of the stairs with the trays and pitcher, Mistuh Hwahruhn had added choice joints from a roast chicken and chunks of honeycomb to their burdens. The stocky, black-bearded Klahrk groused under his breath about the short delay, but Ahzee gave him a single, hard stare; he liked and deeply respected Mistuh Hwahruhn and thought it a goldarned shame that Custuh had been appointed head man.

In the room, Ahzee set the trays and pitcher atop a locked goods chest and drew a couple of smaller bales from the stack in a corner to seat the boys at the improvised dining table. While the older man so labored, the younger stood idly by the door, scraping his feet and whining that if they delayed longer all the choicer portions would be gone at the long tables belowstairs.

Ahzee just snorted, "All you evuh thinks 'bout is yore dang belly, Klahrk, an' it a'ready stickin' out like you's three moons gone, mebbe five! Don't be so dang useless, heanh?

These here younguns is ever bit as much yore 'spons'bility as
they is mine. You jest tek their gut bucket an' empty it an'
mek sure it's a good number of hay balls in t' box. Then you
broach one them bales o' b'arskins, or with no fire, Bahb 'n'
lil Djoh here'll plumb freeze t'death or at leas' come down
with th' dang bloody croup t'night with them thin pallets an'
motheaten blankets."

The wooden latrine bucket in hand, the tall but paunchy
Klahrk paused at the door, his brows knitted, picking with
cracked and filthy nails at a pustulating sore on his chin under the matted beard.

"Sleepin' col' ass one night ain't gonna hurt them lil bastids
none, an' I don' think Mistuh Custuh'd be too happy if I
broke no bale opuned, an' . . ."

Ahzee straightened up and whirled to stand, arms akimbo,
his seamed face revealing more disgust than real anger.

" 'An . . . ? Dang yore lazy ass, Klahrk, you musta been
gone to tek you a piss whin they's handin' out brains! Bestest
thang fer you's t' let a body's got sumthin more'n rotten
ches'nuts in they haids t' do th' thinkin. Heah me?

"You's a wagoner helper, boy. I's a full senior wagoner,
with dang near twenny years awn t' plains, an' I *knows,* boy!
Mistuh Custuh, he won' say pee-turkey bout one dang bale,
oncet he comes to fin' out why it 'uz broached, cause these
here younguns is money, big money. An' evun was he t', he
cain't do a dang thang t' me, he wouldn' dast."

Ahzee grinned broadly. "See, boy, this here train is still the
Stooahrt Comp'ny's, fer all poor ole Shifty's a-layin' back in
Twocityport with jes' one arm an' a leg'll be gimp fer the
resta his life an' his balls a-tore near off him. Mistuh Custuh's
only got charge till we gits back upriver to Looeezfilburkport.
Then, if Shifty cain't tek the train out nex' spring, mos' likely
his brother, Zeek Stooahrt, 'll do it. Don't matter to me none,
boy, 'cause both Shifty and Zeek, they's my son-in-laws, see.

"Now you jes' shake yore stumps an' git 'long bout whut-
all I tol' you t' do. Heah?"

Later, when he had allowed the helper to go back down
the stairs to crowd his way onto a bench and begin stuffing
his face, old Ahzee sat while the boys ate, chatting with
them.

In a casual tone and manner, Bahb shrewdly elicited all
that the wagoner knew of the towns, inhabitants and terrain

of the duchy, but kept his face blank to hide his deep disappointment from both his little brother and their captor. Short of trying to swim the vast and deadly width of the river, Bahb Steevuhnz could comprehend no possible way to win back to the west bank and even a thin chance to regain freedom. Nonetheless, his resolve was firm to continue on with the plan—better to die in honor, fighting to the end, than to become a possession again.

When the boys seemed replete, Ahzee placed the leftover food in the covered dish. Leaving it, the two cups and the milk in the pitcher, he gathered up the rest of the crockery and the lamp and departed, carefully locking the stout door behind him.

The moment they heard the iron lock snap into place and the descending footsteps of the old wagoner, Bahb and Djoh drew forth the three pieces of scrap metal they had managed to pick up near the wagon shop and forge during their brief time in the yard. All during the afternoon, while Bahb had held himself suspended by one arm from the sill of the window and picked at the shallow seating of the two bars, Djoh had been absorbed in honing the other, larger pieces to keenness on a flattish stone he had found and secreted.

While Djoh, mostly by feel in the dimming light from the small, high window, began to slice an edge of one of the heavy bearskins into thongs, Bahb took the longer, slenderer bit of steel he had used on the bars and commenced to patiently work it into the big iron lock securing the chest. Neither of the boys knew what was in this or any of the other wooden goods chests, but with luck they might find better weapons than three clumsy handleless slivers of metal.

Bahb worked the pick deeper, then twisted and turned at it, recalling the movements of the men he had seen thrust similar bits of metal into this and other locks; one bit of metal was as another to him, and he had never heard the words "key" or "lock" prior to his captivity.

Just as he felt the mechanism of the padlock begin to give under his efforts, there were footsteps beyond the door and a key grated in its lock. Then the door swung wide to admit three men—the two trader sub-chiefs and a tall, plumpish stranger.

Chapter VI

Lord Urbahnos rapidly gained a grudging respect for the grubby, smelly little barbarian, Custuh, and could easily see just why the injured Trader Stooahrt had appointed the man his senior deputy. Behind the façade of his talented theatrics, his country-bumpkin-fresh-off-the-farm demeanor, the Ehleen could sense now and again the real Custuh—the born merchant, driving straight for the jugular, thinking on his feet, out to and usually able to squeeze out the best price the traffic would bear.

And Urbahnos just as rapidly came to hate the junior deputy, Hwahruhn, who had not made any effort to disguise, by word or by action, the fact that he despised the Ehleen merchant and detested all for which he stood. Had it been Hwahruhn's decision alone, Urbahnos knew that he would never have been able to purchase the boys. As it was, the junior deputy's barrage of attempts to scuttle the deal had made the eventual purchase price inordinately steeper than Urbahnos had anticipated. For, naturally, the shrewd, cool, calculating Custuh—having sensed that these little Horseclans boys were unnaturally important to the man he was stalking—feigned to seize upon each of Hwahruhn's well-meant objections and points and take them as yet another way to jack the price several *thrakmehee* higher.

But after the two traders had abruptly retired outside to have loud and heated words on the gallery, they had returned for Urbahnos to close the deal with Custuh alone. Hwahruhn simply sat silently beside the other trader and stared at the seller with soul-deep disgust and at the purchaser with murderous hatred and bottomless loathing.

The leathern money belt that Urbahnos lifted from the table and handed back to Nahseer was but a bare shadow of its former, well-stuffed self, but Urbahnos had two copies of each bill of sale. He had been surprised to notice that both of the barbarian traders could write their names—not in civilized Ehleeneekos, of course, but that would have been an unadulterated phenomenon in this benighted land.

Lord Urbahnos was, of course, wrong in his belief that he and he alone was the sole civilized and cultured man from the western slopes of the Blue Mountains to the Great River and beyond.

On the prairie, many and many weeks' hard ride to the west of that river, sprawled the largest camp ever seen by any of its inhabitants. No less than a score and a half of Horseclans made up that camp, and all with their warriors, their maiden archers, their wives, their children, their concubines, yurt wagons, carts, tents, oxen, cattle, sheep, a few clans with goats and dogs, and huge, eddying herds of those mindspeaking horses that were equal partners with these folk rather than their chattels. And even above the incredible tumult of the camp, every day the screams of the clan stallions pealed forth as, with teeth and hooves, they went about settling the question of which was to become the king of this tribal herd.

Present also were more than a score of septs of the Cat Clan. Mindspeakers, like the horses and a majority of the humans, and like the horses equals, these prairiecats were ancient allies of all Horseclansfolk. Had Lord Urbahnos ever confronted a specimen face to face, he would likely have died of fright.

Huge they were, adult males standing nine hands and more at the heavily muscled shoulders, and adults of both sexes bore fangs three to four inches long. The predominant colors of these mighty felines were a tawny brown or a mouse gray, but there were more than a few examples of other hues among them—pure white, jet black, ruddy brown, blue-gray, many shades of yellow and, among the cats of the more southerly clans, traces of the dark spots and rosettes that testified to long-ago breedings with the wild *teegrais*.

In the very center of this vast assemblage stood a yurt the

likes of which few had ever seen before. True, the latticework sides were only half again as high as those of the average yurt—six feet as compared to four—nor did the top tower overly high, but the circumference of the circular dwelling was stupendous to the clansfolk camped about it. Four hundred and eighty and one half hands was its outer measure; more than sixty-five paces might a man take around the yurt's perimeter before returning to where he had begun.

This great yurt was home to Blind Hari of Krooguh—for seventy and more years, the tribal bard—and to his slaves, to the men and women from various clans who had freely joined his household and to one other, the newly chosen war chief of all the Kindred clans, Milo of Morai.

There was, on the surface, nothing too unusual about this man. True, he was taller than the average clansman, with the heavier bones, larger hands and feet and black hair-shot-with-silver of a dirtman (Lord Urbahnos might have taken this new war chief for a Northern Ehleen, what with his aquiline nose and olive skin tones), but a large minority of clansfolk varied—mostly through concubine mothers captured in raids on the dirtmen—from the short, slender, wiry, blond norm to make Milo of Morai's physical appearance pedestrian.

In other ways, there could be no doubt that he was Horseclans born and bred. His mindspeak was superlative with human, horse or prairiecat; he sat his golden-chestnut stallion as if they two were but one creature; his heavy, ancient saber was clearly an extension of his arm, and he was just as clearly a master bowman. And that he was a natural leader of men, a chieftain in every sense of that word, was clear to everyone who met him.

Some sixteen to seventeen winters agone, he had ridden up from the far south on his palomino stallion, accompanied only by two female prairiecats and a packhorse or two. He had wintered over with Clan Morguhn, where Blind Hari also was wintering that year, and with the rebirth of spring he had ridden north with the aged tribal bard.

The story he told—that he was the only survivor of a clan destroyed by a sudden and deadly pestilence—was tragic but easily believable, for a few clans had been extirpated in just such horrible a fashion over the centuries. Other clans had drifted away—to north, south, east and west—never to be heard of again. The Clan Krooguh, Blind Hari's own clan of birth, had disappeared in such a manner ten or fifteen winters past.

Blind Hari himself was an incredibly old man. To the best reckoning of the clansfolk he had weathered at least one hundred and thirty winters, yet still he rode hither and yon, reciting the centuries of the history of the Kindred in rhymes to the plucking of his fingers upon the strings of his harp, collecting the new vital statistics from each clan on his years-long circuit—notable births, heroic deaths, mighty deeds of war or raiding or hunting, ascensions of new chiefs and the like—then weaving the news into his endless rhymes.

But these were not the sole functions of the bard. As he was clanless, he was the full equal of any clan chief, while being but very distantly related to any of them or their folk, and as he knew all of the hundreds of Couplets of Horseclans Law, he was often called upon to break off his circuit in order to serve as mediator between clans on the brink of a feud. And for so many years had he served in this role when called upon to do so that he was the one being upon whom every living member of the Kindred freely lavished true reverence.

Too, there was a mysterious, almost magical quality about the frail-appearing, white-haired and bearded old man. Blind for as long as any could remember, yet it seemed that often he could see more clearly than any sighted man present, and none knew how this was accomplished. Eerie too was his control over the actions of men. On one notable occasion, he arrived to mediate too late. A vicious little melee between the fully armed warriors of Clans Danyuhlz and Muhkawlee had already commenced; Blind Hari had surveyed the carnage from the back of his weary horse—or so it had seemed to those who watched—then he had dismounted, removed his leathern helmet, his saber and even his dirk and eating knife. And, unarmed, unprotected, accompanied only by his prairiecat companion, he had walked slowly and deliberately into that pitiless maelstrom of whetted steel and deadly hate.

Full many had been the horrified cries from the noncombatants begging the irreplaceable old man to come back to safety, but he had not heeded them. He had paced on until he stood in the very center of that small, bloody battlefield. Then he had been seen to raise his hands so that his sleeves fell back from his scarred, withered old arms, and then the more sensitive of the mindspeakers there had felt, they later attested, the vague sense of a . . . a pressure.

While horses in the two camps reared and screamed or went running off onto the prairie, while prairiecats not engaged in the fracas yowled and snarled and spat and clawed at empty air and then, finally, slunk off to hide in tents or yurts or in the man-high grasses, Blind Hari of Krooguh had simply stood, as if carved in stone, he and his cat, with blade of axe and saber and spear and heavy dirk flashing and ringing about them.

Then those gathered about felt that arcane pressure increase, increase until it became well-nigh unbearable, until children began to cry and women to scream.

The twoscore combats ceased—not slowly or individually, but all at once and suddenly, as if the motive power to swing steel or to lift shield had been abruptly denied every man on that field. Bleeding men simply stood in place, arms at sides, panting with exertion, hands still gripping hilt and haft and shaft and handle, staring into the eyes of recent opponents.

Then the pressure had eased slightly and Blind Hari had begun to speak, not loudly, but loudly enough for all to hear. No one afterward seemed to recall his exact words, but only how telling they were. He had spoken of the Sacred Ancestors, of the Undying God-Man who had succored those Ancestors and who had, for more than three hundred years, remained with their own forefathers, teaching, guiding and protecting, giving them law and alliance with horse and cat. He had reiterated the close blood and heritage ties of all the Kindred, every clan, of Ehlai—the Holy City, whence had come the Sacred Ancestors, children, fleeing the War of the Old Gods, which had left them the only true men upon the face of the ravaged land.

He had spoken long of their centuries of bitter conflict with the bestial dirtmen on the verges of the prairies and plains, and of the equally deadly warfare with non-Kindred nomads for control of graze and water. He had reminded them that neither fight was successfully concluded and that since their Undying God had departed them more than tenscore years agone, their only chance of certain survival lay in firm solidarity of the clans, of brotherly love for Kindred brother.

And all at once, whilst the tribal bard still spoke his words of sad admonishment, steel began to ring once more . . . upon the hard, dusty ground. Prized and trusty weapons were dropped to clatter unheeded as hardbitten veteran warriors, whose bloodshot eyes were suddenly a-brim with tears, clasped hands with or fondly embraced those whom they had so lately been earnestly endeavoring to kill or maim.

At the next tribal council, this tale had gone far and wide among the Kindred clans, adding a luster to the very real awe with which Blind Hari of Krooguh was viewed.

Therefore, at the most recent tribal council—the gathering held every five years—when Blind Hari had sung portions of the familiar "Prophecy of the Return of the Undying," "The Song of Ehlai" and "How Strange our Old Lands", and then had presented Chief Milo of Morai for the benefit of those few who had never before met him, commenting upon how exactly the circumstances of his arrival at the Clan Morguhn camp upon the Brazos had meshed with those prophecies in the old songs, a fevered excitement had been generated and was still spreading.

Due to Blind Hari's immense age, there had been but three in the succession of tribal bards since the departure of the Uncle of the Kindred to seek out his own clan of Undying in some far-off land. So the chiefs could be reasonably certain the three musical renditions of history and prophecy—the most crucial of which was "Prophecy of the Return"—had not been garbled by different bards over many, many scores of winters. Furthermore, upon the summoning of the clan bards to the chiefs' council, not by more than a single word were any of their renditions different from that of Blind Hari. The tribal bard's version stated that Ehlai—"by her shining sea"—lay eastward, and a good half of the versions of the clan bards agreed; the others contended that the Holy City lay to the west. The chiefs eventually decided that Hari's version must be the correct one.

Uncle of the Kindred, the Undying God of them all, had not said that he himself would return, only that "one" would return, "from the south, upon a horse of gold"; just so had this Chief Milo arrived, years back, from the south and astride a big stallion of shimmering golden chestnut. The Undying had said that this "one" would be a leader, and this Milo of Morai most assuredly was, and that he would be

one of them, and precious few doubted the Kindred antecedents of the Morai. The Undying had added that, with
the title of War-Chief-of-the-Tribe-That-Will-Return-to-the-
Sacred-Sea, and acting as chief-of-chiefs, this "one" would
lead all those clans with unstained honor on a years-long mi-
gration back to the ruins of the city of the Sacred Ancestors'
birth to reclaim and rebuild.

The tribal council had dragged on and on, far longer than
any other council before it, as the chiefs wrangled and
chewed over the issue. At great length, they had all agreed to
choose Chief Milo of Morai as their first war chief, to be
paramount to all until Ehlai was reached, or Morai died or
named a successor, who must then be approved by the council
before actually succeeding. All the chiefs felt that this final
measure was necessary, for the songs clearly indicated that a
score or more of winters might see the tribe still on the move
eastward. Therefore, few of them would likely see the Holy
City, and, as the Morai seemed to be of at least early middle
years, surely he too would become old and infirm before the
goal had been achieved.

Had he so chosen, War Chief Milo of Morai could have
eased the minds of the chiefs, at least on the final measure.
For his appearance had not altered by one jot through all the
time through which his memory stretched . . . and that was
almost *seven hundred years!*

Where he squatted on a carpet-covered earthen dais, listen-
ing to the circle of squatting chiefs planning and discussing
the order of march, this one called Milo kept his thoughts
well shielded—a thing always necessary in a camp filled with
born telepaths, but especially necessary in his own case. For
he thought it best that none, not even old Hari, know for a
while that he was in reality none other than their deified
Uncle of the Kindred, returned after two centuries of tramp-
ing and riding and sailing the wide world in search of an is-
land where, it was fabled, all folk were like himself, ageless
and almost immortal. —

"But I never found it," he thought ruefully. "Nearly everyone had heard of it in every land I touched, but it was a
chimerical quest, for the information I received was always
the same. It lay just over the next range of mountains, in the
center of the next sea or in a great lake in a great continent
beyond that sea." Deciding at length that he was vainly pur-

suing a mirage, he had begun to retrace his steps, to come back to the only real home and kin he had ever known.

"But haven't they changed?" he thought on. "Who in hell would ever have thought that a bare hundred and fifty or so skinny, frightened, starving, sniveling little kids that I found huddled in an air-raid shelter tunneled into a mountainside could have been the progenitors of these fine men and of all the folk they lead?

"They have adapted unbelievably well to a singularly harsh and unrelenting environment. Their so-called Sacred Ancestors, during that first spring and summer on the high plains, didn't even know how to wipe their butts properly without toilet tissue, while these, their descendants, are fully capable of supplying their every need from the land alone.

"Well, save perhaps the steel for their weapons and a few tools—but Blind Hari avers that very few of the blades came from the east or the south, most being produced by clan smiths who had dug the metal out of ancient ruins. And that's another thing, too. Almost all the easterners and southerners with their anthropomorphic gods and their superstitions are scared spitless of the ruins, the so-called God Cities; yet wherever they come across them the clans camp in them—set up their yurts and pitch their tents in the long-dead villages and towns and cities of the late, great United States of America. Nor do they depart until the graze is depleted, or the game, or the diggings are not producing enough in the way of metals or useful artifacts to make the labor worthwhile, or until they just feel the urge to move on. Worshiping, as they do, only Sun and Wind and, to a limited extent, their swords and sabers—this last a rite that seems to have filtered in from the east in the last two hundred years, for *I* never founded it—these clansfolk harbor hardly any of the debilitating, gruesome superstitions to which most folk in this land and overseas seem addicted, and so they do not fear the supernatural.

"They are truly a feisty bunch, and the few things that they do fear are all completely natural and feared with damned good reason—prairie fire, pestilence, the huge and very dangerous winter wolf packs . . ."

Fleetingly, Milo recalled a wintry day now more than five centuries past when he and a handful of dismounted clansmen had been trapped in a crumbling ruin in the mountains of what had once been southern Idaho by a combination of a three-day blizzard and one of those packs of a hundred or more starving wolves.

"Now *that* was a damned chancy thing," he mused. "If I hadn't lucked across that sealed room of emergency supplies and that scoped rifle with enough ammo to wipe out most of the pack . . .

"No, these people have good reasons for fearing the few things that they do, especially the stinkers and the blackfeet. Those predators are always devilish hard to kill. It's just a damned fortunate thing that there're so few of them, and most of those stalk the elk on the high plains or follow the caribou herds hundreds of miles north of here.

"It's funny, too, back in the days before everything fell apart, a lot of scientific types carried on at length about the mutations of men and animals and plant life that an atomic war was certain to produce in survivors. But unless the mindspeak in which each new generation of these clansfolk seems to be more proficient is such a mutation, I cannot see where any real change has taken place in men.

"*I* am no mutation, at least not of that bit of manmade hell, for I was just as I am today, with every one of my . . . well, oddities . . . sixty years before the Two-Day War.

"The prairiecats are not mutations, but rather the result of a deliberate, scientific, prewar attempt to breed the sabertooth cats back into existence by that group in the Idaho mountains. And that was the origin, too, of these damned beasts they call shaggy-bulls. The journals I read while we were waiting for the rest of the two clans to join us there told it all. *Bison primogenus* or longhorn bison is what that group was shooting for; I think they got them, too, by breeding back the regular, smaller bison and certain of the more primitive breeds of cattle like the Texas longhorn, the Highland strain and the yak, plus—as I recall—the gaur and the European wisent.

"The director of that project who wrote those journals did allude here and there to other, earlier attempts with other species of beasts, and so conceivably those humonguous mustelids could be an outcome of his breeding pens. But I tend to doubt it, for he was trying to recreate extinct species, and I never heard or read anywhere of twelve-or-fifteen-foot mink or ferrets, past or present.

"They . . ."

Blind Hari's voice abruptly broke into his musings. "What says the war chief then? Does the tribe bear to the north and cross the Great River where it is not so wide and swift, or do we rather follow the Traders' Trail and cross over as do they?"

Milo shrugged. "Unless we backtrack far west and then north, we still would be faced with a wide, swift and deadly river before we could reach the headwaters of the Great River. Why should we do that and risk the chance of a much harder winter in a northern land? Let us continue on to Traderstown and see what transpires there. If the dirtmen of that town will not afford us use of their barges for a reasonable fee, then we shall take the barges, the town and all in it by force of arms. It is the sacred destiny of this tribe to return to the Holy City of our Sacred Ancestors' birth, and neither man nor Nature shall impede us."

Stehfahnah lay on her side with her naked body bunched as closely together as she could to conserve its heat, but still her little white teeth chattered. She had been captive in the trapper's cramped, filthy hut for a week, bound hand and foot each time he left for any reason, and as his traplines ran for many miles up and down the riverbanks and deep into the forests, he and his small but sturdy ass were usually absent from a bit after sunrise until nearly dark.

The girl once more ran her dry tongue over even drier lips, wishing for her captor's return almost as much as she dreaded it. It was purest torture to lie watching the bulging waterskin hanging but a few feet distant and not be able to reach it; and torture, too, was the need to forcibly restrain the needs of her body to empty itself during the long hours alone, but the man's hard-swung belt had drawn blood from her bare back on the two occasions she had lost control and wetted or fouled the mattress of grass-stuffed hides whereon she lay.

For a pitifully short time each night and morning he had made a practice of freeing both wrists and ankles that she might eat, drink and void. He did leave her ankles unbound all night . . . but only so that he might easily use her body whenever the mood struck him through the night hours.

Once more Stehfahnah had reverted to the behavior pattern which had sustained her through the long weeks of her previous captivity, separating her mind from her body during the abuse she could not resist, trying not to show pain or any sign of emotion.

She might have experienced loneliness, had she not been a telepath. But the second room of the hut was stall for not only the little ass but for the trapper's other animal, a mare he had captured from the wild years before, and brutally broken to the saddle. During the third morning of her captivity, whilst she had been silently conversing with the two female otters, the previously uncommunicative equine had suddenly joined the "conversation."

Mother-of-Many-Many had just apprised the girl that Killer-of-Much-Meat-in-Water had swum upriver seeking the creature that might be able to help her, the one that they called The-Bear-Killer. Stehfahnah had no idea what sort of beast the otters had in mind. The only impressions she could glean from them were of a huge (to them, at least), dark, furry creature with longish legs, a mouthful of sharp, white teeth and broad feet studded with long, curved claws.

Stehfahnah had known that the mare was a mind-speaker—else she would have possessed no mindshield—but the girl's earlier attempts to converse had been fruitless. Now the small dun mare said silently, "You are truly, then, a twolegs of the Clans. Long has this one been slave to this brutal dirtman twolegs. Sad day it was when you became such, sister."

According to the mare, she had been separated from her herd—a sept of the Horse Tribe attached to Clan Mehrfee—while fleeing a terrible grass fire on the prairie seven years past. Stumbling with exhaustion, she had entered the riverside forest belt, having scented water. She had been taken at a small spring, too tired to really offer much resistance to the big, strong man and his hateful rawhide noose.

Knowing or suspecting that his catch was a Horseclans mare, he never took her onto the prairies when he worked for the traders each spring and summer, boarding her and the ass in Traderstown, where the stable owner also rented out their services now and again.

The girl had had but little "conversation" with the ass. The small creature was intelligent enough, but his mindspeak seemed minimal and had never before been employed with humans.

As Stehfahnah lay there on the smelly hide mattress, a new but familiar thought transmission nibbled at her mind, and abruptly her thirst, the cold, even the aching of her full and distended bladder were forgotten.

"Good-Twolegs," announced Killer-of-Much-Meat-in-Water, "The Bear-Killer swam back down the river with me. He stopped where we came out to eat a muskrat caught in one of Bad-Twolegs's hurt-leg-things. But we must wait until next sun to free you, for Bad-Twolegs and his long-ears are not far."

Eely Maidjuhz led his pack ass—the smallish beast staggering under its load—into the small clearing before the log hut, hung the dwarf antelope he had bagged by chance, then began to affix the day's catch of skins to the drying racks. Once the last skin was up and the antelope's small carcass butchered, he cleaned his knives, took up the ass's halter and led him into the hut and through the front room to join the mare in the lean-to addition.

It was only after he had removed the packsaddle and halter, fed and watered both beasts, brought in the antelope carcass, started a fire on the hearth and spitted the minuscule kill in preparation for broiling when the coals became of the right temperature and consistency that he turned to Stehfahnah.

"Wal, sweetchips, what-all yew bin doin' t'day? Heheheh! Yew glad fer t' see ol' Eely? Yew wawnt me t' untie yew so's yew kin gitchew a drank an' piss?"

Stehfahnah gritted her teeth. "Yes."

The man's grin remained, but his eyes cooled. "Yore mem'ry ain't too sharp, is it, gal?"

Her teeth still gritted, Stehfahnah ground out, "Yes, *master*."

The man nodded his shaggy head once. "But it don' tek much proddin', does it? Come spring thaw time I tek yew in an' sell yew to Miz Soozee fo' her who' house in Traderstown, yew awta be broke in jest raht."

His grin widening, he chuckled. "Then Eely'll jest git word t' pore ol' Shifty Stooahrt wher'all yew is. Way yew hurted up thet gennamun, he oughta be purt' glad t' git aholt of yew agin. An' he won' fergit me neethuh, I figger."

The man kept a slip-knotted thong around the girl's neck while she squatted in the brush, observing her constantly, his steel-shod spear ready in his other hand. Back in the hut, he allowed her to drink her fill from the waterskin before once again retying her, not releasing her again until the antelope carcass was cooked to his satisfaction. Throughout it all and through all the hours that followed, Stehfahnah was aware that Killer-of-Much-Meat-in-Water was crouched nearby, somewhere beyond the log walls.

When the man had gorged himself, he untied Stehfahnah to allow her to consume the remains of the carcass and to drink again from the skin, then tied her for the night, performed his necessary chores, banked the fire and flopped down beside his captive on the hide mattress.

Stehfahnah gritted her teeth, knowing what was surely to happen but as he rolled onto his side and his dirty, greasy fingers began their explorations of her body, there came a deep-chested huffing snuffling at the barred door. Then something began to attack the portal furiously, constantly growling and roaring, striking the door with such force as to slam it back against the bar several times, jar oddments from off the wall shelf near it and even set the items hanging from the wall hooks and rafters dancing and swaying.

Spewing curses, Eely threw off the blankets, rolled out of the bed and, with his spear clasped in one hand, began to stir up the fire with the other, his wide-eyed gaze locked upon the quivering door.

Stehfahnah ranged her thoughts out to the male otter. "Oh, Killer-of-Much-Meat-in-Water, what is happening?"

The reply came quickly. "The-Bear-Killer had thought he could get into the log den, but he cannot. Good-Twolegs must get Bad-Twolegs outside. If The-Bear-Killer does not kill Bad-Twolegs tonight, he will lose interest and go away."

For many long minutes after the attack on the door had ceased, the man stood rooted by the fire, breathing hard, his eyes dilated and the unmistakable stink of terror oozing from his every pore. When there had been no sounds from the outer darkness for about a quarter hour, he took down a torch from above the hearth and kindled it in the fire, padded over to the door and stood with his ear to it for some time.

Standing back at last, he essayed to lift the bar with the point of his spear, but the shaft proved too long to give him proper leverage. Then he tried to find a way to wedge the torch upright in order to free his left hand . . . and almost fired the thatch. Cursing sulphurously, he set aside the spear for but a mere eyeblink of time, then firmly grasped it again.

After a longish moment of just standing and thinking the matter through, he finally padded over to the bed, laid down the long spear and said, "Looky here, gal, Eely's gonna untie yew fum th' bed frame an' yew gonna git up an' lif' th' bar offen th' do'. Heah me? Yew try suthin' an' Eely'll jest run his spear clear th'ough yew an' then th'ow yer carcass out t' whatever critter's awn th' loose."

To the waiting otter, Stehfahnah beamed, "I think that Bad-Twoleg is coming outside, but beware, he has a spear and a torch."

But another mind answered her, a mind unaccustomed to telepathy with humans. "The-Bear-Killer not fear pointed stick. Kill, eat many twolegs, pointed stick not hurt, twolegs all slow, The-Bear-Killer fast, strong. Get Bad Twoleg outside den, The-Bear-Killer kill, eat."

The girl's bound, numb hands were not equal to the task, however, for the bar was not light and the attacks of the creature upon the door had almost torn one of the bar's supports from the wall, causing it to jam tightly into the other.

Finally, she gave up and announced, "I cannot raise it with my hands bound together. I'll need to grasp it at or near each end to get it out."

By the dim and flaring, flickering light of the torch, the man could see that his captive spoke no less than the truth, so, leaning the spear against his shoulder momentarily, he drew his razor-edged skinning knife from the belt that hung on a nearby hook and slashed through the tough thongs. As he did, he reiterated his promise to spear her should she either attack him or try to get away into the darkness.

Stehfahnah took a few moments to flex her stiff fingers and rub gently at her raw wrists, then again attacked the contrary bar. But she was at length reduced to hammering it from beneath with a faggot of firewood until it had been sufficiently loosened to respond to her wiry strength. That done, she stepped back, still holding the bar, and her captor took her place.

Holding the torch before him and inching back the leather-hinged door with the point of his spear, the man crouched on his hairy, thick-muscled legs, ready to stab with spear or smite with torch at whatever beast he might confront; brute and lecher he assuredly was, but not coward or weakling.

Slowly he advanced, moving on the balls of his feet, ever ready to leap forward, to either side or backward, to stab upward or downward or to slash with the knife-sharp edges of the blade of the hunting spear.

When the torchlight had assured him that the immediate area near the door was empty of threat, he raised the torch so that he might closely examine that battered portal and thus perhaps guess just what animal lurked in the darkness outside.

The door hung drunkenly, both central and lower hinges of thick, heavy leather almost sundered from the hardwood. And that dense, well-cured wood was deeply scored and furrowed from lower edge to midway up its height by the down-slashing claws of some powerful beast. In the earth before the hut—earth dampened by the night mist—was a veritable hodgepodge of tracks, mostly one atop the other. However, even those that were a bit clearer than the rest meant precious little to the trapper, for he had never before seen their like.

Stehfahnah mindspoke the otter. "Where is The-Bear-Killer? Bad Twolegs is about to come out."

"The-Bear-Killer sees, female twolegs; he waits in the bad twolegs' path, on side of paw that holds fire. If female twolegs can make Bad-Twolegs look another way for only a moment, The-Bear-Killer can quickly kill Bad-Twolegs."

"I shall try," Stehfahnah beamed silently.

Ever so cautiously, Eely advanced a few feet. Terrible as had been the damage to the door, that and the strange tracks had at least reassured him that it was neither bear nor treecat he faced in the shrouding darkness. Both sets of signs had borne a familial resemblance to a badger, though he could not imagine what on earth a badger—even a vastly oversized badger—would be doing this far from the prairie. Nonetheless, he feared no badger of any size, not with his good spear in his hand.

Briefly, his mind dredged up the memory of a beast he had heard described by other trappers at Traderstown in years past. Some called it "devil-wolf" or "badger-bear," but even if it existed—and he had never met any man who could claim to have actually seen one—its usual haunts were well north of this area, close to the headwaters of the Great River. Rubbish, he thought, dismissing the half-mythical "badger-bear" as but another way of alibing the ill-luck of a bad season for a trapper.

Stehfahnah stood in readiness, her own desperate plan worked out in her mind, and when her ravisher was a few paces beyond the doorway, the girl slammed the door and clapped the heavy bar back into place.

"Why . . . yew lil bitch, yew! Eely tol' yew he'd kill yew!"

Momentarily forgetful in his rage at his slave girl of the menace lurking somewhere out of sight, the man spun about and jammed his spear through the door at its midpoint, his powerful thrust easily penetrating the deeply scored wood.

Through sheerest good fortune, the sharp blade missed Stehfahnah, but in dancing back from it, her foot struck upon the round faggot she had earlier used to hammer up the bar, and she fell heavily, her head striking the raised hearth and her consciousness suddenly reduced to a red-black, flame-shot, whirling tightness . . . and far, far away, she thought that she could hear screaming . . . and roaring. Then there was nothing.

Chapter VII

The morning parade and inspection of his new company done, Captain of Foot Count Martuhn of Geerzburk scraped and stamped sticky mud from his patched boots and climbed the narrow, winding stairs up to the towertop chambers he had chosen as his own in the spanking new fortress the duke had erected in the center of Twocityport, much to the loudly voiced disgust and rage of his wife and her coterie of sycophants.

When Martuhn had set sail up the Ohyoh to recruit this new company, the land on which the fortress presently squatted had been an expanse of stone-built warehouses. Now the stones and massy timbers had been "rearranged" into a fine, small, eminently defensible fortification, its foundations going all the way down to bedrock. The rapacious duke had impressed every able-bodied man—slave, soldier or free—on whom he could lay heavy hand. He had commuted jail time to labor and even taken to shanghaiing drunken rivermen.

The wealthier or more powerful men of the duchy had been allowed to buy out of the construction crews with gold or foodstuffs, stone or timber, or the loan of boats and wagons and teams. And the seemingly impossible had been accomplished, the fortress completed and ready to serve as garrison for the new company upon their arrival.

For all its newness, this citadel of Twocityport felt homey to Martuhn, as it should, for his own big, scarred hands had rendered the plans for the complex, faithfully drawing an exact duplicate of the citadel of faraway Geerzburk.

For all his and Wolf's earlier misgivings, the garrison was shaping up nicely, blending in well with the survivors of his earlier companies with a minimum of friction. Few floggings had been needed to establish and maintain the strict discipline he demanded of subordinates.

Including the "cargo" he had brought downriver, he now commanded a force of tenscore pikemen and fourscore archers. With the lieutenants, sergeants, weapons masters, cooks, wagoners, farriers, smiths and other service personnel, over four hundred men (plus a few women, camp whores, mostly) now called the new fortress home.

As he climbed the stairs to his commodious tower apartments in the chill of the early morning, Martuhn's thoughts strayed back to the sumptuous little private dinner he had shared with his overlord and employer, Duke Tcharlz, on the evening following his morning duel—if the outright butchery of an arrogant but unskilled effeminate could be called such—with Duchess Ann's spy, Sir Djaimz.

His strong yellow teeth having stripped most of the meat from the shank of a roasted lamb, the duke had wrenched it from the larger bone and tossed it to the waiting wolfhounds. Then, raising his voice above the racket of the dogs' snarls and argumentative snappings, he remarked with eyes a-twinkle, "You know, of course, Martuhn, that you were under my eyes from the very moment you entered the outer chamber yesterday morning?"

The lean, scar-faced former count laid aside knife and joint, took a sip from his wine cup and replied, "Aye, my lord, I sensed that you had arranged that little farce. No need to ask why, of course." He frowned then. "But, with all, I'd not have taken the miserable creature's life."

The duke chuckled, his florid face turning even redder. Absently, his guest noted that the noble host was beginning to add a second chin and that his jowls were starting to droop somewhat.

"Martuhn, Martuhn, my good friend, when you had down that bastard's breeks, I thought surely I'd burst with laughter. To think that such things as that strut about with belted weapons and call themselves men!"

Weary unkempt, with fresh mud overlaying old dirt, the

captain and Wolf had paced into the outer chamber and come to a halt before the table and the seated Sir Djaimz.

The young man wore his dark-brown hair at shoulder length, the ends curled. The dark lashes over his pale-blue eyes were long and thick, but his lips were pale and thin, with a cruel twist at the corners. His narrow face was pale and unmarked by any of the scars and calluses that most men had acquired by the time they were knighted. His white-skinned, soft-looking, long-fingered hands looked as if they would find the hilt of the light sword lying on the table before him most unfamiliar.

Neither Martuhn nor Wolf knew the fop. He had arrived from Twocityport more than a month after their departure . . . but both knew his type of old. Nonetheless, Martuhn tried to be polite.

He nodded stiffly. "I am Captain Martuhn of Geerzburk, just returned from upriver with Freefighters. Duke Tcharlz will be expecting me." Then he turned to the left and started around the table, his secret telepathic ability telling him that the duke was quite nearby, likely in the next room.

"*Just one moment, sirrah!*" Sir Djaimz shrilled, in a tenor so high that it verged on falsetto. "No one can see the duke without *my* leave. You hear? Least of all a filthy, smelly, seedy ragamuffin I've never before seen. Likely, the pair of you are nothing more than mean mountebanks hired by my enemies to humiliate me. How do I know you are what you say you are and not just another ill-born liar?"

Martuhn heard the faithful Wolf growl, but sent a telepathic command for peace . . . for the nonce. Turning again to the doorkeeper, he placed the palms of his big hands on the tabletop and leaned until his head was on a level with that of the fop. In a flat, cold, emotionless voice, he said, "Young sir, I have striven to be courteous. I have given you my name and my rank and imparted a modicum of my business with his grace. If you truly require warranty of all I have told you, why simply inquire of any one of the guardsmen here abouts; they all know me of old. Be warned of a few facts, however, young sir. I am at the least as nobly born as you; moreover, *I* am a full man. I have fought more battles than you have hairs in those girlish lashes, and there are precious few *living* men who ever have named me ill-born *or* a liar!"

But a single glance into the frigid depths of the eyes of the big-boned, but rapier-thin, stranger gave Sir Djaimz an immediate feeling of looseness in the guts and a raging urge to urinate. However, knowing how little real respect he commanded among either nobles or base in this savage domicile of the duke he had been dispatched to watch, he stubbornly refused to retrench and let the matter lie.

He curled his lips into a sneer, tilting his carefully coiffeured head to keep his eyes on the big man, who once more stood erect. But when he made to speak, his voice at first declined to obey the dictate of his will; it cracked, soaring high up into the treble.

"*You* . . ." To a chorus of sly chuckles from the guardsmen, Sir Djaimz cleared his throat and started afresh in his normal speaking tone. "You *may* be who and what you say you are, but *if* so, surely you would know better than to seek an audience with Duke Tcharlz while in so disreputable a state of both person and attire. Why not seek your home, if you have one, and bathe, if you know how, and don cleaner, if not better, clothing.

"Return tomorrow morning at the fifth hour—sharp, mind you—and if I feel you are in proper form to see the duke, I shall sell you the very first audience . . . and for a most reasonable price, too. Now, begone! Your stink nauseates me!"

Martuhn had then felt a grudging respect for the pale, slender man, for his telepathic mind could sense the raw fear being held down by force of will. Nonetheless, he knew that he must do what was expected of him in this, Duke Tcharlz's latest, cruel little game.

He breathed a single, deep sigh, then deliberately swung a backhanded buffet against one of those wan, beardless cheeks: not nearly as hard as he might have struck had he been truly affronted or angry, but just hard enough to send the slender young man slamming back into his padded chair.

Sir Djaimz's milk-white hand hovered for a second over the gilded hilt of his small sword, but then, recalling the long, heavy-bladed battle brand belted at Martuhn's side—and how the leather-and-wire hilt was hand-worn to a smooth shininess—he changed his mind. On unsteady legs, he arose and, in as firm a voice as he could muster, issued challenge.

At that juncture, Martuhn sensed excitement and a cold satisfaction from beyond the closed door to the duke's rooms.

And the tall, scarred captain felt dirty, used, as if the last tattered shred of his old honor had been torn away.

The quartet of guardsmen who had quickly—too quickly not to have been prearranged, thought Martuhn—stepped forward had courteously ushered Martuhn and Wolf into one of the guardrooms, seated them, pressed jacks of cold ale upon them and then awaited a visit from a similar quartet, now in attendance upon Sir Djaimz.

At length, the young knight's seconds arrived, were seated and given ale, chatted briefly of the weather and of anything save their mission.

Then the senior of them drained off his jack, arose and announced, "Captain Martuhn, gentlemen, challenge has been issued and legally witnessed by all here. Because I cannot imagine that the renowned Captain Martuhn of Geerzburk would decline a challenge, I simply ask what weapons he chooses and what mode of combat."

Gleeful as malicious boys torturing a stray dog, Martuhn's quartet's suggestions flowed: a-horse, with spear and longsword, in full armor and shield; a-horse, in half-armor, with two-foot targets and heavy, cursive, nomad sabers; a-foot, with full armor and poleaxes. This went on for several minutes until their principal, disgusted, put an end to it.

"Gentlemen," Martuhn growled, "I am as aware as are you that that boy out there is no true knight in any sense of the word, though I strongly suspect he's got a shade more guts than you give him credit for. But I'm a soldier, not a butcher, gentlemen. I choose light rapiers and daggers, a-foot, no armor save face guards, ankle boots, breeches and shirts, and for three bloods *only*. Are my terms clear, gentlemen?"

He left unsaid the fact that he would have refrained from the precipitation of this farcial combat from the start, had he not sensed the malign machinations of Duke Tcharlz in it. Nor did he reveal that he now had, in his own mind, sacrificed the last dregs of the honor of Count Martuhn of Geerzburk in order to retain the goodwill of such a thing as the duke.

An hour later, after a quick wash in the guardsmen's barrack, a shave and a hair trim by their barber, the loan of some clean and lighter clothing and the selection of a rapier from the castle armory, he stood ready, surrounded by his quartet at one end of the inner garden which had been chosen for the encounter. The duke was not visible at any of the surrounding windows, but Martuhn could sense the man's mind now and again, close by, observing, and once more he had the uncomfortable feeling of being but a piece on a gaming board.

As he and his opponent were led to the center of the sward by their respective entourages, Martuhn once more felt respect—an increasing measure of respect—for the willow-slender man he was about to fight. The captain's unusual mind could sense the dark oceans of terror lapping at and around the barrier reefs of will, yet Sir Djaimz's demeanor showed no trace of fear and the only change in his face was a purple bruise on his right cheek, the result of Martuhn's buffet.

Perfunctorily, the weapons and face guards were exchanged and examined by the seconds. Martuhn's left-hand weapon—he had retained his own battle dirk from force of habit—was found to be heavier in the blade and somewhat longer than the wide-quillioned dagger of Sir Djaimz, so one of the men set off at a trot to fetch several shorter, lighter pieces from which the captain might choose.

While they waited, cool ale was offered. Sir Djaimz took a grateful gulp of his and was about to take another when he noted that his opponent-to-be was sipping, barely doing more than wetting his lips and mouth. He began to emulate the veteran captain.

Martuhn smiled to himself. The lad was both intelligent and adaptable. Given time, patience and training, he doubted not he could make a good officer of him. Sword knew he had the sand. This little business proved that for all to see.

Sir Djaimz cleared his throat and bespoke Martuhn, "Sir, I have been informed that I should not address you directly until . . . after these proceedings, but . . ."

Martuhn nodded once. "Speak away, sir. Yon's a custom that's honored as much in the breach as the observance. Do you wish to withdraw your challenge? I'm more than amenable. I've no desire to see your blood."

Sir Djaimz flushed and shook his small head, sending the dark, curling locks swirling on his narrow shoulders. "No, sir, a certain high personage desires my death, and I had as lief receive it from a man I can see than from a wire garrote some dark night or a cup of poisoned wine."

Martuhn shook his own close-cropped head, "I'm no man's

executioner, sir! This duel's for no more than three bloods, mine or yours or both together, not to the death."

Sir Djaimz just smiled cynically. "But, of course, *accidents* do occur now and then, don't they?"

"There'll be no accidents this day," declared Martuhn bluntly. "Unless you go mad and decide to run yourself onto my blade, you'll leave on your own two feet."

"No." Sir Djaimz again shook his head. "I'd not do that, though it might be better for both of us if I did."

The man returned from the armory, and Martuhn chose a dagger that was almost the mate to his opponent's—eight inches of a thick but narrow and double-edged blade, with a crossguard three inches to the arm and a latticework of steel to protect the knuckles. Then he paced to his appointed place.

As the longsword of the arbitrator of the duel flashed downward, Martuhn moved forward smoothly and deliberately; although his conscious mind realized that he was but the instrument of an all but unskilled man's cruel punishment and in no slightest degree of danger, to his subconscious and his physical reflexes, he was approaching another combat, pure, simple and deadly.

Sir Djaimz vainly tried to copy his opponent's footwork, but though awkward, he neither hesitated nor halted. Nor did he flinch from Martuhn's first, powerful thrust, catching and turning the licking tongue of steel on his dagger blade and delivering an upward slash which rang upon the bigger man's face guard, even as the sharp edge of Martuhn's dagger laid open a billow of shirt, barely missing the pale skin beneath.

As they fenced, the tall captain's respect for the pale, slender man became less grudging; relatively weak and certainly unschooled, none of his attacks, defenses or ripostes seemed those of any school of the blade with which the widely experienced captain was familiar—Sir Djaimz seemed to be one of those rare, natural swordsmen. His weapon seemed an extension of his arm, the womanish soft hand inside the kidskin glove but an incidental link between the two.

Martuhn fleetingly regretted not naming longswords or even axes, the proper use of which demanded more strength than he thought his opponent owned, as that same opponent's silvery blade danced and flickered before his eyes, weaving an intricate pattern between them.

He thought, "Had the skinny bastard the foot skill and a bit more muscle to go with it, he'd be flat dangerous!"

He fought defensively, deliberately ignoring seeming openings, until Sir Djaimz showed signs of exertion and he thought that he had finally caught the rhythm of the very unorthodox fighting style. Then he waited his chance and struck—point slashing not thrusting at the already ripped front of the shirt.

He came breathtakingly close, but at the last possible split second, Sir Djaimz's blade beat down his own, so that the slash, rather than opening chest and shirt, severed the pale man's fine waistbelt, the waistband of his breeches and the drawstring cinching his smallclothes. Both items of clothing promptly tumbled down about his ankles.

Apparently unaware of what had occurred, Sir Djaimz made to riposte . . . and fell flat on his face, his bare white and almost fleshless buttocks reflecting back an errant beam of sunlight.

The guardsmen and other watchers, who had been hooting and shouting cruel jests at the downed knight, fell silent as Martuhn moved forward, his face as cold and bleak as a bleached skull. He kicked both weapons from the fallen man's grip, then placed a foot in the small of his back and sank the point of his sword just deeply enough to draw a few drops of blood, once, twice, thrice into the back of the right thigh.

Then he dropped his own weapons and leaned over, placing his big hands under Sir Djaimz's arms. As he effortlessly raised his erstwhile opponent onto his feet, he spoke swiftly and in a low voice.

"This is a good ending, better than you can imagine, my boy. You've been humiliated, and that's a damned good and unquestionable reason for leaving Pirates' Folly while you still have your life and most of your blood.

"Go back to the duchess' court, Sir Djaimz. When the new fortress at Twocityport is completed, I am certain to be named to command the garrison there. Come to me then, and I promise to make a real swordsman of you, with your promise, an unbeatable one.

"What I will do now is for he who watches. Do not take it to heart; it's for your protection as much as anything."

With that, he patted Sir Djaimz's bare buttocks, remarking,

"Soft as a girl's arse. Reminds me of that new whore down at Charlotte the Harlot's place in Pahdookahport." Then he threw back his head and laughed, and, still laughing, he picked up his weapons and stalked back toward the barracks.

Later that same day, Sir Djaimz and his servants had departed Pirates' Folly, riding east toward Twocityport at about the time Martuhn was being ushered in to his dinner with Duke Tcharlz.

When once the remnants of the last course were cleared away and the table bore only a set of small silver cups and a goodly assortment of brandies and cordials, the duke gave over from chitchat and got down to business.

"The Twocityport citadel is completed, Martuhn. I took the liberty of installing in it the bulk of your old company, under command of Lieutenant Mawree, almost a fortnight agone."

Martuhn looked every bit of his surprise. "But . . . my lord, it was no more than a plan when I departed."

The duke grinned like a cat. "Well, nonetheless, it's done, every last stone and timber and treenail of it, and with no less than three clearwater springs inside the walls. A full year's worth of provisions for two thousand men and five hundred horses should be in its magazines by the time you reach it to take command, along with a full complement of wall engines and a well-stocked armory. And none too soon, say I."

He leaned forward conspiratorily, nudging the table with his burgeoning paunch, sweat brought out by the rich foods and strong brandies gleaming on his face. "There've been developments since you left. Duke Alex, that arrogant, overweening, greedy, pig-spawned, dung-eating hound of a sneak thief, has—or so my agents in Traderstown court inform me—entered into a criminal collusion with the witless young jackanapes who now styles himself King of Mehmfiz. Through that supposedly royal ninny, our scheming neighbor is hiring himself an army from anywhere he can scratch up men, but mostly from the northwestern duchies of the Southern Ehleenee.

"Moreover, they—this precious pair of gelded jackasses— have begun to make threatening noises and movements toward certain of my downriver client-states and allies, states that that stunted, imbecilic dwarf Uyr of Mehmfiz has had his eyes on for years. They assume that I cannot but go to the aid of my allies whenever Alex and Uyr scratch up enough personal sand and armed men to actually attack one, and they're right on that score, I'll have to at least send troops down there, possibly even lead them myself.

"But they've not the collective brains of a pissant if they think I'm deluded. I know full well what they're up to. You know it too, Martuhn, and so does every thinking man in my duchy: The one scheme that that prince of deceptions has harbored in his cesspool brain ever since the old duke died has been to rule both Traderstown and Twocityport, that he might control both ends of the transriverine cables.

"Therefore, my dear Martuhn, however much dust these two bastards may kick up downriver, we may be assured that their true objective is Twocityport and its immediate environs, and when once they feel they've engaged the bulk of my forces downriver, they'll strike hard to seize my chief city. My spies at the court of my bitch wife are convinced that she and certain of hers are into this up to their plucked eyebrows, and they're likely right, but I can't prove the case just now, else I'd have her ugly head.

"Now fortifying Twocityport—that is, adding to the existing and somewhat old-fashioned defenses—would not only have taken far too long, but such action would've alerted my enemies that I was aware of what is afoot here. Therefore, I've had it bruited about in the duchy and beyond that this new fortress is, like Pirates' Folly, simply another—albeit an expensive—way to prick Ann's scaly hide. It's an eminently believable yarn, for it's well known up and down both rivers that we cordially hate each other."

"My lord duke." Martuhn held up his hand, palm outward. "If a part of my responsibility is to be preserving the cables from capture, would it not be better to lengthen them a bit, then secure them inside the walls of the citadel?"

The duke grinned again. "Great minds, it is said, run in the same channels, my good Martuhn. Not only are the cables now lengthened and secured within the new fortress, but from the outer walls down to the very lip of the river, they are now housed within very strong and solid stone-built tunnels. Moreover, it is now an open secret in Twocityport—which means that that ewe-raping Alex knows of it—that the fabric of the tunnel is fitted with devices that will assuredly sever the cables if any attempt is made to enter or dismantle the sheathings.

"So, my good Martuhn, now you know as much as do I. Do you think you can hold that citadel against Duke Alex for as long as a year? I'll either be engaged downriver or holding Pahdookahport and the Folly, while my horsemen harry the various besiegers and their inevitable patrols. So you and your garrison will be completely on your own, slam in the center of a probably hostile town—for the bulk of the Twocityporters have always hated me and loved my sow of a wife—and with no hope of relief until I've scared that gutless young Uyr out of this affair and can amass enough of a force to be sure of extirpating—or at the least, soundly trouncing—the Traderstown army in open battle. Well, what say you, Captain Count Martuhn of Twocityport?"

Now, in his towertop aerie, the new-made Count of Twocityport sat down to the spartan breakfast brought up by the faithful Wolf, who had also prepared it, since he felt that he knew his lord's tastes better than did the new cooks. While he ate the fried fatback, cornmeal mush and crisp little apples, washed down with drafts of cider, he read through a pile of dispatches just in from Pirates' Folly, commenting to Wolf, who took notes when necessary in his cribbed writing.

"The duke is taking my advice and retaining almost all of the lancers and dragoons to his personal force."

"A good thing, too," Wolf put in, nodding his hairless, scar-furrowed head. "Horsemen don't do neither side no good in a siege, 'cept mebbe as far-riding foragers for them as is besieging."

"Yes," Count Martuhn continued, "only the officers and sergeants and a score or so of dispatch riders will be mounted in this garrison."

Wolf grunted. "This here garrison his grace promised you had better stir their stumps, if they means to get here afore Duke Alex's folks does. Talk's all over town that he's gonna be a-landing 'fore the end of the month, and any street you walks down, you can hear the spades a-ringing in the backyards with plate and money and all a-getting put under till it's all over."

The captain stabbed a long finger at the topmost letter on the pile before him, bearing the elaborate and gaudy ducal seal. "The first battalion—Baron Burklee's six hundred pike-men, plus two hundred and forty crossbowmen—marched out from Pirates' Folly before dawn this morning, according to this dispatch."

Wolf grunted again and scratched at one of his cranial scars with the nib of his quill pen, heedless of the ink lines he scribed into the skin. "How 'bout the engineers? 'Sides me and my lord and a handful of others, don't nobody know pee turkey 'bout servicing, laying and manning all these here spearthrowers and rock lobbers and such, as his grace's got mounted up on the walls and roofs."

Martuhn frowned. "I don't know, Wolf. I've not yet read all of the dispatch." He fell silent for a moment, then announced, "Ah, yes, here it is. The second battalion, which includes the engineers as well as the surgeons and the rest of the service troops, was originally scheduled to be here before Burklee's, but the duke had to relieve the commander and then reform them to some extent. . . . He doesn't say why, he just says that they'll be on the march soon."

"Which could mean a lot or nothing!" snorted Wolf disgustedly. "Best I c'lect, ever'body as knows anything 'bout 'gines and start a-schooling our comp'ny in how to use 'em. 'Cause sure as can be, that baron's pikepushers ain't likely to know shit 'bout 'em."

The count frowned again. "Go ahead, Wolf, and while you're at it, see if any of ours are fair slingmen. There's no mention of any in the duke's listings. There're siege slings, pig lead and casting sets in the lower armory, I noticed.

"Oh, and I'll want all our officers assembled just before the noon hour, except you. His grace feels that they will get more respect from the baron and the rest of his gentry if they are of the same caste, and, now that I'm a nobleman again, I can knight them . . . you, too, old friend."

The hairless man just cackled. "That'll be the day, my lord! All your of'sers, 'cepting Lootenant Krains, are gennulman borned; ol' Wolf, here, his paw was your paw's servin' man. Ain't no smidgin of gentul blood in him."

Martuhn's lips flitted into a brief, sketchy smile. He had expected just such a response from his old and faithful retainer. "You would then have me disobey his grace, our overlord, Wolf?"

Wolf looked his discomfort. "Well . . . mebbe you could

just tell his grace and ever'body elst that you done it . . . and I won't say no different . . . ?"

"You would, then, counsel that I *lie* to his grace, Wolf?" Martuhn chided solemnly. "Have you not always told me that the truth is easier to keep track of than lies? Or was that another man named Wolf, eh?"

"Well, dammit, Martuhn-boy, it . . . it just ain't right and proper to make a common-borned man like me no 'sir.' "

The count became serious. "Not only is it right, my good old friend, you've earned and more than deserved a knighting threescore times and more in these last hard twenty-odd years. Had I but then had the legal rank to grant it, I would have done so long ago. Now I again have that rank and you will receive your just deserts, but formally and solemnly, after Baron Burklee arrives.

"For now, however, I need you for another task. It's a certainty that the enemy will not try a landing within the range of our engines. The shoreline for miles south of the town is too swampy to make for an easy landing of large numbers of troops, much less horses and supplies, and due north of Twocityport, the bluffs are high and precipitous and march right to the verge of the Great River. However, below the east-west stretch of the bluffs and a few hundred yards eastward of the mouth of the Ohyoh River, his grace's maps show a long, wide beach of sorts, with a track of some description meandering east along the river for a way, then southeast and over a saddle or a pass to come out some miles northeast of us, here.

"Now, whoever drew these charts was no soldier. I've a plan for stinging those bastards, maybe slowing them up a bit and delaying the close of their siege lines for a few days, but in order to use this plan, I'll need better and more exact maps, and that's where you come in, Wolf.

"Take all of our men you think you'll need, take any horses in the fortress and take the existing maps. I need to know how long and deep that beach is, how far it lies from the channel, how high and steep are the bluffs just over it and the exact location, directions and condition of the indicated track. Note carefully all locations along the bluffs at which you think a landslide could be easily precipitated or where your experience tells you a small number of slingers and archers might do a maximum amount of damage while sustaining minimum casualties.

"Take rations and fodder for as many days as you think this will require. If it takes longer, however, don't hesitate to forage. Remember, not only are we on my lands, but a largeish number of the folk in and around Twocityport are sworn enemies of Duke Tcharlz. If, however, you should run across a few likely-looking recruits, by all means bring them back."

Chapter VIII

At Hwahruhn's brusque command, both boys shed their worn and ragged garments. Then the two traders stood by holding a pair of lamps high while the Ehleen "examined" his new purchases. Custuh seemed not to notice the manner in which their customer's soft, beringed hands lingered upon the boys' freckled flesh . . . but Hwahruhn did, and the sight sickened him.

"You kin see, Lord Urbahnos," Custuh said, after a few minutes, "it ain't a earthly thang wrong with the slaves. We's treated 'em good and fed 'em good, too. They's as hale as they wuz the day we ketched 'em, out awn the prairie. No worms, no sores, no pus in they eyes, no loose teeth, no runnin' noses evun. We only carries quality stock, we does."

Urbahnos made his decision quickly. The elder boy was nowhere near as pretty as the red-blond younger one. Too, the elder was already beginning to sprout genital hair—something which no sensitive Ehleen of sophisticated tastes could or would tolerate, had he the choice, in a love boy. Therefore, the younger would be fed to plumpness, clothed fittingly and sent upriver and across the mountains to Karaleenos and the noblemen whom Urbahnos had now convinced himself would see to the nullification of his unjust banishment. The elder would be Urbahnos' plaything until he tired of him, at which juncture he would be sold—with luck, at a good profit—to a brothel keeper.

The Ehleen also decided that the "education" of this new,

blond, exciting love boy would commence this very night, as soon as he could tactfully rid himself of these two barbarians.

Urbahnos was not a mindspeaker. In all of the eastern Ehleen lands, telepathy was considered to be a form of witchcraft and was savagely persecuted by the established religion. Therefore he possessed no mindshield, and his every thought was crystal-clear to the powerful mind of his chosen victim, Bahb Steevuhnz. Though appalled and more than a little frightened at what he read in the roiling mind of his new, degenerate owner, Bahb kept his face carefully blank.

When Urbahnos had announced his satisfaction with the sale, he departed the strongroom, followed by the two traders. Custuh took the lamp he had held with him, but Hwahruhn hung his on a hook let into the wall over the door.

"Now, you lads be careful not to knock this down, hear? I've seen bales of furs and hides flare up like so much oil, and with that rout going on belowstairs, nobody would likely hear your screams until you were both burned to flinders."

Then he just stood for a moment, eying the two naked boys. He seemed to want to say more, but then he snapped his mouth shut, turned on his heel and walked out, shaking his head between bowed shoulders.

When he could no longer hear footsteps beyond the locked door, Bahb once more turned to the now openable chest. He slowly raised the lid and expressed his delight in a single grunt. The lower section was filled with hornbows, each of them wrapped in waxed vellum sheets and packed into a horn-and-leather quiver along with a dozen arrows. Most of the bows were the plainer variety made by all the Horseclans for trade purposes, but the four topmost sets were finely carved and decorated in tooled leather cases marked with the totem animals of Clan Steevuhnz—the bows taken from them, their sister and their dead half-brother upon the day of their capture.

Nor was this all. The two Clan Steevuhnz sabers lay beside the hornbow sets, and in the tray hinged to the lid of the chest reposed the four Steevuhnz dirks and even the boot knives. Bahb immediately seized one of the latter and filled the empty sheath inside his right boot with it, then he began to dress himself, mindspeaking his younger brother the while.

"Don't ask questions, my brother, just heed me. The black-hair who has bought us is like no man I have ever heard of. He cares nothing for females, but rather means to use me as an ordinary man would use a woman. And he means to send for me as soon as he is done with the traders, whom he despises for some reason. So I will not be here to help, though I will let you know what passes by mindspeak.

"With this,"—the wiry boy slapped at his boottop—"I have no fear of the black-haired man, for he is clumsy and more than a little fat, nor does he seem to be overly strong, for all his size and height. So unless he has help, I doubt he can harm me.

"Take a dirk and start cutting one of your blankets into strips; spread the other out flat and I'll roll the sabers and bows in it—that way you can lower them to the ground without damage to them or any noise. I'll take another boot knife and you can take the other two. Then secure all four dirks to your belt. Here, I'll put my belt and the saber slings in with the bows.

"Just before you go out that window, *after* the roll of weapons is safe below, drag something to stand on to the door, take that lamp down and set fire to everything that will burn in this room. No, wait—drag everything you can manage in front of the door before you fire it. That way, maybe they won't know so soon that we're gone."

Barely had the two boys dressed, tied and hidden the blanket full of weapons and gotten the chest closed and relocked than a big, tall, bald man with skin the color of an old saddle opened the door, pointed at Bahb and crooked a finger thrice.

"Our master summons you, boy. Come, or I'll drag you."

Nahseer had been aware of Urbahnos' unnatural vices as long as the Ehleen had owned him, and he secretly felt that, for all the fact he had been gelded, he still was more of a man than his owner had ever been. He had been revolted at the order to bring the boy to Urbahnos' bedchamber, but it had been a matter of either obeying or hurrying the day when the devious Ehleen would sell him to the bargers . . . and he would seek his death, hoping to take as many other men as he could with him into that state.

In the great room below, seated across the dining table from the exultant Custuh, the trader, Hwahruhn, watched the big Zahrtohgahn warrior—still fully armed and obviously cold sober, a fact unusual in this serai full of drunken men—proceed along the upper walkway to the strongroom, unbar the door, lead forth the eldest boy and return with him to the suite of the Ehleen. Then Hwahruhn tore his gaze away, lifted his wine cup and drained it, hurriedly refilled and drained the second just as fast, then refilled again.

Custuh looked up from his calculations and said, with a rotten-toothed grin, "Buddyroll, keep a-drinkin' like thet an' yew won' be in no shape fer t' spin' yore gol', t'morra in Pahdookahport."

Hwahruhn felt the deathly danger so strongly now that it almost eclipsed his own soul-sickness and self-loathing. In that warm, noisy room, cold sweat trickled down his spine and hairs prickled wherever they grew on his body. Near madness glared from his eyes, and he bespoke Custuh in a voice pitched just loud enough for him alone to hear.

"You won't be spending any of that blood money, Custuh, nor journeying to Pahdookahport. You'll be dead by sunup. I've seen your body lying in its blood . . . with the head caved in."

Custuh stared back at his partner and gulped. Then his ire rose above his sudden fear. He slammed a horny palm down on the tabletop, snarling, "Now, damn yew fer a big-mouthed fool, Hwahruhn. Yew knows how superstitious alla these here bastids is. Whut if some o' 'em heered yew, huh? Ah knows it's mos'ly yer likker a-talkin', but they won't. Iffen they all ups an' meks tracks, come t'middle o' t'night, whut we gon' use fer wagoners come daybreak? 'Sides, t'bugtits'd likely steal us blin', t'boot."

Urbahnos stood waiting impatiently by the door to his bed-chamber, temples and groin throbbing with desire bred from his visual and tactile examinations of the two little boys. When, after what seemed centuries, Nahseer entered with the older lad and stooped to examine him for weapons, his master snapped, "Enough, you dung-colored ape! I've just seen him bare and there are no weapons in that room he could have gotten at. Just bring him here to me. But don't leave this room, you hear? Those rascally traders know that I have gold and jewels, and I don't want my throat cut in my sleep."

As his master took the slave boy's arm and propelled him into the inner chamber, then closed and locked the door, Nahseer settled himself into the large, padded chair which

Urbahnos himself had occupied during his dealings with the plains traders, awaiting developments.

The boy moved lightly and could probably be fast as a scalded cat if need be. Another might think the boy's thinness to be all skin and bone, but Nahseer recognized the flat musculature and the wiry strength it portended. Even unarmed, that lad was likely a healthy fight for the master, for even sober he was fat, clumsy of movements and possessed of muscles near to the point of atrophy from lack of exercise. And the master was well into his second drunk of the day, the effects of the first still not fully dissipated.

Nahseer smiled, thinking of the two little knives his sure fingers had detected beneath the felt of the lad's boottops.

"Yes," he whispered softly in his native tongue, "these next few minutes should prove most assuredly interesting."

Within the great room of the serai, the riotous tumult raged at full fury as the wagoners and apprentice traders and the other men of the caravan celebrated the conclusion of yet another summer among the nomads. Several of the serai women had trooped in to sell their shopworn favors in alcoves about the room, the serai musicians—two fiddlers, a banjo, a guitar and a grizzled oldster who performed with hand drum or tambourine, as required—aided willingly (if somewhat off-key) by a drunken wagoner and his reedpipes played loud and lively tunes, but were heard only by those closest to them in the general uproar.

Portuh strolled through from time to time, seeing that the beer, ale and cider flowed freely and without stint, collecting his half from the serai whores and now and then stopping by to share a sip of wine with the morose Hwahruhn and the loud, perpetually grinning Custuh. Before long, Portuh, too, was grinning, for the traders and their men were putting down stupendous quantities of the various potables and his profit from the bill he would present ere they departed on the morrow would be most satisfying, even after the duke's cut was removed.

There had been one killing so far, a fair fight with foot-long dirks between two wagoners. But these things had a habit of occurring when lusty, violent men got drunk, so no one was surprised or upset, least of all Portuh. He just hoped that the sometime mates of the corpse, now lying out in one of the sheds, would decide to burn rather than simply bury him, for his profit would be higher on wood for a pyre than on the digging of a grave.

Suddenly, above the raucous disorder, a shrill, womanish scream rang out from the direction of the Ehleen gentleman's suite. Few of the men gave it any heed, but Trader Hwahruhn came to his unsteady feet so quickly and with such force that he overturned the solid hardwood bench and even set the heavy table teetering onto two legs, sending ewers, cups and mugs crashing to the floor.

Turning, he staggered on unsteady legs toward the stairs, one hand clenched around the wire-wound hilt of his long, wide-bladed dirk.

Custuh rushed after his partner, his every step making squishing noises from the liquor that had poured into his rolled-down boottops. Hwahruhn shook off the first hold that Custuh took on him, but then Custuh threw both brawny arms about the other trader's body, pinning the arms, while shouting over a shoulder to the serai keeper.

"Goddammit, gimme a hand with 'im, heah? He's drunk as a fuckin' skunk an' plumb loco t'boot! We don' stop him, he likely t'kill thet Ehleen up thar."

Portuh grimly reflected that putting paid to that particular bastard of a bag of eastern shit might just be a laudable achievement and would sit most kindly in his mind. Nonetheless, he did not care to have the rich and no doubt well-connected turd die in this serai, so he rushed to Custuh's aid.

Hwahruhn fought them silently and with every ounce of his considerable strength, until, finally, Portuh drew the small, lead-filled cosh from under his belt and fetched the drunken, berserk trader a practiced blow behind the ear. Hwahruhn dropped like a sack of meal, whereupon Portuh and Custuh bore his limp form out into the drizzle, bedded him down in his own, personal wagon and locked him in.

In his drunken, self-recriminating mental haze, Hwahruhn had, of course, assumed that the scream of undiluted agony had been that of Bahb Steevuhnz. Nahseer, closer, knew better, even before his master began to shout.

"*Help!* Oh, please, *no!* Help me, Nahseer, before this little bitch *kills* me!"

A single heave of his thick-muscled shoulder ripped the

fabric of the door's top panel, and Nahseer reached in and drew the bolts, then swung the shattered portal wide.

The Lord Urbahnos, stark naked save for his finger and arm rings, crouched—trembling, whimpering and drooling in terror—at the head of the bed, seemingly unaware of a deep and earnestly bleeding slash down his left cheek. Both his hands were clutching frantically at his crotch. Dark-red blood poured between and over the beringed fingers to soak into the pillow beneath him.

Bahb was still fully clad, although both shirt and trousers were torn and both sun-browned cheeks showed prints left by the fingers and rings of the hand that had slapped him. A short-bladed knife in each grubby hand, the fine steel of both blades clouded with blood, he had been engaged in stalking Urbahnos, even while he mindspoke both his brother and the mare in the serai stables.

Upon Nahseer's entrance, however, he leaped backward to place his back hard to the outer wall. "Brown man," he hissed, holding one blade ready for defense and placing the point of the other just under the hinge of his jaw, "if you try to take me again for *him*, I'll send myself to Wind . . . but I'll take you with me, if I can. Beware!"

Nahseer knew of a certainty that the spindly boy meant every word of it, and he loved him from that moment for his courage in the face of impossible odds—a barely pubescent boy pitted against an armored swordsman four times his size, and the lad with only two little knives.

"Take him alive!" shrieked Urbahnos. "When I've had my will of him, I want him tortured to death, slowly. He hurt me, Nahseer, the little bitch has injured me terribly.

"Well? Move on him, you ape, draw your sword, but hit him only with the flat or I'll have out your eyes. Call the hired guards if you're afraid of him, but *take him*."

Nahseer gazed deeply into the bloodshot, teary, hate-filled eyes of his master. Rage lay in their black depths, rage compounded with pain and the still-fresh memory of cold, crawling terror. He knew that now his master would never sell him, not unless he had his tongue removed first. More likely, the Ehleen would have him murdered soon after they returned to Pahdookahport so that the only living witnesses to Lord Urbahnos' humiliation might be permanently silenced.

Turning his gaze back to the boy, the sometime warrior of far-off Zahrtohgah saw a fellow warrior, for all his lack of size and his tender years. There was no hate in those blue-gray eyes, only a grim determination. The lad stood stock-still, his wiry body seemingly relaxed, but both daggers held steady and unwavering.

With a deep sigh, Nahseer drew his heavy dirk and advanced on Bahb.

Behind him, Urbahnos shrilled, "If you kill him, I'll have your wormy guts nailed to a post and you marched around it until you bleed to death, you whoreson!"

Drawn by the lights and the noise, all the caravansers who had been assigned to stable duty flitted through the misty drizzle into the warmth and clamorous hilarity of the great hall. All but two of the serai stablehands had soon joined them, "just for one or two pots of beer."

Of the two regular hands remaining, the younger was suffering a griping of the guts, and the stables lay nearer to the jakes than did the main building. The other, a much older man, had shed his threadbare breeches and was trying to ease the pains of his arthritic knees by the tried-and-true method of covering the joints with piles of fresh, hot horse manure.

The younger man had just left on his third or fourth run toward the privy when one of the small, ugly prairie-bred mares began to move agitatedly in her shared stall, kicking and snorting. The oldster, the pains just beginning to ease a bit, tried manfully to ignore the equine uproar. But when one, then another of the horses began to emulate the mare, he sighed and, grumbling curses, pulled himself to his feet and stumbled stiffly down the aisle between the rows of stalls.

"Dang half-broke lil ol' nomad critter. Prob'ly spooked by a goldurned rat, is all."

He lifted down a hanging lantern and in the other hand took a grip on a yard-long billet of wood, good for either crushing a rat or dealing with an aggressive equine. At the mare's stall—shared with another of her kind—he held the lantern high and leaned into the cubicle, his old eyes vainly searching the corners for sight of a scuttling rodent.

"Shitfire, anyhow!" he mumbled. "Thet dadgummed boy should oughta be here, a-doin' this—his eyes is a hell of a sight sharper nor mine is." Taking the stick under his lantern arm, he unlatched the lower half of the gate and swung it outward, but before he could take a single step or even re-grasp his protective club, Windswift was on him with flashing hooves and savaging teeth. Within seconds, he was forever freed of the aches of his arthritis. Nor, when he returned, did the younger hand live much longer. Windswift was a trained and veteran warhorse, and these were not the first twolegs she had slain.

The dropped lantern, which had bounced into the stall, had eaten its own oiled-vellum covering, and little flames were be-ginning to lick out at the straw. Windswift quickly kicked and nudged fresh dung onto the device until she could sense no more flame and little heat. It was not yet time for the stable to take fire.

She mindspoke Bahb Steevuhnz that her job was accom-plished, then she and the other, younger mare set about freeing the other two Horseclans mares.

Shortly, little Djoh Steevuhnz trotted in, four dirks at his belt and the bulky roll of the other weapons on his shoulder. There was scant need for actual speech; physical contact en-hanced even his marginal telepathic abilities to the point that he could easily communicate with all four of the mares.

He and Bahb had watched from their window as the vari-ous wagons were parked for the night, and so he had no trou-ble in finding those in which the richly decorated Clan Steevuhnz saddles had been stored. The kaks were too heavy for even a strong ten-year-old to lug back to the stables, but the yard lay empty of all humans save him and the rain and mist made visibility poor at best, so he simply bade the mares to come to him, dragged the gear onto the tailgate and from there heaved it onto the low backs of the small beasts, hop-ping down into the mud to cinch the straps.

Back in the dryness of the stable, the boy squeezed and wrung the water from his dripping hair, then unrolled the blanket and attached bowcase-quivers and sabers in their cus-tomary places on the saddles. The blanket he rerolled and lashed behind the saddle of his own mount, Mousebrown. Horseclansfolk seldom used bridles, except on untrained young stallions, for usually mindspeak and pressure of knee or hand were all that was necessary to guide this breed of equines, who were the partners rather than the chattels of the nomads.

When all was in readiness, Windswift once more mind-spoke Bahb Steevuhnz. His reply was a surprise to them all, mares and boy alike.

Within arm's length of the crouching nomad boy, Nahseer flipped the dirk, grasping the broad blade between thumb and a knuckle. Smiling gently, he said, "Take this, my little brother—it will make for you a far better weapon. But give me in exchange one of the little knives you have used to such good advantage this night, for I too have a few old scores to wash out in the diseased blood of yonder perverted pig."

After a brief silence he widened his smile and added, "And tell the minds outside to saddle and bridle a good, big horse for me. I admire the spirit of your plains stock but they are just too small for a man of my size."

Bahb's eyes widened in surprise. He beamed, "You *mind-speak*, man with brown skin? You are that thing's sworn man, are you not? If you knew of my planning, why did you not tell him? For what purpose do you wish to help me? If you try to do to me what he would have done, I warn you, I will serve you even as I served him."

Nahseer shook his hairless head. "Brother mine, even when still I had my man-parts, I utilized them only in the ways that Ahláh intended, not in the unnatural nastinesses in which some infidels debase themselves." He sighed deeply and aloud, then went on silently.

"And I am no one's sworn man, my brother. I am the pig's chattel, as much a slave as are you. And yes, I can converse mind-to-mind, sense the mind conversations of others and even sense the surface thoughts of those with whom I cannot converse. This talent I was born with; it is not uncommon among the upper castes of my people.

"Why did I not betray your conversations with those outside, why did I fail to inform yon black-haired pig that you bore the two little daggers in your boots? The answers are many and complex, my brother, and if Ahláh so wills it. we will have time and leisure to speak on these matters. But for now, I believe I smell smoke. I imagine that your former cell is blazing merrily by this time, and so I suggest that we put an end to affairs here and depart . . . quickly."

Warily, unsure whether or not to believe, Bahb took both of his little knives in his left hand and snatched the dirk from its profferer, then gingerly laid one of the blood-sticky short blades in the pink palm of the brown-skinned man.

Nahseer withdrew his sword from its case and leaned it against the wall near the boy, then turned and walked to the bedside of his sometime master. Because mindspeak took far less time than did oral communication, bare seconds had passed since Urbahnos had given the order to stun and capture his newest slave.

"What are you doing, you dung-hued cretin?" the Ehleen rasped. "I'll have you flayed and rolled in salt. I'll—"

Nahseer interrupted him. The big man's voice was soft, but the undertone froze Urbahnos to his innermost being. "The only thing you will do now, sweet master, is to hold your flapping tongue . . . unless you had rather lose it, that is. You promised me my freedom whenever you returned to the east, you depraved beast of a liar, yet your true intent all the while was to sell me to the slow, living death of the rowbarges."

His teary eyes once more wide with terror, his thick lips atremble, the Lord Urbahnos shook his head wildly from side to side, sending a spray of bright blood from his slashed cheek in all directions. "No, Nahseer! No, no, no! You are to be freed, *I swear it* . . . my word of sacred honor . . . no, I . . ."

The Zahrtohgahn sneered. "Dear master, we both know that your word is of less worth than a half dram of rat's piss. The only thing in all the world that you hold sacred is profit. As for honor, it surprises me that you even know and can pronounce the word in any language, since you so obviously have never possessed a scintilla of it."

While speaking, Nahseer had used the little knife to cut down most of the bedside bell rope, then divide it into two equal lengths. After tucking the knife into the folds of his sash, he grabbed Urbahnos and jerked him suddenly onto his back on the rumpled, bloody bed. He seized first one arm, then the other and used the ropes to bind the Ehleen's wrists to the bedhead, knotting them cruelly tight. Then he did the same for the ankles, lashing each to a bedpost with strips torn from the linen sheets. Several shorter strips went into a crude but effective gag. Then Nahseer stood back and surveyed his handiwork, while testing the edge of the boot knife on the callused ball of his thumb.

To Bahb, he said, "Bring me the other little knife, please, my brother. That rope is tough and this one has lost the best of its cutting edge. And bring my sword, as well; this thing cannot grab at it now."

"What are you going to do to him?" asked Bahb curiously.

"I mean to geld him," stated Nahseer bluntly and aloud, his words setting Urbahnos to squirming and vainly jerking at his bonds, trying to force words and strangled screams through the fabric of his gag, his features almost livid and his eyes starting from their sockets.

Bahb handed back the Zahrtohgahn's sword. Though he kept the dirk in his right hand and ready, he sheathed the dulled dagger. "This will be the first time I've ever seen a man gelded. Is it the same as gelding a bull calf?"

Nahseer nodded. "Much the same, my brother, much the same." To Urbahnos, he said, "Master, think you back on how many times you have chided me because I have been deprived of the very man-parts you daily dishonor. Recall how often you have spoken to me and of me in public as 'your Zahrtohgahn steer' or 'a creature of uncertain sex.'

"Now, I advise that you lie still, master, for this little knife is razor-sharp. The hilt is small and already slippery with your blood, and if you wiggle too much I might slip and take off your yard, as well. You wouldn't like that, would you, my master?"

Nahseer did not believe in torture, and the movements of hand and knife were quick and sure. Presently he laid aside the blade, grasped a handful of Urbahnos' black hair and raised his head that he might better see what the Zahrtohgahn's other palm held—two bloody, kidney-shaped objects, the Ehleen's testicles. Urbahnos stared, goggle-eyed, then the pupils rolled up and he fainted.

The big man tossed the testicles onto the coals of one of the braziers, stooped and rinsed his hands in the tub of cold bathwater still sitting in a corner, then turned back to the brazier. With the iron tongs that hung beneath the bowl, he poked around until he found a coal to his liking. Gripping this coal between the jaws of the tongs, he lifted it and carefully blew away as much as he could of the white ash, exposing the glowing, red-orange surface of the charcoal.

Returning to the side of his unconscious victim, Nahseer used the fingers of his free hand to hold open the Ehleen's scrotum—now empty of all save the hacked-off stumps of the vesicles and a large amount of blood—then dropped the red-hot, glowing coal directly into the sac.

Lord Urbahnos revived, screaming through his gag, jerking and thrashing to the limits of his bonds, tears jetting from his eyes and mucus from his nostrils, fouling himself and the bed beneath him with the discharges of both bladder and rectum.

"Why didn't you just let him lie there and bleed?" asked Bahb Steevuhnz.

"He might have bled so much that he died, my brother," said Nahseer. "And dead he would have robbed me of my vengeance, you see. No, I want him to live, to live in almost the same condition as have I for so many years.

"Now, let us go into the outer room and gather such things as may aid us in our flight."

The big man wrenched both lock and hasp from off his former master's strongbox, scooped all the coins into the money belt and stowed it inside the breastplate of his cuirass. That done, he stuffed bread, cheese, cooked meats and dried fruits into one set of saddlebags, then filled another set with the metal flasks of brandies and cordials. For want of water, he filled a travel skin with the contents of two jugs of pear cider.

Nahseer knew that no matter how befuddled were those on the floor below, there would be questions were he to try to pass through laden with saddlebags, blankets, waterskins and cloaks and with the boy in his torn and blood-splashed garments.

"Brother warrior Bahb, speak you with your brother below, and ask if the yard between this place and the stables be still empty."

Aware that Djoh was ever difficult to range, Bahb instead bespoke the mare, Windswift, then replied, "All is well outside. One man came into the stables, but he was no warrior, and besides was so dizzy that he could hardly stand. My brother, Djoh, tripped him, jumped astride him and slipped a dirk blade between his ribs. Windswift says that no grown warrior could have done it more smoothly and effectively."

Nahseer tore down the carpet that had been hung over the single small window, wrenched out the entire frame, then sliced one of the large floor carpets into strips, tied them together, passed one end under Bahb's arms and knotted it around his chest.

Lifting the slender boy easily, the Zahrtohgahn put him through the opening feet foremost, then stepped up on the massive table he had pushed into place and lowered him to the muddy yard below. When he had lowered all the items he had decided would be helpful to them, he drew back the improvised rope, rehung the carpet and stepped down from the table.

In the bedchamber, he found that his sometime master had once more swooned. With the lord's own jewel-encrusted dagger, he sliced the man's bonds loose from the bed, then, wrinkling his nose and holding his breath against the thick reek of spilled blood, loose dung and burned meat, he pulled off the gag. Stepping into the corner, he lifted the tub full of cold water, turned back to the bed and flung the entire contents onto the unconscious man thereon.

Urbahnos woke moaning, opened his mouth to scream. But the palm of Nahseer's big hand pressed tightly over it, and the other hand held the slender dagger so that the Ehleen had no trouble seeing the keen edges and glittering point.

"If you make one sound or try to leave this room, Lord Steer, I'll return and complete the job; I'll slice off your prick and stuff it down your throat!" So saying, he sheathed the dagger, thrust it in his sash and stalked out of the suite, then down the stairs. The smell of smoke was now very thick in the upper level, and Nahseer noted that the exposed rafters were all but obscured by layers of smoke.

What with stopping here and there for a word or two of light chatter with the tables of friendly drunks, now and then pretending to take drafts from proffered cups and mugs and leathern jacks, it took the Zahrtohgahn a good quarter hour to reach the vicinity of the big outer door. And there he was confronted with his first real danger.

Ehdee-Djoh Cawl, one of the bravos hired on for the trip by Lord Urbahnos, and far less besotted than most of the men in the main room, had followed Nahseer and confronted him in the relative dimness near the door.

In his native, nasal twang, he said, "That thar knife in yore sayash, thet be yore massa's. I seed it a-hangin' fum oft his belt. He know yew got 'er?"

For all that where they stood was in almost utter darkness

to those in the well-lighted room, Nahseer glanced pointedly
back the way he had come, and Cawl, too, turned his head.
And that was when the Zahrtohgahn's big fist struck the
smaller man, knocking him senseless.

In the middle of the yard stood four small and one large
saddled equines, two of them with riders. Nahseer pulled up
the tops of his jackboots, checked the girths and stirrup
leathers of the biggest horse—a silver-gray gelding that had
been the prized possession of the trader, Custuh—then swung
into the saddle.

Guided by the road, which they kept in sight, they rode
eastward toward the Great River. But getting back across it
would be another matter entirely.

Wolf and his patrol had crossed the barrier of the bluffs
and carefully picked their way along the rocky summits until
they stood high over the beach—a real, shelving sand beach
some eight hundred yards in length, but with real width for
only something less than a hundred yards.

All along the way, Wolf had noted and marked on the
maps favorably placed natural positions or places that might
be easily and quickly improved upon to provide cover and
concealment for units of archers and slingers to harry the advance of an enemy force marching inland from the river.
Also, he had noted that a much narrower and precipitous
track ran along the inland side of the bluffs, averaging twelve
feet below the summit.

When the maps had all been marked and annotated to his
satisfaction, he left the patrol to build a fire and warm their
rations, while he clambered down the landward side to the
track below.

He found a small, low-ceilinged cave and mentally noted it
as a good cache for supplies for men manning the bluffs. Proceeding on toward the higher, thicker stretch of bluffs, he
kept his eyes peeled for more caves . . . and he found one, a
much larger one, with its entrance almost concealed by replaced undergrowth and even sapling trees.

Thinking, as he pushed through the shrubbery concealing
the entrance, that he might have chanced upon a smugglers'
hidey-hole, he loosened in its scabbard the broad-bladed infantry shortsword he favored and was about to do the same

with his dirk when the cave mouth loomed before him, almost blocked by the bulk of a man of the Black Kingdoms, in helm and steel cuirass, armed with bared broadsword and dagger.

Chapter IX

In the dimness to either side of the big swordsman, Wolf saw two very short bowmen—either dwarfs or young boys, and plains nomads by their appearance—each with a nocked arrow in a drawn hornbow. Somewhere behind the trio he could smell horses. Keeping his hands well away from his weapons, the scarred old soldier grinned.

"Comrades, a good day to yer. Now, looky here, I ain't one of Duke Tcharlz's civil marshals, if thet be what yer thinkin'. I be just a ol' soldier, sent out a-scoutin' fer his captain, back t' Twocityport, an' I never had me nuthin' but r'spec' fer smugglers. I swan, wasn't fer smugglers, damn few o' us poor fellers could get us nary a taste o' good likker, whut with these here sky-high taxes ever' mucketymuck an' his friggin' brother slaps awn it."

The swordsman shook his head, the unlaced face plates slapping against his cheeks. "We are not smugglers, soldier. We are escaped slaves who maimed our master, killed freemen, stole horses, weapons and supplies and fired a serai. We now seek a way to cross the Great River, that these youngsters may return to the Horseclan from which they were kidnapped by evil men who sold them into servitude to one of those debauched eastern Ehleenee.

"We know ourselves to be pursued, soldier. That is why I must kill you, lest you betray our hiding place. I am sorry, for you seem a good, blunt, honest warrior."

Wolf saw the brawny, brown-skinned arm go back, readying for the thrust, and the swordsman asked solemnly, "So how would you rather have it, soldier, heart or throat?"

Wolf grinned again, disarmingly, "Of exertion, to be true, Zahrtohgahn"—his keen hearing had sorted out the accent—"after a night with a brace of sixteen-year-old doxies.

"But hold up fore yew murders me. It's a full p'trol, up there 'top of the bluffs, an' they knows I'm down here. I don't come up soon . . . 'less yew thinks one sword and two bows be a match fer a dozen well-armed veterans."

Seeing with relief the muscles of the sword arm relax just a bit, Wolf added, "'Sides, I think I got me a ideer will help us all out a little."

Wolf sank down to a squat, removed his helmet and placed it under his flat buttocks. After a brief pause, Nahseer, too, squatted, laying the blade of his sword across his knees, but keeping the dirk in hand. Neither of the nomad boys stirred, other than to lower the aim of their hornbows to keep Wolf covered.

On a hunch, Wolf tried telepathy. "Do you mindspeak, little comrade?" he asked Bahb Steevuhnz.

He was a bit taken aback when not only the nomad boys—whose people were widely known to have this power—but the Zahrtohgahn, as well, silently replied, "Yes, all of us do, the horses back there as well."

Wolf's grin broadened. This would make things quicker and easier. "I be no enemy to smugglers and I'm no slave taker neither, comrades, an 'least two of them men up on the bluff was escaped slaves when we enlisted them back east. My captain, he ain't too picky about no man's past, just so long's he fights and heeds discipline in garrison or camp.

"Now, being on the run and all, none of you may know it, but this duchy is already at war. Duke Alex, 'crost the river, has got real cozy with the King of Mehmfiz, downriver a ways, and they's both getting ready to hit one of the duke's allies down south of here. Naturally, he'll have to march down and help out his buddies, and the mosta his troops with him.

"When he's too far away to do no good, it's a sure thing that Duke Alex is gonna invade this duchy and try to take Twocityport, so's he can hold both ends of the barge cables. My captain's job is to hold the new citadel at Twocityport until the duke be done down south. My captain's been promised a hundred score of soldiers, but I ain't gonna be-lieve them till I comes to see them marching in the gate.

"So part of the mission of my patrol was to bring back any likely-looking recruits we could lay hand to, and to my mind, you three is the best I seen all this week past. It don't matter none what size the boys is, long's they can shoot straight, and I never heerd tell of a Horseclansman what couldn't. As for you, Zahrtohgahn, you got you that look. I'd say you're the same as me, you been soldiering mosta your life. Ain't I right, now?"

"Yes," agreed Nahseer, without pause, "before I was sold into servitude by a powerful man I had wronged, I was an officer in the armies of my native state, a noble-born officer, commanding a mixed brigade, as had my father and his fa-ther before him."

Wolf nodded. "I thought so, and I ain't often wrong about men. If my captain was to get the duke to give you three freedom *and* amnesty, would you fight for him against his foes?"

"Could such only be so," replied Nahseer, "it would be a true godsend, a sweet gift of Ahláh. But our former master is a rich and powerful merchant of Pahdookahport; not only did we attack him and rob him, but I maimed his body be-yond any hope of forgiveness."

"Nahseer gelded the bastard," put in Bahb gleefully. "Then he put a live coal inside his scrotum. But I was the first to blood him. I laid open his cheek and stabbed him in the crotch when he would have stuck his yard up my arse."

"No matter how rich and how powerful your master be, there be strong laws against sodomy—especially when such nastiness takes the form of forcible rape of either free man or slave—and it is my understanding that Duke Tcharlz, for all his other faults, detests sodomites and sees the laws he has enacted against them enforced to the last jot and tittle," Wolf assured them.

"But that matter aside, the duke is even now going through the duchy with a fine-toothed comb, seeking out able-bodied slaves and apprentices and offering them freedom, pay, keep and, perhaps, loot, will they serve in his army. As the senior sergeant of the Twocityport citadel, I've the power to make you three that same offer and to enlist you on this spot if you all be so inclined.

"Understand me, please, comrades, it be your decision, and yours alone, to make, but there is only death or recapture for you here. You and your beasts could never get across the river without help, and if you stay in this place and the slave takers don't chance upon you, then you'll assuredly be slain or taken when Duke Alex lands his army on that beach beyond this bluff—for that is where my captain thinks he will land, and my captain is seldom wrong on matters of a military nature."

"How do we know," Nahseer inquired bluntly, "that you will not get us to your citadel and disarm us or take us in a drugged sleep, and chain us and send us back to him from whom we fled?"

Wolf shrugged. "You have only my word, of course, but no living man has ever questioned it."

It was, to Nahseer's way of thinking, a good answer, and he already was beginning to like and trust this bluff, scarred old soldier. But he felt that he must be as sure as possible before putting himself and the boys in a jeopardy which could prove fatal. "But what of your captain? He may have bigger fish to fry, so his thinking may be different from your own. Understand, old warrior, the fiend from whom we escaped will not simply stripe us, he will have us all slowly tortured to death."

"As I have soldiered with my captain for almost thirty years, I can speak as truly for him as for myself. He detests sodomites as much as does the duke, and he detests the vile institution of slavery even more, wherever and by whomever it is practiced. This be why he has never been loath to enlist runaway slaves or apprentices in his companies. He and I have fought off slave takers to protect men who had freely enlisted . . . and I can say that he and I would gladly do such again."

The clouds which had been scudding westward over the valley of the Ohyoh River banked lower, denser and dirty-gray as the afternoon progressed and, in the premature darkness of what should have been sunset, began to let loose blinding sheets of water, along with crackling stabs of blue-white lightning and shuddering rolls of thunder.

But all of the patrol, horse and man, abided warm and dry in the commodious bluffside cave, along with Wolf's three newest recruits, sharing food and drink and swapping tales. The storm passed in the night, and in the bright sunshine of the next morning, all set out for Twocityport by way of a tiny, rural hamlet, where they were to pick up a brace of husky farm boys who had promised to meet them there. Wolf had taken their enlistment oaths on the way out from the citadel.

The broken, hilly area just south of the bluffs was brushy and alive with small game, and Bahb and Djoh Steevuhnz strung their bows and impressed Wolf and the soldiers to a high degree by arrowing, seemingly without aim or effort, above two dozen running rabbits.

Wolf set a slow and easy pace, and, just shy of the sun's zenith, the patrol arrived in the minuscule square of the farming hamlet. Only a few hours' ride from Twocityport, the community boasted no inn, only a hwiskee house—which sold mostly ale, beer, cider and a cheap, sour wine, despite its announced purpose—which stood on one side of the square, adjacent to the smithy.

At an outside table sat Wolf's two farm boys, passing the time with a checkerboard, coarse bread, pickled pork and mugs of cool cider. Between them and the square, at the long rail, nearly a score of horses were hitched, and anyone could see that the beasts had been ridden hard and long. Yet the sweaty, huffing equines had not been unsaddled, nor had the girths been loosened, and no one was walking the mounts to allow them to gradually cool after exertion.

Wolf shook his helmeted head, sneering to himself at the stupidity and cruelty of whoever led this pack of halfwits.

Spotting him, the two farm boys folded and stowed their game, wolfed the last crumbs of their food and upended the cider mugs, their throats working, then came trotting to the head of the column—blanket rolls slanting across chest and back, war bags in hand and one with an old, worn dagger under his belt.

At Wolf's query about the ill-served line of horseflesh and the loud hubbub of men's voices from within the hwiskee house, one of the boys replied, "Ahh, them varmints be but a passel of plains traders and Crooked Portuh's men from the big serai on the Pahdookahport road and a few hired bravos, out a-lookin' fer three runaway slaves. This be the second time they been th'ough here, cain't seem to find 'em, and we folks hopes to God they never does neither."

To his patrol archers, Wolf gave the hand signal to string bows and nock arrows. At the same time, he mindspoke Bahb and Djoh to do likewise. Then, hoping to the last to avoid a confrontation or a fight, he urged the two farm boys to mount a brace of the led horses at once.

But it was already too late. A pair of men came out of the hwiskee house, their arms linked, holding foamy mugs and bawling a lusty song. And then the song died on their lips. One man dropped his mug and ran back inside, shouting, "It's *them*, Mistuh Custuh, sir. They all three out inna square. A passel of sojers done took 'em."

There was a brief delay as both Portuh and Custuh tried to make use of the narrow egress at the same time. The heavier Portuh won that contest, but Custuh was hard on his heels, followed by the big, rawboned bravo Djahnbil—representing the Lord Urbahnos on the hunt—and his sidekick, Buhbuhtchuhk, trailed by the other trader, Hwahruhn, and then most of the other hunters, most of them bearing mugs or jacks and still chewing.

Wolf warily eyed the mob of men, judging their potential, and felt somewhat reassured. All bore arms of one kind or another, but only five were fully armed and armored—Custuh and Hwahruhn wore the boiled-leather armor of the plains nomads, with swords and dirks; the two bravos' bodies were protected by steel scale shirts, their shoulders, arms and thighs by steel plates, and their heads by steel helmets; Portuh was encased from neck to knees in a fine and very expensive ensemble of Pitzburk plate armor topped off with an old leather cap which had been split to fit over the dirty, greasy bandages swathing his head from the ears up.

Portuh, recognizing Wolf as the adjutant of Duke Tcharlz's favorite condottiere, Captain Martuhn, approached him, followed by Hwahruhn and the two bravos. But the other trader, Custuh—basically hotheaded, in addition to being hot, tired, dirty, saddlesore and, after a week of fruitlessly crisscrossing the sector of the duchy between Pahdookahport and Twocityport, frustrated to the point of tears or murder—rushed up to Nahseer's place in the column and grabbed the gray's bridle, snarling, "Git t' hell off'n m' hoss, yew no-good, thievin' shit-faced bastid, yew!"

Before Nahseer could even start to free boot from stirrup and kick the man away, the war-trained gelding reared, lashing out with deadly steel-shod hooves. One of those hooves took Custuh just above the eyes, cracking his skull like an eggshell and smashing on into the brain. Custuh's lifeless body spun off to flop into the dust of the square, blood and gray-pink brain tissue contrasting with splintered shards of white bone in the place where his forehead had been.

Hwahruhn shuddered and moaned softly. This was just the way he had seen his partner die many times over in his fevered dreams of weeks past.

Custuh might have been the only casualty, had rational men been vouchsafed the time to take charge, but such was not fated to pass. Hwahruhn's nightmares of blood and death for the men of the caravan of kidnappers was swiftly to become reality.

"Thet dang Zahrtohgan bugtit done kilt Mistuh Custuh!" shouted the bravo Djahnbil, drawing sword from sheath with a sibilant *zweeeep*. "Let's us git 'im!"

"*No!*" yelled Hwahruhn, turning and starting toward the bravo. "It was the horse killed him, an accident . . ."

But it was too late for words in the tense confrontation of the two groups of irritable and nervous men. The two sword-holding bravos had taken no more than three steps in Nahseer's direction when, with a *twanng* and a *thunnk*, Bahb and Djoh Steevuhnz had each sent a bone-headed hunting arrow through the left eye and into the brain of each of the mercenaries.

As the two dropped with a clashing of their scale shirts, the mob before the hwiskee house began to mill and move forward, with the nooning sun glinting on bared blades. A ripple passed through the double column of soldiers as the bowmen presented and drew, awaiting only Wolf's signal to loose.

Wolf had been watching the mob when, out of the corner of his eye, he saw Portuh grasp the hilt of his longsword. Wolf's short, broad, heavy model was out first, and with the flat he cudgeled Portuh's bandaged head; the serai keeper dropped to his knees, holding his head and groaning.

Wolf reined about to the right flank and raised his sword above his head, roaring, "Archers, one volley, target to right flank, fifteen yards. *Loose!*"

To the accompaniment of screams of pain and fear, six war arrows and two more hunting arrows of Horseclans make thudded through clothing and into the vulnerable flesh of those men unlucky enough to have been in the forefront of the mob of would-be slave catchers. Several of the men in the rear faded back into the hwiskee house. Running down three slaves, and two of them little boys at that, was one thing; taking on a fully armed and mounted squad of the duke's dragoons was another thing entirely.

Automatically, the veteran archers nocked a second arrow and awaited orders, the non-archers loosened swords in the scabbards and wheeled their mounts about to face the foe, gleefully awaiting an order, for men who could afford to frequent a hwiskee house must perforce have money, and once they had been hacked to death they would have no further need for money or anything else.

The surviving trader, Hwahruhn, stood aghast between the mob and the column. All of his worst presentiments and forebodings were come to terrifying life.

Second Oxman Bailee sat spraddle-legged in the dust, both his hands lying limply between his thighs, the gray-fletched shaft of an arrow protruding from his front while the blood-dripping point and more of the shaft stuck out of his back. Bailee said not a word, he just rocked to and fro, whining and coughing, deep coughs that brought up frothy blood to spray onto his legs and dribble down his chin.

Wagoner Sawl Krohnin had a black-shafted nomad arrow in his eye, and so too did one of the apprentice traders, Bahbee Gyuh. One man—Hwahruhn could not see his face—was stumbling into the door of the hwiskee house, the steel point of a war arrow winking out just below his left shoulderblade. And First Wagoner Tahm Gaitz had driven his last team across the prairie, having taken an arrow squarely between his eyes. The other three downed men were Portuh's, and Hwahruhn could not recall their names.

Slowly, the trader raised his hands, palms open placatingly. To the remaining slave catchers, he said, "Put up your steel, men. More than enough blood has been shed here over something that was none of our business to begin with.

"The slaves are all the property of that Ehleen, and no reward he could offer would be enough to pay for your lives or your suffering. These men are soldiers of Duke Tcharlz. They have the slaves, and I am sure that all will be made right in time. Take your friends back into the hwiskee house and see to their hurts; I'll deal with these gentlemen."

Most of the mob gladly took this excuse—the voice of authority—to put stout log walls between their unprotected skins and those sharp-biting arrows, but a knot of three or four of the caravan men stood their ground, grumbling. At length, Tahm Lantz stepped a few feet forward and said, "But Mistuh Hwahruhn, is we jest gonna let them bash mah cousin's haid in an' git away with it?"

Hwahruhn sighed. "In the first place, Tahm, the horse killed Mistuh Custuh, not the rider. In the second place, there is not and never was any reason, any excuse, for us to have picked a fight with these soldiers. But certain of us did so, and you can see and hear the consequences. If you, personally, and your friends there want to commit suicide, speak to the sergeant here. I'm certain that some of his troopers will accommodate you."

Then Hwahruhn turned his back on the late Trader Custuh's cousin and bespoke Wolf. "Sergeant, there has been a terrible misunderstanding this day. We are peaceable men and had been about a lawful, civic duty: the recapture of three slaves. I see that you have taken them, but you were wise to disarm them, as well, for they are directly responsible for the shameful maiming of their master and indirectly responsible for the deaths of several men, the partial destruction of the serai on the road from Twocityport to Pahdookahport, the burning of most of our caravan's best goods from this last trip and the theft of five horses and other items."

Wolf shrugged. "You should oughta have tol' all o' thet to them firs' two buggers drawed steel and come a-runnin' at my column, mistuh. Hell, my men and me had us no way to know who or what your outfit was," Wolf lied, blank-faced. "First off, some loonatick comes a-runnin' up and grabs the bridle of Trooper Nahseer's hoss and the hoss gits hisself spooked and kicks that crazy's head in."

"It was Custuh's gelding," said Hwahruhn. "The Zahrtohgahn slave stole it out of the serai stables. But you're right, of course, he should've gone about things differently. He always was a hothead."

Wolf smiled grimly. "Wal, he's a busted-open head now.

But why'n hell did them other two have t' draw steel and come at my column? That's what really touched the thing off, y' know, Mistuh."

Hwahruhn sighed again. "They were hired men in the service of Lord Urbahnos of Pahdookahport, the master of the three slaves, the man who wanted them back. He had offered a huge reward for their recapture, alive."

"Wal . . ." Wolf leaned forward in his saddle and spoke slowly and distinctly. "He ain't a-gonna git them, mistuh, nor nobody elst, f'r that matter. All three of 'em's enlisted in the comp'ny of Captain Count Martuhn of Twocityport f'r the rest o' the war, and then—by the orders o' His Grace Duke Tcharlz—they gets their freedom!"

Knowing that he had precious little time to spare, Duke Tcharlz and his columns descended on the phony war downriver with frightening speed, marching something over a hundred miles—cavalry *and* infantry, and much of it cross-country—in a few hours less than five days. The young King of Mehmfiz and his three marshals, one of them an actual nobleman of his court, the other two mercenary captains, strove to fight delaying actions in keeping with the king's promises to the Duke of Traderstownport; therefore, to that planned end, they separated . . . and this was their downfall. One after the other, the wily duke forced them into open battle and decimated them, pursuing the shattered ranks far southward across the border and deep into the Kingdom of Mehmfiz itself.

Nor did he and his troops simply war on fellow soldiers as his columns returned northward. They razed and raped, looted and burned and slew; no structure of less strength than a walled and well-defended town was safe from their savage depredations.

And, as Tcharlz had known full well they would, the court of Mehmfiz was quickly agitated by the grumblings of the nobles whose northern lands were being hardest hit by this large-scale raiding, even while the streets and alleys of the young king's largest city were becoming clogged with lowborn refugees, each of them with grisly and horrifying tales to recount.

There was now but a single army left free and unpummeled in the north. It was the personal force of King Uyr, and, despite himself, Duke Tcharlz was beginning to develop a degree of respect for the young man, who seemed able to avoid trap after trap, to wriggle his force out of situations instinctively. Nor could this military expertise be that of mere experience, for the royal ruler of Mehmfiz was not that old and he had never before personally warred so far as the duke and his informants were aware.

The manuevering had now crossed the border and was taking place over the battered northern provinces of Mehmfiz itself. Save for the two armies, these provinces—formerly among the richest of the kingdom—were become virtual deserts, empty of man. The fine crops not yet harvested had been either burned or trampled into the earth by hooves and booted feet. Harvested crops had been either looted or burned while the structures that had held them, fine halls and hovels alike, were become roofless ruins, their former occupants either fled southward or lying—their scavenger-picked bones scattered and bleaching on the ground—in or nearby those ruins.

Knowing that King Uyr's intemperate alliance had already cost him and his kingdom dearly, and certain that—with but the single, small army to back him—the kinglet would be unable to further menace the states to his north, Duke Tcharlz was upon the verge of breaking off and marching his force back to Twocityport. Then into his camp came riding a delegation under a flag of truce.

The meeting between the two leaders took place within the open parkland of a ruin that Tcharlz well remembered. It had been here that he had almost lost an eye to the toothsome, red-haired noblewoman he had been raping. Such had been his admiration of her spunk and spirit that when he was done with her he had, rather than turn her over to his officers and troopers, gifted her with a good horse and a purse of gold and even allowed her to keep her jewels.

King Uyr seemed anything other than the utter fop that northern rumor named him to be. He was very short, but such was his dynamism that the duke found himself forgetting the difference in height. There was an intense vitality in every movement of the young king's wiry frame, and intelligence of a high order glinted from the depths of his gray blue eyes.

When wine had been sipped—each had brought his own

—and after the opening amenities, King Uyr had leaned back in his scorched chair—both chairs and the heavy table having been dragged from out of the nearby ruins for the meeting—and, smiling ruefully, commented, "Well, my esteemed Cousin Tcharlz, you've played merry hell in these my northern counties, have you not?"

Tcharlz shrugged. "There is only one way to conduct warfare, lord, and that is to fight to win; the harder and bloodier you make it for your enemy, the quicker you win."

The king nodded. "You have made it hard for me, cousin, damned hard indeed. Half a dozen of my richest, most powerful and most influential counts are constantly badgering me and would likely be fomenting a rebellion, had I not had the foresight to summon them all to my army, where I can keep an eye on them. It is partially at their behest that I meet you here."

The young monarch leaned forward. "What would you say if I asked that you and yours return north and I and mine return south, eh? You were wise to agree, cousin, for by this time Duke Alex has already at least invested your capital, if it has not indeed fallen to his arms."

Tcharlz smiled lazily, catlike. "The town proper may be in that arrogant popinjay's hands, King Uyr, but not my new citadel, I'll wager you; and unless or until he holds that fortress, he'll have no use of the port or of much of the town."

"A half-finished fort won't delay his army long, cousin," said the king.

"Oh, ho, ho," laughed Tcharlz. "I've stolen a march on you, lord king, that I have. The fortress is completed, completed *and* garrisoned *and* in command of a veteran captain, Martuhn of Geerzburk. He's a born nobleman of the eastern kingdoms, driven from his patrimonial estates by a greedy overlord. Now I've invested him with another county, and it is to his own interest to hold that citadel for me; and he can if any man can. The merchants of Pahdookahport have hired on their own mercenary troops, and quite a strong contingent of them, too. So have the rulers of my client states to the north of the Ohyoh. They're none of them strong enough to go on the offensive, but if that dung-eating hound Alex should be fool enough to attack either of them, he'll be badly singed.

"So, my dear enemy, I can see no reason to curtail my romp here in the rich lands of Mehmfiz. Over the years of late, I've been vegetating, growing old and fat, while attending to affairs of state and letting hirelings do my fighting for me. After these last few weeks, though, lord king, living again the hard, strenuous, spartan life of a soldier on campaign, I feel and—so my gentlemen attest often—look at least twenty years younger than my actual years.

"Since this raiding and riding and fighting so well agrees with me, and since, as I have told you, there is nothing of an urgent nature to summon me back to mine own lands, and since I have no lines of supply to hamper my movements or disturb my sleep—this, because my forces and I are living well off *your* lands, lord king—I can see no reason to desist just yet.

"Perhaps after I have razed a few more of your counties and have finally chivvied you and your remaining forces to panting, bleeding tatters you will truly regret your and Duke Alex's little scheme to forcibly divest me of that which is lawfully mine.

"Now"—Tcharlz shoved back his chair and stood, hitching his sword back around for easier walking—"unless my lord king of Mehmfiz wishes to begin discussion of the terms of his surrender, I've matters to attend to in my camp."

The young king's eyes flashed the cold fires of outraged anger for a moment, even as his knot of retainers snarled and grumbled curses at the impudence of this mere duke, but Uyr's anger dissipated as quickly as it had appeared.

"As you wish, Cousin Tcharlz, as you wish. I have little need and no intention of surrendering to you. Rather, I came this day to suggest that we call it a draw and retire to our respective capitals.

"As you are well aware, you have left me insufficient strength to risk an open battle with you. However, because I am operating in lands I know well and because our two minds seem to function similarly, I seem to have scant difficulty in escaping your envelopments.

"As for the damages you are doing to these counties, perhaps the injured counts will, upon your eventual departure, have sufficient to occupy them at home that they will bide there for a few years and stay out of my hair in Mehmfizport."

Duke Alex had made his landfall on a stretch of beach just below the bluffs to the north of Two*river*city—he insisted on calling it by the name it had had prior to the coming of his hated rival, Tcharlz—but the invasion had been a disaster almost from the moment the ships and towed barges had left the waters of the Great River.

His plan had been to send a bevy of shallow-draft sail-and-row galleys ahead to run up on the shelving beach and discharge enough men to hold the landing area against possible attack until the big, clumsy barges could be towed out of the channel and rowed in to land horses and men to scour the immediate area and make it safe for himself, his staff and the mountains of supplies, stores, weapons and transport to be put ashore.

In theory it had been a good plan, but it had reckoned without the keen mind of Count Martuhn and *his* staff.

First, a lucky long-range shot from one of a pair of medium-light war engines which had been concealed atop the bluffs over the beach holed and sank one of a string of overloaded barges in midchannel. The barge ahead cut the sinking craft loose, but before the trailing barge could do so, the weight on the connecting cable had pulled its bow so low that it began to ship water and founder as well.

Then, without awaiting orders, the masters of the galleys began to make for shore at flank speed, rather than with the slow caution Duke Alex had intended, said masters knowing that on the beach they and their ships would be out of either sight or danger from the deadly engines atop the bluffs.

Some half of the ships beached safely. Of the unlucky ones, two were holed by sixty-pound boulders hurled by the eingines, and yet another was set afire by a pitchball from the same source. The rest, within but a few yards of the beach, ripped out or seriously damaged their bottoms on underwater obstructions unmarked on even the latest charts.

The loss of life was not really heavy, not even among the slave rowers, for the water was too shallow for any of the ripped galleys to sink deeply. But the hulks made the subsequent landings of men and horses much more difficult and far longer in accomplishment . . . and, all the while, boulders and pitchballs continued a constant hazard to the ships and barges from near shore to the center of the channel.

At the duke's command, his larger warships, at anchor in the channel, had attempted a counter-battery offensive with their own deck-mounted engines. But, as the ship masters and army officers could have told him, the range was just too great for these lighter engines, and most of their shots fell among the already hard beset shorebound vessels, while the few that actually struck the face of the bluffs did sore hurt to the troops gathered at the foot of those bluffs to escape the showers of arrows and slingstones with which they had been greeted upon landing.

Raging at the dashing of his plan, Duke Alex ordered that the warships cease fire until they had upped anchor and sailed closer inshore. However, when the bowsprit of his flagship was neatly sheared off by a stone from the bluff-top battery, new signals fluttered aloft: "Return to channel anchorage."

Only the fall of night saw the eventual landing of the entire force, less casualties, for the lanterns which the barges and lighters had perforce to mount to avoid rammings provided winking, blinking targets for the engines, bowmen and slingers high on the bluffs.

In the gray light of dawn, a hundred picked marines from the galleys scaled the towering, mist-slippery rocks of the precipitous face of the bluffs. But they found nothing atop the bluffs save piles of stones for engine or sling and a single broken hornbow. They also found tragedy, however, for when a dozen or so of them congregated on a spot near the edge, the lip of rock suddenly collapsed, hurling them all to a quick if messy death on the beach far below and crushing or injuring men and horses on that same beach. One of the chunks of rock—a stone of more than the weight of two armored men—bounced once, then splintered its way through the foredeck of a beached galley to smash the keel and exit from the side planks.

With men, animals and equipment at last ashore, Duke Alex saw the wagons and carts assembled and loaded, the teams hitched and the men in column. Then he sent a strong advance guard of mounted men ahead and set out along the beach, bound for the track that Duchess Ann's people had sworn would serve to place his army over the bluff line and within a short march of Tworivercity.

At the place where that narrow, winding track mounted

upward, the van met the battered remnants of the advance guard, most of them wounded and only a few still mounted. After hearing their tale, Duke Alex realized his error in sending cavalry into such ugly, broken terrain and dispatched, instead, three companies of light infantry, stiffened by a detachment of his marines, to scout the route of advance.

The wounded he sent back to the beachhead, to be rowed out to a ship and returned to Traderstownport. With them went a nobleman messenger with orders to come back with reinforcements, supplies to replace those lost or ruined during the landing and more horses. Then, after allowing time for the slower infantry to gain an interval from the main body, he advanced.

Captain Barnz was the fifth-eldest son of the Archduke of Tehrawtburk—a principality that lay a month or more east and north of Pahdookahport—and had had to swing steel for a living for most of his life. From his beginning as a pink-cheeked ensign in the condotta of a renowned captain, he had advanced to the command of a full regiment of light troops—six companies of infantry, two troops of lancers and a large support company of artisans and the like; a total of nearly a thousand men.

He had enjoyed a fair measure of success in recent years, choosing the proper contracts and managing to emerge from each of them with his full wages and usually a bit of loot besides. Shrewd investments in his homeland had by now assured him a comfortable retirement whenever age or wounds necessitated such, so now he fought for the sheer love of campaigning, and a large part of his profits went to recruiting the best men and officers and fitting them all out with the finest in weapons and equipment. Such had become his fame that he had not had to seek out contracts for years, while younger sons of noble lineage came from as far away as the Middle Kingdoms—far to the east, on the shores of the salt sea—to vie for places in his companies.

Rather than detailing the dangerous chore to a lieutenant, he was presently leading these three companies with a spirit of vengeance. It had been one of his troops of lancers that had been chewed up while serving as advance guards, and he meant to see blood for it. He did, more than he would have preferred.

They had marched more than a mile from the beach, the

track mounting ever higher, the scale-shirted men sweating, envying the officers and sergeants their horses. For all that the drums were covered and mute and the column proceeded at a route step, every man was a blooded veteran and knew that he was in enemy-held territory and in imminent danger. They marched with targets strapped and gripped, one dart ready in hand and the other five loose in the quiver. The archers, every fifth man, marched along with their infantry bows—heavier and longer-ranging than the cavalry horn-bow—an arrow nocked and an additional two shafts in the fingers of the bow hand. The officers and sergeants rode with bared blades.

Even so, the wickedly planned and well-executed ambush took a heavy toll of Captain Barnz's prize companies.

In a place where generations of smugglers had improved upon and shortened the former game trail through the expedient of digging a cut through a knob and deeply ditching on each side to prevent erosion from restoring the natural contours, a deadly chorus of twanging bowstrings and the hissing hum of whirling slings heralded the descent of a shower of death from within the woods atop the slope to the right.

Looking back to see dozens of his men flopping and screaming or lying still, sprawled unnaturally in the dust, Barnz waved his long sword horizontally and roared to his subordinates, "Ditch to the right flank. Get them into it, the dartmen. Get our archers into the left-flank ditch and get them returning fire at the bastards." But then, as the first men to obey his orders hurled themselves into the brushy ditches, Barnz and those men received another painful surprise.

Dartman Seth of Libberyburk had just been remarking to his marching companion, Dee Lainee, that the brush-filled ditches would make splendid habitats for snakes. But now Dartman Dee lay in the roadway, coughing out his life with an arrow transfixing his throat, and Seth forgot the possibility of snakes diving into the protection offered by that same ditch.

Seth began to scream, however, even before his body struck the ground. He screamed with the white-hot agony of some something piercing through his leather trousers into and then through the flesh and muscles of his thigh. And his was but one in a veritable chorus of screams and shrieks from up and down the lengths of both roadside ditches.

Those men unhurt cleared away the brush to find that it concealed a thick sowing of solid wooden stakes, the sharp ends of which had apparently, from the look and the stink, been soaked in fermenting dung.

With at least half of his command dead or wounded from arrow or slingstone or the devilish stakes, Captain Barnz halted his survivors where they lay. Let the main column catch up with *him*. His contract with Duke Alex committed him and his regiment to siege warfare not the steady and costly attrition of counter-guerrilla combat.

But the noble nincompoop in command of the detachment of Duke Alex's marines profanely insisted that the wounded be left behind for the main column to collect if the enemy had not slowly butchered them by that time, while the hale men pressed forward into the forbidding country ahead. When Barnz, no less profanely, had made it clear that where he and his much reduced three companies were was where they were going to stay until the arrival of the main force, the fuming young officer formed up his detachment and went marching up the road. No one ever saw any of that detachment again.

That night, in one among the labyrinth of bluff caves, Count Martuhn squatted, his eyes smarting at the smoke of the fire before him but showing a rare grin withal.

"We've slowed them and stung them, which is about all that I aimed for to start. We just lack the strength to do more."

Nahseer nodded. "Were all the lands between here and the city broken, hilly and wooded with but a single, narrow track, we might continue to nibble away at them until they broke and mutinied or, at least, lost heart for a protracted war. But once they are through the saddle there, it were suicide to attempt opposition. We are far too few and mostly unmounted, and their horsemen would ride us down at will."

When, shortly after he and the boys rode in with Wolf, the Zahrtohgahn had lowered his mindshield that Martuhn might survey his training and experience, the new-made Count of Twocityport had quickly realized just what a treasure had fallen into his hands and had willingly entrusted the delaying action to his newest lieutenant, leaving him and Sir Wolf free to attend to the multitudinous minutiae attendant to preparing the fortress and its garrison for a siege of uncertain length. But when, after the first messenger to deliver word that the enemy fleet was standing off the beach below the bluffs was not followed by another, Martuhn had taken a small escort and ridden up to the cave that had been marked on the maps to serve as Nahseer's headquarters.

The Zahrtohgahn had simply said, "I sent you word that they were about to land, my captain, and they landed, although we made that landing difficult, time-consuming and costly to them. But nothing untoward happened after that and I had suffered no casualties, so I could see no reason to afflict you with a horde of riders who could only have told you that our affairs here were proceeding as planned. Did I displease you, sir?"

"You displease me?" Martuhn shook his head vehemently. "Anything but, my good Lieutenant Nahseer. But it has been so long since I have had any officer save Sir Wolf who was capable of thinking on his feet and properly handling a protracted action without seeking my help or advice that it is difficult for me to reaccustom myself to one such as you."

Changing the subject, he asked, "And how are our little nomads faring? I was loath to send boys so young on this mission. Wouldn't have, had not you and Wolf been so insistent."

Nahseer smiled. "Bahb and Djoh, for all their tender years, are the best archers I command and better field soldiers than men two and three times their ages. They both have shown a quick, sure grasp of tactical principles, and the fact that they are telepaths, as am I, allows me far better view over and control of an ambuscade than any nontelepathic commander could have."

Martuhn nodded. "I know that feeling well, my friend. The fact that Wolf and I can communicate silently and over a distance has been vitally useful on more than one occasion over the years.

"But getting back to the subject that brought me up here, you do plan to withdraw before the enemy reaches the plain and traps you with cavalry? I could ill afford to lose so many archers and missilemen out of my garrison at the citadel."

"And I," replied Nahseer, "have no slightest desire to die trying to digest a lance point. For all the joy it has given me to once again command warriors independently, when the van of the Traderstown army comes within sight of the gap, my rear guard and I will assuredly spur for the citadel; the main body should be there by then. I doubt me not that the wagons bearing those engines that served us so well are at the gates even as we speak."

Martuhn, much relieved of mind and feeling even more blessed in Wolf's finding of the huge, tough and intelligent Zahrtohgahn, rested men and horses through the rest of the night and set out for Twocityport with the first light of the new day. While he would have enjoyed the acceptance of his new subordinate's offer to stay and watch the last big ambush of the enemy, he had ever been a slave to duty and he knew that there was much yet to be done in the citadel.

Chapter X

Stehfahnah awoke shivering lying on the floor beside the cold hearth, but her first instinctive movements set off such waves of blinding red agony in her head that she sank sobbing back onto the icy floor of packed earth. It was some time before the twin forces of her will and the cold enveloping her naked body could force her to risk again the crippling effect of that hellish pain. And it was even longer before she could will herself to rise to a huddled sitting position, the lowest part of her back pressed against the mortared stones of the hearth, her arms hugging her small breasts, rocking and moaning softly with the rhythm of the splitting pains in her head, even while her white teeth chattered and the rest of her shuddered with the agony of the cold.

Finally, after what seemed to be eons of time wherein a third force, that of raging thirst, commenced to drive her, she commenced a snail-like crawl to where the water skin hung. It required every ounce of her strength to pull her body up onto her wobbling legs, but the first cool gush of water into the dry desert her mouth and throat had become revived and revitalized her to a great extent, though it did nothing to alleviate the pain.

She wisely decided not to try walking yet. Rather did she sink back as gently as possible onto her haunches, then crawled over to the bed and the precious warmth of its thick blankets. Hardly had she wrapped herself against the cold than consciousness again left her and awareness of the pain with it.

Thump, came the loud noise. *Thump thump thump, THUMP.*

Stehfahnah slowly came awake, dragged back to awareness by the insistent thumpings. Then the adrenalin rush of fear brought her upright on the bed. *The man,* he was trying to break down the door!

But a quick glance at the battered door showed it unmoving, and even in the gloom of the hut she could see that the steel spearhead and at least a foot of hardwood shaft still projected from it.

The pain still throbbed in her head, but it was become a bearable agony. The renewed thirst was not bearable, however, nor was the aching of her bladder.

THUMP, thump thump thump thump!

She crawled back over to the water skin and again pulled herself erect. Once she was upon her feet, her legs seemed far more willing to hold her than the last time. She greedily guzzled the tepid water, then allowed some of the stuff to cascade over her face and chest. This proved even more of a refreshment than had the drink.

In no way willing to go out the door naked and unarmed when *the man* might be waiting just beyond it, she half-squatted over the ashes on the hearth and emptied her aching bladder.

THUMP THUMP THUMP! Then a splintering crash from the rear room of the cabin. Arising from the hearth, Stehfahnah lifted down one of her own finely balanced horn-tipped spears from a wall rack and, lightfootedly and silent as her condition allowed, she approached the closed door leading into the shed, her weapon ready for either stab or throw.

Bracing herself for immediate combat, she threw open the door and drew back her spear arm, then sank back against the frame of the door, pouring out her tension in a flood of tears and laughter.

Working as a team, the mare and the little ass were backed up to the outer wall of the shed and were well on the way to kicking out a section of it. But at sight of the girl, the mare ceased to flail at the wall. She mindspoke petulantly.

"Well, what did you expect us to do, twolegs female? Starve or die of thirst?"

"You'd hardly starve, horse sister—the male twolegs fed and watered you both last night."

The little mare snorted angrily and stamped a forehoof. "You are wrong, twolegs. This is the second sun since the cruel twolegs male has seen to our needs. There is no more grain, no more hay and no more water. I first tried to reach your mind but I could not, so there remained nothing more to do except free myself. Will you now feed us? Will you give us grain and hay and water? Or are you truly as uncaring as the other twolegs?"

Setting aside her spear, but keeping it near to hand just in case, she emptied the second, larger water skin which hung near the door to the horse shed into the section of hollowed-out log that served as a trough, tried to lift a sack of grain and pour the feed bucket full as she had watched *the man* so often do, but ended by scooping out the grain a double handful at the time. While the mare and the ass avidly munched the grain, she gathered an armful of dried grass from the corner pile and dumped it in the wicker rack.

"Are you now satisfied that I am not as the cruel twolegs male, dear horse sister?" inquired Stehfahnah.

Her sarcasm was lost on the mare. "I never truly thought that you were, clanswoman, but I was so very hungry and in need of water and . . ."

But another message beamed into Stehfahnah's open receptive mind. "We all thought you dead, twolegs sister. We could not reach your mind, so we thought the male twolegs had slain you when he thrust his big, long, pointed stick through the moving-dead-wood at you." The girl recognized the mindspeak of the female otter, Mother-of-Many-Many.

"Where is the male twolegs, my sister?" she demanded. "Is he near to this place?"

"He is in many places," the otter answered. "After The-Bear-Killer slew the twolegs, he ate the best parts, laid up for one sun, then went away. Then the eaters-of-old-kills came and ate and bore pieces of him away to their dens. What is left of him lies where The-Bear-Killer dragged it, in a copse near the side of the water.

"But you would not want to eat of it now, sister. It is old carrion and stinking. Wait, I will catch you a good fish."

Scarcely able to believe that she was really free of *the man*, the girl moved to the door, used the same cudgel to knock loose the bar and swung it wide, letting a wealth of golden sunlight in to flood the fetid dimness of the tiny cabin.

Just at the verge of the clearing, she could see the sleek, brown form of Mother-of-Many-Many moving toward the river with the humping scuttle which was the gait of otters on land.

When she had assured herself that nothing threatened her from without, she went back inside and searched until she found her boots and clothing, for despite the sunlight there was a distinct nip in the outer air. Dressed for the first time since *the man* had captured her, she took the monogrammed dirk from where it hung from a hook on *the man's* belt and reaffixed it in its proper place on her own belt. Then she set about worrying the steel-bladed spear out of the door.

Before she left, she drained the smaller water skin into the trough in the horse shed, then slung both skins over her shoulder and headed for the river. By the time she had rinsed out and refilled the two skins, the sun had sufficiently warmed so that she suffered scant discomfort when she stripped and swam briefly in the river. Its waters were bitingly cold a bare two hands beneath the surface, but she felt a driving compulsion to lave the stink of *the man* from her body.

For all her wiry strength, Stehfahnah Steevuhnz soon discovered that she simply could not carry both filled skins at once, and, while making the two trudging trips, she was considering fashioning a small travois from one of *the man's* drying frames; for, given the wealth of skins and hides, supplies and gear to which she was now heir, there would be no need to kill animals except for food, even if she found it necessary to winter here.

Then she thought of the ass, once *the man's* and now hers. For all his minuscule size, the little beast was amazingly strong, capable—so *the man* had once assured her—of bearing the carcass of a full-grown buck deer, which in life had weighed more than the ass. He would be perfect for bearing back the filled water skins, in future.

She had just rehung the larger water skin when Mother-of-Many-Many humped through the open door, bearing in her sharp white teeth a silvery, feebly flopping fish a third as long as her own sinuous body; behind her humped the larger Killer-of-Much-Meat-in-Water, his own teeth impaling a big catfish, swollen with roe.

Fish of any description had ever been classed as a treat by Horseclansfolk. After a week of subsisting on *the man's* hideous stews and half-burned, half-raw venison and rabbits, Stehfahnah fairly drooled at sight of the offerings of her otter friends.

While the fire burned down to the coals needed for proper cooking, the girl squatted in front of the hearth, using one of the half-dozen skinning knives to skin and clean the two fish. As of old, when she had lived in the woods downstream, the two otters crouched before her, avidly devouring the fish guts and lights, which they preferred even over the firm white flesh.

It was not until she gobbled the first mouthful of raw catfish roe that she realized just how ravenous she truly was. Therefore, to take her mind off her growling belly, she asked the otters again about the beast—surely fearsome, for had he not slain a full-grown man?—they had brought down to deliver her from her captivity.

"Where is The-Bear-Killer now?"

The big male otter chewed his way up a rope of roe as he beamed, "Not here; he never stays anywhere for long. If he did, all the meat-beasts would leave, for he will eat any fresh-killed creature, from the greatest to the least."

"Why was he willing to come so far to help me, a twolegs?" asked Stehfahnah puzzledly, knowing that the strange beast's action had been totally unlike the usual behavior of even the most intelligent of wild animals.

"When he was little more than a kit," the male otter answered, "he was caught in a twolegs' shiny-leg-biter, then taken to a place where many twolegs denned. He was kept, half starved, in a deep pit and forced to fight other beasts while twolegs watched.

"One night, a tree fell over the pit and he was able to climb up a big branch and escape. He hates all twolegs, but most of all he hates the twolegs who use the shiny-leg-biters. I told him one such denned here and he swam down the water to kill it. He is a mighty killer of twolegs."

As the Sacred Sun went to rest, Stehfahnah hunkered near the hearth on which a dry log blazed atop the coals of the cooking fire. With the careful, patient strokes of long practice, she was honing new edges onto the spearblade dulled by being thrust through the door at her.

Outside, all around the snug cabin, a cold wind soughed, rattling the branches of the trees and shrubs. All the signs indicated that the first snows were only weeks away, perhaps only days. She had been born and reared on the prairie, and so she knew full well the suicidal folly of setting out now to seek her clan, even mounted on the mare, well armed and equipped and with the ass to carry supplies and a small tent.

Better to winter here and seek Clan Steevuhnz with the coming spring. True, the cabin and its meager furnishings were stinking and filthy, but all could be cleaned. Fresh clay could be brought up from the riverbank to cover the greasy floor, the tabletop could be scoured with sand and water and the greasy sooty walls, as well. She could wash the dirt-shiny blankets and, with fresh deerskins and tips of cedar and the rare pine, she could fashion a new and more comfortable mattress, lashed and sewn with sinew and placed upon a frame of sapling trunks and woven willow switches.

There were several bags of dried grain for the mare and the ass, but while the weather was still good, she would have to fashion travoises for both of them, take the sickle and go west to the prairie verge of this woodland to cut and bear back enough hay to last the two herbivores through the cold time.

Far westward, upon the tall-grassed prairie, the Kindred clans were slowly trickling into the huge, sprawled Tribe Camp. Of sheer necessity, the camp moved east a few miles each day, leaving behind it a clear, flat-tramped and close-grazed sign of its passing more than two miles wide.

The tribe now numbered forty clans of the Kindred. From the high plains of the west had come Clans Ohlszuhn and Danyuhlz and Kehlee and others. From the far south, Clans Rohz and Morguhn and Rahs and more; and from the northern prairies where winter was already making itself felt, Muhkawlee and Mahntguhmree and Maktahguht and Pahlmuh and Makbeen and Keeth and Stynbahk. A few came from the east, and one of these was Clan Steevuhnz.

Of a sunny autumn morning, a small party of riders wended their way through the vast herds of horses, cattle, sheep and a few goats ringing the tribal camp about. In hair, eyes and features, the leading rider bore a striking resemblance to both Stehfahnah and Bahb, which was perfectly natural, for he was their and Djoh's father, Chief Henree, the Steevuhnz of Steevuhnz.

Henree looked every inch the chief, a leader of men, cats and horses, from the spike of his helmet of mirror-bright steel to the soles of his high boots of red-dyed doeskin. He bestrode a handsome, spirited black stallion, the horse fitted with a tooled saddle the same shade as the boots and inset with hooks and rings and decorations of steel, brass, copper, silver and ruddy gold.

The Clan Steevuhnz was a wealthy clan, and part of the duty of a chief of such a clan was to wear clear evidence of that wealth, to richly deck out his mount and to bear fine, expensive weapons.

When at last Chief Henree stood within the circle of chiefs while his clan bard sang his long pedigree, which was also the history of Clan Steevuhnz, replete with all the many deeds of valor of his forebears, Milo of Morai noted that for all the costly and colorful clothing and adornment, the gray eyes of the Steevuhnz were dark-ringed and sunken and his lips were set in a grim line.

When, after Blind Hari and Milo and the assembled chiefs had formally recognized that Clan Steevuhnz was indeed of the true Kindred and that Henree was its lawful chief, being the eldest son of the eldest sister of the previous chief—over the years, some clans had adopted this system of inheritance of the chieftancy, while others had clung to the system of primogeniture—and had taken his place in the expanded circle, Milo spoke to him aloud.

"Perhaps if my brother Henree Steevuhnz speaks of his sorrows to his brother chiefs, wrongs to him may be put right."

Like a summer storm filling a dry streambed, the words rushed out in a flood. A peaceful party of clan hunters set upon in treachery by a caravan of eastern traders. Henree's third-eldest son murdered, two younger boys and a daughter of his get captured and borne back eastward to what terrible fates no one knew.

"We would have known nothing of any of it," said Henree sadly, "save that my brave, dead boy had left the cat that had accompanied the hunters outside the camp when he and his brothers and sister rode in, bidding the cat stay hidden lest she frighten those eastern men and the beasts they enslave. So this young cat, Cloudgray, saw it all, every infamy.

"From the descriptions she gave, I can but believe that the

caravan was that of the trader Stooahrt, called 'the Shifty Man.' Steevuhnz warriors have many times ridden out and back as hired guards for this Stooahrt.

"Cloudgray said that all my folk were invited to eat the meal and sleep within the trader camp and then eat with them again at sun birth. But the meal was hardly well begun when first the young boys and then the girl dropped their bowls of stew and fell upon the ground. My brave son arose and, though staggering as if he were drunk, drew saber and dirk and fought his way through the knot of traders to his mount, leapt onto her back and had ridden almost to where Cloudgray crouched, when one of the traders hurled a dart which pierced through my young warrior's back and burst his mighty heart.

"Being a young cat, with no war training and little experience other than some hunting of beasts, Cloudgray did not immediately run back to fetch the clan warriors, but rather remained crouched in the grass until the traders packed and hitched and set out eastward at the next sun birth.

"She saw these accursed murderers put the two young boys into one wagon, the girl into another. They stripped the body of their victim of everything of value, then tumbled him into a hole in the ground, rather than sending him decently to Wind."

A foreboding rumble of rage passed around the circle of squatting chiefs. Only dirtmen sank their dead beneath the ground to rot and stink and be consumed by loathy beasts. Horseclansfolk were always sent to the home of Wind, their spirits rising up with the smoke of their pyres. To simply bury a Horseclansman constituted one of the deadliest of insults to his clan.

Henree then continued his tale. "When the traders moved on east, Cloudgray set out on the week's run to my camp, south and west of the spot on which this shameful deed was done.

"Unfortunately, in trying to take a saberhorn fawn for food, the young cat was seriously gored by the herd bull, and so was almost four weeks in stumbling into my camp. But before she died, she told all, beamed detailed descriptions of the evil men and of the country and landmarks between.

"Leaving only enough force to guard the camp, I rode forth with my warriors and maiden archers and most of my adult cats. The king stallion followed with two spare mounts for every man, maiden and cat. Riding by sun and by moon, as well, we won to that ill-omened spot on the prairie in less than four days.

"We had packed wood and oil with us, and we dug up my son's pitiful, putrid body and sent him properly to Wind." Hot tears of grief and frustrated rage cascaded over the scarred and weathered cheeks of the chief of Steevuhnz, and many of his brother chiefs wept with him; for though stoic to non-Kindred, with their own they could be very emotional.

"We camped that night in the spot whereon the murderers and kidnappers had camped the second night after they had done their wickedness against Clan Steevuhnz. Then we rode hard upon their trail and did not pause for longer than a few hours at a time until we came in sight of the fort that lies at the limits of the lands owned by the dirtman chief of Traderstown.

"I made to ride in with my sons and my subchiefs to speak to the subchief of that fort, with all bows cased, and all blades put up and even the lance points toward the earth, a bit of white rag fixed at the butts. But they would not even speak. They hid atop the walls and threw stones and loosed many sharp arrows at us, killing two horses and my second-eldest son and injuring two of my brothers."

Milo looked around the circle of grim-faced men and used his powerful mental abilities to skim their surface thoughts. All were enraged to the point of blood and death by the appalling arrogance of the subhuman dirtmen to so dishonor the most ancient and revered symbol of parley. He knew that should he or Blind Hari of Krooguh call this minute for a discussion and vote upon the matter, within an hour there would be two thousand or more fully armed riders bearing down upon that still distant border fort.

Further, knowing the minds of Horseclansmen as he did, it could be only a matter of time—and a short time, at that— before one or more of the chiefs demanded that some or all of the clans ride forth to mete out punishment to the dirtmen.

Milo had no compunction about leveling the tiny fort and butchering its garrison—for, after all, he had personally slain thousands of men and had been responsible for the deaths of numerous other thousands during his hundreds of years of life. But his scheme for getting the tribe over the Great River was to move suddenly and quickly across the lands of the Duchy of Traderstown, overrun or set siege to the city itself, and force out of the rulers of the duchy the use of their cable barges.

A premature attack upon the border of the duchy would but serve to warn those rulers that the prairie nomads were now gathered in unheard-of numbers and grant the dirtmen the time to gather unto themselves allies and mercenary companies and the wherewithal to make Milo's tasks harder and longer of accomplishment.

Henree of Steevuhnz went on to the end. "That night, we camped out of range of their arrows and of the things that throw big rocks. The subchiefs chose a clansman to replace my son slain that day and my wounded brother who died soon after we made camp. Then it was decided that, with the next sun birth, we would simply swing wide, bypass the fort and then swing back to cut the trail of the caravan, for we were gaining on them hour by hour.

"But when we tried to carry out our plan the next morning, the dirtmen sent out almost sixscore of mounted fighters to head us off. We drew up in battle line and, when those accursed dirtmen came into bow range, we gave them two loosings from every bow in the party. Then I led the warriors in under the cover of the maidens' arrow storm, which rained down up to the very minute we struck them.

"My brothers, that was a fight! I had ridden from out my clan camp with less than twoscore warriors, plus a half-dozen war-trained but unblooded boys, so we were seriously outnumbered, but the courage and honor of Clan Steevuhnz has seldom been matched, as any bard can sing you.

"Of course, the volleys and the arrow storm had taken a heavy toll of both men and mounts, and besides, when ever were any four mere dirtmen a match for a full-grown and armed man of our Holy Kindred? My warriors and I, we smote them, broke them and sent those craven curs still able to ride or to run back toward their fort as fast as their legs or their mounts could bear them.

"We pursued, harrying and slaying the bastards, sabering and lancing them until arrows and stones from the fort began to fall among us. Then we trotted back to just out of range of the walls, uncased our own bows and dropped many more of those cowards before they could put stone walls between us and them. But not all had been spineless, some had fought hard, well and long, and, in consequence, some Steevuhnz warriors lay dead and red with their blood and others were so seriously wounded that—though it grieved our hearts full sore—we all knew that we must break off the pursuit of the stealers of our much-loved kin and return to the clan camp.

"But before we left that field, we stripped those foemen left lying upon it and had the king stallion and his subchiefs bespeak all the sound horses and mares left outside the fort; of course, most of them joined the Steevuhnz sept of horses.

"This fine steel helmet"—Henree pulled off the spiked headpiece, now decorated with red-dyed horsehair and the bushy tail of a fox—"I took from the chief of the dirtman warriors. With some gentle persuasion," he explained, with a grin as cold and humorless as that of a winter wolf, "he told us that he himself had seen the trader Stooahrt and his wagons loading onto the barges to cross the Great River two days before we came near the fort.

"Therefore, my Kindred brothers, let us move quickly to cross that mightiest of rivers, that we may the sooner free from the filthy men of dirt my little sons, Bahb and Djoh, and my daughter, Stehfahnah. It is a duty owed by us all to our Holy Race and to the honored memory of our Sacred Ancestors."

As Milo had known would happen, immediately Chief Henree ceased to speak and sank back upon his haunches, Steev, the Dohluhn of Dohluhn, stood and, while scratching at the sections of scalp bared by his thinning, dark hair, said flatly, "I doubt not that you stung the scum badly, brother Henree, for I know well that Clan Steevuhnz breeds stark warriors. But deeds of such dishonor—if, truly, anything could dishonor a mere dirtman—call for death, not just crippling.

"Now Clan Dohluhn's full warriors number twoscore and eleven, and there are ten more unblooded."

Another balding chief sprang to his feet. Pat, the Kehlee of Kehlee, announced, "Clan Kehlee numbers a full threescore blooded warriors and almost a score of unblooded. All of us will ride with the valiant chiefs of Steevuhnz and Dohluhn."

"I had better," thought Milo, "defuse this thing before it

gathers more momentum. Once they get the bit in their teeth, these stubborn bastards are going to be hard to handle."

The war chief arose from his place beside Blind Hari on the dais. "Chiefs, Kindred brothers, vengeance will be taken on this batch of dirtmen, but like a stew of the flesh of a tough, elderly bull, it will be more enjoyable to us if we allow it to cook for a while.

"This fort lies on the way to, in the very lands of, the dirtmen whose ferry we needs must have in order that all our tribe may safely cross the Great River."

Milo talked on at great length. Then Blind Hari stood up and added his not inconsequential powers of persuasion against any rash, early attack. As usual in any "discussion," the circle of chiefs grumbled and groused, argued and shouted, but finally decided that the war chief and the clan bard were right.

Chapter XI

Although all of the court of Duchess Ann and more than half the residents of Twocityport cordially despised their duchess' husband and openly welcomed her invading brother-in-law, Duke Alex of Traderstown, the folk of the farms and hamlets and villages of the countryside loved or at the very least deeply respected their overlord—he who had wiped out the ferocious river pirates, had kept alien invaders off their lands, had decreed and seen strictly enforced just laws, many of which had served to protect them from the depredations of the nobles and gentry. He had broken up the huge estates of the old families and made yeoman-farmers of men whose fathers had been landbound serfs, and his heaviest tax bites fell upon those able to bear it: merchants, foreign factors, rich ship owners and the like.

The duke's soldiers, retreating before the enemy army which vastly outnumbered them, had but to say the word and the non-city dwellers did their duty.

Duke Alex, as he advanced into the rich farmlands north and east of his objective, quickly realized to his dismay and rage that his plan of feeding his army off the country of his foe was doomed to failure. Storehouses and granaries gaped as empty as every house and barn, and the few unreaped fields now sprouted only charred stubble. Aside from the occasional stray goat or half-wild pig rooting in the midden of a deserted village, nothing that might possibly be of use to him and his host remained. Cursing sulphurously, he sent yet one more messenger riding back the way they had come, with orders for supplies to be ready for barging across the Great River as soon as he had secured the surrender of the ridiculous little pile of stone that went under the misnomer of "citadel." It would be ten days or two weeks, he estimated, probably only half that time.

Just outside the low walls of the city, Alex set up camp and, while he met with his sister-in-law, her retainers and courtiers and the chief men of the city, his troops were marshaled and groomed to give the best appearance. Then on the morning of the third day, to the cheering of the city folk lining the street—High Street, which led straight from the North Gate to the Palace Square in the exact center of the city— beneath the bunting-draped shops and homes, he and his army paraded in, with drums beating and banners unfurled. And Duke Alex felt every inch the liberator he had convinced himself he was.

This heady mood lasted all the way to the Palace Square. As soon as the square was jam-packed with his soldiery and Alex was staring in horrified awe at the bulk of a completed citadel in the lower reaches of the city, a number of black specks were seen arcing from the top of the inland walls, growing steadily larger as they neared.

The boulders slammed sanguineously into the massed troops, shattering against the pave in deadly, flying shards or bouncing high—once, twice, sometimes thrice—to mash out the lives of still more men. And the carnival atmosphere was become, in a matter of short seconds, purest pandemonium and screaming panic.

Nor did the second volley of bushels of smaller stones or the third of blazing pitchballs help to calm the terror-stricken throngs. It was later reckoned that as many or more were trampled to death trying to flee the Palace Square as actually died from the engine missiles.

Duke Alex thought it, in toto, a most inauspicious beginning for the siege.

And the following weeks went no better. Early on, it was discovered that the usual trenching manuevers would be impossible anywhere in the Lower Town, for no sooner was a trench deep enough to give a minimum of protection than it commenced to fill with groundwater from the high riverside water table.

Therefore, on the advice of his staff, Duke Alex had many

nearby homes and other buildings demolished and the rubble carted to fill in the canals the trenches were fast becoming. Then the rest of the rubble was used to give some measure of cover to the crews of his engines.

But no sooner were his stone and spear throwers in place and taking their first, ranging shots at the walls of the citadel than their crews and Duke Alex were made painfully aware of the error in the staff's reckoning. Not only brick, stone and mortar had gone into the filling of the trenches and the erection of the protective wall, but much splintery wood, lengths of dry, dusty timbers that flared like brushwood at the impact of the first pitchballs. The fire spread with unbelievable rapidity, its heat driving the crews away, crackling flames leaping in every direction, soon adding the wooden portions of the engines to the conflagration. Slowly eating into the wetted wood in the trenches below, the fire smoked and smoldered on for days.

The oldest portion of Tworivercity or Twocityport (which bore a third and still older name, Tworivertown) was the riverside section, in the center of which the citadel now squatted, ringed about by its moat. A hundred and more years agone, when the ancestors of both Duke Alex and Duchess Ann were nothing more than river pirates, who sent their swift galleys beating out to levy tolls on or board and plunder passing river traffic, the lower section had been all the urban area there was and the only edifice on the stretch of bluff behind the town had been a watchtower to warn of the approach of prey from up- or downriver.

It was only after the town became richer and conquered much of the inland farmlands and small towns and the then rulers began to style themselves high nobility and hire on soldiers to protect their holdings and add more by conquest that the first part of the bluff-top palace was built, and the present city had grown up around the palace. In the beginning, only mansions of the nobility and gentry and the quarters of the soldiers had occupied the newer section of the city.

In more recent decades, however, pursuant to the many and sweeping changes wrought by Duke Tcharlz—and much to the screaming outrage of the old nobility, whose wealth and power had declined precipitously in the wake of the new duke's reforms—non-nobles, newly rich ship owners and merchants had bought or built in the once exclusive Upper City.

Prior to the erection of the new fortress-citadel, the Old Town had been entirely given over to huge warehouses, mean bordellos and low dives frequented almost exclusively by river sailors and low-ranking mercenaries, fringed at north and south by a ramshackle aggregation of the huts and hovels of the poor, the aged, the outcast and the indigent.

Wisely, Duke Tcharlz had raised the landward walls of his new fortress several yards higher than called for in the original plans, that they not be overshadowed by higher elevation of the bluff-top city. However, as days became weeks, Duke Alex, frustrated at every turn in his attempts to open a normal siege on the citadel in the old town, determined as his sole real advantage the fact that the bluff area, which he did fully control, was almost on a level with the walls of the objective and that it was the only feasible place, both within range and affording some measure of protection, on which to mount his batteries of engines.

Although only a little better than half of the promised troops to garrison the citadel had ever arrived, Captain Count Martuhn still felt well served and secure in his firm belief that he could hold the fortress as long as might prove necessary. True, he was devilishly short of archers, having only those from his own mixed company and the unit of crossbowmen from Pirates' Folly. But in the absence of any attempt at a frontal assault against the fortress, he had as yet had no need of them.

A more serious problem might have been the nonarrival of the company of engineers and artificers, save for the multi-talented Lieutenant Nahseer and two happy turns of fortune.

Quite a few of the yeomen-farmers who had stripped and deserted their land in the face of the invaders had come through the Upper Town to the Lower and sought admission to the citadel. Most had brought their whole families, their livestock and wagonloads of personal effects, furniture and victuals.

After cogitating the ticklish matter and discussing it with Wolf and Nahseer, Martuhn had admitted a few, but only those who had relatives among the garrison or those who were retired soldiers. And that was how he acquired not one but two veteran engineers' artificers, one a company sergeant, one a sergeant-major, with a total experience of nearly fifty years between them.

With a few simple adjustments and a few days of drilling the amateur crews, the two sergeants had rendered the existing engines more flexible, longer-ranging and harder-hitting. The missing spearthrowers they had replaced with an ingenious device consisting of a wooden framework holding a wooden, V-shaped trough to support the spear and springy boards to propel it. When both of the retired noncoms flatly refused the offer of commissions, Martuhn transferred Nahseer from his personal staff to the command of the fledgling engineer unit, promoting him at the same time to senior lieutenant.

Well aware from times past of the inherent dangers of idleness among soldiers, especially under the present conditions, Martuhn made certain that every member of the garrison had work of a sort to perform for almost every hour of daylight. The men, of course, grumbled at the unending rounds of drills, weapons practice and inspections, but it was the good-natured grumbling of professional soldiers and to be expected in any command.

In the absence of a real bowmaster, Martuhn, hesitantly at first, placed Bahb and Djoh Steevuhnz in charge of the small contingent of bowmen, with Sir Wolf to back them up was their authority to be questioned. But Wolf soon returned to the commander requesting a more urgent assignment, remarking that every bowman deeply respected the deadly and matchless accuracy of the two boys and was more than anxious to himself acquire such a degree of skill.

Martuhn too respected the nomad boys, and not solely because he had never known them to miss any target—still or moving—at which they had loosed their short, black-shafted arrows. Under his and Nahseer's tutelage, Bahb and even the slower-witted little Djoh had rapidly learned the Game of Battles and a session or two in light brigandines with dulled lancer sabers—Martuhn taking a blade somewhat shorter to allow for his longer arms—had pleased the veteran captain immensely. The wiry older lad was as fast as a greased pig, though he depended little on the various point attacks, seeming to prefer the hack and the slash and the drawcuts of a horseman. But that the boy was a quick study and highly adaptable was proved early in the second session, when he startled Martuhn by employing the entirety of an attack he had seen but once and penetrating the older man's guard almost to the juncture of contact.

"I tell you, Nahseer," he had averred that night, when once the two boys had been packed off to their bedchamber, "if Bahb had been but a wee bit bigger with no more than three more inches of arm, he'd have had me. A perfect thrust to the high belly or low chest. And I know he could've learned that bit from no one but me. The only things those nomads ever stab with are their dirks and their spears. All their saber drill is pure edge fighting. Some of their sabers don't even have real points.

"But he'd only seen it once, man, and that in the midst of a very brisk bout of fence."

Nahseer, lounging back in one of the four chairs set at the table-cum-desk, which with the narrow bed and a trio of clothes and weapons chests made up the only furnishings of the captain's spartan chamber, sipped at the cup of cool apple juice—cider which had been briskly boiled to rid it of the alcohol that was forbidden him by his religion. "Yes, Martuhn, you, I, Sir Wolf, any man would feel proud to be able to name as his get such sons as Bahb and Djoh, especially Bahb.

"You obviously stand high in the regard of the duke, your sometime employer and now your overlord. And your lordship of this city and its environs is worded to be a hereditary one. But, my friend, your age is a bit advanced to go about the siring of heirs, if you mean to see them grown and properly reared. So why not, once this silly little war be concluded, prevail upon the duke to legalize your adoption of these two boys and make Bahb your legal heir?"

Martuhn sighed. "Would that I could, my dear Nahseer, but they two talk of nothing else but a return to their clan and their prairies."

Raising a shaggy eyebrow and nodding, Nahseer replied, "Yes, I know, but I also know, as do you, what they do not. Returning them to the prairies were difficult enough, reuniting them with their clan a virtual impossibility, as it could now be hundreds of miles away in any direction. As they get older, the boys will come to appreciate just why they could not be returned to their savage relatives. Of this I am certain, my friend."

"I promise to think on your idea, Nahseer," agreed Martuhn, "and to discuss it with you and others at more length once Duke Tcharlz comes to lift the siege and affairs of the duchy normalize once more."

In the press of everyday affairs, Martuhn had almost forgotten Sir Djaimz Stylz. Then, one night, pikemen and a sergeant of infantry marched that very man before him. This Sir Djaimz, however, looked more like a half-drowned rat than like the precious young fop that the captain remembered.

With a crashing salute of his poleaxe, the sergeant intoned the ritual phrases, then got to the meat of the matter. The prisoner had swum the moat and had made sufficient racket to draw the attention of the wall sentries. They had, of course, called for the sergeant of the guard, who had, in his turn, sent for the officer of the guard. That worthy had had a rope lowered that the sodden, shivering swimmer might be hauled up the outer face of the wall.

"He don't know nary a one of the passwords, m'lud count, but he tawks like gentry and he swears he be a friend of m'lud, so Lootenunt Brysuhn ordered he be haled afore m'lud. It was a sword strapped 'crost his back, a dirk at his belt and a dagger in the boots he had slung 'round his neck, but he ain't armed now, m'lud."

"Very good, sergeant," Martuhn said. "You have done well this night, as has Lieutenant Brysuhn. Return to your duties."

With another crashing salute, the sergeant ordered his brace of pikemen to face about, then marched them out of the chamber and down the narrow, spiraling stairs.

"So, Sir Djaimz, we meet again. But whatever possessed you to take such a deadly chance, man? Had you not lucked onto a set of level-headed sentries, you could now be on the bottom of the moat or floating toward the river with an arrow or two in you."

However, despite the heat radiated by two large braziers, the chattering of the young man's teeth made his reply all but unintelligible.

"Wait, Sir Djaimz, hold on." Martuhn sprang to his feet and crossed to one of his chests in two long strides. From it he removed a thick blanket and tossed it to his visitor. "Strip those wet clothes off and wrap up in this while they dry; hang them from those hooks, there, near that brazier."

Then the captain filled a jack three-quarters full with strong honey wine, added a generous dollop of barley hwiskee, pulled a loggerhead from among the coals of the other brazier and blew off the ash before plunging it into the jack, releasing a small cloud of fragrant steam. He proffered the jack to Sir Djaimz, then filled another for himself.

"Get yourself outside this, lad, and you'll have another. Now sit you down and tell me why you risked your life to join me this night."

"My lord count did, after all, invite me," said Sir Djaimz, bluntly. "He offered to teach me, to make me into a true knight and soldier, not simply one of Duchess Ann's lapdogs."

"You'd forsake your sinecure then, Sir Djaimz? I am certain that Duke Alex would've taken you into his army, if you've just a taste for the life of a soldier. Then you'd have still had the good graces of her grace to fall back upon, if you chose to return. By coming to me, man, you've burned your bridges behind you, with a vengeance . . . unless . . ." Martuhn rested his elbows on the table and, with hooded eyes, stared at his blanket-wrapped guest over steepled fingers. "Unless you are doing your mistress' bidding by coming here. Are you, Sir Djaimz?"

When the young man made to speak, Martuhn raised a hand in warning. "Wait, before you say a word, I do not hold it dishonorable to perform the dictates of one's overlord . . . or lady, as the case may be. But if you are doing such by coming here, tell me now and I'll have you put outside tomorrow morn in health and honor.

"For if you say not and I later discover the lie—as I will eventually—you will die very slowly and painfully in humiliation and dishonor, as befits a spy and a forsworn liar.

"Do I make myself clear, Sir Djaimz?"

The head of water-plastered hair sticking out from amid the folds of the gray military blanket nodded wearily. "Abundantly clear, my lord count, but all that I shall tell you will be the unadorned truth. I swear this by all that I hold dear. I have done many things for her grace, a few of them of a base nature, but I have never and would never perjure myself for her . . . or for any other man or woman.

"Lord count, I am born of that class now known as 'the Old Nobility.' My late father owned twenty-five thousand acres of rich farm and pasture lands, woodlands and fish ponds. When I was barely three years old, Duke Tcharlz dispossessed my house of all, save only our hall and our townhouse in Twocityport, neither of which we could afford to staff and keep up without the income from lands that were no longer ours. Our estate was parceled out to the serfs who had worked it. The duke freely gave these rural scum title to that which should have been the patrimony of me and my brothers.

"My father died shortly after he had been plundered, in an ill-conceived attempt to exact a measure of vengeance from the flesh of Duke Tcharlz. My widowed mother and my brothers and I were taken in by Duchess Ann, who is a distant cousin of my house. My brothers and I were reared in her court, fed and clothed, educated, trained and equipped by her charity."

Martuhn felt his heart go out to the young knight. He too knew how it felt to be bereft of lands by a greedy overlord, to be cast into a hostile world with only his wits and the strength of his sword arm to sustain him . . . but he was also Duke Tcharlz's man and must try to defend the actions of his overlord, no matter how reprehensible.

"Sir Djaimz, your class fought Duke Tcharlz—openly and in secret ways—at every turn, almost from the day of his ascension. He had no choice but to break them, render away their wealth and strength. Nor was that all; to your late father's generation, the men and women who actually worked the land were little better than slaves, lived far worse than slaves in most cases and often starved even when the harvest was good, which was damned poor incentive to work hard, you must admit. Since his grace broke up the estates and parceled out the land to those serfs and their sons and a scattering of old soldiers, yields have doubled and redoubled to the point that no one who is willing and able to work starves any longer. And this duchy, which formerly was obliged to *im*port beer and ale now *ex*ports both, to the vast profit of a large proportion of the folk of the duchy, directly or indirectly. Why, his grace . . ."

Now it was Sir Djaimz who held up a hand. "Hold, my lord, please hold. You need not waste your time in convincing me. A few weeks agone, yes, but not now. There is another side to the duke, this I have always known, though I have long pushed that knowledge to the back of my mind.

"Even though my father tried to take his life, and, in fact, wounded him sorely, five years later the duke saw to it that my mother was paid a good price for Stylz Hall and the acreage hard by it. Furthermore, at his own expense, he had every stick of remaining furniture, paintings, carpets, every movable of value, carted to our townhouse in Twocityport. Would a true tyrant, an ogre such as the duke is painted by Duchess Ann and her court, have done so much for the widow of an enemy? I think not.

"When first Duke Alex arrived, I—along with the duchess and all the rest of the court—welcomed him, hailed him as a liberator, a savior . . . but I have had reason to reconsider. Using as excuse that there is nowhere nearby the citadel to set up his tents, this unbearable man has quartered his men and officers on every household in the Upper City, to be housed, clothed, fed and . . . entertained, with no hope of any reimbursement. By this time, I doubt there's a girl or a woman of the lesser gentry or the commoners between the ages of ten and sixty who has not been raped at least once. Yet Duke Alex merely laughs off any complaints for redress, and the duchess dotes on him, cannot praise and honor him and his pack of raping, thieving, guzzling cutthroats enough. I can but be thankful that my own poor mother is dead, for she was a comely woman.

"The Stylz townhouse, the last single piece of real property left to me and my brothers, was one of the row of buildings Duke Alex chose to raze to provide him material for that wretched little useless wall of his. But, to add insult to injury, he and his officers trooped through my house and all the others just prior to the demolition and had them stripped of anything that caught their eyes or fancies.

"When they would have forcibly prevented such blatant thievery, both my younger brothers were cut down, coldly butchered. I was in attendance on the duchess at the time, but neighbors and servants apprised me of these atrocities. By the time a messenger fetched me and I got back to what had been my home, it was fast on the way to becoming a heap of rubble.

"My just complaint to the duchess brought from her the answer that I and every other soul in *her* cities and lands were hers to do with as she wished, and that my poor brothers had been criminals for attempting to save our possessions from Duke Alex. That night, trying to sleep in the mean quarters assigned me by the palace majordomo, I began to compare the two dukes—Tcharlz and Alex—and to sift through the lies and distortions that had been my daily fare for most of my life.

"After some week or more of soul-searching, I thought upon you and your offer to one who had treated you with naught save contumely. I thought me that I had wasted enough of my life in service to a blind hatred of a man who had truly done much good for the duchy and who, even at his worst, was far and away a better man, a more just and honorable man, a more noble man in all senses than his rival will ever be.

"Had his grace been at Pirates' Folly, I should have hied me there to humbly beg that I be allowed to enter his service in any capacity he might deem fitting. But he is on campaign downriver, so I came to you, my lord. Will you have me?"

Sir Djaimz's mind, because he possessed no scintilla of telepathic ability, was as an open book to Martuhn, and nowhere in the roil of confused thoughts could the captain sense that the young knight was trying to delude him. He decided to add this former foe to his staff for a while. When he had proved himself, he could be trained for duties of a military nature.

In his final instructions to Captain Count Martuhn, Duke Tcharlz had bluntly granted his surrogate much latitude in defense of the citadel. "Martuhn, as matters sit that city is not worth a pinch of cow shit to me; most of its residents cleave to that fat bitch and hate my guts, despite all I've done and tried to do for them. So don't be afraid to bombard or even fire the city, if it comes to that. You'll hear no complaints from me. The damned palace, too, for all I care!

"I would prefer that the cables and the docks remain more or less intact, but if push comes to shove, cut the frigging cables and render the docks to gravel and splinters. If you wish I'll put all this in writing, legally witnessed and sealed, that there be no misunderstanding."

Martuhn had taken his overlord up on that last offer and the written, witnessed and sealed orders now reposed in his strongbox, in the hollow under a certain stone in the floor of his tower room. And for this reason, he had no compunction in ordering the engines to return fire against the cleverly concealed enemy engines at the edge of the bluff.

After a day of being too busy dodging stone shards or bouncing boulders or the collapses of battered-down house walls to get many missiles launched at the citadel, the engineers of Duke Alex elected to recommence by night. After all, they knew the distance and direction, so there was scant need to actually see the target.

Their first boulder produced Martuhn's first casualty of the siege when it knocked down a merlon which, in falling, broke the leg and crushed to paste the foot of a sentry. It was then that Martuhn decided to teach the enemy not to repeat this night's work.

Fifteen minutes after their initial loosings, the engineers atop the bluff heard the long-drawn-out creakings, then the basso *thuummpps*, and cringed despite themselves, recalling the carnage and destruction of the past day. But no single stone fell among them. Rather a hail of red-glowing, hissing, spluttering, fire-tailed pitchballs passed high over them to fall onto and around the palace. After the first volley of pitchballs came a second, a third and then a fourth.

No more missiles were thrown at the citadel that night or on the day following. The engineers and every other man, woman and child, slave or free, were far too busy trying to prevent the city from burning to the ground.

Two months to the day after he had landed with his army on the beach north of Tworivercity, Alex, Duke of Traderstown, sat alone in a room of the south wing of the singed and charred palace chewing at his thumb in a high dudgeon. He and the army were in serious trouble, and well he knew it. His support within the city was fading away like morning dew under a hot sun, and even Duchess Ann was beginning to whine at him.

"No wonder," he thought, "that Tcharlz keeps so far away from her. Were the fat slug my wife, had I wed her instead of her sister, I'd likely have slit her damned gullet by now, and shut her yapping mouth for good. Tcharlz must have far more patience than have I."

Absently, Alex chose a strip of jerked meat from a plate

before him and gnawed at the hard, stringy stuff. It was about all the victuals that he or anyone else in the city would have until supplies from Traderstown could be gotten to him. The supplies he had brought with him and those received shortly thereafter had mostly gone up in the same smoke that had taken almost all the stores of the city on the night the engines of that accursed citadel had fired so many buildings.

When his big yellow teeth had worried off a chewable piece of the jerky, he masticated for a while, then sipped from a goblet of honey wine to dilute the salt and mask the abominable flavor of the meat. And his mood was as foul as his repast; servants and retainers tiptoed past the open doors to the room, for he had already injured one man with a thrown dagger.

Duke Alex was by now convinced that all the world had turned against him. The damned little fort down yonder refused to surrender, refused to face the fact that Duke Alex held the city. Due to the high level of the groundwater in the Lower Town, the fortification could not be properly invested. None of his many and varied attempts to pound down the walls of this thorn in his side had been successful, and now he and his staff were loath to even try, again; should they, they feared that the satanic bastard who commanded might very well finish the burning down of the upper city.

Even his ally the King of Mehmfiz, that craven little fart Uyr, was turning against him, reneging on his sworn word. The plan had been for him to leave behind sufficient force to hold Tcharlz and his forces in the south, then to sail upriver with the bulk of his men and attack from the dock area, while Alex attacked from the landward side. But the puling bastard had never sailed upriver, and each succeeding message from the forsworn scoundrel was more evasive than the last.

Nor had the coward even been able to hold Tcharlz in the south as he had promised to do. Tcharlz himself had been identified leading the strong force of dragoons, lancers and irregulars that had captured or destroyed three of the last five supply trains bound for the city, had eradicated smaller patrols of Duke Alex's cavalry and had fought pitched battles with larger bodies.

The weather had become frightful, freezing cold long before its time, with little cordwood and less charcoal and no way to secure more. So many officers and men of his army had been assaulted or murdered in the streets recently that they were now forbidden to venture abroad in lesser numbers than a full squad, by day or by night, nor had salutary executions of suspects or hostages picked at random seemed to do any good.

It was become very difficult to feed the horses properly, and the beasts were, moreover, beginning to disappear. His own favorite stallion had been taken from a guarded stable; later the animal's glossy hide and a few of the larger bones had been found on a midden pile. Watching the stable guards die slowly had done little to assuage his grief.

So sorely beset, Alex was no longer sleeping well. He was drinking more than had been his wont, which meant that when sleep he did, he invariably wakened red-eyed, with throbbing head and queasy stomach and nerves taut as the ropes of a catapult. The rough and paltry food available even to him had so addled his belly that he alternated between painful constipation and debilitating diarrhea.

Why would not that damned little fort surrender? He had offered generous and handsome terms, all refused.

A few hours later, Duke Alex watched in impotent rage as Duke Tcharlz and his horsemen swept down upon the southbound supply train, butchered guards and drivers alike, then drove off the wagons and carts in triumph. And still later that dreadful day, he gazed dejectedly from a window of the palace to the square below, where citizens and his own soldiers fought like starveling dogs for the basketloads of offal and refuse hurled into the city by the engines of the citadel.

For the sake of his slipping hold on sanity, it was perhaps as well that Alex, Duke of Traderstown, was not aware that his real troubles had not yet begun.

Chapter XII

The winter was as hard as any that Milo of Morai could recall. It came early, howling in from the far north, and it necessitated a measured scattering of the painfully gathered clans in order to provide graze and to preserve as much live-stock as possible. He and Blind Hari of Krooguh could but hope that the clans would reassemble at the appointed place if spring ever arrived.

Nor was the winter any whit easier on Duke Alex, his army or the folk of the Upper Town. What remained of the invading force was now all foot soldiers with no transport, all oxen and horses and even the mules having either been slaughtered by the troops, with or without orders, or stolen by groups of ravenous civilians.

The besieged besiegers had scoured and rescoured the Upper Town, completely ridding it of pigs, goats, dogs, cats and even rats. Now rawhides and leather were being boiled up over fires fueled by chopped furniture, while mixed bands of soldiers and citizens willingly risked the deadly attentions of archers and crossbowmen on the walls of the citadel in order to secure one or two of the huge wharf rats on the streets and in the alleys of the old town.

Duke Tcharlz, who was in actuality nowhere near as hard, uncompromising and unfeeling a man as he would have had the world believe, permitted an early exodus of nursing mothers and young children. At length he began to allow supply trains to reach the city, and finally when unusually heavy ic-ing brought river traffic to a standstill, he and his men de-

144

livered dozens of wagonloads of cordwood, charcoal and nonperishable foodstuffs to just beyond bow range of the city's low walls.

By then his infantry had marched back up from the south, and he well knew that come spring, those scarecrow-defended walls would present little obstacle to his army. Nor would King Uyr of Mehmfiz present a problem any time soon, for, was the intelligence correct, that unhappy young man and what was left of his hired army was hotly engaged in putting down scattered rebellions on his northern marches.

Messengers passed with the greatest of ease between the duke's field army and the "beleaguered" citadel in the Lower Town. Tcharlz was inordinately pleased with and proud of his selection of Captain Martuhn, nor did he hesitate to express his good nature toward him and his garrison in every way possible.

"I think, Sir Wolf," Martuhn chuckled, "that his grace would adopt me, name me his heir and gift me half his duchy, did I but drop the word that such would please me."

"Then why don't you, my lord count?" Wolf mindspoke. "I think I'd enjoy serving a duke's heir."

Martuhn just shook his head. "No you wouldn't, old friend, you'd have to guard not only my back but taste all of my victuals, as well, and eventually you'd get a fatal bellyache of it. Too much politics of a poisonous nature goes on among the higher nobility to suit me. Count is as high as I will ever aspire, thank you.

"But if you'd rather enter Duke Tcharlz's service, I could easily arrange . . ."

Sir Wolf looked wounded. "My lord should know that I'd never leave him, in good times or foul."

Aware that his barb had penetrated more deeply than he had intended, Martuhn laid a hand on his old retainer's shoulder. "Oh, Wolf, I was but jesting. You're ever so serious."

Lolling in a chair, Nahseer had been observing while sipping at hot, spiced cider. Now he said, "Whilst your overlord be in a good mood, Martuhn, would it be too much to ask that you get my freedom and that of the boys in writing? You could get your adoptions of them legally attested at the same time, you know."

"Oh, aye," responded Martuhn, "and my last messenger to

Pirates' Folly requests those very things, among others. But he has not yet returned with answers."

"But you sent the last messenger over a week agone," Nahseer said worriedly. "He should be back, long since."

"Why so perturbed, friend Nahseer?" smiled Martuhn. "Likely the fellow was trapped somewhere for a few days by last week's blizzard, or his horse could've turned up lame, or he could've reached Pirates' Folly only to find the duke in the field with his cavalry. He'll be back, soon or late."

Nahseer squirmed in his chair, his features revealing real concern. "You're most likely right, Martuhn. Nonetheless, I'll not feel even marginally secure until I can hold in my hand the legal documents that declare Bahb Steevuhnz, Djoh Steevuhnz and one Nahseer ibn Wahleed al-Asraf Ahkbahr to be free and unindentured or apprenticed.

"And I warn you, my good friends Martuhn and Wolf, do not ever make the error of underestimating Lord Urbahnos of Karaleenos. He is shrewd and cunning. But then, most successful merchants are so; such traits are needful in their work. But in addition, the Ehleen is stubborn as a cur with a bone when he truly wants something. He has vast wealth and influence in high places, and he is utterly without morals or scruples.

"Urbahnos desperately needs little Djoh to gift to some high-ranking pervert in Karaleenos, hoping that in return that man will see to the reversal of the order of exile that sent Urbahnos hence, years agone. Bahb he will probably torment until his spirit breaks or he dies. Me he means to torture to death, very slowly.

"Had matters progressed his way, he meant to sell me into the hellish living death of the barges. But, too, he meant to take his family upriver just far enough to be out of Duke Tcharlz's sphere of influence, then sell them, his own wife and children, into slavery!"

Few men had ever seen the peculiar cold light that then beamed from Martuhn's eyes . . . not and lived to tell of it. "You're not describing a man, Nahseer, but rather a beast, a loathsome monster. I wonder if his grace knows the truth, knows that his duchy holds so debauched and terrible a thing?"

"If he did not before, he will as soon as my messenger

gains his ear," said Martuhn grimly. "And then I would not care to be in this Lord Urbahnos' shoes, my friend."

However, although Martuhn was not to know of it for some time, that messenger never reached Pirates' Folly or Duke Tcharlz, and no trace of him was ever found until, with the final melting of the deep snows, his remains and those of his horse were discovered in a deep gully . . . and by then it was too late.

Milo of Morai and Blind Hari of Krooguh had worried needlessly. With the spring thaw, all the clans of autumn plus a few new arrivals, began to converge at the chosen location. At the first full meeting of the Council of Chiefs, Chief Rahn, the Patrik of Patrik, arose, cleared his throat and said, "War chief, revered bard of the tribe, brother chiefs of the Holy Kindred, we all have waited patiently through a long winter, but now it is time. Let us gather our warriors and our maiden archers and help our brother, Henree of Steevuhnz, avenge himself upon these despicable dirtmen. How says the war chief?"

Milo's head inclined. "Yes, my brothers, it is time. But I have had word that three other clans are on the march and nearing this place. Let us delay for two weeks, that their warriors and chiefs be not cheated of a chance to share in this mission of honor.

"But, although we delay the war ridings, yet will the tribe continue eastward, for all must be across the Great River ere next winter's snows overtake us.

"Plan to divide your fighters into three war parties, for there are three of those little forts along the border in our line of march, and if we strike but the one, the others will try to come to its aid.

"Chief of the cats," Milo mindspoke the huge, gray brown, winter-shaggy prairiecat that sat in the circle, thick tail lapped over its big forepaws, red-pink tonguetip slightly protruding from between its three-inch incisors.

"Yes, war chief?" replied the immense feline, Elksdeath.

"Choose six of your best to accompany the twolegs scouts. It will be the mission of the twolegs to observe everything about the forts and the mission of your cats to see that no dirtmen live to tell that the scouts are about."

"The cat chief hears and will obey, war chief."

Stehfahnah, the mare and the ass had wintered well. She had had time to clean the cabin, rechink its walls with new clay, chop and stack a decent amount of firewood and mow a good supply of wild hay grasses before the really bad weather commenced.

Soon after the first, deep snows, she located a deeryard not far from her cabin, and so seldom lacked for fresh meat to eat herself or trade to her otter friends for fish or smaller game. Her only moment of real danger came when a big, solitary male wolf began to openly stalk her as she bore home parts of a butchered doe, but two quick-loosed arrows crippled him enough for her to be able to finish him with *the man's* fine, heavy spear.

She still used her low-topped felt boots inside the cabin, but for outside wear, she had fashioned for herself a pair of thigh-high boots such as she had seen on some of the traders. Drawing liberally upon *the man's* store of cured hides, pelts, skins and hanks of dried sinew, and adding her own expertise at felting and compounding fish glue, she whiled away the long hours within the cabin working by firelight.

The finished footwear was fine by any standards. Soles were compounded of no less than four thicknesses of shaggy-bull hide, triple-stitched with heaviest sinew and sandwiching thick coatings of fish glue. She had even made provision for easily attaching the high, horn-sheathed wooden heels of her felt boots when she took to horseback in the spring.

The uppers, which came to midthigh, were of two thicknesses of soft, pliable deerskin, with a layer of her felt quilted between them. She had found in rechinking the walls a small leather bag containing a double handful of the discs of gold, silver and copper that dirtmen used in trading, and these, plus discs of horn and bone, had gone to decorate her new boots.

But boots were not all that she fashioned or improved upon that winter. By the time that the winter ice began to weaken, then crack apart to be swept downstream on the high-surging waters of the river, she was well clothed and equipped for however far she might have to travel to find her clan.

Following the receipt of a shattering message, and a hurriedly concluded conference with Duke Tcharlz—which had included some highly painful concessions, among them a document conferring full ownership of the transriverine cable and all its appurtenances to the Duchy of the East Bank (which was Tcharlz's newest title for his holdings)—Duke Alex was allowed to make use of the cable barges to ferry his decimated and dispirited army back across the river to his own domain. For his lands were now threatened by a horde of prairie nomads, who had overrun three of his border forts and were presently playing merry hob in the croplands and raiding to within sight of the very walls of Traderstown.

Besides his guard of hard-faced cavalrymen, Duke Tcharlz brought with him to the citadel a large, fattened ox, a wagon-load of other eatables and a wain the sole lading of which was a full hogshead of splithead cider—a very potent variety of tipple, so called because of the aftereffects of imbibing too deeply of it.

After he had reviewed the garrison, the duke first praised them, then thanked them in blunt, simple terms for their help. Then, in view of every man jack of the assembled troops, he formally invested their captain to be the count of the city and of a broad swath of farmland and pastures and forests round about it. When the men had cheered themselves hoarse, they were dismissed to gather about the massive hogshead and the beer barrels, with empty but expectant jacks, cans and buckets. And Martuhn led his overlord up the stairs to his tower chambers.

While they awaited the serving of their meal, prepared by ducal cooks brought along for the purpose, and of course far more elaborate than the simple roast ox, cabbage and potatoes the garrison would soon enjoy, Martuhn described in detail the farcical investment of the citadel by the inept or unlucky Duke Alex.

The duke, draining off flagon after flagon of beer, was clearly in a rare good humor throughout, but at one point he threw back his leonine head and rocked the very stones of the tower with his deep laughter.

"So after burning up all their stores and a good part of that traitorous city, as well, your engineers threw your garbage, by the bushel, into the palace square? Ah, Martuhn, Martuhn, I've always said it, you're a man after my own heart. Had I but an hundred like you, I'd be master of every acre from the Great River to the Eastern Sea.

"I've but just come from the palace, you know, stopped there on my way here from Pirates' Folly. The court of the duchess is much reduced and she and they are no longer at all popular among the commoners and lesser gentry of the Upper Town. The palace itself is a bit charred in places; the north wing is mostly roofless and may have to be torn down entirely.

"I was cheered when I rode through the gates of that city up there, Martuhn; *cheered*, do you hear, by folk who've hated my guts for as long as I can recall!"

A smile flitted across the captain's scarred face. "I know the feeling, your grace. For all the death and destruction and terrible suffering I hurled upon them, whilst Duke Alex the Feckless squatted with them, yet did they seem most fond of me when my guards and I visited the Upper Town yesterday."

The duke just nodded. "And well they should, Martuhn. Your holding of this citadel gave them all a salutary, if painful, lesson. They learned just how spineless and fickle is their formerly esteemed duchess and just how little she really cares for them and their welfare. They also learned that, with friends and allies like Alex and his minions, they will never have need of enemies.

"They now love you because you were the first to fight against the man who quickly became their oppressor and exploiter. And it is well that love you they do, for you must rule over them for the rest of your life."

He allowed Martuhn to refill his flagon yet again, then went on, flinging the beads of moisture from his drooping mustachios with a hard, browned hand, the back of which bore a fairly new scar, broad and jagged.

While the duke talked on of his own campaigns, both the southern one and the eminently successful guerrilla war he had waged in his own lands against Duke Alex's cavalry— while the beasts still were war horses, rather than siege-beef—and in the swift, merciless raids on the supply trains, Martuhn noted to himself that his grace had seldom looked better.

Gone was any trace of surplus flesh at waist, hips, or jawline. Duke Tcharlz once more was the hard, weather-browned, intensely masculine fighting lord who had first hired Martuhn and his ragtag company on ten years agone. Gone were the dark half circles and pouches from under his eyes, and those eyes were once again clear and piercing; gone were most of the showy rings from fingers no longer chubby, but ridged with hard callus, with nails square-cut and neither buffed nor polished.

Moreover, it was obvious to Martuhn's experienced eye that the duke still did not stick at risking his own skin, for the quillions of the plain, heavy saber he had hung on the sword rack before he sat down showed the nicks and dents of many a close and vicious combat.

At length, the duke said, "I saw her grace, of course. Most contrite, she would appear, and weighing less than she has in at least twenty years. Still plug ugly, of course—that's one thing fasting can't cure—but shapely enough now to look beddable." He chuckled. "Being a man, I thought of it, naturally. I thought me of closing my eyes or of decently hiding that caricature of a face in a pillowcase or a bean sack. But all along I knew I'd not touch the bitch, for I want me no spawn out of such a graceless, demented creature. I'll name one of my flock of bastards my heir, if it comes to that . . . but I'd rather leave my lands and cities and folk in better hands, in the hands of a man who thinks like me, a man of proven worth and valor and perception, a man of honor who will rule by love and respect, not by brutality and fear. And such men are an exceedingly rare breed. Martuhn, I thought me for long and long that I'd never find one of them.

"Is there any honey wine in this place, Martuhn? I've swilled me enough beer, for the nonce.

"Now, where was I? Oh, yes. How old are you, Martuhn, do you know?"

"The winter just past was my thirty-eighth, your grace."

The duke frowned. "Hmmph, you look older than that, but you've no reason to lie, and you've led a harder life than do most men; that could account for it.

"Well, Martuhn, my boy, I'm old enough to be your father, more than, considering the tender age at which I started swiving serving maids, peasant girls and suchlike. Last winter was my fifty-fifth, and few are the men, even of our class, who see more than threescore winters."

The first courses of the expertly prepared repast had long

since been served, but the duke talked on between mouthfuls, motioning Martuhn to do likewise.

"Now, my boy, we two have soldiered together for the best part of ten years, and I think that I probably know you as well as I know myself. Furthermore, I've always held that a man should only be allowed to assume high rank or office when he is at least forty years old, with a sound mind and body, and no stranger to warfare, women, men and horses . . . not necessarily in that order, you understand." He grinned, then ripped most of the meat from a chop with his strong teeth and tossed the bone over his shoulder to his waiting wolfhound, who nabbed it in midair, crunched a couple of times, then swallowed and continued to sit, an expectant gleam in his yellowish-brown eyes.

"Now, true, my boy, we two differ in some small ways. For one thing, you're far less lecherous than am I, but for all that, I know you're no sodomite." His eyes twinkled. "Oh, yes, my dear Martuhn, there are others who watch you when I cannot . . . and they all report back to me. So I know of the Lady Behti—fat as a lard sow or as my wife used to be, but most skilled, 'tis said, in some rather esoteric modes of mattress play.

"I know, too, of the black-haired Dohlohres, in Pahdookahport; talk about contrasting taste, man, she's skinny as the scarecrows in the Upper Town. How is it that you never ruptured yourself on those protuberant bones, Martuhn?" He chuckled again.

Then all trace of humor flew from his voice and demeanor. "Martuhn, you're a perceptive and a highly intelligent man, and I've not the slightest doubt that you know in advance just what I've been building up to these past few hours."

Martuhn did know, he had read it all in the duke's surface thoughts, and it had almost stunned him. "But my lord cannot mean to . . . but, your grace, I am so unworthy."

The duke smiled again, this time most warmly. "Yes, my boy . . . my *son*, I mean precisely that. And I—whose word is law in these, *our* lands—I say that there is none *more* worthy from one end of the Great River to the other."

The duke withdrew a flat leather case from his belt pouch and from it extracted a cigar. Piercing one end with the point of his tableknife, he dunked it into his brandy, then puffed it to life over the flame of a candle. Waving to disperse the thick cloud of bluish smoke, he added a few more words.

"Think on the matter, Martuhn. I believe we can spare a few weeks. Mehmfiz will not be bothering anyone until they get their own house back in order, and Alex will certainly have no idle hands with which to meddle in the affairs of others, not with western nomads over his borders. Things are winding down to normal again. We'll talk this over at another time, but I wanted you to know my mind, my boy."

In his mental confusion, Martuhn completely forgot to ask about the written evidence of full freedom for Nahseer or of a formal document of adoption of Bahb and Djoh Steevuhnz for himself. There was no time the next morning either, for the duke rose with the sun, quaffed a hurried stirrup cup and then thundered out the gate and across the bridge at the head of his horseguards.

"Son Martuhn," began the letter that arrived ten days later, "you are reputed to have presently among your garrison three escaped slaves: a Zahrtohgahn castrate of some thirty-five years, one Nahseer Something-or-other; and two nomad boys, a twelve-year-old, Bahb Steevuhnz, and a ten-year-old, Djoh Steevuhnz. These three were the property of Urbahnos of Karaleenos, a merchant/factor of Pahdookahport, and they all escaped from him sometime last fall, partially burning my serai and lifting five horses, the property of a band of plains traders.

"Now, my boy, since informants assure me that the castrate Zahrtohgahn was once an officer of the Kaliphate and proved himself quite useful to our arms in the course of the late unpleasantness to the point at which you saw fit to rank him among your officers, I consider him to have earned his freedom and the attached document proclaims that fact to all the world hereabouts; this Nahseer is now his own man, or yours, if you so wish it. I respectfully advise that you keep him on and if his asking price is more than you can just now afford, I'll be pleased to advance it to you.

"Despite their tender years, the minor boys are said to be superlative archers, known to have slain two, possibly three grown men during their escape and four after enlisting in our forces, so I would free them as well, save that their former master, this Urbahnos, has already done so. Furthermore, he has legally adopted both of them, the adoption (copies of the orders included herein) having been enacted by my sworn surrogate, His Honor Judge Baron Yzik Lapkin of Pahdook-ahport, shortly after Duke Alex's precipitate withdrawal. Therefore, these boys must be returned to their adoptive father.

"The last document should not be taken seriously; it is included merely for your amusement, my boy.

"Insofar as the claims of the plains traders are concerned, Master Hwahruhn, their leader, is not pressing them very hard, so ignore them; I am so doing. Portuh and his losses are another dish of oats. Although I am his silent partner, at the times of his losses, *you* were unofficially his overlord; his taxes would have been paid to the county not the duchy, so I leave his claims to your capable hands to settle as you think best.

"In that comical fourth document, you will see that this Urbahnos—a sly and oily bastard if one was ever born!—lays claim to everything from a shirt of chain mail and a sword supposedly valued at *ten pounds of silver*—and, my dear Martuhn, you and I both know that there aren't any three swords in the duchy worth that much, nor would any man arm a slave with such a prize!—down to and including the cotton drawers that this Nahseer was wearing on the night of the escape.

"I have instigated some preliminary investigations of this Ehleen. He's too wealthy for my liking, but his tax records appear to be in order, and he will soon be sailing upriver back to his homeland. This is why it is imperative that the adopted boys be returned without undue delay, that they, his wife and the children of his loins may be ready to accompany him east.

"With a true paternal regard for your welfare,

"Tcharlz, Duke of the Duchy of the East Bank."

And near the bottom of the last page, below the ornate, beribboned seal, "This by the hand of Ken Kohtz, Scribe to His Grace Duke Tcharlz."

Among the documents was a folded square of extra-fine vellum, all of its folds and edges sealed with a layer of wax and in two or three areas impressed with the duke's thumb ring. Inside, in Tcharlz's own, sprawling script was a short note.

"As regards this adoption business, Martuhn, I too was suspicious at the first, but now I can see his reasoning. Although he has added no suffering price to his overlong list of claims against the Zahrtohgahn, the knowledge is fairly well disseminated that, ere he took his leave, this Nahseer overpowered Urbahnos, stripped him, bound him to a bed and had out both his stones, then packed the empty bag with glowing charcoal.

"Both his sons by his wife are puny, unsound little things, the eldest afflicted with the falling sickness, to boot. So, since he can never again sire sons, I suppose he feels that these nomad boys, already proven warriors, will carry the name of his house well and honorably.

"Baron Lapkin avers that the Ehleen provides well, if not lavishly, for his family. The baron also swears that Urbahnos is an honest businessman, but this statement I must take with a grain—nay, a double handful!—of salt, for I've never seen or even heard of an honest Ehleen.

"Tcharlz."

When he had skimmed over the letter and the note and glanced through the various documents, Martuhn bade the messenger, one of Tcharlz's bastards, Sir Huhmfree Gawlin, bide the night in the citadel and ride with his reply on the morrow. Then he sent for Wolf, Nahseer, Bahb and Djoh.

The duke's next letter was shorter.

"Son Martuhn, your accusations against this Ehleen seem, on the evidence available to me, to be pure and unfounded libels. Baron Lapkin solemnly avows that Urbahnos of Karaleenos truly and deeply loves his wife and his children. Yes, before his maiming last fall, he was often seen in the brothel district of Pahdookahport, but I, for one, do not consider such peccadillos in any way reprehensible even in a married man, perhaps especially in a married man.

"The only man I have thus far found who supports even a portion of your allegations is one of the plains traders who captured the boys and sold them to Urbahnos, one Master Trader Hwahruhn. And even his testimony may be tainted more than a little by the fact that Urbahnos has filed a suit against this Hwahruhn for a refund of the purchase price on some complicated legal ground understood by Judge Baron Lapkin, but certainly not by me.

"Martuhn, my dear boy, you know that I have great plans

for you, for *us* and *our* duchy. You know that I deeply re-spect you, and therefore I would much dislike being com-pelled to order you to accede to my request. But I have many things to consider, and Baron Lapkin and his minions are at me night and day in regard to this matter of the nomad boys. Please send them to me or to him or directly to Urbahnos, that this troublesome baron will grant me a few days of peace.

"No, there is no legal way—and here I am bound by my own laws, states the judge baron—in which I may set aside the Ehleen's adoption of the boys in favor of your own. I would that all this turmoil could be so easily settled. You are yet a young man, with all your parts still in place and in good working order, I presume, so you can sire your own heirs on women of good bloodstock. You can rear them to be as brave, as honorable and as *dutiful to superiors* as are you, my boy.

"Paternally, Tcharlz."

Martuhn put down the letter and sighed gustily.

Young Sir Huhmfree asked politely, "Will it take my lord count long to draft an answer this time? I would doubt that his grace expects me back much before tomorrow, so my lord need not make haste."

Martuhn had heard much of Sir Huhmfree's previous visit to the garrison's officers' mess. This particular ducal bastard was said to be affable, to hold his liquor well and to be possessed of a good singing voice and skill on several musical instruments, so he had a host of admirers among the younger officers.

He forced a half-smile. "My hospitality and that of my of-ficers is always yours for the asking, young sir. Stay you the night, if you wish. But my answer in the morning will be ver-bal and no whit different than what I now say.

"Pray inform his grace that my answer to this letter and the reasons therefor are contained in my letter replying to his first one. Pray inform his grace, also, that although I truly re-spect and honor him in all ways, I have come to love these sturdy little boys as sons and I shall willingly forsake all that I might ever possess, sacrifice anything to which I may ever aspire, rather than accede to the delivery of Bahb and Djoh Steevuhnz to a man who will subject them to lives of pain and shameful degradation."

Sir Huhmfree gulped audibly. His face had gone white as curds under the campaign tan, and his dark-blue eyes were dilated with shock. But his voice was firm.

"My lord count, will you but repeat the message once more, I shall deliver it word for word. But I pray, my lord, reconsider, for much as his grace respects and cares for you, you must know that he will not and cannot tolerate rebellion in any form. If I deliver such a message, he will certainly march on you with force, seize these two boys, and relieve you of your command and rank, if not of your life."

Martuhn nodded wearily. "Thank you for your kind concern, Sir Huhmfree. I've known his grace for ten years and I know as well as do you what his certain reaction will be, but, you see, I cannot do other than what my conscience dictates.

"But wait, sit you down and partake of that ewer of wine. I'll summon Bahb Steevuhnz to tell you of what occurred on the night this Urbahnos bought him."

". . . and so," Bahb concluded the tale unabashedly, having recounted it so many times, "when the black-haired pig tried to tear off my breeches, I stabbed him in the crotch, just to one side of his yard, with one dagger; and when he clapped both hands to himself, I used the other blade to open his ugly face.

"When Nahseer came in, fully armed, he was ordered to take me alive for torture and promised torture and the loss of his eyes should he chance to slay me. Instead, he gave me a better weapon, his dirk. Then he tied the dog, spread-eagled, gagged him and cut out his nuts and threw the things onto the coals of the brazier.

"Then Nahseer thrust a chunk of hot charcoal into the swine's emptied scrotum. You should have seen him then, chief's son—I thought his little pig eyes were going to pop out of his head and roll onto the floor!"

Sir Huhmfree, who had tried to evince disinterest to begin, had clearly been moved by the lad's sorry tale. His mobile features were a study in ill-suppressed rage, his lip line thin as a whetted blade and his eyes slitted, while a tic jerked at one cheek and his right hand clenched and reclenched around the hilt of his dagger.

"Mere deballing were far too good for such an unspeakable and depraved animal. The Zahrtohgahn should have had off his damned yard, as well, and his two kneecaps. It had been hoped that his grace had either eradicated all such unnatural creatures from his lands years ago, or at least made them understand that his duchy was a most unsalubrious climate for such subhumans as they.

"My lord count, due in part to the well-known fact of my paternity and to my personal efforts over the last few years, I own some small power and I am become influential in some circles. Now you know as well as do I that his grace is as stubborn as are you and will not back down or appear to change his mind on this or any other matter without good and clearly spelled-out reason. Mayhap I and my resources can supply that reason, can his grace but be kept mollified for the time it may take.

"Will you not now rephrase your reply?"

Martuhn tried, but his mind refused to conjure up lies and he could not bring himself to write down the suggestions of Sir Huhmfree, Wolf or Nahseer. Finally, Sir Djaimz Stylz, who had been one of the duchess' scribes, penned a letter composed by himself, Wolf, Nahseer and Sir Huhmfree. Then they all badgered Count Martuhn until he signed it, and the next day Sir Huhmfree bore it back to Pirates' Folly.

It was the first of many such over the next few weeks, citing illnesses of varying, but believable, sorts as the reason why the boys could not travel—first they were said to be suffering a bout of the bloody flux, then a mild case of camp fever, then a siege of large, painful boils in highly sensitive areas of their bodies.

The young knight was too shrewd to openly name the fictitious maladies. Rather did he describe the symptoms with an almost clinical accuracy—this achieved with the clandestine aid of Martuhn's Zahrtohgahn garrison surgeon, Medical Sergeant Hahseem ibn Sooleemahn—leaving the duke to draw his own conclusions. Nor did Sir Djaimz further compromise Martuhn in this most dangerous game. He took to signing his own name over the official seal of the county, adding below, "Chief Scribe to the Most Honorable Sir Martuhn, Count of Twocityport."

Sir Huhmfree made no more appearances at the citadel during this period of subterfuge, but rather sent messages by way of one or the other of his squires.

"My lord Martuhn," he wrote, "there is a 'place' along an alleyway just off Shippers' Row in Pahdookahport. You may know of it, for its open activities are legally licensed; it is called the Three Doors, and is ostensibly owned and operated by an old harridan who calls herself Lady Yohahna. The first door leads to a big hwiskee house and inn for sailors and other riffraff, the second door to a mean and dangerous gambling den, the third, of course, to the bordello. But I have determined that there is a fourth door and another and most shameful operation housed therein.

"At this point, all that I write is mere hearsay and my own suppositions, for some very powerful person (or persons) seems to be protecting this 'place' and so difficult is firsthand information to obtain that I have determined to have the so-called owner seized and brought to a place whereat I can have the truth wrung out of her, at leisure.

"What little I have thus far learned points not only to this Ehleen, but to certain of his grace's most trusted officials and at least one of his advisers. But perhaps, when the 'owner' feels her bones leaving their sockets and sees the irons heating, she will give me and my witnesses some names and solid facts.

"Your servant and admirer, Sir Huhmfree Gawlin."

But it could not last for long. The duke was not a stupid or unperceptive man, else he never would have risen to his present power. Near to the nooning of a day, it all came to a head.

Baron Hahrvee Sheeld, commander of the duke's personal guard, arrived before the citadel with half a troop of the black-cloaked and -plumed horseguards. The baron had served the duke as long as had Martuhn, and though each respected the courage, prowess and accomplishments of the other, they had had their differences and had never been friends.

With his troopers in formation a few paces from the end of the drawbridge, the baron rode into the citadel alone. In Martuhn's ground-floor command office, the grim-visaged visitor removed his helmet and cradled it in his arm, but brusquely refused offers of a drink or a chair.

"Count Martuhn, you have rendered his grace most wroth by your refusal to accede to his requests. I have here his warrant"—he reached under his breastplate and withdrew a folded document bearing the ducal seal—"to bear to him at his castle the persons of the two boys, Bahb Steevuhnz and Djoh Steevuhnz, be they sick or well, living or dead.

"You may accompany us back, if you wish. But my candid advice would be to shun the duke's proximity for a while.

"I presume that you have mounts for these boys. If not, they can double up with a brace of my troopers as far as the Upper Town and the palace stables.

"Please have them fetched at once. I am due back at Pirates' Folly by dark."

"I'll see the warrant first, if you please, Baron Hahrvee." Martuhn spoke with as much cool formality as had the baron.

"Of course, that is your right, Count Martuhn." The black-cloaked nobleman proffered the document.

Martuhn broke the seals and read. The warrant was cold, impersonal and brief. It simply empowered any officer of the duchy to seize the boys by any means necessary and to convey them to the duke. However, there was one thing wrong with it, and Martuhn grasped at this single straw.

"Baron Hahrvee, I would be bound to honor this warrant, save for one detail."

"And what, pray tell, is that, sir?" demanded the short, thickset, powerful-looking man.

"It is not signed by his grace," answered Martuhn.

"Now, by my stallion's balls, sir," swore the baron hotly. "Yon's a legal document, drawn up by the clerk of the Court of Pahdookahport and signed by the Honorable Baron Yzik, judge of that court. Baron Yzik is also his grace's deputy and voice in Pahdookahport, just as you are—so far—in Two-cityport."

Martuhn shook his head, knowing that his very words were damning him, but desperate to buy time, no matter the cost. "Not good enough, Baron Hahrvee. Baron Yzik, whatever else he may be or not be, is my inferior in rank, and I cannot be legally bound by his decrees or warrants. Present me a warrant signed by his grace and we'll go further into the matter."

The officer shook back his shock of black hair, grinned and relaxed a bit. "I had hoped that your answer to this warrant would be something similar to what you just said, Count Martuhn. I, and some others at Pirates' Folly, are deriving a measure of true amusement and no little satisfaction in watching you destroy yourself in the eyes of his grace.

"We all saw you rise above your betters, too fast and too far. Your imminent fall will be interesting to observe.

"You well know how his grace deals with rebels. I just hope that I am on hand to view your execution, Count Martuhn."

Redonning his plumed helmet, the baron spun on his heel and, with a jingling of spur chains and a clanking of his saber scabbard, stalked out to his waiting horse.

A week later, the duke himself arrived before the citadel with a full brigade of his army and a siege train.

Chapter XIII

Even before the last clumps of snow had melted from under the shrubs and around the rocks, Stehfahnah had begun to exercise herself, the mare and the ass—toning and toughening muscles, perparing for the long trek ahead. She pulled the nails and removed the shoes from both of them, carefully trimmed and filed down the winter growth of hoof, then reshod them as best she could. Some of the poorer clans rode their mounts unshod or, in rocky country, wearing close-fitting 'horse boots' of rawhide and leather; but Clan Steevuhnz was one of the larger, wealthier clans, and the girl had seen horses shod since she had been a toddler and knew well all the intricacies of that art.

The nights she spent in constructing two travoises—a set of two long trailing poles of hardwood with a net of woven strips of rawhide between, one of customary size for the mare to draw and a smaller one for the ass; for, in addition to her weapons, equipment and supplies for her journey, she intended to bear away with her all the furs and hides, all the metal tools and every single one of the steel traps with their chains. No single tiny scrap of metal went to waste among the thrifty Horseclans, and the girl could already picture the delight on the face of Dan Ohshai of Steevuhnz when he saw and hefted the weight of the cluster of traps she would bear into camp.

She fashioned two more water skins, larger than those she had inherited from *the man*, sewing the seams as tightly as she could with wet sinew—which would shrink as it dried—then smearing all surfaces, inside and out, with a compound of beeswax and pine resin. She had to make sure they would last, for it was sometimes far between springs or watercourses on the vast stretches of the prairie.

She dug a long, narrow pit in the clearing, constructed a rack of green wood with forked posts to hold it, then built a low, smoky fire and began the curing of strips of flesh from the carcass of a lean springtime deer and fillets of fish brought ashore by the three otters.

At long last, as the flowers began to drop off the dogwoods along the riverbank, Stehfahnah led out mare and ass, saddled them and lashed the pole ends of the loaded travoises in place. As a parting gift for the otters who had done so much for her, she left the carcass of a small-horn buck anchored in fairly deep water near the underwater entrance to the den of the mustelids to make it difficult for other predators to rob her friends. She had taken only the needle-tipped, six-inch horns and the liver, which she munched raw as she rode west toward Sacred Sun's resting place.

Despite her lack of a saber or any armor worthy of the name, Stehfahnah considered herself well enough armed to deal with any contingency. Over the winter, she had strengthened the wooden dirtman bow of *the man* with strips from the long, thick horns of the shaggy-bull she had taken on the night *the man* had captured her. Carefully, patiently, she had carved and smoothed the edges of the horn strips, affixed them with fish glue and tightly bound them with fresh deer sinew. The result was, while not a true Horseclans horn-bow, considerably better than the bow had been to start with. She also had a deerhide, water-repellent case for the bow and two others to hold the thirty-two arrows she had made, fletched and tipped with fire-hardened bone.

She had shortened the shafts of her pair of horn-tipped spears and balanced them for darts, then made a case for them and for the throwing stick. *The man's* belt axe she had fitted with a longer shaft, and it now hung in its rawhide case at the mare's withers. The handsome silver-mounted dirk with its S monogram was at her belt, as were a couple of other knives from the cabin in the woods.

She had considered reshafting the steel spear as well, to make it longer and more like a horseman's lance. But with no time to properly cure the wood, even if she could find an unflawed sapling of the proper species, size and length, she had wisely reconsidered.

Horseclans-fashion, her long hair had been braided and the two thick braids lapped over the crown of her head, secured in place with thorns and some thin slivers of bone. Atop her coiffure, she wore the only piece of armor *the man* had owned—a plain steel helmet, lacking both nape and face guards, pitted with age and lack of care, dented here and there and with only a hacked-off stub of metal where the spike should have been.

Aside from the hide-and-horn bracer on her left arm, the girl's only body protection was a double-thick deerhide jerkin, into which she had quilted strips of horn and antler and, over the most vulnerable areas, the few odd strips of metal from the kit *the man* had kept to repair his traps.

Through all of the first day of travel, the mare had incessantly mindspoken complaints to Stehfahnah about the weight of the load she must bear and draw. Meanwhile the patient little ass trotted along at the end of his lead rope, having to take two steps to the mare's one, and bearing a proportionately heavier load without pause or complaint.

The petulant equine was even more indignant when, at that night's camp, Stehfahnah hobbled *and* picketed her, while only picketing the friendly, good-natured ass.

"Horse sister," the exasperated girl finally told her, "when we reach the camp of my clan, you will be unsaddled and may then run to the high plains, to be eaten alive by wolves, for all I care. But for now, you are the only one big enough for me to ride, and for your size and strength you are far less burdened than is sweet Brother Long-Ears. You are staked and hobbled for the very good reason that, despite the fact that I kept you alive all winter and have delivered you up out of bondage to a dirtman, I simply do not trust you not to run away in the night and leave me afoot. If you don't stop your complaining, I'll give you no grain this night."

On the afternoon of the third day, now well into prairie country, with the riverside expanse of forest far behind, extreme good fortune favored Stehfahnah. She cut the trail of a clan on the march. The hoof-trampled and wheel-rutted expanse was a good half mile wide, nowhere straight and probably a month old. New grass sprouted up all over it, but the girl could easily recognize it for what it was. There was no way to tell which clan it had been, of course, but it could be none other than a Kindred clan, all non-Kindred clans having been driven out of this part of the prairie or exterminated long years past. Moreover, it was headed in the direction Stehfahnah had selected as her best bet, northwest, so she followed it the rest of that day and camped on it that night.

She had been sleeping. Suddenly the little ass began to bray loudly, his uncertain mindspeak projecting incomplete message-images which told only of a horrendous danger out in the man-high grasses a hundred yards distant.

The hairs prickling on her nape, the girl shucked off her blankets and crouched, her back against the load of the larger travois and her steel-headed spear clutched in both her grubby hands. When there was no immediate attack, she lit her small fire of cattle chips and some splintered wagon spokes she had collected during her day's ride.

In the sudden flare, she saw a pair of eyes reflecting the firelight, just at the edge of the higher grasses beyond the new growth in the clan trail. And the eyes were large, set as high as her waist above the ground. Wolf? Not likely. Bear? They were fairly common on the high plains to the west but rare on the eastern reaches of the prairie. Then what . . . ?

Hesitantly, she sent out a mental beam. "Cat brother? Cat sister?"

The answer was immediate and beamed with the well-remembered power of a mature prairiecat. "You were sleeping soundly, twolegs sister, so I have been conversing with our horse sister. She tells me that you are of the Kindred and are riding to seek out and rejoin your clan. She also tells me that you have been most cruel to her and that you are uncaringly overworking her." There was an undercurrent of dry amusement in the cat's mindspeak as he related the mare's complaints of Stehfahnah's misuse of her.

"That miserable mare is lazy, treacherous and rough-gaited, and nothing would please me more than to get a decent mount between my legs again. But why does not my cat brother or sister come into my camp?"

"Cat brother, it is, Kindred sister; I am called Steelclaws and I was cat chief of the cat sept of Clan Danyulz last spring; now I am a subchief of the tribe's Cat Clan. I will come in if that strange, woolly, horselike beast with the ears of a desert rabbit will stop making those terrible noises."

The campaign that Duke Alex had tried to wage against the nomads had been even more of a disaster than had been his ill-starred incursion into the lands of Duke Tcharlz.

Once his army was back on its own side of the river, he let them rest in Tradertown for only as much time as it took him to scrape together horses and mules to remount most of his cavalry. Then he marched southwest toward the border, with the primary intention of remanning the forts situated at the points at which the three principal trade routes from off the prairie entered his duchy.

The forts had first been erected fifty years prior to Alex's birth and improved upon or at least kept in repair by most of his predecessors. The steady flow of monies from the transriverine cable had seen most of the original sod interior buildings rebuilt in brick and the more vulnerable stretches of the outer works—gateways and corners—done in brick and stone, with the addition of deep, broad, dry ditches fronting the gates and winch-controlled bridges to span them.

But what the conquering nomads had left of the three formerly stout fortifications caused Alex to rant, blaspheme and chew his fists in rage. He would have to forget about regarrisoning until there was time and peace for extensive rebuilding to be accomplished. The stretches of wooden palisade between the masonry strong points were become rows of charred, jagged stumps, and everything within that was susceptible to the ravages of fire had been subjected to it, which meant that not one building retained a roof. Weapons, armor, horses and their gear, wheeled transport, metal tools and artifacts and everything else that a nomad might fancy had been lifted, of course. Only the unburied remains of the defenders were left.

Even though his recent luck was bad and his judgment sometimes faulty, no one ever had need to question Alex's personal courage. Sending the foot back to Traderstown, he rode on at the head of his dragoons and lancers—although many forked scratch horses and half-broken mules with no hint of war training—deliberately seeking out the bands of nomad raiders, widely acclaimed as the most savage and dangerous light cavalry known.

There were, over the next weeks, a few inconclusive running skirmishes between small bands of raiders on their speedy, skittering pony-size beasts and units of his heavy-armed force on their larger, slower mounts. He lost a few troopers and the occasional nomad was killed, but the bands always escaped onto the prairie with their loot and captives—mostly nubile girls—leaving their pursuers sweating, red-faced and drooping and their mounts near foundering.

Duke Alex then did the only thing that he could under the circumstances. He sent riders to every rural hall and village. Their message was simple: in its present poor condition, his army could not offer any measure of protection against the inroads of the nomads, and the border forts were no longer tenable. Therefore, they all should gather up their families and serfs, animals and valuables, and leave the land to seek the protection of Traderstown's high stone walls and numerous well-armed soldiers.

Alex himself stayed in the field with his cavalry, returning to the city only long enough to draft and dispatch requests for troops, *materia militaris* and as many trained war horses as could be quickly located to King Uyr of Mehmfiz and to his late mother's nephew, Ehvin, Grand Duke of Ehvinzburkport. Then he scraped again the already scraped barrel and, with the scanty supplies, replacements and remounts thus obtained, he went back to his sorely tried field troops.

Even with sails, favorable winds and a full complement of husky oarsmen on the benches, the war galley took an entire week to reach Ehvinsburkport up the winding loops of the river and against its swift current. In receipt of the plea from his cousin, however, Grand Duke Ehvin IX—reflecting on the plaintiff's well-known wealth and upon the possibility that he, too, might be in so tight a difficulty sometime or other—moved quickly and generously.

The first ships to arrive were loaded with foodstuffs for both man and beast. The next ships brought a full squadron of mercenary dragoons and their mounts, with wages paid for a month, at which time their contract with the Grand Duke would expire. Ehvin had found their terms crushingly expensive, and he felt that Alex, rich as Croesus, could better afford them.

Ehvin also cleaned out some old armories and sent down a shipload of archaic but still serviceable weapons and armor.

Last, he shipped some two hundred horses and sixscore mules.

He also sent a letter. It profusely apologized for the fact that, lamentably, he was unable to bring his own huge armies downriver to the aid of his esteemed cousin in the hour of need. It gave as explanation the fact that the bulk of those armies were, even as he wrote, massing in his northern marches for the full-scale war that now seemed imminent, in the wake of the repeated raids and other treacherous acts of the brazenly aggressive Duke of Tehrawt.

Alex saw to it that neither the mercenaries nor the remounts remained within Traderstown for any longer than it took them to disembark, form up and trot through the streets to the West Gate. His conscience told him that with the advent of nearly six hundred fresh cavalry, he should give at least that number of his run-ragged veterans a couple of weeks to rest and refit in Traderstown. But he knew that he could not, that he dared not, for he had urgent need of every man and mount.

In the tribal camp, which still sat upon the eastern verge of the prairie, Milo of Morai and Blind Hari of Krooguh squatted on the dais in their huge yurt, facing each other across a low folding table laid with mutton, cheese, fresh milk and dried fruit. At Hari's side sat a gangly year-old prairiecat cub, whose vision the bard used whenever he needed to see something.

"The chiefs are all exultant," remarked Hari. "They and their tribesmen are growing rich on the pickings of these raids, and precious few warriors of the tribe have even been wounded, and only a very small number slain. Many have said to me that had they but known how weak, how vulnerable and defenseless this particular aggregation of dirtmen really was, they should long since have banded together—a dozen or so tribes at a time—and regularly plundered them."

Milo shook his head. "Had they been so rash, we'd now have considerably fewer Kindred clans, Hari. We have been very, very lucky, you know. Those three forts' garrisons were at half-strength or less. Had they been fully manned—built, situated and equipped as they were—I assure you that they would never have fallen to the attack of unsupported light cavalry.

"As for the success of our raids, the earliest were made against no opposition worthy of the name. I have questioned captives, and all told me that the chief of this land and people—one Alehks, whose title is 'Duke'—had called up all his subchiefs and their warriors, had all but stripped the forts and the city of fighters and had hired on hundreds of warriors from far-distant tribes in order to cross the Great River and make war on a rival chief, one Tcharlz, also called 'Duke.' He had been across the river for some moons when we struck his forts.

"More recent captives say that this Alehks suffered great reverses in his war-making across the river. They say that he lost many men, all his horses and oxen, all his wagons and supplies, many of his weapons and armor and gear. They also say that those who survived to return with him to this side of the river had nearly starved to death during the winter past.

"I can well believe these stories, Hari, for the warriors who have recently been opposing us were fine-drawn when they first rode against us, most of them riding mules or poor crowbaits that were likely pulling dung carts a week before. But, old friend, our luck will not hold forever. It is a certainty that sooner or later this Alehks will bring in fresh, well-equipped and well-mounted troops. When that day comes, any chief or subchief who tries to deal with them as the clansmen so often have with the poor exhausted bastards we've faced up to now will find some sharp, painful surprises and all will probably awaken in the Home of Wind."

Hari smiled, showing teeth worn down almost to the gums. "I think you exaggerate, war chief. I know, I know, you carry your duty to husband the tribe's warriors, so your intentions are good. But our horses can easily outdistance these dirtman breeds, can run rings around them. And our bowmen . . ."

"Hari," put in Milo, "recall the breed of horse that the chiefs of the traders ride, the tall ones with the long legs and the small, fine heads. You've observed races between them and clansmen on our horses, haven't you?"

At the bard's nod, he went on, "Well, have you ever seen a Horseclans mount win one of those races?"

"Yes," answered Hari slowly, trying to bridge the gap of years. "It was a . . . young subchief of Clan Makinnis, I believe."

Milo snorted derisively. "All right, one win out of how many races, eh? Those horses, Hari, are of the eastern breed of warhorses, but those of the traders are far from the best examples; those are either culls, rejects from war training or retired warhorses. Even so, they are invariably faster than our own short-legged, big-headed breed over a short stretch. Also, being bigger and bulkier and heavier, they will be able to bowl over our mounts as easily as a prairiecat knocks over a lance-horn buck.

"As regards our bowmen, and the maiden archers, they've inflicted frightful losses on those scantily armored wretches, true enough. But properly equipped heavy cavalry are going to be armored from knee to pate, Hari, and all of steel, mind you—mail or scale or plate, but steel, none of this leather boiled in wax and, perhaps, covered with thin sheets of brass. Now, Hari, I would stake great odds that nine out of every ten arrows in this camp are tipped with either chipped stone or fired bone, both of which materials are cheap and first-rate for hunting; and, loosed at the proper angle and at close enough range, they'll even pierce good-quality leather armor.

"But, my wise and musical friend, a clansman or maiden could loose such shafts at a steel-armored man all day and still do him no harm; both bone and stone shatter against steel plate or scale, as I know of experience in the far south among the Mehkskuhn tribes.

"So pray start informing the chiefs not to try to make a stand or play any of their bloody games against any new bands of warriors they encounter. You'd better also tell them to get every smith in this camp to the task of forging every available scrap of iron or steel or even bronze into arrowheads."

Hari said drily, "The mighty war chief speaks, the aged and most humble bard obeys."

"*Humble*, you?" Milo chuckled, then licked the grease from his fingers and began stuffing his pipe.

The squadron of heavy cavalry—for all that they were well-disciplined veterans, splendidly equipped, masterfully led by hard bitten and intelligent officers and sergeants, and mounted on fresh, big, powerful warhorses—accomplished far less of a positive nature than Alex had hoped. Within a week in action, they had taken casualties of near a hundred killed and wounded and had lost at least a half of that number of their highly valuable chargers to death, serious wounds or capture.

The squat, beetle-browed, very muscular commander, Captain Sir Jaik Higinz, in conference with Duke Alex was crushingly blunt.

"Yer grace, I knows you ain't too pleased with my boys and me, and I cain't fault you none, rightly, 'cuz I ain't no way pleased with the sitch'ation my own se'f. So I tell you what I'll do: I'm contracted to the grand duke till the end of this month. He done sent us here to fight fer you, and I'll 'bide by my sworn word till the time runs out. But that's gonna hafta be it, Yer grace. God knows, I'll like as not be down to half a squadron or less, in thet little time. I's to sign on with you fer any longer, them screechin', howlin' little bastids on their ugly, runty hosses will've most like kilt us all."

Duke Alex nodded stiffly, though he had the overwhelming urge to hang his head in despair. He knew that the fine, fresh troops had done their best, all that could reasonably be asked of men and horses. He was getting the nagging thought more frequently as disastrous day followed disastrous day that nothing could or would stop this horde of nomads—not him and all his horsemen, not the infantry or the walls of Traderstown, not even the Great River.

Knowing in advance that it was hopeless, still the unhappy duke made a try. "If it is a matter of stipend, captain, fortunately I can afford to pay a higher figure for your services than could my esteemed cousin . . . ?"

"No, yer grace." The captain shook his shaven head. "The squadron ain't afeered of no civilized troops on either bank of the whole damn Ohyoh Valley, but what we're up 'gainst here is another kettle of fish, and I've done had to hang or stripe some deserters a'ready.

"And I'm not the onliest one, neither, yer grace. My old comrade Captain Barnz, his contract with you expires 'bout the same time as mine with the grand duke does. Him and me figgers to merge what's left of our troops by then and sail downriver to the Kingdom of Mehmfiz where a civilized war's going on.

"Now, yer grace, I ain't a edjicated man; I thinks God give all the brains to my older brother, along with the title and all, but in near on twenny-eight years of sojering, I done learned me a few things here and there. Fergive me fer putting it like this, yer grace, but you done got your parts in a crack and them Horseclanners are 'bout to lop 'em off.

"But yer grace ain't the only one's almost eyebrows deep in the shit, 'cause we took us a wounded nomad las' week and afore he died, he tol' me that all of them clans, forty or fifty of 'em, means to cross the Mizipi—what you folks 'round here calls the Great River—and then they means to march on due eas' till they gets to the salt sea, living off any lands they come onto and killing anybody tries to stop 'em.

"And so, yer grace, it seems to me—a poor, iggerant wight of a perfeshunal sojer—that you should oughta mend yer fences with yer brother-in-law, 'crost of the river, and let him know what-all's going on down here 'fore it's too late for him or anybody elst to help you out.

"If the two of you's to fight together, mebbe you can stop them scrawny devils or at least head 'em in a diffrunt direck-shun. Seems to me it's come up a question of hang together or hang one at the time . . . no disrespect meant, yer grace."

Tcharlz had as quickly, if not as painfully, learned just how difficult it was to bombard the fortress he had built. He knew better than to try to dig emplacements in the Lower Town, of course, recalling the cofferdams that had been necessary in order to get the walls and foundations down to bedrock. Therefore he tried to add to and improve upon the charred ruins of the semicircular protective wall that had brought a disaster to Duke Alex's abortive siege.

There was no wood to be fired in Tcharlz's construction, but this did not deter Captain Martuhn, nor did it save the duke's siege engines. After raining a few bushels of small stone over the emplacements to keep the engineers pressed close to the wall and away from their own engines, the massed engines of the citadel accurately hurled large crocks of oil to burst and soak the engines, then followed these in short order with blazing spears and fire arrows.

From the Upper Town, Tcharlz watched his engines burn-ing merrily and cursed them because he could not yet bring himself to curse Martuhn, for all the man's rank insubordina-tion and disloyalty to him.

When first he had arrived before the citadel at the head of

his troops, Tcharlz had sent in a messenger with a letter of demand that Captain Martuhn come out, unarmed, and bringing with him the two boys, whose adoptive father had accompanied the army.

The messenger returned with an oral message from the captain that neither he nor the boys would come out. However, the duke was welcome at any time to come inside, alone.

Tcharlz then sent in another messenger bearing an order for all troops within the citadel to come out with their arms and beasts and join the siege brigade in bringing the rebel, Captain Martuhn, to the duke's justice.

After a wait of several hours, the messenger returned . . . with a scant dozen common soldiers and two shame-faced officers. At this, Tcharlz rode into the citadel alone, as invited by his rebellious officer.

Stiffly, formally, he explained his purposes to Captain Martuhn, who then had all of the citadel's garrison assembled in the forecourt to hear the duke. Duke Tcharlz made no threats, he simply reminded them that they were his troops— either natives of his duchy or client states, or mercenaries hired by his order and paid by his gold—and that their loyalty belonged to him, not to any of his officers, and especially not to a former officer now in open rebellion against the duchy. Then he asked that all men and officers who would accompany him out of the citadel and help in the overthrow of Sir Martuhn—formerly Captain of Ducal Infantry and Count of Twocityport—take two paces forward.

Not one man or officer moved from his place in ranks, and the duke's face reddened, while his jaws worked and his left hand tightened on the hilt of his broadsword until the scarred knuckles stood out as white as snow.

At long last, one officer left his place and approached the livid duke, who growled with the beginning of a grudging smile, "Well, Baronet Fahster, you took long enough to make up your mind. At least one of you assholes knows which side his bread is buttered on."

The tall, blond man shook his head forcefully. "Your grace, I'll not be leaving with you, but in fairness to you, I felt you should know why. Have I the permission of your grace to speak?"

"Talk away, rebel bastard," snarled Tcharlz, all hint of the smile fled from his lips. "I trow your next speech to me will be from the gallows at Pirates' Folly . . . just before you swing for your treason."

"Lord duke," began the baronet, "I have served your arms long and faithfully. I have taken agonizing wounds in your service, but you rewarded me graciously and you have been a generous patron."

"Then why do you now turn on me, Baronet Fahster . . . Hal?" For a fraction of a second, the deep, hidden pain tinged the old nobleman's voice, glittered from out his eyes. "You and I, lad, we're natives of the same county. Your father was one of my dearest friends, a staunch supporter whose courage and strong right arm did much to put me where I am today. When he died in my arms, he committed you to my care, and I reared you and sponsored you as if you had been my own flesh and blood.

"So, why, Hal? What have I now done to you that you would forsake me?"

The young man's own inner turmoil was patent; tears coursed down his cheeks and his voice shook with emotion. "Your grace has ever been good to me, to all my house, and is loved for his goodness. But, your grace, I now must follow the dictates of my conscience, which tells me and all these other soldiers and officers that your grace—who is, after all, but a mortal man like us—has been ill-advised and misled by those men closest to him and that he is, therefore, in the wrong to so persecute one of his best, bravest and most loyal officers in an attempt to force him to turn over two of our young comrades to an alien and unnatural creature who has already offered one of them shameful abuse.

"It will hurt me more than anyone can know to draw my sword against your grace, but I—on my honor—can do no other unless your grace relent in his purpose."

The duke whirled on Martuhn. "What have you done, damn you? Bewitched them all?"

"Your grace," answered Martuhn in a quiet, controlled voice, "I simply told them all your side, my side and my decision. Then I allowed the boys to tell of what had befallen them and Lieutenant Nahseer to speak of what he knew from his years of slavery about this Urbahnos' true nature. What the men and officers then decided was of their own choice."

Turning back to the assembled troops, the duke roared,

"You'll live to regret this defiance of the law, of the duchy and of me, every man jack of you!" Then he jumped down from the platform, found his stirrup and hurled himself into the saddle of his dancing stallion. Jerking the reins from the horse holder, he almost rode over the man as he spur-raked the big horse into a fast canter toward the gate.

A few miles to the southwest of Pahdookahport lay the ruins of a long-deserted hall, one of the victims of Duke Tcharlz's land reforms, two decades and more agone. Although the complex appeared to have been slighted, it actually had not. Rather, two generations of the new breed of yeoman farmers and stockbreeders had used it as a quarry—carrying away brick and cut stone, roofing tiles and even massive timbers, when and as they felt the need.

The larger, less easily manageable stones of its outer walls had been carted away by the duke's men and were now incorporated into the fabric of Pirates' Folly, while nearby smiths and countless vagabonds had torn or prised away all reusable metal of any description.

But though the half-picked skeleton of the once gracious home lay with most of its interior exposed to the effects of wind and weather, now only providing permanent lodging to birds and bats and the small, scuttling creatures of the fields, the deep, roomy, extensive cellars were almost intact. And of a late, stormy night, they were used by Sir Huhmfree Gawlin and certain of his retainers.

Within the large, earthen-floored subcellar room once used as a winecellar, a small slice of hell had been constructed and was in use. Brightly lit in its center by torches and lamps, and thick with their smoke and the commingled stenches of sweat, spilled blood, charred flesh, dung and heated metal, there were chairs to make some of the observers comfortable and devilish devices to inflict varying degrees of discomfort upon the flesh and bones of the one female in the room.

Despite the oppressive heat, all five of the men seated in the chairs were voluminously cloaked, with hoods and masks that made identification impossible.

The woman, on the other hand, was naked. Her gross, corpulent body hung by its wrists from a rope threaded through a big iron pulley spiked to a ceiling beam. All parts of her fat body showed the marks of whip or sharp knife or heated iron or pincers.

Her name was Yohahna and she had for many years operated and claimed to own a Pahdookahport "business," the Three Doors. Her swollen and discolored feet and nailless, charred toes hung a few inches above the floor, and blood from various parts of her battered, horribly disfigured body had dripped down to form a clotting pool on the hard-packed earth.

Her hands had been tied behind her back before she had been hoisted up; her immense weight had long since dislocated her shoulders and she now hung, panting hoarsely in agony, her one remaining eye bulging and bloodshot.

"Would it not be better to lower the wretch while she ticks off her silent partners for us?" inquired one of the cloaked men, aged by the sound of his voice.

The cloaked man on the far right shrugged. "She's as comfortable where she is as she could be. She can no longer stand or sit, you see. I suppose that we could put her on the rack again . . ."

The woman's hoarse panting was suddenly replaced by a low, bubbling whine, and the blood trickling from her burned and mutilated pudenda was briefly diluted with urine. "Aw, don' hurt me no mo'," she whimpered huskily. "Pleez don' hurt me no mo', mistuh. I'll tell yawl enythin', everthin'. Yawl wawn' gol'? I c'n show yawl where two hunnerd pounds is bur'ed. Jest, pleez, pleez Gawd, don' hurt me no mo'!"

One of the other cloaked figures, not sounding anywhere near as aged as the first, remarked, "The fat bitch sounds considerably different from when last I spoke with her about that matter some years back of kidnapped girls. This exercise in chastisement has obviously purged her of her unseemly arrogance. She now has recalled how to properly address her betters."

The aged man said rebukingly, "You say too much. She is of scant use to us dead, so it is imperative that she be given no clue to our identities . . . yet." Then, to another of the hooded ones, "Are you ready, then? Take down every word from now on spoken in this room. Identify us and yourself as numbers one through five, counting from left to right. Her, you'll list by the letter Y, but note the full names and ranks or offices of anyone she mentions; there must be no mistakes or omissions to legally trip us up."

"All right, Yohahna," said the man at the far right, "you will now repeat for these gentlemen what you told me earlier. First, who are the actual owners of the Three Doors?"

There followed a chorus of gasps and exclamations of incredulity as the tortured woman whisperingly stuttered the list of more than a dozen names—nobles, gentry and commoner-merchants of the duchy.

The man on the right spoke again. "And how, Yohahna, do you usually recruit your whores?"

"I buys me purty slaves, if I can," she gasped. "But I got me this gang of fellas, goes outa the town and tries to get farm and village gals to run away with 'em. If the gals won' the mens ushly knocks 'em inna haid and brings 'em back to me. Then I gentles 'em down till they is broke proper."

"These girls you have kidnapped, Yohahna—are they all the daughters of citizens of this duchy?"

"Yessuh, far's I knows they is. None the slaves is," she replied. "I buys *them*, leegul and proper, I does."

"And these partners you have named, do they all know just how you obtain your girls? Of your highly illegal methods?"

"Sure they does," she affirmed. "Lak I done tol' you, suh, oncet the baron hisse'f tol' me which gal he wawnted took up and brought to mah place. It'uz the daughter of some piss-poor gentleman, and the baron, he'd offered her a dang good living to be his mistress and the crazy lil wench'd turned him down flat, and he had the itch, bad, had to get in 'er, he did."

He of the aged voice growled, "And did you kidnap this gentle-born girl, then, you piece of filth?"

"I got 'er inna place, a'right," the dangling woman replied. "But it won' no gentling 'er, and me and my mens tried near everything we knows, short of flat-out raping her—and we couldn' do thet 'cause the baron was set on being the firstest man in 'er.

"Fin'ly, the itch got to 'im so awful bad, he come down and took 'er by main force. But after he'd done had her, she come to git holt of his dagger and come at him and afore he could git it away from 'er, he'd done kilt 'er."

The man with the aged voice snarled behind his mask like some beast of prey and started up from his chair, his heavy dirk half out of its sheath. But hands on either side gently restrained him, murmuring to him until he had regained his composure and sheathed his weapon.

The man on the right then asked, "And the Ehleen merchant factor, Urbahnos of Karaleenos, Yohahna—is he, too, one of your partners?"

"He useta be, suh, but he just up and sol' out his shares to me'n the baron, 'cause he 'uz going back eas', he said, as soon's he'd done got him back them two lil slaves what had got 'way from him."

"You mean his sons? The two nomad boys he'd adopted?" her main questioner prodded.

"Aw, naw, suh. That there adopshun was jus' a way him and the baron come up with to keep from him having to pay part of what-all they costed him to whoever caught 'em. The lil'es' one he was gonna give to some Ehleen mucketymuck in the place he come from what likes to bugger lil boys as much as Urbahnos does; then this other Ehleen was s'posed to make it right enough that Urbahnos could go back home.

"He offered to sell me his wife afore he left, but I figgered she's a mite too old, and b'sides, her paw was to find out she'd done been sol' to me, *that*'d be a purty mess. So I tolt 'im to wait till he got upriver, somewheres pas' Ehvinzburkport, and then sell her and his kids."

They went on, the hooded gentlemen, until the scribe had run out of materials. Twice the woman fainted and had to be revived by the application of hot irons to her vulnerable flesh.

At length, the man of the aged voice said, "All right, we have what we need, more by far than was really needed to achieve our aims. Confine the hag closely, but see to it that she is well fed and nursed back to health and strength. For at the conclusion of this, I want to see her last a long time, a very long and painful time, impaled on a thick stake. Then and only then will justice be truly served."

Chapter XIV

Count Martuhn had been performing one of his periodic inspections of the magazines wherein were kept the garrison's food and supply stores when Wolf's messenger found him. As the citadel had been victualed and supplied for the needs of two thousand men—and Martuhn's command had never numbered more than fifteen hundred, including noncombatants—for a year-long siege, he figured that it would be months still before there was any dearth to consider. But he still checked the magazines every ten days on general principles: it kept the quartermaster sergeant and his staff on their toes.

The pikeman Wolf had sent found the count still chewing a chunk of the pickled pork from a cask he had had sprung at random.

"My lord, Sir Wolf bids me report that a barge is starting across the river on the south cable. It soon will be within range of the engines, and he asks if he should sink it."

"Only the single barge, soldier?" Martuhn asked around the pork.

"Yes, my lord, only one. And it one of the smaller ones."

"Wait, I'll return with you, soldier." Martuhn turned to the quartermaster sergeant, "Aye, Les, that's good old-fashioned campaign pork. Have your lads reseal it and bear it up to my tower. I often want something solid to chew on in the night."

By the time Martuhn stood beside Wolf, the small barge was well out into the river and, for all the efforts of the unseen men pulling the heavy oars in steady, even strokes, was

179

making very slow progress and straining against the thick cable high above. It was now within easy range of the wall engines, and Wolf's shift of engineers were all standing ready at the stone hurlers and spear throwers, awaiting but the word of command to release the triggers of their deadly devices.

Martuhn used one hand to shade his eyes against the bright noon sun. He spied the reflections of sunlight on a bit of polished steel, but could discern little at that distance through the glare.

"What do you make of it, Martuhn?" Wolf mindspoke.

The count shrugged and beamed. "No reinforcements for Duke Tcharlz, certainly. Even if the men on the benches below were soldiers too—which I tend to doubt, for the tempo is too strong and regular to be aught but trained slaves—still they could not get more than a bare hundred men on that cockleshell. Could be a messenger from old Alex, so leave it be, let them land: that man brings trouble if not doom to everything and everyone he touches. His grace has surely seen the barge, too, or his men have, so don't fire on any party he sends down to the dock."

As the greeting party and the westerners rode past the citadel, it could be seen that one of them was Duke Alex himself, accompanied by a bare handful of his gentry and noblemen.

"Now just what," mused Martuhn to himself, "is that feckless bastard up to now?"

His answer was not long in coming . . . in the person of Duke Tcharlz, who approached the outer works the next morning, just after it had become light enough to recognize men's faces at a distance.

The duke rode almost to the verge of the moat, opposite the main gate, in the middle of the south wall. He looked up at the works just above that gate for a moment, then roared, *"Martuhn*! Are you up there, lad? Let me in, we must talk."

Martuhn was: so too were Wolf and Nahseer.

Wolf muttered, "What the hell is that sly old fox up to now, milord count?"

"I have no idea, Sir Wolf," Martuhn replied. "But he's alone and unarmored and . . ." He peered harder. "I don't think he even has his sword on. Scant harm he could do."

To the soldiers inside the tower that housed the machinery

controlling gate, portcullis and drawbridge, he snapped, "Lower away, soldiers, and raise the grille, but don't raise the bar until Sir Wolf says to.

"Wolf, wait until he's at least halfway across the bridge, then, if no assault party has come into view, open the right valve only, and close it the minute he's through it. Hear?"

Martuhn and Tcharlz met in the grim, spartan little ground-floor office, and the older man came directly to the point. "Martuhn, son, I need your help."

"Your grace needs *my* help?" Martuhn sounded his incredulity, but his voice quickly acquired an undertone of cynicism. "The siege is become too expensive to maintain, your grace? I fear I've very little to lend, but . . ."

The old duke seated himself without invitation. "Martuhn, my boy, I don't blame you a bit, but you of all people know just how murderously violent I become when I'm thwarted. It's not a thing I enjoy admitting, for it's a serious weakness in my character, but, hell, man, I can't help or control myself.

"Have you got a few quarts of beer left? I've been up all night with Alex and my staff—talking, talking, talking, all of us, when we weren't scheming and planning and weighing possibilities—and I'm dry as a salt fish."

While a pikeman went to fetch beer, the tall captain planted the sole of a booted foot on his desktop and, leaning over, snapped, "All right, your grace, what do you want from me? It is, you will admit, most singular for the commander of the investing force to come to ask the help of the very man he's besieging. But I suppose you have your reasons and I also suppose they mean something . . . at least, to you."

The duke shook his head. "Not just to me, my boy, but to you and to Alex and to every man, woman and child in both duchies, these two threatened duchies.

"But, you were speaking of investments and sieges; well, there is no longer a siege. My men are packing their gear and breaking camp at this very minute. There never should've been a siege to begin with, Martuhn, I can see that now, though I couldn't then, of course.

"You are my *chosen* son, the best of the best, my heir presumptive, the strong right arm of an old and very tired man, and I should've remembered that before I tried to bend you to my will against your own. What matters it what some alien merchant wants or does not want, really, eh? *I* am the real law, not that doddering, maundering old fool Lapkin.

"And I say that the boys are yours, Martuhn, now and forever. I beg you, my son, please forget or at least forgive my harsh words and harsher actions against you and them. I'll not reinstate you in your rank and lands and title, for to my mind, you never were disenfranchised, all right?"

And what, your grace, am I expected to do in return for all the largess of My Lord Sir Tcharlz, Duke of the East Bank?" asked Martuhn in tones of mock humility.

"Why, simply resume your rank of senior captain of all my infantry, Martuhn, my dear boy. Leave only enough of them here to maintain civil order and ferry the bulk of them over to Traderstown, then assume command of the town and all the troops therein."

Martuhn strove not to show his surprise and total bafflement at the request. "And what is Duke Alex going to think when one of your officers takes over his capital? Or has your grace managed to cozen him out of his duchy?"

The duke chuckled. "Not quite that much, Martuhn . . . not yet, anyway, though that too may well come in time. No, Alex is in complete accord that you—a man, I might add, whom he deeply respects, despite and likely because of the drubbing you gave him last fall—take command of the city and hold it against the Horseclans nomads while he and I with our cavalry try to get those Satan-spawn into a real battle on open ground, whereon our heavy horse can fight to best advantage.

"As soon as heavy barges can be brought across and loaded, Count Bart is taking over all my lancers and dragoons. I'll be following with the heavy horse as soon as I've handled some of the more pressing affairs at Pirates' Folly. I'll be at my castle ten days, at most; that should give you time to marshal the footmen hereabouts, assign temporary duties within this duchy to ones you consider least effective for combat, and ready the rest to embark immediately my horse is landed over yonder.

"But, Martuhn, I cannot allow you to take those boys over the river. Now, hold, hold! I have a very good reason for it, and please believe me, my son, there are no hidden reasons, only the one, open one.

"Martuhn, those boys are nomads, Horseclan nomads, and

those people hang together more firmly than ticks on a hound. You know the boys and love them and respect them and *trust* them. I do not trust them and I'll not have them placed in a position from which they might do our arms considerable damage, were they to find themselves torn between old loyalties and new.

"Leave them here, Martuhn, in this fortress, and if you're still worried that I may be acting in bad faith, leave Wolf or Nahseer to guard them. I'm no mean swordsman myself, but I'd think twice before I drew steel to go against either of those two."

Arrived back at Pirates' Folly, Tcharlz threw himself into a whirl of activities. Ensconced in his private office, he kept messengers scurrying in and out, while five or six scribes hunched over their portable tables, trying hard to keep up with his staccato dictations of messages, and the chief scribe sat at another table with a goodly supply of melted sealing wax, ribbons and the weighty ducal seal.

Noblemen, gentry officers and their retainers only just sent home upon Duke Alex's precipitate cessation of hostilities and withdrawal to his own, now hotly embattled lands needs must be recalled with haste; supplies and transport must be arranged for; small, speedy ships must be dispatched up both rivers to try to seek out unemployed mercenaries (if, with a civil war in Mehmfiz and another war building up between the traditional rivals, Ehvinzburk and Tehrawt, there were any to be found, at any price).

He knew that he also must find time to arrange a meeting with the council of merchants and the council of shipowners. For to pay whatever mercenaries his agents might scrape up, he would have to float a loan on next year's taxes, and he well knew that those two packs of skinflints were the only ones who could quickly raise the sum he had in mind. But he did not relish the thought of asking the rich, supercilious commoner-bastards and arrogant foreigners for anything; he had avoided doing so in the campaigns against Mehmfiz and Traderstown, but this new calamity found a treasury virtually drained of fluid resources.

Such was Tcharlz's dislike of what he knew he must do that he briefly flirted with the idea—actually, it was his prerogative to do so, if in his opinion (and who else's?) the good of the duchy required so radical a step being taken—of marching into Pahdookahport with all the armed men he could quickly gather and seizing the members of the two councils. Then he could either squeeze the monies out of them with threats of torture, mutilation and death, or hold them for ransom to be scraped up by their peers.

But that would be killing the goose, he reflected; the last river lord who had tried that stratagem had gotten every ounce of gold that he needed for that particular project, but while he was otherwise engaged, the merchants and shipowners had loaded their families and portable possessions onto their ships and set sail for healthier ports. Some of his Pahdookahport shippers and merchants were, in fact, a portion of that very exodus.

If he could only lay hands to as little as a hundred pounds of gold . . . But the duchy was bled white, legally, and this distasteful business seemed the only way.

The merchants' council was the first group to come to the castle, and, although their rates were as steep as he had known that they would be, they seemed to know just how far they could push him and did not venture beyond that point; and, save one, all were in favor of extending the duke a sizable loan. The one dissenter was Urbahnos, the self-styled "Lord," though the man held no title that any ruler along the Ohyoh River would recognize and honor.

The duke wondered if it was his imagination working upon the open secret of the Ehleen's terrible mutilation that made him think to hear a higher tone to the unfortunate man's voice.

"Your grace is quick to come to us when *he* needs assistance—and very expensive assistance at that—but when is he willing to assist us, eh?"

Old Gaib Fai, senior of the council in age, wealth and standing, spoke in his usual whining voice, constantly rubbing together hands that looked as fleshless as the feet of a bird. "Urbahnos, yer outa place to tawk to the duke lak thet. Duke Tcharlz, he's allus bin a good'un, not oncet has he evun thawt 'bout doing suthin' to his honest, law-'biding merchants and factors and shippers, lak a puling pocket-king I kin recawl done to me and sum others, oncet."

Urbahnos' lips twisted in a mirthless smile. "I'd lay long odds, old man, that Duke Tcharlz has, indeed, *thought* about doing that very thing . . . and more than once; but he knows better than to commit such a folly.

"No, the only nomads who interest me are my two dear little adopted sons, illegally held for many long months by the infamous Count Martuhn at the citadel in Twocityport. Baron Lapkin himself pled my case before your grace many weeks past, and your grace at that time did promise the return of my two sweet sons—although your grace refused to force this ducal officer to pay blood price for my two valued and loyal retainers slain by this officer's troops; nor would your grace even make the effort to bring to justice my escaped slave, Nahseer—a ruthless, sadistic and highly dangerous man, who injured and robbed me before escaping.

"As for those nomads across the river, I have no fear of them for I am leaving Pahdookahport immediately your grace makes good his sworn word and returns to my loving arms my two small sons, Bahb and Djoh. My house is sold, and my animals, slaves and bulkier effects, but I refuse to be a party to this loan, not to a single bent copper of it. Do you all hear? This trouble is not my affair and I'll not be involved in it."

Tcharlz inwardly squirmed for a few moments, then the perfect solution to the problem occurred to him. "Master Urbahnos, I have expended time and resources in attempting to obtain those boys for you, as I promised you I would; I still would be so engaged, had not this nomad threat arisen, so do not try to throw the lie in *my* teeth, Ehleen.

"Count Martuhn is a very stubborn man—every bit as stubborn as am I—and it is his desire to adopt those boys himself, nor does he trust you. He thinks that your plan is to get the boys out of my sphere of influence and then sell them as slaves. Do you have this intent, Master Urbahnos?"

Dark blood suffused the Ehleen's features and his black eyes blazed with what appeared to be anger. "Of course not, your grace! The concept is outrageous, ridiculous. I . . . I . . ."

"If you'll hold your temper and your tongue for a few moments, Master Urbahnos," Tcharlz admonished, "I'll tell you and these other men—in strictest confidence, understand; if one word of it comes back to me from whatever source, my operatives will surely trace it back and excise the loose, flapping tongue—of how you may lay hands on the nomad boys.

"In all legal matters, masters, possession is now and has always been nine-tenths of the law, which is why I had to resort to using diplomacy against Count Martuhn. But if you, Master Urbahnos, were in possession of the boys and a-ship for points east . . . d'you get my drift?"

"I should just ride a coach into that citadel, I suppose, big as brass, and say, 'Lord count, I have come for my sons.' Is that it, your grace? *Fagh*, the man would let that savage, Nahseer, kill me . . . if he did not do it himself!" Urbahnos answered hotly.

Tcharlz shook his head patiently. "Within ten days—less than that, I hope—both I and Count Martuhn will be on the other side of the river and neither of us will be able to return quickly; the boys will be alone in the citadel with a bare handful of guards, if that. Hire you some tough men, ride to Twocityport and retake what is legally yours, man. That's what I'd do, in your boots."

The next day, as he was on his way to his conference with the council of shipowners, a few of whom were also on the council of merchants, he was approached by one of his host of bastards, Sir Huhmfree Gawlin, and three other gentlemen.

"Huhmfree, lad!" Grinning, he clasped the young man's hand in his own big paw and clapped him on the back affectionately. "Have you, then, raised your lances so soon? Now, here's an obedient subject for you, gentlemen—never one to dawdle when his duty calls."

"Your grace," said Huhmfree, "my force and I shall be in the appointed place at the appointed hour. However, these gentlemen and I, we have a matter most urgent which we must discuss with your grace . . . in private, if it be your pleasure."

The duke frowned, then shook his head vehemently. "However important or urgent, Huhmfree, it will just have to wait until I've driven off those damned Horseclanners, over the river yonder. At this very moment, in fact, I'm due to grovel before a pack of commoner swine for a few pounds of gold to buy me troops and horses and supplies."

"Your grace . . . Tcharlee?" The eldest of the group of gentlemen, a venerable, white-haired and -bearded figure with the still-erect bearing, the movements and the stance of an old soldier, stepped from the knot and extended a veined and bony hand to touch the duke's arm.

His every feature radiating true and unabashed pleasure, the duke half turned to embrace the ancient warmly. "My steel, but it's good to clap my eyes on you again, Uncle Peetu. You frequent my court far too seldom, in recent years, and I find myself often yearning for the sight of you, for the sound of your voice."

"You know why I am so infrequently in public, Tcharlee . . . ah, your grace," answered the old man softly, his faded-blue eyes misting slightly.

Tcharlz nodded once, stiffly; his lips became a thin line. "And you know that I, that we all, grieve with you, uncle, though perhaps not so broodingly as you. Were you ever able to determine just what happened, what was the exact fate of your granddaughter?"

The aged man nodded his grim-faced head, his eyes hard and frosty as arctic ice. "I but recently learned, thanks to Sir Huhmfree's invaluable assistance, who bore sweet Mahrtha away, to where and at what powerful man's order, and I learned how and by whose hand she was murdered. I come to you seeking justice, Tcharlee, although were I a younger man or were my sons still living, I'd handle the matter myself."

The duke pursed his lips. "Is this the matter of great urgency of which Huhmfree spoke, uncle?"

"A part of it, Tcharlee," replied the old man.

"Well, then, I'll just have to make the time," stated the duke baldly. Turning to his chamberlain, he ordered, "Sir Rahdjuh, have a keg of the dark beer and a few decanters of brandy—my private stock, mind you, man—taken to the shipowners and make your apology that I keep them waiting. Don't go into any details with them . . . affairs of state, et cetera; you know it all, man, you've alibied me often enough."

"But, your grace . . ." the chamberlain began, until a curt gesture of the duke's hand cut him off.

"Not a word. Sir Rahdjuh! I feel the press of time as keenly as do you, but here's a man I cannot deny. Before you were born, was Sir Peetuh Bohwlz risking his life and truly beggaring himself to help me consolidate lands and power. His five brave sons died while fighting under my banner, and his daughter's husband suffered such grievous wounds that he has not walked again in thirty years.

"But never has Sir Peetuh been willing to accept a single acre or one ounce of silver from me in return for all his and his house's sacrifices. Now he comes asking an hour or so of my time. How can I refuse him, Sir Rahdjuh?"

"But, your grace . . ."

"I said, not one word, Sir Rahdjuh. I have given you a task to perform elsewhere. Do your duty, sirrah!"

The chamberlain knew better than to argue with his master when his voice acquired such a tone.

As soon as most of the foot soldiers had been called up and assembled in and around Twocityport, Martuhn scraped together enough mounts, of a sort, to place almost a hundred of his own mercenary infantry in saddles and sent them into the countryside by squads, each in command of a veteran officer or sergeant or, at least, a corporal. Their task to flush out any sound, sturdy beggars or vagabonds and bring them back for impressment into the ranks, to recruit among the uncommitted farmers and villagers and to chivvy along supplies due but not yet delivered to the marshaling point.

Because the heavy horse was to embark first, Martuhn kept his infantry units camped at a short distance from the city, leaving the closer campgrounds vacant for the imminent arrival of the cavalry, the only exceptions being his own company, the garrison archers and crossbowmen and the citadel engineers, whom he suffered to remain in the citadel.

Tirelessly, he threw himself and his staff into the tasks of organizing the minutiae of the call-up and movement of above ten thousand warm bodies; inspecting weapons and equipment and repairing or replacing, where necessary; sending home any who chanced to be seriously ill or diseased, especially if their ills were of a contagious nature; ruling upon the pleas for exemption, and these were many for many of these men were but bare weeks returned home from the last campaign when summoned again; receiving and inspecting supply shipments, then apportioning them, marking them for the various units and for their shipping times.

Whenever he was not in the citadel courtyard, which was now become a supply dump, or in one or another of the far-flung camps, he could be found on the cable docks, attending to the embarkment of supplies, remounts and replacements for the lancers and dragoons of Duke Tcharlz's force already engaged against the nomads . . . and suffering as badly as had the men of Duke Alex, if the steady stream of casualties said anything. Nor was this intelligence unknown or unnoticed by the marshaled troops; desertions or attempted desertions rose afresh with each arrival of a bargeload of maimed, mutilated and demoralized lancers and dragoons from the fierce fighting on the west bank.

All that Martuhn could do was to order larger and stronger camp-security details posted on a twenty-four-hour basis and to supplement them with roving patrols of mule-mounted men from his own company of professionals. That, and hope that Duke Tcharlz and his heavy horse arrived on time or, best of all, ahead of schedule, that he might the quicker embark his foot.

The "hour" was now approaching three hours, since Tcharlz had closeted himself with Sir Peetuh, Sir Huhmfree and the other gentlemen of their entourage. He had pored over the entire "testimony" of the madam, Yohahna, twice and then reread portions a third time. The chamberlain had intruded three times; he was ordered out twice, and the third time Tcharlz had thrown his belt dagger at him.

Finally, he slumped back in his chair. "Uncle, Huhmfree, gentlemen, had you or anyone else lodged such charges against some of these men, unsupported, I'd have adjudged you madmen. But how to discount such lengthy and detailed testimony . . . ?"

"I am only sorry that there is no way I can be around to see these malefactors dragged here to Pirates' Folly and fitted with fetters and lodged on the lower levels to contemplate until they can be brought to trial. The witness, this female monster, she still lives?"

Sir Huhmfree answered, "Oh, yes, your grace, we . . . I . . . have taken exceeding care in her regard. Those nursing and guarding her are all my good and unceasingly faithful folk."

"Beware she doesn't bribe them, boy," growled Tcharlz. "After all in which she and these other scoundrels have been involved over the years—and not one single cent of taxes paid to me out of their nefarious enterprises, I'll wager you!—she must be richer than Duke Alex, over yonder."

Sir Huhmfree smiled like a cat with a mouse between his

paws. "She already tried that, your grace, and the folk she would've bribed came directly to me. I bade them behave with her as if she'd bought them, but to demand at least a part of the bribe in advance. They did my bidding, and thus I was able to get my hands on her hidden store of gold . . . all of it. And that, your grace, is how I have, this day, delivered to Sir Shawn Bailee, your treasurer, two hundred and six pounds of pure gold, about half in the form of various coin, the rest in two-, three- or five-pound sandmold bars."

At this, Duke Tcharlz beamed beatifically on his bastard, Sir Peetuh and the others. *"Sir Rahdjuh!"* he roared. *"I know damned well you're out there. To me, immediately!"*

When the chamberlain had edged warily into the room (he knew that the duke did not have another dagger, but all five of these knights had at least one), Tcharlz, appearing to be in a rare good humor, told him, "Chase those parsimonious, beer- and brandy-swilling swine of shipowners out of the castle. We no longer need them or their lousy monies.

"Wait, before you do that, send me my chief scribe; tell him to bring two more scribes, wax, ribbons and the seal. I'll be issuing some arrest warrants for immediate service, so have Baron Hahrvee Sheeld stand by, and alert Master Kahks, down belowstairs, that we'll need a good dozen of his lowest, dankest, slimiest cells, plus that many sets of the heaviest fetters to be fitted and riveted."

The chamberlain nodded, rapidly making notes as the orders were given. Then he looked up and asked, "Your grace, if you will be issuing warrants, perhaps Baron Lapkin might be of an assistance? He has just ridden up from Pahdook-ahport and now waits in the anteroom of your audience chamber."

At his words, the chamberlain was deeply shocked to hear a snarled string of foul curses and epithets issue from the aged lips of Sir Peetuh Bohwlz, from whom he never could recall having heard a single harsh or off-color word.

Softly, but firmly, Tcharlz said, "Hold your place, and your temper, just a bit longer, Uncle Peetuh. You'll have every last gram of your vengeance soon enough. But this is a duchy of law and things must be done legally.

"Sir Rahdjuh, courteously request that the learned and *most honorable* Baron Lapkin join us . . . oh, and I'll have six of my foot guards outside the door to this chamber, at once."

Baron Sir Yzik Lapkin, ducal deputy for, and high judge of, the city and environs of Pahdookahport, strode solemnly into the small chamber. When he removed his flat cap of plum velvet and cloth-of-gold, his bald scalp reflected the light of the lamps as fully as did his exposed teeth and dark eyes.

Bobbing the shortest bow permissible, he nodded, "Your grace." Then his smile, which at no time went beyond his mouth, was turned toward the others. "Ah, young Sir Huhmfree and . . . why, my word, is it truly you then, Sir Peetuh? Why, I've not seen you in . . . How long is it? Years, anyway. We two old ones should get together more often, you know.

"Sir Benedikt Railz, what in the world brings you from your lovely hall? Oh, of course, the duke's muster. And that would, of course, account for your presence, too, Sir Leeoh. But, Sir Clai, have you then recovered enough of that smashed kneecap to once more ride to war?"

Before any of them could even start to frame answers, the duke said, "Lapkin, we're about to issue up some arrest warrants for certain malefactors. Sit you down there at the end of the table. I'd have you read a copy of the testimony before the scribes arrive, that all may be in proper order."

"Of course, your grace," said the baron, adding, in a condescending tone addressed to the knights, "you see, wise as is our lord, he is ever ready to seek out expert and loyal counsel."

But he had read no more than two pages when all of the blood drained from his face, the hands that began to rip and tear at the statement were seen to tremble and the voice that he finally found had developed a quaver. "Your . . . your grace *must* not, *cannot* believe a . . . a single word of . . . of *this*! The . . . the woman has obviously gone mad and . . . and besides, look at what she is. Harlots and madams, they . . . they're *all* liars, everyone knows that! Does my dear lord suppose that I . . . that for one moment I . . . no, my lord, mayhap these others named are truly guilty of . . . but not me, my lord, not *me*!"

"No, Lapkin," said Tcharlz, a hint of sadness in his voice, "I am inclined to think you guilty of all those charges, of them, and probably of much, much more which the woman, Yohahna, was unaware of or did not mention."

The baron slid out of his chair onto his knees and crawled abjectly to the duke's side. Raising his tremulous hands beseechingly, he stuttered, "N . . . no, my l . . . lord, no!"

Tcharlz looked sternly down at the groveling man. "Yes, Lapkin, yes! It stand to reason, man. There is no way that bitch and her minions could have engaged in all but open smuggling, kidnapping and extortion and all the sorry rest without protection of them and their activities by a very powerful man. And who more powerful than a man who was, at once, my deputy and the high judge?"

"My . . . my lord has already convicted me!" wailed the baron. "Perjured test . . . testimony . . . a trial . . . right to face my . . ."

The duke's voice was become warm honey flowing over steel. "Oh, yes, Lapkin, you'll get a trial, an open trial, just as soon as I get back from Traderstownport. Meanwhile, because I suspect that you and your criminal cohorts just might take it upon yourselves to take a voyage for reasons of health, you will be availing yourself of the hospitality of Pirates' Folly. My good Master Kahks is already preparing a private room for your occupancy—a cool, dark, quiet one, wherein you may have the peace to reflect upon your treachery to me and my folk."

Tcharlz raised his voice a few notches. *"Guard!"*

Chapter XV

"Wolf, you will be in overall command of the citadel,"
Martuhn stated at a last conference in his towertop home on
the eve of his departure for Traderstown. "I'm leaving you a
score of pikemen along with Corporal Hailee, a couple of
cooks, plus Quartermaster Sergeant Lestuh and his men. His
mission is to ferry over supplies in the proper order, as we
come in need of them, as well as to receive and stow and
record any late-arriving consignments for the garrison of
Traderstown.

"Neither he nor you will be troubled with remounts or supplies for the various contingents of horse. All those are to be
handled by and through the big cavalry camp just north of
the upper city; Chief Quartermaster Sergeant Renuhlz bears
that onerous responsibility. I believe you two are acquainted,
of old."

"Aye," Wolf mindspoke to save time, "it's many a quart
I've downed with him. He be a good man, for all he's a
damned lazy horse soldier."

Martuhn continued, "The citadel will also be host to a
dozen ducal messengers and a selection of mounts for them,
as well as hostlers to care for them and a farrier and his boy
to keep them properly shod; principally because he can both
read and write, and also because I trust him in all ways, Sir
Djaimz will be in charge of the messenger service."

The senior captain turned next to the hulking Zahrtohgahn.
"Nahseer, your responsibility—and your only one until my
return—will be the boys, Bahb and Djoh. For all that this

193

Urbahnos has been declared 'outlaw' by his grace and is being hunted the length and breadth of the duchy, I still fear for their safety from him. Don't ever stray far from them. And both you and Wolf be damned careful of who is let into the citadel and of how many they number."

To Bahb and Djoh, he beamed, "Obey Nahseer and Wolf, lads, they'll have your best interests in mind."

Then, back to Nahseer, "I think it would be best if the three of you lodge up here in my chambers, for there are certain built-in safeguards, as well as a long climb, for any interlopers who might come seeking you. I'll demonstrate them all to you before I'm done. There're foods and various potables up here, and this chamber and Wolf's offer the only routes of access to the roof and its cistern."

A week earlier, Baron Hahrvee Sheeld had ridden into Pahdookahport, his belt pouch bulging with ducal warrants, and ordered the commander of the city guard to bar all gates immediately, no man or woman to enter or exit until he gave leave that they do so. Next, he had visited the office of the harbormaster and served notice that until further orders were forthcoming, no ship, barge or boat of any size or description was to leave wharf or dock or mooring. All with whom he spoke knew his status, and none offered arguments.

When his two troops of household guards were inside the city and the last of the lumbering, ox-drawn prison wagons had rumbled through the north gate, he set about his mission.

The tough, tactiurn horseguards went through Pahdookahport in a manner akin to the proverbial dose of salts. Most of those men arrested were long-resident aliens, but not all.

The high bishop of the Most Ancient and Most Holy Church of Remembered Glory (who was also the brother-in-law of Baron Lapkin) was dragged from his palatial residence screaming at the top of his lungs, "Never would I attend or frequent such a sinkhole of inequity, I assure you. The stock that I hold was simply a good investment for church monies!" His protestations gained him nothing, however; the guards tossed him most ungently into one of the wheeled cages . . . after an iron "scolds' bridle" had been locked securely around his head and under his jaws to prevent him conversing with his fellow prisoners.

Right soon was he joined in the wagon by four of the other

"investors." Ten, in all, of the eleven warrants were executed that day; five of the malefactors were lodged in each of two of the wagons, while the third was the repository of every ounce of gold and silver, every piece of coinage or of jewelry that the troopers could uncover in meticulous searches of the homes and/or businesses of the prisoners. These seizures, too, were performed by authority of ducal warrants, Tcharlz holding that such specie or gems or ingots would effect partial payments of the years of taxes of which he had been cheated, since no one of the men had ever reported this large hidden income.

Baron Hahrvee saw to it that all buildings in which the prisoners had holdings were closed, locked and sealed, the families and employees of those men he had seized being driven, willy-nilly, into the streets. Port guards were posted on the ships owned by the prisoners, and the grim baron ordered the steering gear chained into immobility, the crews cast out, the holds scaled.

Lastly, although he bore no warrants to that effect, the baron seized every sound horse and mule occupying the mews of the soon-to-be defendants, as he knew that the duke would soon have need of every mount and pack animal upon which he could lay hands.

He and his men did not quit the now roiling city until well after dark, sweeping it from top to bottom and from end to end in an unfruitful search for the subject of the eleventh warrant; but they could find no trace of the person of Urbahnos of Karaleenos, hunt as they might.

Captain Martuhn, Count of Twocityport, felt an uncomfortable sense of gathering doom from the moment he set eyes upon the city of Traderstown at close range. The ancient walls had apparently never been higher than twelve or fifteen feet, with towers hopelessly small and placed too far apart to give each other any meaningful support in an assault. Moreover, it appeared to have been at least a century since those walls had been afforded any repairs to speak of, and in places, mostly along the now critical western face, half the previously existing height had tumbled inward or outward, while elsewhere the stones were so loose as to rock underfoot.

In a conference with the two dukes shortly after the last

contingents of eastern troops had been set ashore from the barges, he said as much, in his usual, blunt speech.

"Your graces, we can only hope that the cavalry wins a crushing victory against the nomads, for the city of Traderstown will prove indefensible against determined or prolonged assault."

He went on to detail the many faults—the walls, the towers, the dearth of effective emplacements for modern engines and of convenient rallying points for the defenders.

Then he asked, "My Lord Alex, whatever possessed you to fill in that fine, broad moat? The city might have had a fair chance, properly manned of course, did the moat remain, along with a few outer defenses."

Alex sighed and shrugged. "I allowed myself to be swayed by the thrice-damned merchants and factors, who wanted land under the walls whereon the returning caravans could camp; they hoped that thus the caravaners would tend to stay longer and spend more money in the city and possibly have to sell more of their goods in Traderstown, rather than barging them across to the east bank. It was greed, pure and simple, Captain Martuhn, theirs . . . and mine, too."

"Then, too, Martuhn," put in Duke Tcharlz, "you must understand that Traderstown has not been attacked on the landward side for—what, Alex, a century or more?—well, at least for a considerable period of time."

"As for those nomads," the other duke added, "they never have gathered in such stupendous numbers before; nor has anyone ever heard of any nomad or group of nomads penetrating this far east other than in peaceful ways."

"Then why do you think they're here now, My Lord Alex?" inquired Martuhn.

"Well, my good captain," Duke Alex answered, "the tales of wounded and captured nomads lead me to believe that this invasion in such force is the doing of a new element, a sort of 'chief of chiefs.' He is said to be a big, tall, black-haired man from the south—which could make him a renegade Ehleen from their Southern Kingdom, but I don't think so. His name is not Ehleen, for one thing; he is called Maylo Morré and is most probably one of those troublemaking, warmongering Mehkskuhns."

"And, be this supposition of Alex's true," added Duke Tcharlz, "we have us the answer to where these Horseclan-

ners learn how to maneuver and fight so cannily. The accursed *Emperador* would not have sent just anyone north to
disrupt our trade; no, this Morré is most likely a trained and
veteran noble officer, and we're going to have to start opposing his savage horde differently, are we to win. Poor Alex
here and his horsemen did not dream that they were come
face-to-face with a professional, to begin, and they sustained
very heavy losses as a result.

"But now we both know. Therefore, we must utilize the
textbook tactics, with an overriding strategy of getting the
howling little bastards into a position in which our heavy
horse can get a good crack at them—a goodly stretch of flat,
level ground, firm and free of brush or trees. *Then* we'll give
them a fatal taste of civilized steel, I trow."

During the ensuing weeks, while the two dukes and their
horsemen maneuvered over and through the farmlands and
woodlands of the Duchy of Traderstown, parrying the thrust
of nomad raids, even as they sought a means of persuading
the foe to commit the bulk of his force at one time and
place, Martuhn drove his men fiendishly and himself much
harder in a vain attempt to ready the city to withstand the
prairie horde, just in case.

For all his exalted title, he quickly found that his real authority held only over his own infantry and that of Duke
Alex. The city merchants and shippers and factors refused re-
peatedly to tender him and his hard-working forces aid of
any nature; further, they right often impeded the nonstop
work by complaining formally of the incessant noise or of the
occasional drunken soldier, by refusing to allow the use of
needed docking facilities to galleys and sailers when the
slaves manning the row-barges had been formed into chain
gangs by Martuhn to work on the walls, and they kept their
warehouses solidly locked, forcing all supplies for their defenders to either be shipped over from the east bank or to be purchased—sometimes sight unseen—for scandalous prices.

Martuhn finally decided that he thoroughly despised the
entire pack of venal skinflints after his first meeting with
Hatee Gairee, a merchant-banker whose family owned
several of the large warehouses near the docks.

There were no men to spare to care for the wounded men
who kept trickling in from the skirmishing cavalry, and with
the available medicines obtainable in Traderstown only at

outrageously inflated prices, Martuhn had continued to send any injured or wounded across to the east bank, where the palace complex and several of the larger Upper Town buildings had been converted into hospitals.

The river sailers and Duke Tcharlz's and Duke Alex's war galleys—which brought supplies on the western leg and took back the pitiful debris of conflict—were nowhere as capacious as the cable barges had been, and so a wounded man might lie moaning on a wharf, ill tended, robbed by city scum or nibbled at by rats, until a bottom was available to bear him to the eastern shore.

One short visit to one of those docks, become in his mind a slice of veriest hell, was enough to convince Martuhn that he must find a place near the docks wherein all wounded could await the ships and galleys in safety if not comfort with at least enough attendants to drive off the rats and the human scavengers. He thought that one of the warehouses near the wharves would be ideal, but when he had the men whose goods therein resided approached, it was to discover that they only leased the buildings from various members of the Gairee family, commoners but extremely wealthy.

The family was, he found out, headed by a fiftyish woman, who made all decisions affecting income or outlay of any size. And she arrived at his headquarters in the style of a high noblewoman—a large, ornate and luxuriously furnished coach, uniformed coachmen, postilions and outriders astride finely bred, sleek, well-groomed horses, and two little slave girls to attend her.

She was a tall, very slender woman, with a wealth of gray hair, streaked here and there with strands of the dark-brown color it once had been. Her every finger bore at least one ring of gold; from her small ears depended weights of gold and gems that Martuhn was certain must be uncomfortable. The additions of the golden neck chain and pendant, gold bracelets and armlets and brooches, as well as a headpiece of golden wire set with a profusion of tiny pearls and other gems, caused the captain to reflect that the woman was no doubt wise to have armed her male attendants and riders.

Her clothing was in keeping with her ostentatious display of gold and gems, being all silks and satins and tooled, dyed leathers and—regardless of the enervating combination of thick humidity and blistering heat—fur-trimmed velvets. And she was soaked with some heavy, hellishly expensive scent.

But despite all the rich jewelry and clothing, at close range her perfumery failed to cover the stench of a human body long unwashed. The few teeth remaining behind the carmine-painted lips were stinking and rotted brown, and under the dazzling brilliance of the cut stones, her clawlike hands were dirt-streaked and grubby.

Her manner, when Martuhn had outlined his needs, was blunt to the point of discourtesy. "Cap'n, this here ain't my affair nor my fam'ly's. Wouldn't be no fighting atall, if our pigheaded duke had done what the commoners' council had tol' him to do first off. He should oughta pay off them nomads, alla them savages don' want nothin but loot and hwiskee and a few good-lookin slave girls to screw."

Martuhn had not heard earlier of this conference. "You mean that you and the rest of the citizens were willing to pay a ransom to the nomads to prevent hostilities?"

The old woman drew a goodly breath into her bony, nearbreastless chest and exploded, "Hell no, cap'n! That young fool of a duke is richer than anybody elst in this whole fucking duchy. Let *him* pay the frigging ransom, him and his hoity-toity nobles.

"We all tolt him we'd give him good prices awn the stuff the nomads was gonna want, but aw, naw, he hadda start a-buying up hosses and mules and hired fighters and all."

Hatee suddenly thrust the four fingers of her right hand between two buttons securing the front of her silken dress and scratched vigorously, the huge ruby of her thumb ring flashing the light from its surfaces. The stone itself was obviously hundreds of years old and had probably been scavenged from a dead city of the Ancients, for no one today was capable of cutting and finishing stones in that fashion.

After examining the fresh layers of dirt now under her fingernails, she went on, "Cap'n, I know you means well and all, but ain' nobody here in Traderstown gonna empty no warehouses and get the flo's all dirtied up with blood and piss and shit and puke and I don' know whatall, like them docks is right now. You gotchew any idear what it cos' to buy and feed and put clo's awn good, strowng slaves, these days? And I reckon it'd turn out to be our slaves had to shift all the stock and then clean up, after Duke Alex either comes to his senses or gits hisself kilt out yonder.

"But I'll tell you what I will do for you, cap'n. I'll lease you some tarps and poles I got me, cheap. And, 'sides that, I'll let you use some of my older slaves inta the bargain— they ain't none of 'em got what it takes to work awn no wawls, no mo', but they could all shuffle 'round enough to fetch water and chase 'way rats and all."

"And what, pray tell," replied Martuhn dryly, carefully holding himself back from the violence he longed to wreak upon the stinking flesh of this vile, vulgar, parsimonious and self-centered bitch, "would be the cost of your generosity?"

She steepled her stained fingers and eyed him over their apex, "Well, them tarps is almos' new and soma the poles *is* new, but sincet you'll be a-feeding the slaves while they's a-working for you, let's us just say a round one ounce of gol' the day, eh? Now ain' that a good pricet, cap'n?"

Martuhn heaved himself out of his chair, his face gone white as fresh curds; he kept his hands tightly clenched and a vein was throbbing in his temple. "Mistress Gairee, I have been a soldier for the most of my life, living in camps and garrisons. But not even among the whores who follow the armies have I ever met a woman as filthy, foul-mouthed, deceitful, callous of suffering and coldly mercenary as are you."

"Well, I just love you to pieces, too, you foreigner cocksucker!" snapped Hatee, her brown eyes blazing. "You just as dumb as our asshole duke and them shitheaded gents of his'n, think you kin git anythin' you wawnts for free. Well, we'll learn you fuckheads diffrunt yet!"

"*Enough, woman!*" Martuhn slammed the callused palm of his hand down on the desktop so hard that several items were bounced off onto the floor. His other hand came down less violently, and he leaned across the desk to meet her hot glare with a murderous look that set her innards to quaking.

"Had His Grace Duke Alex empowered me to arrest citizens of my own warrant and for my own reasons, you and your overpretentious finery would presently be immured in the deepest, darkest, dankest cell I could find for you, but my powers here are limited, alas, so I must release you. However, you have well earned and you fully deserve punishment, and I think I know of one that will hurt such a stinking bitch as are you more than fetters and whips and hot irons.

"I am fully empowered to commandeer to the duchy all riding or draft horses and mules, as well as all wheeled conveyances which might be of use to the army. Therefore, as of this moment, your coach-and-six and the mounts of your outriders are become the property of His Grace Duke Alex of Traderstown. Upon the victory of our arms or a cessation of hostilities, your property will be returned to you, if then living or intact. Dead or destroyed beasts or items will be replaced either in kind or in specie."

Leaping to her feet, the skinny old woman clenched both bony fists, raised her arms above her head and shrieked at the top of her lungs. But neither her screams nor her protests nor the incredibly obscene names she called him nor the tears to which she finally resorted altered Martuhn's decision.

And, in the end, all of it was for nothing. The superhuman labors on the crumbling walls, the constant feuding with the merchants and the bankers, the shipowners, the artisans, the factors and the landlords; all were for nought in the final analysis.

Their numbers reduced in the steady attrition of indecisive skirmishes with the innumerable bands of raiders, in ones and twos to hidden bowmen and in larger numbers to wily ambushers, the two dukes at long last got the "advantage" toward which they had been manuevering.

Martuhn saw it all, from start to sanguinary finish, under the ancient, inadequate walls of Traderstown itself. At the very end, when both ducal banners had gone down and the few pitiful survivors of the two duchies' cavalry were fighting desperately, their backs to the city walls, against the waves of screaming, blood-mad nomads on their ugly little horses, Martuhn used his few engines and his massed archers and crossbowmen to drive back the foe long enough to allow a regiment of pikemen to march out, form to repel cavalry and slowly withdraw, still in formation, when the last of the battered and bleeding cavalrymen were through the gates.

Several of the surviving horsemen had seen Duke Alex and his bodyguards go down under a wave of nomads, while others told almost identical tales of how Duke Tcharlz, beset on all sides, had finally rallied a couple of hundred still-mounted men and personally led a charge deep into a huge knot of the massed Horseclanners . . . never to be seen again. All of which tended to leave the reins of power in both duchies clearly within the grasp of only one man, Captain Count Martuhn.

As he had been certain they would, the nomads attacked a stretch of low, incomplete wall shortly after dawn on the day after the defeat of the cavalry; Martuhn's spirited defense threw them back, all four waves of them. But he also took casualties, more than he would have liked, and mostly the direct result of the inadequate defensive works. And that night he made his decision.

When the last of the wounded and ill men were across the river, when all supplies and extra weapons had been landed on the east bank and when the last of the families and personal effects of the original garrison of Traderstown had been evacuated, Martuhn commenced the taking off of his troops, beginning with the now nearly-useless remnants of cavalry and their few remaining mounts. After them he sent his service troops, then the pikemen and dartmen, saving his archers and crossbowmen until last.

Early on, in the military exodus, his orders had seen all sailing ships and galleys not already in his hands seized at glittering swordpoint, and those few unusable—for whatever reason—had been scuttled or set afire and adrift to deny their use to the nomads who would certainly come swarming over the soon-to-be-undefended walls.

It was while he was supervising the loading of the last units of archers onto the three huge cable barges, his own fast war galley awaiting him on the other side of the long cable-barge dock, that he became aware of the clop-clopping of hooves and the rumbling of heavy transport proceeding along the streets of the city and drawing ever nearer the dockside.

Presently, the head of a long procession of assorted wains, wagons and other wheeled vehicles wound into view. Perched on the bow of the leading wain—a huge one, drawn heavily by two span of hefty oxen and laden high with chests, trunks, cases and bales—was Hatee Gairee; her two little slave girls trotted alongside. On or about the vehicles behind, Martuhn recognized numerous other merchants, bankers and an assortment of the wealthier commoners of Traderstown.

When her repeated summonses effected nothing, the tall, flashily garbed old woman finally climbed down from her seat and strode out onto the dock, ill-concealed rage in her every movement.

Without pleasantries or preamble, she snarled at Martuhn, "Whut's this here 'bout you a-seizing fo' of my ships, then setting t'others afire and letting 'em drift down t'river? Just how d'you think me an' these here other folks is gonna git 'crost the damn river 'fore them fucking nomads is in t'city?"

Martuhn grinned like a wolf at a crippled hare, but his voice was soft and his tone mock surprised. "Why, Mistress Gairee, why would you and these others wish to flee the nomads? I thought you knew them and their simple wants so well? You surely will have no trouble dealing with them, will you? A few pretty slave girls? A few pounds of silver? Jewelry and some bales of cloth?"

"You damned bastid, you!" hissed the old woman. "You knows damn well the sitchayshun's done changed, what with the duke daid and the dang cavalry, too. And now you done sent alla the pikes and archers crost the river; it won't be no dealing with them damn Horseclanners now. They'll just come in and take what they wants, all they wants, and likely kill halft the folks in t'city."

"And now you done took or burnt up alla our ships, you gotta take us 'crost in yore cable barges . . . and soon, too."

"I believe firmly in repaying my old debts, Mistress Gairee," said Martuhn slowly. "Therefore, I shall give you and your kind all the willing aid that you have given me these last weeks. When the last of my troops are safely landed over yonder, if there are no nomads in sight from midstream, I shall allow three—and only three—barges to dock. They will remain on this side only as long as it is safe for them to do so, but no longer than half an hour, in any case. All not aboard at that time will stay behind or swim. Is that clear, Mistress Gairee?"

Leaving Hatee Gairee spluttering in wordless rage, the tall captain returned to his supervisory duties.

But the barges did not return that day. For when Martuhn had his small galley rowed back to midstream a few hours later, it was clear that the nomads were swarming through the streets of the city, and he was completely unwilling to risk the loss of more of his men on the chance of rescuing such undeserving types as Hatee Gairee and her ilk.

It was well after dark before the overworked Captain Count Martuhn of Twocityport was able to ride down into the Lower Town and walk his weary horse slowly over the bridge through the open main gate of the deserted citadel, followed by his staff and a few mercenary dragoons who had survived the carnage under the walls of Traderstown and whom he had summarily adopted as bodyguards.

Les, the quartermaster sergeant—identifiable only by a pair of bronze arm rings, the flesh of his face picked down to bare bone by crows or ravens—lay dead in the main courtyard, with two of his assistants and a cook nearby. It was evident that all had gone down fighting, and the bodies of two strangers testified to the effectiveness of their efforts.

Without the need for orders, the veteran dragoons dismounted and strung their hornbows, while Martuhn and the rest unslung targets and loosened swords in scabbards. But a hurried search of the headquarters complex and the nearer barrack rooms revealed them to be deserted and undisturbed, although another dead cook was found in the kitchens. It was also clear that he had taken his death-wound elsewhere and dragged himself into familiar surroundings to die.

With a burden of deep, dark foreboding, Martuhn at last led his small contingent to the central tower . . . only to find its outer door closed and secured firmly from within. When repeated shouts elicited no response audible to him and the others, Martuhn sent his mind questing the height of the winding stairs to the topmost rooms. Beamings from Nahseer and Bahb Steevuhnz immediately answered.

"Lord Urbahnos and a gang of waterfront scum from Pahdookahport came into the citadel hidden in a supply wagon, three days since, Martuhn. We fought them as long as we could out there, but when Les was slain and Wolf wounded, I brought him and the lads up here. They have been besieging us since."

"How is Wolf?" beamed Martuhn.

"Dying," said Nahseer, simply and bluntly. "But he swears that he will live until the lads are once more delivered into your hands."

At Martuhn's terse directions, a heavy timber was fetched and soon brawny arms were regularly crashing it against the ironbound door to the tower. It took time, for the tower had been designed and built as a last, strong refuge against an attacker who had overrun the outer defenses. But first one hinge gave way, then another, then the bars began to crack and the triple panels to sunder. Then, suddenly, what was left of the reinforced portal crashed inward and a knife thrown from the darkness within dropped one of the troopers who had been swinging the ram.

Martuhn had the dragoons drop the timber, draw back a few paces and loose a blind volley through the yawning doorway; two very satisfying screams of agony resulted. Then he, his staff and the dragoons charged through the portal, blades bare and shields up.

The fight in the large ground floor chamber was short, brutal and very messy, but the common toughs were no real challenge to veteran armored mercenaries, most of the bravos being armed only with knives and cudgels or the occasional hanger. Soon all the living murderers had been driven up the stairs toward the topmost levels, followed closely by the coldly raging count and his merciless professionals.

The next-highest level was lit with lamps and cressets. The invaders had apparently been using it as siege headquarters for the last few days, and it was here that they made their last, doomed stand.

Martuhn took the ringing hack of a thick-bladed hanger on the face of his target, angling the attack to the left and downward, while he drove the point of his sword into the man's bearded and unprotected face. Another blade clanged onto the visor of his helmet and flashed momentarily before his eyes, then his peripheral vision recorded the sweep of a dragoon saber and his ears the gurgling shriek coming hard on the heels of a meaty *tchunk*.

And then it was done. Five of the bravos lay dead or dying about the room and a big, black-haired man in half-armor stood with his back pressed against a wall. The crest had been raggedly shorn from atop his open-faced helm of eastern pattern, and he was just in the act of dropping a broken shortsword.

Martuhn dropped his target, tossed his bloody sword to a trooper, then unbuckled and removed his helm. "What's your name, bastard? Urbahnos, perchance?"

The dark man drew himself erect. "*Lord* Urbahnos of Karalccnos, barbarian. What are you waiting for? Kill me."

Martuhn shook his head. "My steel were too easy and far

too honorable a death for the likes of you, pervert. Before he went to his death, Duke Tcharlz proclaimed you outlaw, and there awaits for you a short, wide, blunt stake, in Pirates' Folly; *that* should tickle your buggering bum until you scream your rapture."

Urbahnos paled to true ashiness. "Duke Tcharlz . . . d . . . *dead*? Then who . . . who rules?"

Martuhn shrugged. "I suppose that I do, since all his retainers save me went down with him under the walls of Traderstown."

The Ehleen cleared his throat. "Then we should be able to come to a mutually profitable agreement, you and I. You will be in immediate need of funds, of course, and I will be more than willing to pay a most handsome sum for my freedom and a passage up the Ohyoh. Five pounds of gold? Ten?"

Martuhn spat at the Ehleen's feet. "You are an outlaw, you pig, and as such everything you once owned is mine anyway. I loathe you and all you stand for. Moreover, you and your pack of hired dogs have here slain a number of my men, several of them friends—old and very dear friends, two of them.

"Now, there are a number of cells below us that are dank, ever cold, slimy and dark and constantly at least a foot deep in muddy water, so that the rats have to swim to get at you."

Urbahnos had again paled; he gulped wordlessly, his fleshy lips trembling.

"But," Martuhn went on, "I think me I have a better place for you to bide until I'm ready to put you to death. I have it on reliable authority that you are a castrate. You are obviously strong, and such wounds as you've suffered this day are but mere scratches."

Turning to a short, wiry, blood-splashed dragoon sergeant, the count said, "Byuhz, take this prisoner down to the docks, strip him to the buff, then turn him over to the overseer of one of the cable barges. It will do my heart good to think of the bastard pulling an oar for his keep."

"B . . . but . . . but you *cannot*!" Urbahnos wailed. "I . . . I'm not a slave!"

Martuhn shrugged. "You are whatever I say you are, dog, and I say you're a barge slave . . . until I'm ready to make you a corpse, that is."

Chapter XVI

Empty of human life, save for occasional parties of mounted nomads clattering through the streets, Traderstown lay sacked and smoldering. The clans had taken such slaves as they wished of the conquered, then driven the rest out into the countryside beyond the camps and herds. The loot of the city had been incredibly large, rich and diversified, and no clansman or woman was not happy in the sharing-out.

But the war chief, Milo of Morai, was anything but happy. It had never been his intent to take and sack the city. He had only wished to use the threat of such to force from the townsfolk use of the cable barges to transport the tribe and its herds across the otherwise impassable stretch of muddy brown water.

Now there were no longer any folk with whom to treat in the city. All the cable barges were on the eastern bank of the river—which meant that, in effect, they might as well have been on the moon—and so, too, he assumed, was every other bottom of any usable size.

True, some had been sunk at the docks or close inshore and he and the nomads might be able to raise a few and refloat them, but there were nowhere near enough to ferry many folk and their herds. Besides, not one of the nomads knew aught of sailing, so such boats as did set out without the firm support of the transriverine cables might well be swept clear down to the Inland Sea, if not to destruction on some sandbar or mudbank.

The tall, saturnine man thought hard on his possible alternatives, twisting idly on his finger the fine, ruby-set, golden ring which had been a part of his share of the city's loot. At length he decided upon a plan that might work, were the commander who had headed the city garrison the kind of man he reckoned by available evidence. At least six centuries of weighing human actions and human nature backed his judgment.

Duchess Ann had never recovered her health after the cold and deprivations of the siege of Twocityport. During her hated husband's hurried embarkations, she had come down with what her physicians had at first diagnosed a bloody flux, but it had worsened, despite their nostrums and purges. Moreover, an infection of her lungs had also set in, complicating the matter.

On his first, last and only audience with the hereditary duchess, Count Martuhn could feel Death in the chamber; he could smell it in the close, too warm air, could see it in the deep-sunk but fever-bright eyes of the woman. He dutifully knelt and kissed the trembling hand she held out to him from her place on the huge bed.

Her ladies had washed her and dressed her and arranged her hair and done the little that they could to impart healthy color to her face. They had even anointed her bed, body and clothing with rich scents and strewn the floor with a deep layer of flower petals, but still the mingled stenches of illness and medicines were more than evident.

Her first attempt to speak suddenly became a racking fit of coughing which bent her body almost double before it was done. When the attending ladies had wiped the bloody mucus from her lips and chin, she spoke in a husky whisper.

"*He* is truly dead, Count Martuhn? You *saw* him die?"

Still on one knee, Martuhn shrugged. "As good as, your grace; I saw Duke Tcharlz gather his surviving nobles and bodyguards and launch a charge into the very thickest of the nomad hosts. Very few of them came back, but he did not . . . and the nomads were taking no captives. And a sergeant of dragoons, Lee Byuhz, saw a nomad on a horse that he is certain was the duke's charger that day.

"So, yes, your grace, all the evidence points in the direction of the duke's death. But he died bravely, in honor, and he—"

He was cut off by the duchess' cackling laughter, which was in its turn ended by another of those terrible fits of coughing. When once more her ladies had wiped away the red-and-yellow residues, she breathed. "Then I've outlived that evil monster, I've truly, truly outlived him; not by much, alas, for I'll be dead meat inside a week myself. But I can now die content that that terrible man is burning in hell while vermin gorge on his rotting cadaver.

"Count Martuhn, never speak the word of honor in the same breath with the accursed name of my late and unlamented husband. Although he fancied to use the word often in public, he never really comprehended its meaning, nor did he ever harbor in his body or his soul a scintilla of it. He possessed much, it is true, of one quality that you men put great store by: great physical bravery. Otherwise, he was base, treacherous, deceitful, murderous, lustful and rapacious.

"My poor old papa, frantic that his lands not be ravaged and sundered upon his demise, had me wedded to the man, despite my pleas and against the good advices of all his councilors. Papa gave Count Tcharlz his daughter and his trust, then the back-biting bastard had papa poisoned; I have always been more than certain of it.

"The shameful practices to which he literally forced me in the privacy of our chambers aside, he was the very soul of kindness and courtesy to me in public . . . so long as papa still lived. But with papa laid to rest down in the crypt, he took over Papa's suite and banished me to the far end of the north wing, while he filled the palace with his cronies and his whores, and the very air with the rotten reek of his open adulteries. And not a one of my own ladies and maids but suffered sore at his callous hands—those he could not seduce, he forcibly raped, then often as not turned them over to the evil men of his coterie for further abuse. At least three of my ladies slew themselves out of shame after being so used."

Martuhn had heard many of these same tales before, during the more than ten years he had served Duke Tcharlz, but had heretofore tended to dismiss them as the highly exaggerated maunderings of the duke's political opponents. A death bed statement, however, recounted by the duke's wife, and he already dead, was difficult to dismiss as mere fable. He began to see the bluff, supposedly uncomplicated nobleman who had for so long retained him in a new and different and decidedly sinister light.

After another bout of coughing—which portended ill, producing as it did not threads but rather great gouts of blood—the dying duchess continued her narrative.

"In dear Papa's day and for generations before it, the duchy had been ruled by the duke *and* the ducal council—membership in which had once been purely hereditary but had become appointive in the time of Papa's grandpa.

"They, the council, to the eternal honor of their gallant souls, tried to oppose the malicious machinations and schemes of my *husband*—" the duchess spat the word—"whereupon they began to die—the younger ones in clearly provoked duels with certain of the duke's clique; some were found dead in their beds of no clear cause; a few were done to death on the benighted streets, presumably by footpads.

"With more than half the old councilors dead, the rest quickly retired to their estates outside the city, the wisest and most perspicacious pausing only long enough to convert assets into gold, gather their families and pack their transportable goods and flee the duchy entirely.

"Those unable or unwilling to flee their ancestral homes and lands finally organized most of the country nobles and gentry and mounted an armed rebellion against the murderous usurper, but it was doomed from its inception; for while almost all of the nobles and gentry were well-mounted, well-armed veterans, the bulk of their force was a vast mob of untrained peasantry, all afoot and armed with a miscellany of agricultural implements. Crushed as they were under the heavy taxes levied by the new duke, they could afford but few mercenaries, and those few chose to go over to the duke at a crucial point in the decisive battle on the land northeast of the city.

"Beset with such treachery, the rebels were defeated with terrible losses, Count Martuhn, leaving the very flower of the duchy dead or dying on the field . . . and much of the precious rootstock, as well, alas.

"Tcharlz and his southern ruffians and forsworn mercenaries pursued the broken columns of survivors for miles, ruthlessly murdering any they caught of gentry or noble houses. But the wretched peasants he simply disarmed, dispersed and sent home, unharmed for the most part."

Martuhn could detect perspicacity in such a move. After all, hands were needed to work the land, else the whole duchy would starve, and the peasants had likely been forcibly impressed into the rebel army anyway. Under the old system, their mean, dehumanized status would have remained the same no matter who won the rebellion.

The duchess had begun to cough again, even more violently than previously; the spasms went on and on for long minutes and were followed by more minutes of choking and gagging. A white-bearded and stooped physician left his place at the foot of the bed and motioned Martuhn to arise and depart, but the old duchess would have none of his attempt to exercise authority.

The deathly-ill woman flopped weakly back against the piled mound of cushions, but—though she perforce must speak through a mouthful of blood and mucus which dribbled the while down her chin to drip onto her bodice— her voice was as strong as ever.

"Count Martuhn, keep you your place. And you, you blathering old imbecile, get out of here! See you now how much good was done me by all the nauseous doses you made me swallow? By the unholy messes of oils and herbs you made me endure? If you must be active at something, fetch me that Zahrtohgahn, Master Ahkmehd. His drugs can at least render my death easier."

"Hush, your grace, hush," murmured the lady who bent to wipe the duchess' lips and chin. "You are very ill, true, but you are not . . . are not dying."

"Nonsense, Mahrtha!" The duchess patted the freckled hand of the red-haired woman tending her. "I know it and so do you; I'm dying, all right. But my consolations are that the ravening beast who dishonored us both and most of the duchy as well is dead before me and most of his jackals with him, and that this birthright of mine will finally pass into the strong, capable hands of the kind of man Papa should have found for me to marry—this man, Count Martuhn—and I mean to live until I can tell him what he needs to know if he to rule long and wisely over my people."

When Martuhn finally left the chamber of the dying duchess, he was of two minds about the late duke. He did not doubt that the non-bereaved widow was telling the whole and unvarnished truth . . . as she had perceived it. But still he felt admiration for much that Tcharlz had done for the duchy—however he had come to the ascendancy—and was he, Martuhn, to rule here, he could discern little or no reason to go back to the old order and ways, which was what the duchess had been advising in a roundabout way.

Insofar as Duke Tcharlz's personal habits were concerned, the duchess, who obviously had been reared in a sheltered and insulated environment by an adoring and overly indulgent sire, might be shocked to her innermost core, but Martuhn had known or known of far worse lechers than her dead husband. His hereditary overlord, Duke Lin of York, for example, had set aside his wife to take up the violent rape of three or four young virgins a week; and as he had gotten older, the victims he chose were younger, with many of the prepubescent children dying as a direct result of his abuse of their immature bodies. At length the monster had been overthrown and slain by some thoroughly disgusted nobles, and Martuhn had lost his patrimony in the ensuing dynastic struggles.

That the late duke had poisoned (or smothered; there was more than one tale of old Duke Myk's demise abroad) his father-in-law, long years agone, did not sound at all like the man Martuhn had known and respected, even while opposing him in the matter of Bahb and Djoh Steevuhnz. Besides, it had never been aught save suspicions mouthed by men and women who actively and openly hated and despised Tcharlz on other grounds; no one, not even her grace, had ever possessed a shred of hard evidence.

The deaths of so many of the councilors of the preceeding duke were another matter, of course, but here again the personal, straightforward stamp of Tcharlz just would not adhere, in Martuhn's mind, to poisonings or garrotes and envenomed daggers in the dark. So what really had happened in those distant days was anybody's guess. Most likely, Martuhn reasoned, some or all of them had been slain by Tcharlz's then retainers, but probably not on his direct orders.

The way that Tcharlz had summarily broken the power of the nobles and gentry—seizing their hereditary lands and thereby so impoverishing them that their only options were to cleave to him, flee the duchy or slowly starve—had, in Martuhn's opinion, been a stroke of rare genius; and that Tcharlz had not then—as many a high noble would have done—parceled out the seized lands to supposedly loyal new landlords, but had rather freed the peasantry and redistributed the land to them to own and work had without question immeasurably richened and strengthened the duchy. And that he had done precisely the same to those lands he formerly had ruled as a count had proved that it was not simply a punitive action but part of a carefully conceived plan.

Of course, the actions and the suddenness with which they had been taken were very hard on the affected landlords—upon whose sufferings, admittedly pitiable, the stricken duchess had dwelt at length. But the overall outcome had been good and more than good. The lands were now more productive than ever they had been. The majority of the nobles and the gentry were unswervingly loyal to the overlord (so loyal, in fact, that the vast proportion of those of fighting age had gone down to death behind Tcharlz's banner at Traderstown) and the peasants-cum-yeoman-farmers had proved time and again where lay their allegiances.

But there were those nagging other things haunting the honor and the honest soul of Martuhn, and not solely because of the fevered accusations of the dying duchess. Despite the wholly admirable system of laws, law courts and judges instituted by Tcharlz to replace the ancient hodgepodge he had inherited, the captain had heard rumors as long as he had been a resident of the duchy that—were a large enough sum paid to a high enough authority—favorable judgment in duchy courts could always be purchased.

The recent apprehension and incarceration of the sly and treacherous Judge Baron Lapkin of Pahdookahport had, he had thought, put an end to it all. But now, in the light of the information given him by the duchess, he was no longer so certain. Some of the most flagrant examples of bought judgments had, it seemed, well predated the ill-starred appointment of Baron Lapkin to the bench. Possibly, he mused as he rode toward the citadel, that very appointment had been effected for the same reason a skilled captain would readjust his pike line behind a screen of manuevering cavalry . . . and the late Duke Tcharlz had been, if nothing more, a superlative field captain; no mistake about that.

He and his entourage were recognized long before they rode onto the bridge, but still the wall commander—knowing damned well that Martuhn's instructions were never issued lightly—insisted that all the riders bare their heads and faces and that the proper word be given before he would order the grille raised and the gates unbarred and swung open.

Before the main building, Martuhn swung down from the saddle of his big white riding mule and surrendered the reins to his waiting groom. Then he strode up the steps and into the dim coolness, slapping dust from his boots with his shucked elbow gloves.

But gone forever was the near-empty building he had loved and remembered. As the seat of the now supreme power in the duchy, the corridors and rooms swarmed with the necessary staff of clerks and scribes and petty officials, with messengers and suppliants thronging so thickly about that his bodyguards and a double brace of pikemen from the entry had all that they could do to force through a clear path to the larger and far more elaborate offices his staff had had to occupy.

Awaiting him in the antechamber were Nahseer, Dragoon Sergeant Lee Byuhz and a tall, black-haired man he did not know. Ignoring the stranger and the sergeant for the moment, Martuhn questioned Nahseer.

"How is Wolf? He still lives?"

Nahseer sighed, nodded. "Yes, my lord count, the noble Wolf still breathes, but he dies a little more with each passing day. The physician, my countryman, can do nothing more for him, save to administer the drugs that keep him free of pain.

"But is my lord to see him, it had best be soon, for I think that he now craves death."

Martuhn nodded wearily. "Immediately I'm done here, I'll come, Nahseer.

"Now, my good Byuhz, what have we here?"

Once the stranger was seated with him in his private office, with brandied wine poured for them both, Martuhn stated, "I'm glad that your command of Trade-Mehrikan is so good, *Señor* Morré, for yours is one language I've never learned, since I never soldiered for or even near to the empire. I truly regret that you were left behind when we withdrew from Traderstown—I had thought that I had gathered together and brought safely out all of the nonresidents, but obviously I erred.

"But that aside, tell me, why did the nomads send you over here to me?"

Señor *Don* Maylo Morré, merchant and noble ambassador of His Imperial Majesty Benito IV, Emperor of all the *Mexicos*, sipped delicately at his goblet before answering. And in that moment of waiting, Martuhn essayed to read the surface thoughts of his guest's mind; he failed miserably. He never before had contacted so powerful a mindshield, and he reflected that such a contact was akin to butting one's bare head against a stone wall.

Setting down the goblet, Morré answered, "*Don Conde*, the Horseclansmen now hold some hundreds of *caballeros* and *mercenarios* as prisoners, a few of them sound, but the most wounded to greater or lesser degrees."

Martuhn's face darkened. "And the barbarian bastards want to sell them back to me, eh? All right, I always try to stick by my warriors. How much gold do they want? But I warn you in advance, gold is all they'll get from me—no horses, no women."

But when the foreign nobleman put the ransom demanded by the nomads into his halting, heavily accented Mehrikan, Martuhn looked every bit of his amazement.

"*They what?* Those plains rovers must think me bereft of any wits at all. Such would be akin to not only opening the door to the wolf, but courteously helping him over the sill, as well. I saw what your noble savages did to the lands of Duke Alex, and I'll not abet them in visiting the same on the lands and cities of this duchy."

"There were good reasons why the Duchy of Traderstown was so despoiled," began Morré mildly.

"There are always 'good reasons' why invaders rape and pillage," snorted Martuhn derisively. "I've been a soldier for most of my life, and I know them all. A man hungers or thirsts or covets or lusts, and where no law is enforced, it is always far easier to take one's wants at the point of a sword than it is to haggle a sale."

"If the illustrious my host will please to allow for me to finish . . . ?" Morré inquired politely.

Wolf's mind, still sharp and quick despite the wounds from which he was slowly dying and the drugs administered for the hellish pain, immediately sensed the matters troubling Martuhn. Mind to mind was presently the only way in which the grizzled man could converse, so smashed and damaged were his face and jaws.

"If you doubt this Morré's true motives and identity, my lord, why not hustle him down to the cellars and put him to the stringent question?"

"No, old friend." Martuhn, too, beamed silently. "He sailed over under a white flag, so his person is as sacrosanct as is that of a herald, and my suspicions may be entirely ungrounded—he may well be just what he claims, a captured Mehkskuhn merchant sent over by the nomad chiefs.

"But, Wolf, although he is clearly not of the Horseclanner breed—he's too big-boned and tall and dark to be one of them—his name is very close to the name given by that wounded nomad the late duke captured across the river as the so-called war chief, or overall commander, of that tribe's warriors—Milo of Morai. I know, I have the transcript of that interrogation; the spelling is different, of course, but I would bet that the two names are pronounced the same in speech."

"Nonetheless," stated the dying Wolf, "you sense him to be an honor-bound man and you will sail back across the Great River with him. I will not be there to guard your back, as of old, Martuhn, so I pray you, take Nahseer with you. He is a doughty fighter, that one, and is now as faithfully your man as ever I was."

Count Martuhn, surrogate Duke of the East, stood in the blunt prow of the small row-barge and watched the citadel—gleaming almost white in the westering sun—grow larger with each ordered stroke of the oars. The dark-skinned, heavy-thewed Nahseer stood just behind him, conversing softly with Daiv Ghyp, master of the barge. On every other square foot of the deck lay or sat wounded cavalrymen, mostly mercenary dragoons or lancers, but with a sprinkling of gentry and petty nobility from both duchies. And on the docks of Traderstown, more survivors awaited the arrival of another, larger cable barge.

After that, a number of mounted chiefs and older clansmen would be barged over to scout out an easy, short and, with luck, frictionless route for the tribe's passage through the duchy. His agreement with the Council of Chiefs had been that the crossing of the river by the horde would be delayed until all the duchy's crops were harvested. Further, the chiefs had given their sworn word that no folk of the duchy would be harmed, no villages or farms looted or burned, no lands deliberately ravaged in their passing, and Martuhn believed them. Now all he had to do was convince his staff and the folk of the duchy.

Once landed upon the western bank, a bare week since, the count's suspicions of Morré's true identity had been fully confirmed, but he could not fault the war chief for the subterfuge. It had been a necessary, military expedient and had really wrought much good.

Neither he nor Nahseer had been required to surrender their weapons or doff their armor, but they, the two boys and Milo of Morai had been escorted at a polite distance by fifty or more well-armed clansmen with strung bows, as they rode through the shattered city of Traderstown.

In the Clan Steevuhnz enclave, after Count Martuhn had formally returned the boys to their sire along with vociferous praises of their bravery, cunning and war skills, and when Bahb and Djoh had opened wide their minds and memories that their father might know of all the striving and scheming that the count had performed in order to keep them out of the perverted clutches of Lord Urbahnos, the Steevuhnz of Steevuhnz flatly refused to allow the two easterners to leave his camp.

So Martuhn and Nahseer had, perforce, bided the two nights and a day it took Milo to assemble the council in the camp of Clan Steevuhnz, as deeply honored guests. There he first met a prairiecat and was thoroughly impressed at the high intelligence of the beast, as compared to horses, which were the only other animals with which he had mentally communicated.

Nor were the human clansfolk quite what he had expected. For all the grim, blank-faced taciturnity they showed the world, among themselves they were a merry, active people, living by a strict code of honor—both personal and clan— bound together by loyalty to their clan and duty to their chief.

As for the myth of "stinking savages," he had found it to be a patent falsehood. No member of the clan but washed or was washed at least once each day in the waters of the lar-

gish creek that separated their camp from that of Clan Mak-
loor—often in large, mixed parties of young and old, male
and female, and always with much horseplay and laughter—
and most seemed good, if unorthodox, swimmers. Clothing
and most of the horses were washed by slaves. A few of the
cats swam on occasion, but most avoided the water except
when thirsty.

From the first hours in the Steevuhnz camp, Martuhn felt
oddly as if he had returned home after a long campaign. He
could not recall feeling so much that he was in his rightful
place since his exile from Geerzburk.

"I could live with these good folk," he thought. "I could be
truly one of them and happily live out the rest of my days as
a nomad. I wonder . . . ?" Then he sighed, as reality once
more confronted him, dashing hopes and daydreams alike. "I
could, oh, aye, were it not for these damned duchies and my
cursed responsibilities, my sworn word to a dead man."

Martuhn's flexible mind had quickly accepted the differing
customs of the clansfolk, even the unabashed nudity and the
frequent and openly sexual fondling of couples, young and
old. But when, just as he was settling into his bed in the
chief's yurt on that first night, none other than the chief's nubile daughter slipped from the surrounding darkness to press
her warm, naked body close to his and nibble at his ear while
her hand groped downward toward his manhood, he was appalled. The very last thing he needed or wanted was a row
with these folk over the matter of a debauched maiden.

Stehfahnah read his surface thoughts, inchoate though they
were, and mindspoke him matter-of-factly, "Maiden? Oh, you
mean untried. You'll find none such in this camp, Chief Martuhn, and fear you not my father. What I do is as fitting as it
will be—I believe—enjoyable. Both his younger wives are too
near to their foaling to receive your seed safely; one of his
new concubines has her time of the moon and the other is
with him. So my sisters and I cast the bones for you—I
won."

"But, my dear child," Martuhn began in a whisper, "I am
more than old enough to myself be your fathmmmp!"

She stifled his words by pasting her hot, wet mouth firmly
over his own, her little pointed tongue thrusting deeply into
his mouth, there to twist and writhe like a maddened serpent.
One of her little hands clasped the back of his thick neck,

kneading at the corded muscles under the skin; the other crept to his crotch and began to knead that which it found there.

"Oh ho," she mindspoke him amusedly. "You misled me, Chief Martuhn; you are not so aged as you would have me believe. But as the proof of a stew is in the eating, so the proof of a new horse is in the riding. We must try your gaits and stamina, my stallion."

Neither Martuhn nor Stehfahnah slept very much that night ... nor the night following.

In the end, his staff proved harder to convince than did either of the duchy councils, noble or common, but all came around eventually.

A balding, sun-browned yeoman-farmer hailing from somewhere down in the late duke's home county stood in the commoner council and stated their reasoning bluntly and succinctly.

"We'uns all would hev his worship fer our new duke, an' if thet means a-herdin' five hunnert winter wolfs th'ough the dang duchy, we'uns'll do thet too!"

In the much-shrunken council of nobles—which numbered a few graybeards, but was mostly filled by the fresh young faces of younger brothers or distant cousins of those men who had followed Duke Tcharlz's banner to their deaths—Sir Manfred, Baron Kehrbee, had the last words prior to the oral vote.

"My lords, I do not stomach the idea of a horde of nomads traipsing across the duchy any better than I would a dish of rotten stockfish, but Count Martuhn believes their assurances of a peaceful passage, and I believe *him*. And I'll speak true, far better them, who only wish to pass through and then be gone forever, than the incursions of foreign armies who mean to stay ... and we'll have just that unless we immediately unite behind Count Martuhn and acclaim him publicly as our new overlord.

"You all, even you younger lords, know what usually occurs when the overlord of one of our neighboring states dies with no legal heir—the countless assassinations, the chaos and, like as not, outright civil war, with three or four or more factions jockeying back and forth. One always wins eventually, of course, but by then the land has lain idle for too long, the humbler folk have been butchered or driven into hiding, the treasury has been scraped clean and the flower of the nobility either hacked to death or hanging from gibbets in chains. Over the years, Duke Tcharlz took advantage of more than one such debacle to enlarge our duchy.

"Well, now Tcharlz is dead and precious few of his male issue—legitimate or otherwise—survived him. But our duchy is fortunate in that he legally adopted and named as his heir none other than his long-faithful captain, Count Martuhn of Twocityport. I mean to tender Count Martuhn my fullest support, and I shall expect all true noblemen of this duchy to do no less.

"Moreover, before she died, Duchess Ann authorized a long and deep investigation of Count Martuhn, received him and spoke with him in private for several hours, then exacted the solemn oaths of all her followers to support him as their new overlord.

"You younger men will not recall, of course, but I was a man grown when old Duke Myk died. The duchy was neither so large nor so rich then, but it was strong; and it was strong because it was united—every man of breeding or substance was solidly behind his overlord. It is a very good feeling to live in such a state . . . and we can have it again in this homeland of ours, do we but give our unqualified support to Duke Tcharlz's chosen heir, Count Martuhn."

However, despite the unanimous support of the councils, despite the open-handed hospitality of the gentry and nobility, the unrestrained cheers of the common folk who ran out to see him whenever his cavalcade rode through a city or village, Martuhn could not make the final and irrevocable decision to allow himself to be invested with the rank and the privileges, the duties and the responsibilities, he had long since shouldered.

And the busy months passed into history. The early harvests were in and the farmfolk were assiduously sharpening scythes and sickles and corn knives for the long, weary labor which lay just ahead.

And in the bright, hot afternoon of a day just like the one before, a small band of horsemen clattered through the Upper Town, to draw reins before the palace into which Martuhn had recently had to move his headquarters, though he still returned to his citadel quarters most nights when he was in Twocityport.

The leader of the horsemen stiffly dismounted, shucked the billowing road shirt which had protected his rich attire from the dust of miles, then unwrapped some yards of sweaty, dust-caked cotton cloth from his head and face, donned a battered but polished helmet and stalked toward the guarded doorway.

Duke Tcharlz had come home.

Chapter XVII

The Great River lay many long leagues behind even the slowest of the herds now, and at the average of four or five miles per day, the tribe had been more than a month on their eastward trek. A few of the intervening statelets had been crossed in peace, after overawing or negotiating with the owners; most had not been entirely peaceful and some had had to be hacked through with twanging bowstrings and dripping blades.

The season was growing older, and although the days still were stifling, the nights were cool to nippy. As soon as he had stripped, given his dirty, sweat-tacky clothes to the waiting slave girl and washed in a barrel of water still tepid from the hot sun of the day just past, Senior Subchief Martuhn Geer of Steevuhnz made haste to his bed of hides and blankets and the warm young wife who awaited him therein.

Much later, when both were near to exhausted sleep, lying a little apart that their two sweaty bodies might more quickly cool, Martuhn thought back to other times, far less happy times, such as the return from supposed death of the duke.

Tcharlz had embraced him warmly and even brushed lips to his cheek, though speaking in tones of stiff formality. In the privacy of the office, however, the worn old nobleman had drained off a half-dozen jacks of beer, belched loudly, farted even louder, then begun to speak, familiarly.

"You've obviously kept the reins firmly in hand, my boy, and by my steel, that's a relief. Those stinking savages hunted and harried us for days, drove us far downriver, and then we had to travel even farther down, ere we could find a way to cross to the east bank.

"I knew, though, all along, that if you survived you'd do the right thing; you'd hold my duchy for me. But until barely a month ago, I had no idea what had happened to you, the fort or Traderstown itself.

"I finally got back across with over a hundred mounted men, yet the bare dozen I rode in here with and a few wounded men I left in the south, in my home county, are all that are left of that force. We first landed in Ehleen territory, and it was either fight our way out or be enslaved by the black-hearted, boy-buggering bastards.

"The folk who bide between the Ehleenee and the southern marches of the Kingdom of Mehmfiz are a primitive, savage and most inhospitable breed. And more men were lost to long-range sniping and ambuscades.

"In Mehmfiz, our troubles should have been over for a bit, but we had the bad luck to ride directly into an ongoing battle and had to fight to survive. I merged my force with what looked to be the larger, stronger, better-led group, only to flee with them when the other side was overwhelmingly reinforced."

With a rueful look, the trailworn old duke added, "And, as Fate would have it, we had not even wound up on the side of the right and the king, but allied with a group of noble rebels and in support of a would-be usurper, one Count Djoolyuhn. Since I could fathom no way to set the matter aright—get us safely over to the royal side—I threw in our lot with the rebels, arranged an audience with this Djoolyuhn whereat I revealed my true identity and took over full command of the sorry agglomeration he called an army.

"To be succinct, my boy, once I had gotten his troops properly organized and distributed, trained his officers to drill and handle them and imparted to him and them a modicum of theoretical strategy and tactics, I undertook a campaign that virtually cleared his county of royalists and the county to his westward, as well.

"Then I turned his army back over to him and told him to clear the county to his north. He is a quick study, that lad, and he did just that, with scant delay and little loss of troops. So I put him against the next county north, then the next and so on, until I and my survivors could safely cross over into friendly lands.

"Thanks to me and my military genius, Martuhn, Count Djoolyuhn now has more than quintupled the size of his original army and has effectively split Mehmfiz—holding as he now does a succession of counties stretching from the southernmost border to the northernmost. He may very well actually become the next king, and, as such, he will make me a splendid ally. Though lacking my genius at war and state-craft, Djoolyuhn is much akin to me and I understand him.

"So, anyway, we rode north through the client states in short, easy stages, resting frequently at this little town or that country hall, putting it out only that we were a handful of survivors of the cavalry battle at Traderstown, riding up here to seek the last of our pay. And so, my dear boy, here we are, home safely at last. And thanks entirely to you and your loyalty, it's still home."

Stehfahnah's hand came to rest softly upon his chest, and her mindspeak gently probed. "Are you sleeping, my husband?"

Martuhn snapped back from the past to the present, from the tile-walled office in the Twocityport palace to the felt yurt so many miles and weeks away. "No, my dear, not yet."

She raised herself to rest on an elbow and let her fingers trace along the numerous furrowed scars on his chest and shoulders. "I saw you today, my husband, when you led your money fighters to the in-saddle council that the war chief had convened.

"I watched you from a distance. You sitting your fine, big stallion among the chiefs, with Sacred Sun making your ar-mor gleam and sparkle like pure, polished silver.

"You towered over them all, even the war chief, and when you had listened for long and you finally spoke, their respect for your wisdom and valor held them all silent until you were done.

"And I said to myself, 'That is *my* man there, so tall and handsome. He is mine and I am his and one of the sons he will get on me will be the chief of Clan Steevuhnz.'

"And, oh, my dear, dear husband, I felt so full with my pride that I thought I should surely burst of it."

The girl sighed. "So very, very proud." She leaned to brush

his lips lightly with her own, then snuggled herself against his side, pillowing her tousled head on his shoulder. Presently, her regular breathing told Martuhn that his young wife lay asleep.

Upon being apprised of the death of Duchess Ann, the duke had elected to take over the urban palace complex and Martuhn had more than willingly removed himself and his military staff back to the familiar, homier environs of the citadel. It had been a real relief to the captain to leave the self-seeking, ever-scheming bureaucrats to the man who had first chosen them and trained them to the ungentle art of power-mongering.

A few days after his arrival, the old duke had had every soul in the entire city assembled in the palace square and had then publicly announced that, henceforth, Captain Martuhn, his good and faithful liegeman and the count of their city, was his legally adopted son and the heir of all his lands, titles and goods. The cheering and joyous shouts of the throng was deafening, and the old man seemed quite pleased with the effect his words had wrought.

But his pleasure did not last. For one thing, the old nobility, the folk of the court of his late wife, were as unremittingly hostile to him as ever they had been when yet she lived. However, they seemed to honestly like Martuhn, and this phenomenon did not long escape the notice of the duke, quickly planting and nurturing in his ever-suspicious mind a seed whose evil flower was soon to almost plunge the duchy into civil war.

Because his public announcement had gone over so well in Twocityport, Tcharlz decided to repeat the performance at Pahdookahport and set about organizing a suitable cavalcade of nobles, gentry, soldiers and servants. He ordered Martuhn to have Urbahnos brought up from his cable-barge row bench, as he intended to join him with his co-criminals in the other port city and there execute them all as part of the celebration.

Had he not been aware who the fettered man plodding barefoot behind the troopers' horses was, Martuhn would never have recognized him for the once dapper, arrogant and evil Ehleen.

Urbahnos' few bare months in the fetid near-darkness of

the row-deck had drastically altered his appearance and bearing. His long, matted beard and hair were almost uniformly gray. His nose was mashed and canted far to the right, so that he now breathed noisely through his mouth and the gap where his front teeth had once been. He seemed oblivious to the flies which swarmed and buzzed about him, feeding in avid clusters on the open, crusty-edged sores of his whipwhealed back and shoulders. The gleaming, hate-filled eyes Martuhn remembered now were bloodshot, dull and uncaring, as blank of expression as those of a weary plow ox. Martuhn could almost feel sorry for the broken wreck of a man.

The captain did retain the prisoner in the citadel overnight—long enough to have him completely shaved and deloused, soaked and thoroughly scrubbed, his sores treated, his body clothed and shod and then given a quantity of decent food. The next morning, Martuhn's smith fitted the prisoner with fetters, and he was mounted on a mule and borne up to the duke and the palace dungeons, and throughout it all, he had spoken no single word to either guards or benefactors.

The cavalcade took the best part of a week to reach the city on the Ohyoh, cheered in every village and hamlet and greeted with an overwhelming reception in Pahdookahport itself. But hardly had they arrived, when the duke abruptly announced an indefinite postponement of the celebration, took his guards and his prisoner and rode north in an obvious rage. He left Martuhn and the rest of the party lodged in the palace—only slightly smaller than the ducal one at Twocityport—which had formerly been the property of Baron Lapkin.

And there they hunkered in idleness for a week more, while Martuhn silently fretted about the condition of the dying Wolf or the possibility that Milo of Morai might have tried to send messengers to him for one reason or another. He was, in fact, on the very point of gathering his people, calling for his horses and riding back to Twocityport when the duke's curt summons arrived from Pirates' Folly.

He knew himself to be in bad grace from the coolness of the horseguards who escorted him from the city, as well as by the bare civility shown him by the palace people upon his arrival. Therefore, he was prepared for the dark, glowering demeanor of his overlord, though not for the groundless accusations that soon followed.

"You back-biting young bastard!" was the growled "greeting." "It's lucky for me that I rode in when I did, else I might have—no, would have—had to fight to win back my own damned duchy from you. If I could've raised an army, that is, which is doubtful, the way you've poisoned the people against me."

"My lord," began Martuhn, "has evidently been misled, for what reason I know not; but he should know above all others that I ever have been his true man."

Gripping the hilt of the bared sword that lay on the desk before him, gripping it so hard that his scarred knuckles stood out white as virgin snow, the old man hissed but one word.

"*Liar!*"

Stunned, Martuhn stood mute while the duke let go the sword, poured a small goblet brimful of strong brandy and regained a measure of composure, after draining it off.

"Martuhn, I trusted you, I even was coming to love you as a father should love a son, and, regardless of our differences in that matter of the nomad boys, I had deluded myself into the belief that you reciprocated. But I was deluding myself, I can see that clearly now.

"The outlaw Urbahnos stated to me that when he came before you, you openly admitted that the supposed killing of me by the western nomads had but saved you the trouble of having me murdered."

"Your grace," said Martuhn, puzzled that the duke would so easily believe such calumnies of him, "Urbahnos would say or do any ill he could toward me. He and a gang of scum invaded the citadel whilst I was holding Traderstown, slew a number of my cooks and quartermasters, and were beseiging the central tower when I arrived. Urbahnos was the only one taken alive, and as he and his pack had so severely wounded my old retainer Wolf that even now he is slowly dying, I had the outlaw sent to serve in the cable barges. Naturally, he hates me."

Regarding Martuhn with smoldering eyes from under his bushy brows, the duke heard him out. Then he said, in a soft and almost conversational tone, but with a hard intensity underlying it, "Captain, lying tongues that flap too often and too long and, in any case, unbidden can be easily torn out; I have ordered such before, nor am I loath to order such again.

"As for the Ehleen pig, he swore to the verity of his original statement, over and over, even under severe torture."

Martuhn was of a mind to point out that under severe torture, most men would say whatever they thought their tormentors wanted most to hear, but instead he demanded, "Under your laws, your grace, I have the right to face my accuser."

The duke squirmed ever so slightly in his armchair and rubbed two fingers over his chin between lower lip and beard. "I had intended just that, here and now, Martuhn, but it is no longer possible. Somehow, for all that his front teeth were gone, the bastard managed to gnaw through the flesh of his wrists to the big veins. When men were sent to fetch him up here upon your arrival at Pirates' Folly, they found him dead and stinking."

Martuhn nodded solemnly. "He knew that he could not face me and still fling such heinous charges."

The duke sighed. "Possibly, possibly; the word—sworn or otherwise—of a felon is ever suspect, and were that the only or even the greatest ground for my suspicions, I'd dismiss it all and set myself to forget it. But there is more, Martuhn, much more.

"There's the council of nobles, too. Most of the elders are still mine, but almost all the younger members seem to idolize you. Thank God I'd not yet gotten around to naming you to the council. Otherwise, I'd soon find myself in one of those cells down there or in exile and on a boat, while you ruled in my stead.

"More sinister yet, all the so-called 'Old Nobility' worship you and make no bones about the fact that they would much liefer see you duke than me. And what's this about you talking to my sow of a wife before she finally freed me of her carping corpulence for good and all?"

"Her grace was rumored to be near death, your grace," replied Martuhn. "She sent for me and I attended her for a short while. She wished to know if I had seen your grace fall and if I thought you truly dead."

The duke snorted derisively. "And I can hear that bitch, even now, chortling that she had really outlived me. She always swore she would, you know. I but regret she didn't live just a little longer, long enough to know that still I lived.

"And I suppose, knowing her and how she loved to dredge

and redredge choice turds from her cesspool of a mind, that she spoon-fed you twenty years' worth of exaggerations and outright, whole-cloth-cut fabrications to prove to you what an unmitigated bastard I'd been throughout my misspent life, eh?"

Now it was Martuhn who sighed. "Your grace, her late grace spoke precious little of you that I had not heard as tavern rumors and camp gossip over the more than ten years I've served you."

"I suppose she trotted out that ancient slander that I had forcibly raped every woman and girl in her retinue; that would be like her, dying or no. Well, Martuhn, I didn't. I did seduce a goodly number of the sluts—only the younger and better endowed ones, of course—and possibly"—the duke grinned slyly—"a few seductions were a wee bit more forceful than the rest, but most succumbed easily enough to my manly charms.

"Of course, the tales with which the strumpets alibied themselves to her were likely an entirely different kettle of fish. But what the bloody hell did that tiresome woman expect? She had never been a proper, willing wife to me, and after her father died she removed herself and her entourage clear to the end of the north wing of the old palace and kept her chambers barred and locked to me, her lawful husband, while she daily ate herself fatter and fatter until in the end she resembled nothing so much as some bloated, loathsome garden slug."

The duke poured and quaffed another goblet of brandy, took several deep breaths, and asked, "Did you swear oaths to her? 'Tis rumored that you promised to wed her sister, Alex's widow, replace the present nobility with scions of the older houses and restore the ancient system of landownership, relegating all of the presently free farmers to the status of landbound serfs."

Martuhn shook his head. "Her grace required no oaths of me, your grace, and I swore none."

The duke nodded. "That much, at least, I'll believe of you, Martuhn. I discounted the rumor when first I heard it, and it's obvious that none of the farmers and none of my gentry put any stock in it either. Otherwise, you wouldn't have such strong support in those quarters.

"And that's really my case, Martuhn. There are numerous

other scurrilous tales have been brought to me, but I don't believe one in ten. As for the matters just covered, I honestly don't know whether you're the prince of all liars or simply a born leader and ruler and too honorable for your own good. But you have become a threat to me and to my continued reign. One of us has to go, and it will be you.

"Probably a prudent man would either have you quietly assassinated or hang you on trumped-up charges. But you served me well and faithfully for too long for me to stomach that, Martuhn. But go you must, and soon.

"It's now a week and two days shy of the new moon. When that moon is old, I shall expect you and your company to be on the road. You might go east—King Ehvin is still embroiled, I understand, and consequently hiring mercenaries. Or south—for that matter, the civil war in Mehmfiz is far from resolved and both sides are rich, as is the looting."

Martuhn hung his head briefly, then straightened it and his body to the erect, unmoving posture of a soldier receiving orders. "It will be as your grace wishes, of course. But, your grace . . . ?"

"Yes, captain?"

"My . . . agreement with the nomads, you will honor it?"

"Of course not, man!" snapped the duke. "Don't be a fool. It was a good ploy to get our wounded back though, I grant you that much."

"Your grace, I gave the chiefs my word of honor and—"

"And, as I said earlier, you may have too much belief in your honor for your own good, captain. Those bastards will get no uncontested passage over my lands, I trow, not after they butchered most of my nobles and hunted me and the rest like beasts of the chase. If cross they will, let them go north for a few hundred miles to where it's a mere stream."

"But, your grace, my pledged word . . ."

Tcharlz had once more grasped the sword. He raised it and brought the flat crashing down on the desktop, his eyes sparking with rage. "*Enough,* I say, captain; I'll hear no more of this matter! And if you want to keep your tongue to leave the duchy with, I advise you to recall my previous warning. *Dismiss!*"

At last, the guttering lamp flame flared once and died and Martuhn could no longer see the interior of the yurt or even the young woman who lay pressed close against him. He could now feel her soft warmth, smell the clean fragrance of her hair and sense the muted thunder of her heart. He realized before his thoughts again wandered back into the tumultuous recent past that he was beginning to truly love Stehfahnah.

Immediately he had returned to the citadel, Martuhn sent Nahseer across the river to seek out and fetch back the war chief. Milo returned with the Zahrtohgahn in the small, speedy little sailing boat that same day, and the captain put the recent events to him bluntly.

At the end, he said, "And so, if your folk are to cross on the cable barges, it must be done soon. Nor will you be able to count on a peaceful transit of the duchy; now you must all be prepared to fight for every foot of ground. Tcharlz is no tyro at any aspect of arms or armies, and he bears intense hatred for you all, based upon your defeat and pursuit of him. If he can quickly raise an army—"

"You doubt, then, that he can, Martuhn?" asked Milo.

The tall captain nodded. "It's possible that he won't be able to soon muster any effective numbers, for various reasons. To wit: Before the debacle at Traderstown, he had legally adopted me, recognized me as his heir and made me count of the city of Twocityport, as well as his senior military commander. When it seemed that he was dead, both the older nobility and his own, newer noble houses pledged themselves wholeheartedly and unasked to me . . . and they, none of them, seemed at all pleased at his return.

"I am certain that both the dukes had expected me to hold Traderstown to the last man against you and yours, but I could see early on that it was indefensible against any determined assault, so I opted to withdraw in good order with all my infantry—the bulk of whom were drawn from the free farmers of this duchy—and all those others I deemed worth saving. The result of that action is that the common country folk of the duchy now hold me in far higher esteem than they do Tcharlz."

"So, you don't think they'd willingly respond to a call to arms from their duke?" inquired Milo.

"From the way all the people—noble and common alike—spoke whenever I stopped to bid someone farewell on my way back here from Pirates' Folly, those who didn't actually refuse would most of them assuredly drag their feet mightily. You see, they all recall that Tcharlz made war on me, besieged me in this very fortress once before—that was in the matter of the Steevuhnz boys, you may recall—then suddenly forgave me everything and secured my alliance to go to Traderstown and fight you. They now seem to feel that this present business is but another family spat that will sooner be done with if Tcharlz and I have only our personal troops to carry it on, and the duke has precious few after Traderstown.

"Nor can he summon up the specter of 'barbarian invasion' to spur a muster, for—thanks in no small part to the public relations done by you and your chiefs when you were scouting out your proposed line of march through the duchy—the country folk know that you are men like themselves, not the howling, unwashed savages you have so often been depicted as being."

Milo wrinkled his brows. "But how about mercenaries? Even if your own company remains loyal to you, there must be others that Duke Tcharlz can hire on."

Martuhn nodded. "Normally there'd be plenty wandering along the river valleys in search of employment, but with a full-scale war going on some days east of here, on the north bank of the Ohyoh, and a multisided civil war in Mehmfiz to the south of us, the few companies not working aren't worth anybody's hire.

"Now Tcharlz just might get more support from his home county, but the north-south roads have never been well maintained, for strategic reasons, so it will take them a bit of time to march up here. And, even with those, if he can raise an overall total of four hundred troops, I'll be more than surprised."

Milo still looked worried; the lives and well-being of thousands of his clansfolk rode on his decision here.

"You are dead certain then, Martuhn, that you can hold this place *and* protect those cables with the small number of troops you have?"

"I am certain I can hold the citadel, Milo. I once held one just like it for over two years . . . and with a garrison of mostly untrained peasant pikemen. But so far as protecting the cables goes, well, I am critically short of seasoned bowmen, and, frankly, I'd expected to borrow a couple of hundred from you."

Milo compressed his lips and pinched his chin between thumb and forefinger for a moment, then raised his head and nodded briskly. "All right, two hundred archers; they're yours. I'll start them over as soon as I get back. However, with the possibility of hand-to-hand fighting to hold our landfall, I can't deprive the tribe of any of its warriors. Far too many of them were lost in the battles across the river, as it is. I'll send you two hundred maiden archers—unmarried women of between fourteen and sixteen years; they'll all be experts with either bow or sling, and fully war-trained, too, if push comes to shoving spears or swinging honed steel.

"Will female archers be acceptable?"

"If you don't mind some of them coming back pregnant," grinned Martuhn. "Most of my men are unmarried, too, and so far as I know, none of them are celibate, by inclination at least."

Milo returned the grin. "As you've learned, Horseclanfolk are most uninhibited; none of those two hundred will be a sheltered virgin, of that you may be assured. So yours should be a happy garrison for however long the siege lasts."

And it had been as Martuhn had predicted. By the time Duke Tcharlz had realized that the nobles, gentry and farmers of the more northerly portions had no intention of responding in any numbers, by the time that some less than two hundred foot and horse had marched up from the south, thousands of the nomads were already within the confines of his duchy and their warriors could even be seen on the hills west of Pirates' Folly. Nonetheless, being a stubborn man, he set out for Twocityport with his pitifully tiny force.

Milo had ordered that none be slain unless necessary, and none were. Almost all the force finally made it to their set objective . . . afoot, which was the way that they had made most of the journey. On the second night out from Pirates' Folly, a dozen of the great prairiecats had infiltrated the sentry patrols and stampeded the horses and mules. And each time more beasts were obtained from the free farmers and country gentry in any meaningful numbers, the same thing occurred despite stringent safeguards.

For this reason, among many others, Duke Tcharlz was in

a mood of exceeding foulness as he paced the horse he had borrowed from the upper city across the cleared area to a spot just opposite the gate on the far bank of the moat.

Raising the faceguard of his helmet, he roared, "*Martuhn,* lower the goddam bridge! I've got to talk to you."

Once again seated in the captain's grim little ground-floor office, Tcharlz pulled off helmet and padded coif, ran the fingers of both hands through his short-cropped hair and whuffed a few times, then drained off the large flagon of beer his "host" had provided.

"Martuhn, you disobeyed me. I told you the nomads were not to cross over here, and you let them anyway. Nobody obeys me anymore around this duchy! I called for a general muster and the only troops that ever showed up were this piss-poor lot from my home county. And no sooner were they on the march with me than those big panthers of the nomads drove off every head of riding stock.

"I should be furious with you to the point of murder . . . and I am in a way. But, too, I've been tumbling an idea around in my old head and now it's smoothed off into a sure-fire plan.

"How do you think this nomad war chief would react to an outright gift from me to him of Traderstown to be a nomad duchy? In return, I would want some thousands of his warriors to add to my army . . . but for a very special purpose, mind you; they're little use for set warfare.

"As you know, for years, I've wanted to expand east along the Ohyoh, but other matters have always cropped up to take the gold that I'd need for enough troops to succeed. So what we'll do is turn those thousands of savages loose on the Duchy of Maryuhnburk and, when they've bled the bastards white, I'll magnanimously offer my assistance to that young whippersnapper of a duke, Frehdrik. Once that duchy is safely annexed, we can do the same thing to another of our dear neighbors. I'll be a king yet, Martuhn!"

Martuhn sighed, knowing in advance that the duke was not going to like all that he now had to say. "Your grace, yes, I disobeyed you, and you know why. In that honor which you deride I could do none else. But also, you *had* dissolved our contract, so I truly owed you no service of any kind.

"So far as your granting ownership of Traderstown to the Horseclansmen is concerned, I think me that Milo of Morai and the other chiefs would laugh you out of their camp should you make that offer. They already hold that entire duchy by right of arms, and I doubt not that they could continue to hold it in the same way . . . if they wanted lands and city. But they want neither, your grace. Nor will they ever serve you as mercenaries in your never-ending schemes to see a crown set upon your head."

"Then they must not be allowed a free passage over my . . . over *our* lands, my son, and you must join with me to halt them. If we *both* call for a general muster, I've no doubt but that our people will arise. Considering what seems to be their line of march, the best place to stop the savages would be—"

Martuhn shook his head slowly. "No, your grace, I shall never serve you or this duchy again for any consideration or amount. Immediately the last of the tribe and their herds are across the river, I shall quit this citadel with all my company. We will then trek eastward with the tribe until opportunity presents itself. There is always a market somewhere for good fighting men, especially for a company of veterans."

Tcharlz snarled, "Then don't look to me for letters of reference, you whoreson blackguard! I'll damn you the length of both rivers as a forsworn would-be usurper, see if I don't. And I'll stop these goddam unwashed swarms of barbarians myself."

Martuhn realized that he should have held his piece, but he asked gently, "And how will you do that, your grace? The only reason you arrived here at all was that I asked Milo to order that you and your men be spared, if possible."

The duke arose, his face empurpled, his eyes bulging. For a moment he could only splutter, such was his rage. Then he burst out, "And what gave *you* the right to beg a stinking, murdering nomad for *my* life? Better to have let them do your dirty work for certain this time around. They could've brought you my severed head as warranty of a job well done. Then you could have named yourself duke without any opposition."

"Dammit, your grace," snapped Mahrtuhn in clear exasperation, "how many times must I tell you that I do not want your damned duchy, ere you believe me?"

"How can I believe a clear lie?" snapped Tcharlz in quick retort, adding somewhat bitterly, "For the duchy *is* yours even now in all save name. Why even in my own home county, the only fighters who answered my summons this time were my own relatives of various degrees of kinship and a few old comrades of days long gone.

"I don't know what you did or how you did it, Martuhn. The whole business smacks to me of witchcraft, if you'd hear the truth, but you are become the sole power in this duchy.

"D'you recall our progress from here to Pahdookahport, Martuhn, d'you recall how I canceled all my grandiose plans and rode down to my palace, all a-seethe with my rage? D'you know why?

"It was because in every little hamlet, at every hall and farm and on every stinking pig track, the people didn't cheer and laud their duke, just returned from the dead, the fuckers cheered *you*, every last mother's mistake of them. It was 'Long life to our Count Martuhn!' first, then a few remembered to shout for me, their lawful lord.

"When that stringy-haired harridan held her snot-nosed brat up above her head, she didn't shout for it to look on and remember Duke Tcharlz—oh, no, it was 'Look, Hwil, see the tall man dressed all in gray. That's Count Martuhn—God bless him—who brought your papa and uncles home safe from Traderstown! You remember him in your prayers tonight.'

"And when we got to Pahdookahport, it was the same story, Martuhn, magnified by the larger crowds. And that was all that I found myself able to stomach."

Tcharlz refilled his flagon from the big ewer, drained a good half of it off, then said candidly, "I strongly considered having you killed. I had even sent for a trusted assassin I've used in the past, but then I reconsidered and sent him away. Nor was that reconsideration from any love of you—I've never in all my life loved anyone enough to allow them to stand between me and anything I really wanted—but rather the simple realization that, were I to have you killed, the entire duchy might well rise up against me—all classes and orders. That was when I decided that you must quit the duchy forever."

The duke rose to his feet. "But now"—taking the short single step to the desk, his right hand moved up from his side in a blur of motion and its horny palm cracked against Martuhn's scarred left cheek—"it is become obvious to me that one of us must die before the other can reassume control of this duchy.

"So what will it be, Martuhn? Longswords or short? Axes or spears? We're both of us masters of them all. Shall we fight ahorse or afoot? In private now, or in public later? You say your wishes and I'll go along . . . within reason, of course. I just want to get the beastly business over and done with and get back to collecting my taxes and hiring on some decent fighters and continuing my expansion. Well, Martuhn?"

The tall captain had gone pale with anger under his weather-browned skin, and the imprint of the duke's buffet glowed red over the long, purplish scar, but he shook his head. "No, your grace, I have no reason to kill you. I do not want your damned little duchy. Yes, I was tempted when we all thought you dead and the people needed an overlord, but more for them and their welfare than for me and mine.

"If a death you must have, open your veins or fall on your sword, but don't look at me to make it easier for you; my becoming an executioner was never a part of our contract."

With a feral snarl of bestial rage, the older man slapped the younger again . . . and again, palm and back, back and palm. Finally, Martuhn's own hands closed on the duke's wrists in an armor-crushing grip.

"Enough, your grace." His voice was low but there was steel in his tone. "You have overstayed your welcome within these walls. It's time for you to leave."

With a glare of pure hate, but no other words, the duke stalked from the office and the building, swung up on his mount and rode out the gate and back over the bridge at a fast trot.

Despite the drugs, Sir Wolf could not sleep this night. He lay still on the bed, his nostrils cloyed with the reek of medicines and sweat and suppurating flesh. He felt cheated by life and fate. This was no way for a fighting man to die; a warrior's death should be delivered quickly, with clean, sharp steel, while he guarded his lord's back. Not a slow, endless torment such as he had endured these last months.

The buffet of the mace had taken him in the small of the back, and from that moment he had been as dead from his waist down, for all that his upper, living body had been con-

tinually racked with spasms of an agony both fierce and in-
describable.

The drugs that alleviated all but the worst of the pain also
took away his appetite, so that the flesh had gradually wasted
away from his big bones, leaving only blotched and wrinkled
skin lying in folds on a weakening frame that was dying by
slow inches.

"Oh, damn him!" he raged silently as so often before.
"Damn that scurvy, worm-crawling bastard of a lard-sow and
a poxy he-goat! Why the hell couldn't he have crushed my
frigging skull and been done with it—that's what a mace is
for, anyhow."

He did not hear either door open—the one to the hallway
or the one to Nahseer's room—but he was suddenly aware
that at least one other person was now with him in the chamber, near to him and moving nearer, but almost soundlessly.
He said no word, made no movement except to close his
eyes; let Nahseer think him asleep.

But the hand that touched his withered right arm was not
Nahseer's. A needle-pointed blade came to rest swiftly and
surely, despite the stygian blackness of the room, just over his
heart, and an unfamiliar voice breathed, in a hoarse whisper,
"One peep out of you, old one, and you're dead meat. Get up
and come with us, show us to Captain Martuhn's chamber
. . . and I just might spare you your life."

Soundlessly, frantically, Wolf tried to raise Martuhn's
mind. "My Lord Martuhn, beware. Assassins. Armed enemies
are at large in the tower."

But Martuhn, sleeping soundly after a lengthy love-bout
with Stehfahnah, who had come to the citadel as one of the
archers, could not be roused.

Even as Wolf croaked, aloud, "Kill me if you will, but I
cannot arise—my legs are lifeless since my backbone was
crushed in battle," he was beaming to Nahseer in the next
room, "Nahseer, I can't wake Martuhn. Arm yourself and
guard him. Assassins are in my room seeking him."

Nahseer, who had often in past months of nursing the dying man been awakened by telepathic means, made no answer of any description but rather rolled silently from his
bed, armed himself with saber, dirk, helmet and a small target, then padded barefoot toward the hall door.

But the valiant Wolf, thinking that his message had failed

to reach Nahseer either, made one last, heroic effort. Filling his lungs, he roared out in that booming voice which had risen above the din and clangor of so many hard-fought battles, *"To arms, soldiers, guard your captain!"*

Cursing aloud, for sounds didn't matter now, the unseen man plunged the slender blade into Wolf's chest, skewering the mighty heart. After wiping the weapon on the sheet, he sheathed it and turned to go back the way he had come, but the sudden ringing clash of hard-swung metal on metal, the scuff of feet on the stones and the huffing of exertion told him of an open fight—not at all his preferred form of activity—in the corridor.

Feeling his way, catlike, among the cluttered furniture, the intruder found a wall at right angles to the corridor and felt along it until he located a narrow doorway. The room beyond was as small and as dark as that he had just quitted, but when he gently cracked open the hall door of this one, a thin sliver of light from the watch lantern gave his inordinately keen eyes enough illumination to discern that the room was tenantless.

There was a high-pitched scream from the corridor, then a babbling, bubbling whine in a voice that the intruder recognized. Apparently, Roofuhs Rat-face had taken a death-wound.

The intruder never carried a sword, only a dagger, a small leathern bag of lead balls and a wire garrote, so he cast about the room for something with which he might hope to fight his way out of the tower. At last he lifted down a hunting spear from its place on the wall, opened the door just a bit wider and slipped silently out into the corridor.

There had been three of them—all unarmored, clad in tight-fitting dark garments, with soft slippers rather than boots and no weapons but hangers and daggers. Even stark naked save for his baldric, dirk belt and helmet, Nahseer was better-armed than any of them, so now one lay nearly decapitated in a widening pool of blood, one sat hunched against a wall, trying in vain to hold back the coils of gut exiting the foot-long lateral slash across his abdomen, and the other was backed into an angle of the corridor, while the hulking Zahrtohgahn stalked toward him at a half-crouch, his target and blood-smeared saber held before him.

For all his intentness toward his victim, Nahseer heard the

creak of the door and the pad of swift footsteps behind him, but before he could turn, his chest was filled with a white-hot, agonizing pressure. He tried to scream, but his lungs would take no air. However, even as a murky, steaming, spiraling red blackness seemed to infuse him, he took the last step forward and drove his dripping saber unerringly into the body of the screaming man trapped in the angle of walls.

The intruder jerked the broad blade of the spear out of the back of the naked warrior as he fell. But before he could take even a single step toward the down-spiraling stairs, his right thigh was struck hard, penetrated by something that felt to be as huge and hurtful as the gore-splotched wolf spear he had just used. Nor would the leg support him longer, but still he tried to crawl to the stairhead.

But it was too late for him. Soldiers of the guard—all armored and with bared blades—came stomping and clanking up the stairs, while from behind him, from the level above, came striding another naked men. This one was tall and deep-chested, and where the speared saberman's skin had been uniformly the dark brown of an old saddle, the skin of this one was pinkish-fair where not weathered darker by sun and wind. He bore in his big right hand a bared longsword, and a bedsheet had been hastily wound and wadded about his left hand and forearm.

Beside him was a small, fine-boned young woman—looking tiny beside his tall massiveness. Her long, red-blonde hair hung loose down her back, and she was as naked as her companion, save for a bracer of metal and leather on her left forearm. In her right hand was a short, thick hornbow and also a couple of black-shafted, steel-headed war arrows, mates to the one which the intruder now could see had so cruelly skewered his thigh.

All three of the soldiers closest to the intruder raised their swords to end his life, but the big, nude man spoke.

"No! Before this one dies, I'll have at least one answer, though I think I know it already. Someone take that shaft out of him, bind his wound and his hands and take him below. I'll be along presently to question him."

Somehow, sometime, without his being aware of it, it had begun to rain. A soft rain, it was, but insistent. It made gur-